Praise for
The Little Old Lady
Who Broke All the Rules

'This lighthearted caper is f
but also weaves in   ality
of life in today's   p,
following recent   o
Climbed Out the
Exotic Marigold   ople continue
to live life to its over-the-top fullest.'
—*Zoomer Magazine*

'A good-natured, humorous crime caper.'
—*The Independent*

'A funny, smart and heartwarming look
at aging disgracefully.'
—*Canadian Family*

'A quirky, offbeat delight and a heartwarming
reminder that one is never too old for some
mischief and adventure.'
—TOM WINTER, author of *Lost and Found*

'Reminded me of the more mischievous moments
of *One Flew Over the Cuckoo's Nest*.'
—J.B. MORRISON, author of
The Extra Ordinary Life of Frank Derrick, Aged 81

'The funniest book this year.'
—*Magazine Familjen* (Norway)

'Criminally fun!'
—*Bonniers Bokklubb* (Sweden)

'A hilarious farce. . . . Highly entertaining
with very well-crafted characters.'
—*Fréttabladid* (Iceland)

'It has humour, brilliant dialogue, irony and warmth.
A light-hearted and enjoyable detective comedy.'
—*Pro Pensionären* (Sweden)

THE LITTLE OLD LADY STRIKES AGAIN

THE
LITTLE OLD LADY
STRIKES AGAIN

CATHARINA
INGELMAN-SUNDBERG

Translated from the Swedish by Rod Bradbury

HarperCollinsPublishersLtd

Published by HarperCollins Publishers Ltd

First published in 2014 by Bokförlaget Forum, Sweden,
under the title *Låna är silver, Råna är Guld*

First published in Canada by HarperCollins Publishers Ltd
in an original trade paperback edition: 2015
First Harper Perennial trade paperback edition: 2016
This mass market edition: 2018

HarperCollins books may be purchased for educational, business,
or sales promotional use through our Special Markets Department.

HarperCollins Publishers Ltd
2 Bloor Street East, 20th Floor
Toronto, Ontario, Canada
M4W 1A8

www.harpercollins.ca

Library and Archives Canada Cataloguing in Publication
information is available upon request.

ISBN 978-1-44345-458-2

Printed and bound in the United States of America
QUAD 9 8 7 6 5 4 3 2 1

To Lena Sanfridsson, Barbro von Schönberg and Inger Sjöholm-Larsson – my warm and sincere thanks for an unforgettable effort!

One thing is certain,
you can never drink too much champagne . . .
—Martha, aged seventy-nine

THE LITTLE OLD LADY STRIKES AGAIN

Prologue

When seventy-nine-year-old pensioner Martha Andersson put the cheese, the Argentinian sausage and the delicious lobster pâté in her big flowery bag, it marked the start of a new life.

Humming contentedly to herself over the buzzing of the supermarket's overhead air conditioning, she thought a drink of cloudberry liqueur with some tasty snacks would be perfect before the evening's gambling session. Martha just loved living in Las Vegas – it was the place where anything and everything could happen.

Eager to return to the comfortable suite at the Orleans Hotel & Casino, where she was staying with her four oldest friends, she turned and, as bossy as ever, announced to the pensioners trailing behind her:

'My friends! Let's go back to the hotel and recharge our batteries!'

She pushed her short white hair under the wide brim of her yellow sun hat and took a firm grip of her shopping bag with her nicely manicured hands. Her black Ecco shoes sounded loudly as she led the way. Her fellow pensioners, Oscar 'Brains' Krupp, Bertil 'Rake' Engström,

Anna-Greta Bielke and Christina Åkerblom, nodded and paid politely for their goods at the checkout before they followed Martha out of the shop. It was just over six months since they had left Sweden after making it onto the Most Wanted list with their Robin Hood–style art robbery. They had been keeping a low profile ever since. But now they had had enough. Their motto was: *If you are bored, you are not living.* So it was high time to do something fun.

Outside the department store a dog was waiting for them alongside their walkers. The cocker spaniel yapped and jumped up at Martha's aromatic bag. The five friends – or The League of Pensioners, as they sometimes called themselves – helped to exercise Barbie, the hotel receptionist's dog. Martha bent down to stroke and calm the dog and then, when everyone was ready, she strode forth, leading the way again.

The white hotel buildings towered high above their grey heads, and the pavement glistened. The neon signs blinked, the heat was oppressive and a police car drove past at high speed. After just a few steps, Martha was soaking with perspiration. Panting, she turned into Hayes Street, pulled out her fan and started to hum a jolly traditional Swedish children's song about climbing mountains. Soon the League of Pensioners would make themselves as unforgettable in Las Vegas as they had in Stockholm.

1

The staff in the De Beers diamond shop farther along the street ought to have behaved with more caution. But instead the security doors were opened immediately and the guards politely stepped aside when the three bearded, impatient young men entered the shop. Two of them had guide dogs, and the third helped his friends across to the counter. The female assistant gave them a welcoming smile, her look full of friendliness. The men courteously said hello and asked to look at cut diamonds. Then, to reinforce their meaning, they whipped out their pistols and yelled: 'Give us the diamonds!'

The shop assistant and her colleagues reacted instinctively and discreetly started groping about for the alarm button. At the same time, they pulled out all the drawers with the shimmering diamonds. Their hands shook as they placed the diamonds on the counter. Two of the men pushed the guards up against the wall and disarmed them while the third man quickly stuffed the diamonds into specially sewn collars worn by the guide dogs. The glimmering diamonds were quickly followed by a dark blue sapphire and some rough diamonds, from the workshop, that had not yet been cut. The robbers emptied the drawers and didn't notice when the assistant finally managed to press the alarm button. When the alarm sounded, they swept the last of the gemstones into the dog collars, then zipped them shut and hurried out. The last of the three men to leave had short-circuited the electrics so that the security doors would lock themselves after he stepped out the door.

Out on the sidewalk, the three men took off their wigs but kept their sunglasses on. Then they calmly walked down the street as if nothing had happened. The trick with the guide dogs was something they had used before. It worked well and made people less suspicious. Now the men just looked like completely ordinary pedestrians, and they leisurely went round the corner and into Hayes Street, where their car was parked. After a hundred metres or so, they couldn't resist looking back to see if they were being followed, but in doing so they took their attention off the path ahead and managed to bump right into a gang of pensioners who almost filled the whole sidewalk. The five elderly men and women were singing for all they were worth and took small dance-like steps behind their walkers. All the robbers could do was stare at them.

'Watch up!' Martha exclaimed, her English not being its best if she didn't have time to think. Then she and her elderly friends continued along the street towards the three men and their dogs, singing a jolly children's marching song. They had sung in the same choir for thirty years, and they liked singing loudly and happily together.

'We stride across the dewy mountains, tra-la-la . . .' they sang in parts and, as always when they sang this song,

4

they became a little sentimental and started to long for their home country. They were in their own little world, unaware of the goings-on around them, and they weren't in a hurry either as Barbie had lots of exciting things to sniff at. Walking down the street, they had passed lots of restaurants, casinos and jewellery shops, and Martha enjoyed it all. Las Vegas was a town for adventurers, and she and her friends belonged there.

'Move out the way!' shouted the men with the guide dogs.

'Why don't *you* move out the way!' Martha responded, but backed up when one of the dogs in luminous-yellow coats bared its teeth. Best to be friendly to the canine, she thought quickly and fumbled in her bag for the Argentinian spicy sausage. Brains had had the same thought and was pulling out the pâté. The big German Shepherd ignored the delicacies, growled threateningly and leapt across to try to bite Martha's leg. Thankfully, Brains managed to push his walker in between them, and the next moment the dog got caught by its collar in the walker basket. That was when Barbie reacted too.

Confronted by the huge German Shepherd, the little dog panicked, yapped rather pitifully and pulled so hard on her leash that Christina lost her grip. Howling, little Barbie dashed away with her leash trailing after her, upon which the other guide dog, a black Labrador, also got loose and charged after her. Barbie was, one might add, a rather sweet little doggie, and, to cap it off, was in heat.

'The dog collar!' the men shouted when they saw the Labrador disappear with the diamonds. Two of them rushed after the dog. The German Shepherd was still caught in the walker basket, and one of the stressed-out robbers was trying to get it loose.

'I am sorry,' said Martha.

The man swore in response.

'If you take it easy it goes better,' Martha went on, leaning forward and giving good advice, in fact doing her very best in broken English. But the man ignored her and just tugged and tugged without managing to release the dog collar. Suddenly several police sirens could be heard. At the sound, the entangled robber gave a start and pulled the dog away so hard that the collar broke and was left hanging from the basket. In full panic he then set off down the street with the dog after him.

'Hey, stop! You forgot your dog collar in the basket!' Martha shouted, gesticulating wildly, but, instead of stopping, the man ran to his car. His companions had also heard the sirens and they gave up chasing the black Labrador and fled towards the vehicle too. Once there, they unlocked the car and threw themselves inside. With screeching tires, but without any dogs, they disappeared round the corner.

'Weird way of going about things! They don't seem to need their guide dogs at all,' Martha mumbled to herself. Then she unhooked the dog collar just like she had suggested to the man. After that she caught her breath, shook her head slowly and muttered: 'Why do people so rarely heed good advice?'

Martha's good friend, Brains, took a quick look at the dog collar.

'Put that in the basket for the time being. We can phone the owners later. Their name will certainly be marked on the inside.'

They all thought that was a good idea and as soon as they had succeeded in getting Barbie to come back to them, they walked off towards their hotel. Now they had a new addition to their party – the black Labrador was in tow – and once they arrived at the hotel Martha realized that they would have to look for the dog-owner too. She took off the dog's collar and put that in the basket as well, just as the receptionist came up to them.

'Thank you so much,' he enthused, lifting up his little Barbie before disappearing with quick strides into the lobby with his darling in his arms. The Labrador started yapping and ran after them but wasn't quick enough to sneak in before the big glass doors were shut in front of its nose. Broken-hearted, it stared a long while through the glass before dejectedly wandering off with drooping ears. The League of Pensioners were left with two dog collars.

'I've got a magnifying glass up in our hotel room. There's bound to be something written in small print on the leather or there'll be a little note inside that zipped pouch,' said Martha, and then they all took the elevator up to their suites on the eighth floor.

'That's what's so strange about life: you never know what is going to happen, do you?' she chirped a while later when she had laid the table for the evening's drinks and snacks, and pulled out her magnifying glass. 'Now, let's see what it says here.'

Martha examined the inside of the collar but, however

carefully she looked, she couldn't see any letters or initials. Finally she unzipped the pouch on the collar to see if she could see a name tag inside. Then something suddenly fell onto the parquet floor. Rake bent down, picked up the pieces that had dropped on the floor and placed them on a plate.

'Doggie snacks in the collar – that's practical!'

2

'Doggie snacks? I'm not sure about that,' said Martha and she felt one of the little pieces. 'If that were the case, the dogs in Las Vegas would hardly have any teeth left. Feel them – they're hard as rock.'

They all leaned forward, felt the tiny objects and held them up against the light. Silence followed, then gasps could be heard.

'My God, they look like diamonds. Real diamonds!'

Outside the hotel window, the city lights glowed. Advertising signs flashed on and off, and neon rushed around in colourful tracks. And the League of Pensioners had just stumbled across a heap of diamonds.

All five of them stared at the gemstones, put them in the palms of their hands and stroked them very gently before reluctantly putting the diamonds back on the coffee table.

'We don't know where they come from, or who owns them. Either we go to the police or we can donate them to the Robbery Fund,' said Martha, who looked after the interests of the joint robbery fund. That was where they kept their stolen money. They also made donations to needy institutions and less fortunate members of society from the accounts.

'But the police . . . What if we handed them in and they thought we had pinched the diamonds? No, it would be better if we took care of the gemstones ourselves,' Anna-Greta said, having worked in a bank all her life. 'We'll sell them and transfer the proceeds to the Robbery Fund. All additional income is welcome.'

They all nodded in agreement. Despite them all being around about eighty years of age, they worked now more than ever. They could have named their robbery fund 'The Revolving Door' because the money came in and went out again almost straight away. As soon as the old friends had stolen something, they gave away the booty. In Las Vegas alone there were almost seven thousand homeless people and back home in Sweden there were a lot of people in need too. So they had started to save and set a target of accumulating at least five hundred million kronor and letting that money work for them. The dividends would then be used to pay for geriatric care, culture and other things back home even after they retired from their life of crime. After all, they couldn't go on stealing for the rest of their lives.

A week had passed since the remarkable encounter on Hayes Street and Martha and her friends were drinking coffee and munching some tasty chocolate wafers in the hotel suite that the three women were sharing. Since the meeting with the diamond thieves, they had kept a low profile. In fact, they hadn't even set foot outside the hotel and the receptionist had had to take little Barbie out himself. The friends understood that the diamonds in the dog collar must be stolen property and the robbers would now be searching for them. Unless, of course, the police had already locked them up.

'Can we agree that we should take care of the diamonds ourselves and from now on regard them as our own?' Martha wondered out loud when they had all drunk their coffee.

'Absolutely! The diamonds *are* ours!' the League of Pensioners exclaimed in unison and cheered, because what they liked the very best of all was to steal something that had already been stolen. In that way it was as if they had been given it. The pile of diamonds lay glistening next to the coffee pot, and when the sun shone in through the panoramic window, the gemstones glimmered in colourful cascades of light – faceted gems, drop-shaped, clear and coloured diamonds. Somebody had owned these gems, but who? In Las Vegas, there were as many diamond shops as there were hot-dog stands back home in Sweden, so the owners would surely be impossible to trace. It would be best to take the gems home to Sweden, sell them there and put the proceeds into the Robbery Fund.

That decision must be celebrated! Rake got up and fetched a bottle of champagne and five glasses. He had been a waiter on the cruise ship MS *Kungsholmen*, and with a practised and elegant touch, he opened the bottle without the cork hitting any of the others, or the chandelier.

Nor did the champagne bubble over the edge of the glasses. No, he was a real pro and not one drop of champagne was wasted.

'Well, then, cheers to you all, you crooks!' said Martha and they all joyfully trumpeted a few bars from *Champagne Galop* before raising their glasses and drinking. A pleasant atmosphere immediately spread in the room. All five of them were touchingly in agreement, and now the diamonds must be smuggled home. In fact, Martha and Brains had already made certain preparations. The handles of Brains's walker was unscrewed and awaiting the stolen loot.

'Are we really going to hide the diamonds here?' Christina wondered out loud and put a few of the precious gems in one of the handles. She then shook the walker so it rattled. 'Just listen to that: we could be discovered!'

'Pah, we simply fill the handles so they don't rattle, or we could put the diamonds inside our walking sticks instead,' Brains chipped in. He was the engineer and inventor in the gang, and now he waved his cane to accompany his idea.

'Yes, perhaps walking sticks would be better,' said Martha.

'Okay, we'll mix the diamonds and gravel in the handle of one of the walking sticks. The other walking sticks we will fill just with gravel. And we'll pack them so tight that they won't rattle. We can put all the walking sticks in a golf bag. That ought to work,' Brains decided.

'Oh how clever!' said Martha. 'You always have such good ideas.'

'But the diamonds worry me,' Christina fretted. 'I think we ought to travel home tomorrow.'

'Not before the coup,' Martha protested. 'Don't forget why we've come here. We can't just abandon all our plans simply because we happened to stumble upon a few gemstones. Even if we include them, we still need millions more for the Robbery Fund. Remember that geriatric care is always in need of more money.'

'Yes indeed. Nowadays, most things in society need financial support to work properly,' Anna-Greta agreed.

They fell silent. When society no longer functioned as it should, others must intervene, and the League of Pensioners had taken that burden upon themselves. In a world where the rich became even richer and the poor even poorer, they felt compelled to commit crimes to support the less fortunate members of society. They were like Robin Hood – stealing from the rich to give to the poor. For a whole month the friends had been planning to rob a casino in Las Vegas. That would give them lots and lots of money, so a few diamonds were not a sufficient reason to drop the idea.

'Yes, I suppose we must carry out our plans, then,' said Brains tentatively. Martha had said they would carry them out tomorrow. She had so many ideas all the time, sometimes it was hard to keep up. Brains looked around the room. For several months they had played roulette and raked in the equivalent of more than one hundred million kronor, but now it was time to round it off. They had felt the looks of the security guards. The men muttered into their earphones and stayed close to the tables every time the five of them turned up for the evening's gambling. They were beginning to get nervous. You should never go on too long, or aim too high, he thought. Brains did a few sums in his head. During the last year, if they counted all of their various robberies and deceptions, they had collected two hundred and forty million kronor for the Robbery Fund. With the diamonds, they would certainly have reached about three hundred and forty million. So they still lacked about one hundred and sixty million before the dividends could finance the donations for geriatric care they had planned, which was why Martha had agreed to Christina's idea of robbing casinos. Stealing from a casino was a lot quicker than winning the money at roulette, Martha thought. She was always so impatient.

'Okay, let's pack this in tonight. We'll carry out the robbery tomorrow, and then go back to Sweden,' said Martha.

'But why should we carry out this giant coup? Isn't it safer to steal at home in Sweden?' Brains suddenly asked. He had grown up in the small suburb of Sundbyberg near Stockholm and, although he knew five languages, he had never lived abroad and felt a bit uncertain so far from home.

'But my dear friend! We need those hundred and sixty million. What will happen otherwise, when we are too old to commit crimes?' said Martha. 'Here we can hit the real jackpot. Not until our children can live on the dividends from what we have invested with the money we've stolen can we retire for real.'

'You've got big plans, Martha dear,' Brains sighed.

'But of course we must go on stealing. The banks pay such poor interest on savings accounts nowadays,' Anna-Greta added.

'Yes, that's true, of course,' mumbled Brains, who wasn't particularly well versed in financial matters.

'Well, then, cheers for the Robbery Fund *All Inclusive*,' Martha said and smiled.

'All inclusive?' Rake looked puzzled.

'Of course. The Robbery Fund must be made larger. Now that welfare has collapsed all over Europe, the Robbery Fund should also cover health care, schooling, other social—'

'But, Martha, that sounds like an awful lot. We mustn't lose control,' Brains said, as he was beginning to find it all rather confusing. 'One thing at a time!'

'I agree with Brains,' said Anna-Greta. 'We can't start handing out money we don't have.'

'Oh yes we can – a lot of countries do that. If they can, so can we! Besides, the casino plot is watertight. We're going to get lots of money,' Martha said and threw out her arm in a foolhardy gesture. Her face creased in pain. She had completely forgotten that she had overstrained her arm when she had sat half the night in front of one of the slot machines.

Was the casino plan really watertight? The others looked somewhat worriedly at each other and, above all, they looked at Christina. She was somebody who worried about most things and, more than once, she had put them in awkward situations. She came from Jönköping, had had a strict religious upbringing, and was always hesitant before she dared to do anything new. While they had been in Las Vegas, her friends had done all they could to build up her self-confidence and they had succeeded only too well. Now she didn't seem to have any inhibitions at all.

Martha got up and fetched a bucket from the bar. It was full of gravel and sand that she had fetched earlier that day. She determinedly unscrewed the handle of her walking stick.

'And as for doing robberies here in Las Vegas . . . well, it's been a while since we committed a crime,' Brains said, trying yet again. He cleared his throat: 'We're a bit rusty. Are you suffering from hubris, Martha, my dear? I mean to say, this isn't just a little Swedish bank robbery. You want us to carry out a raid on one of the best-guarded casinos in the world. They have armed guards, CCTV everywhere and—'

'Now, now, Brains. Just think what a delightful challenge it is!' exclaimed Martha and she started filling the walking stick with gravel and diamonds. 'It'll all work out all right, you'll see,' she went on and gave him an encouraging pat on the cheek. 'I bet you one hundred thousand dollars we'll succeed!'

'Just listen to yourself! You've become a compulsive gambler,' he groaned and looked glumly at his fingernails, which were now chewed to bits.

'A little more coffee, perhaps?' Martha said to change the subject. 'I'll get some cups, you can open the wafers,' she said as she got up.

After Martha had served the coffee, she sealed the handle of her walking stick. Then she went to fetch the plan of the casino. Robbing a casino in Las Vegas was not just any old robbery; in that respect her friends were right. It would be difficult, and it was her duty to support and encourage them.

'I know we've looked at these building plans a thousand times, but as an exercise I think we should try to memorize the layout by tomorrow. Nobody will make any mistakes with a door or a corridor then,' she said as she laid the building plans out on the table.

'You never give up, do you?' Rake sighed. 'Do you want us to do a round of gym exercises after coffee too?'

Martha pretended not to hear him. She was admittedly very particular about them all keeping in good condition, but now was not the right occasion for exercising. All their focus must be on the robbery. It would be a last, but necessary, coup before they left America. They needed the proceeds from their criminal activities. If the League of Pensioners could help people to a better life, they would have achieved a great deal. Then she and her friends could give up their criminal activities and live a good life in the years they had left.

The next day they packed all their belongings and prepared themselves for the journey, and followed this with their usual afternoon nap. At dinner time the mood was undeniably a little tense, but they all put on a brave face – as brave as they possibly could. After a fortifying meal with lobster and champagne, they all felt well prepared for the evening's adventure.

Brains and Rake put on their stylish black suits, while Martha, Christina and Anna-Greta dressed in silk and tulle, and wrapped themselves in long, wide shawls. In suite 831 there was a smell of perfume and shaving lotion, and when the zips of the long dresses needed to be pulled up, Brains and Rake hurried to assist.

Brains looked uncomfortable, but he always did when he couldn't wear his usual 1950s trousers and checked flannel shirt. He felt so uncomfortable dressed up in a dark suit with a tie and a white handkerchief in his top pocket that he'd blown his nose on the handkerchief and then put it back in place, which made Martha quickly find a new one for him. The charmer Rake was right at home in his elegant clothes and carried his suit with a straight posture and a confident smile. Christina was wearing a light blue dress with shoulder straps and a large pink hat, while Anna-Greta strode across the floor in her rustling evening gown, which was so old-fashioned that she looked as if she came from another – indefinable – century. She wasn't interested in clothes and she really didn't care what she looked like. If she could have, she would have put on an old tracksuit. Or even better, she would be happiest the day somebody invented a clothes spray so you only had to spray yourself and you'd be dressed.

When they had all got dressed and fortified themselves with a cup of coffee, Martha pulled out the building plans.

'The staff room is diagonally behind the bathrooms beside the emergency exit at the end of the corridor. This ought to be a quick grab-and-run robbery,' she said, tracking with her finger slowly across the paper.

'Grab and grab, and run and run. Have you ever seen running wheelchairs?' muttered Rake, who had a weakness for sarcasm. On this particular evening they would not have their usual walkers with them, but would instead carry out the robbery in electric-powered wheelchairs.

'Well, they can go pretty fast, that's for sure!' said Brains smugly, with a mischievous look on his face. For a brief moment Martha was worried, because she had seen him working on the wheelchairs with his tools all afternoon. But Brains would certainly have done his best. He had a great talent for technical things and so far he had not disappointed her. She decided to trust him.

'Don't start arguing, boys, but just try to remember this,' said Martha and she held up the building plans, which were full of markings in various colours. A large X indicated the staff room and some smaller ones showed the escape routes. Some mumbling and throat-clearing could be heard while the five of them memorized the building plans a final time. Rake fidgeted with the tie around his neck.

'Everybody says it's impossible to commit crime in Las Vegas, but you, Martha, think we can fool the lot of them.'

'Yes, it's inspiring to try, isn't it?' answered Martha quickly. She knew, deep inside, that something could go wrong but she kept that insight to herself. Anything else would have been destructive for the group's confidence.

'Now that we've made up our minds, we mustn't start doubting ourselves,' advised Christina as she pulled out her lipstick. Of course she was worried too, and didn't even dare to think about the fact that they might end up in an American prison. But since she was the one who had mostly been responsible for the idea, she wanted to go through with the robbery. One day when she'd been on her way to the ladies' room to touch up her makeup, she'd noticed that the door to the casino staff room was ajar. She peeped in and saw that the betting chips were kept there and there wasn't a guard in sight.

Naturally, Christina told her friends about this. 'If one could get at those chips . . . Well, you understand my meaning.' And of course they all did.

Christina didn't need to say any more to kick-start the adventurous spirit of the League of Pensioners. The five friends saw the sparkle in each others' eyes, and that was that. Now it was time to act upon it!

'Righto, next stop the casino,' said Martha and put the building plans down on the table. 'Good luck to everyone. We'll rendezvous in the parking lot, okay?'

A murmur of agreement was heard from the others.

'Oh, do you have the tickets?' Martha asked. She wanted to make sure every part of their plan was accounted for.

'Stop treating us like children,' Rake responded churlishly.

Martha blushed. It was hard for her to keep track of everything and everyone while at the same time refraining from getting too bossy. But, after all, she had persuaded her friends to embark upon their criminal path last year at Diamond House. She had masterminded their escape from the dreary nursing home and then organized their great art heist. So, as the ringleader of the group, it was up to her to stop them running into difficulties.

Martha just couldn't stop herself from adding, 'Just one last thing. Don't forget the balloons!'

'Yes, indeed, or the CCTV system,' mumbled Rake.

'And don't drink too much during the evening,' chimed in Anna-Greta.

'No more than will make us *naturally* confused,' giggled Christina.

'No more than usual, in other words,' said Brains.

Martha picked up the building plans, got up and pushed them into the document shredder.

'Let's hope we remember everything now,' Christina commented anxiously as she watched the scraps of shredded paper emerge from the other end of the machine. 'What if we forget something?'

'We won't,' said Rake, squeezing her hand encouragingly.

'And we can't walk around holding a map while we commit a crime,' Anna-Greta said as she pushed her 1950s glasses up onto her forehead.

'Indeed we can't,' Martha agreed, and she picked up the paper scraps and flushed them down the toilet.

3

The casino floor, with its plush red carpets, had no windows, and there were no clocks to be seen. Those who entered the casino did not want to be reminded of the time; they were there to enjoy themselves. The high, dark tables with their roulette wheels attracted hordes of people, most of them tourists. You couldn't always tell who the compulsive gamblers were, but they were there among them.

A muffled buzz of voices lay like a blanket over the room. Fat men in suits or Hawaiian shirts walked around between the tables, treading nervously on the red carpets. Ladies in long dresses and glittering jewels leaned over the tables, pushing heaps of betting chips out and fidgeting with their manicured nails. In the background you could hear the distinctive noises from the slot machines.

'We'll play with the highest stakes tonight of course,' said Martha as she came close to colliding with Anna-Greta after accidently steering towards a table in her electric wheelchair. Anne-Greta, who was as tall as a drainpipe and looked as though she had come straight from that movie about Mary Poppins (only the umbrella was missing), veered out of her path at the very last second. She gave Martha an irritated look.

'Take it easy! We practised manoeuvring yesterday. And for goodness' sake don't crash into anybody – because then the security guards will hear about it.'

'No traffic accidents here,' Martha started to say but abruptly fell silent. Across the room, she could see that the security guards were already emptying out of the staff room: their shift for the evening had begun. She snuck a look at the doorway. They had all agreed that they must strike as early as possible in the evening, while there were still lots of betting chips in the room, but as quickly as this . . . ? They had hardly had time to get to the roulette tables and blend in with the other gamblers.

'What a weird lamp up there on the ceiling. I didn't see that yesterday,' said Rake, who had parked himself by the long side of the roulette table. He looked up towards a shining bowl-shaped object right above the table.

'Pah, it's only another camera,' said Martha, trying to sound plucky. 'Don't worry about that. They must have a whole wall of TV screens in the security room, and one more doesn't make any difference. They're probably looking at us this very minute.'

Rake pulled out his steel comb and tidied his part. It was a reflex reaction. He always wanted to look smart and he enjoyed other people admiring him. His friends claimed that he deliberately filled his pockets with coins when he went through security checks at airports – it was just like Rake to draw attention to himself, and they were convinced that he was hoping for a body search by one of the female guards. Rake slipped the comb back into his pocket, straightened his bangs and put his straw hat on. It wasn't fancy, but it was necessary this particular evening.

'Don't bother about the cameras. We'll be out through the doors before the guards have time to react,' Martha went on cheerfully. She tried to sound confident, but her heart was pounding. She moistened her lips, nodded to the others and, for the sake of appearances, pushed a few chips onto the roulette table. 'We mustn't forget to place some bets, you hear!'

Martha always wanted to win, but this evening they had decided to lose as much as they possibly could. They didn't want to attract the attention of the guards. The croupier spun the wheel and then spun the ball in the other direction. Out of habit, Martha bet on a colour. Today it would be black. Then she remembered that she shouldn't double her bets this evening; they had agreed that they wanted to lose, so she quickly pushed a big heap of chips on the double zero. That never came up.

'No more bets!' said the croupier and looked at all the players. He eyed Martha a bit longer than the others, as if he suspected her of something, but then he spun the ball, which whirled around before bouncing off the sides a few times and then falling down. On the double zero.

'Oops!' said Christina and pushed her sun hat higher up on her head. A win – that wasn't part of the plan. Martha looked up at the ceiling again. The new camera seemed to have zoned in on their table. Best to lose it all now, she thought, so she left all the chips on the double zero again. That very same moment she saw the door to the staff room being opened as one of the guards went in. Martha moved her hand to the wheelchair control joystick.

'Brains, it's time!' she hissed but she wasn't able to say any more before the door closed again. That same moment the ball fell onto the numbers and landed on the double zero again.

'What in the name of heaven . . . I've never seen anything like it!' she stuttered and looked on with a dim-witted expression as the croupier pushed a pile of chips across to her. Some security guards with earphones approached the table, stopped and stood right behind them. I *must* lose now, Martha thought, and bet all her chips on black.

'Please, please, let me lose now!' she said silently to herself. And then, just then, the door to the staff room opened again at the same time the ball fell down onto a black number. One of the security guards pulled out his cellphone.

'What the—' Martha gasped.

'Have you seen them? That gang of old people are here again,' said Stewart, a middle-aged supervisor, as he glanced up at the nearest TV screen. 'Wow, they're winning a lot there, first the double zero and now black. Those idiots will bankrupt us. I bet you there's something fishy going on.'

The security room above the casino looked like a TV shop with all the televisions turned on at the same time. All round the walls two rows of screens flickered with images from different rooms and tables. In the middle was a large elliptical table where the security the staff sat. Now and then they zoomed in on somebody who looked suspicious.

'Just because they're having a run of good luck you think they're up to no good. Take it easy. Soon they'll lose it all again,' answered his colleague, who was called Bush. He had curly hair like the former president and was just as cocky. The only difference was that he hadn't started a war.

'Good luck? You've said that every day and you've always been wrong. No, let's grab them!' Stewart slapped his palm hard on the table so that his cellphone hopped.

'Take it easy. Let them carry on awhile; this is good entertainment.'

'But the balloons on the wheelchairs, what about those? It isn't Thanksgiving yet, damn it. And just look at those sun hats. They must be crazy, the lot of them.'

'This is amusing! And have you seen they've got electric wheelchairs today? What if they crash into something?'

'I didn't bloody well take this security job to go chasing old people in wheelchairs. No, let's throw them out. I've had enough. We'll check that guy over by the blackjack table too. A card pro. He's got sunglasses on and probably has a transmitter there.'

'A suspect simply because he hasn't won several days in a row? No, hold your horses, Stewart.' His colleague yawned. 'By the way, the old lot are moving across to the bar. Just look at that, their baskets are full of betting chips. I hope they spend it all on something fun.'

Stewart leaned towards the TV screen and zoomed in on them.

'No, they aren't going to the bar. They're on their way to the bathrooms.'

'I'm not bloody well chasing them there!'

'But five people wouldn't go to the bathrooms at the same time. I'm telling the security guards.' Stewart picked up his phone and dialled the number.

For a moment Martha stared at the pile of betting chips that the croupier had placed in front of her, then she swept them all into her basket. She glanced again at the staff entrance. The guard had been hovering at the door and now looked as though he might be leaving the staff room. They couldn't wait any longer. She put on her sun hat and poked Brains in the ribs.

'Action!' she whispered and raised her hand as a sign to the others. Christina, Anna-Greta and Rake put on their sun hats too and followed after her.

Brains steered his Flexmobil Classic wheelchair in the direction of the bathrooms, and, just as he passed the staff room door, he had a bad coughing attack. When the guard was on his way out, Brains leaned forward and coughed out his false teeth. The security guard paid scant attention to the bent-over old man, and strode off towards the gambling hall with a security bag in his hand. Brains looked up with a grin and made a thumbs-up sign to the others. He had been spot on target. His loose teeth lay on the threshold and the door had not closed properly.

'I must just powder my nose!' announced Christina loudly, her sun hat pulled low over her head. She pretended to drive off towards the bathroom, but just outside the staff room she made it look as if the electric wheelchair had gone wrong. Determinedly, she pushed the joystick back and forth so that the chair twirled round a few times while Brains cautiously held the door to the room open. 'The balloons!' Martha indicated with hand signals, and when Brains released them they elegantly hovered up by the ceiling. Christina then manoeuvred her chair over the threshold and backed into the room at full speed, closely followed by Rake and Anna-Greta.

As long as they cover the camera lenses properly, Martha thought, but said instead: 'Okay, go, go, go!' And she also sped into the room. Finally, Brains looked around, adjusted his sun hat and followed the others.

Once they were all in the staff room with the door pulled shut behind them, Christina quickly yanked out the wheelchairs' seat cushions, which she had filled with cash boxes similar to those used to keep the betting chips in. It hadn't been an easy task for Brains to transform the bag-in-boxes into false cash boxes, but tinfoil and silver paint had done the trick, though unfortunately they had managed to spill some wine on the tinfoil while Brains was making them. Christina sniffed at the mock cash boxes. They still smelled of wine, but it was too late to do anything about that now. Besides, the wine had been good so they had all had such a nice evening. Brains and Martha had already made their way along a corridor to open the storeroom, where the casino kept its aluminum cases of cash boxes full of betting chips.

Brains had to mess around a bit before he managed to

pick the cases' complicated locks, but suddenly his face lit up and a distinct click could be heard as the first lock was opened. The gang rapidly started to switch their empty fake cash boxes with the real ones from the casino. When they had finished, Christina zipped the boxes with the chips inside the wheelchair cushions before putting them back in the wheelchairs. Then Brains locked the cases and put them back on the storeroom and closed the door.

'I hope the guards didn't see that,' Martha muttered with a prayer up towards the ceiling. 'There might have been a gap in the balloons.'

'That's why we had the sun hats, have you forgotten?' said Brains. 'Right, let's get out of here!'

'What about the balloons?' said Christina.

'And the false teeth,' Martha added.

'Don't worry about the balloons, and I've got a spare pair of teeth!' Brains shouted.

For a moment it was all a bit chaotic, but in the end they got things in order and were all seated in the electric wheelchairs ready to move again. Somewhat tense, they grasped their joysticks and set off at full speed towards the door, without bearing in mind that Brains had tinkered with the engines of each of the wheelchairs. They now shot off like New Year's rockets.

'What the . . .!' exclaimed Anna-Greta and almost lost her hat.

'I told you I had improved their performance,' Brains panted.

But as they emerged from the staff room, they had to suddenly brake. Standing there were two security guards.

'What are you doing? You're not allowed in here!' the tallest and beefiest of them shouted, blocking their path.

'The bathrooms? They were here yesterday,' Martha answered quick as a flash.

'Oh dear, they are farther down the corridor.' The younger security guard pointed.

'No, they were here yesterday, I know that for a fact!' Martha insisted.

'If you go to the right by the entrance, then—'

'Oh no, that's where the betting tables are, you can't fool me.'

Then the big guard grabbed hold of her wheelchair and turned it to point down the corridor. 'That way!' he said.

'All right then,' said Martha and she pressed the joystick as far as she could. 'Bathrooms next stop! Goodness, how fast we're going!' she managed to add before she disappeared at full speed towards the ladies', closely followed by the others. Brains and Rake went to the men's and after a few minutes they all rolled out to the designated meeting place in the parking lot.

'How did it go?' Martha asked. 'Did you get your radio transmitter in place?'

'Yes, I sure did. I fixed it behind the mirror in the bathroom,' confirmed Brains.

'Good, now we can send a message to the security guards if we need to. You are clever, Brains,' Martha said. They smiled at each other, nodded and then drove off as agreed back to their hotel. In the lobby they stopped in front of the elevators.

'Eighth floor, but make it snappy!' said Martha.

'Don't say that Brains has tinkered with the elevator engine too!' said Anna-Greta with a sigh.

Once they reached the eighth floor, they made a bee-line for Martha's room, where they hastily pulled out the cash boxes from the cushions.

'That's better. I couldn't have put up with that hard metal in my back for another second!' said Rake, rubbing the curve of his back and then handing over his boxes to Brains. His comrade then picked the locks, took out the betting chips and began to put them into the wheelchair baskets.

'These are the genuine things – and we can cash them in,' cackled Anna-Greta, rolling her eyes in delight at the sight of the colourful piles of chips.

It was quite a fiddly task to empty all the cash boxes and fill the baskets, but in the end they managed to get all the betting chips out and covered them with shawls and sun hats.

'Now the hardest part remains,' said Martha. 'We must pretend that this is just an ordinary win and that this evening is just like all the other evenings when we have won lots.'

'Then why did we try to lose earlier this evening?' Rake wondered.

'To avoid attracting attention, have you forgotten?' Martha cut him off, but had to admit to herself that per-haps she hadn't thought it through properly – because it would indeed have seemed strange if they hadn't won anything during the entire evening and then had gone to the cash desk with chips worth several million. Being a criminal required a lot of brainwork, Martha thought. It was much better than sudoku, crosswords or self-help books for keeping the mind active.

'What if the staff get suspicious?' said Christina, worryingly pointing at the basket jam-packed with betting chips.

'Pah, we just behave as though we are confused,' said Martha. 'Now let's go. Time for the next move!'

The League of Pensioners took the elevator down to the lobby, rolled out of the hotel and returned to the casino. To be on the safe side, they had covered the betting chips over very carefully, but, even so, Martha thought that the security guards looked curiously at them when they approached the cash desks. And indeed one of them adjusted his earphone, joined his colleague and stopped them abruptly.

'Excuse me, madam, but will you please follow us for a security check.' The guard looked strict.

'Goodness me!' stuttered Anna-Greta.

'Pah, we simply forgot to cash in our chips,' said Martha nonchalantly. 'To think one can be so absentminded!'

'Yes, I think we drank too much champagne,' Christina added with a nervous giggle. The security guard picked up one of the chips from her basket and held it up against the light.

'Hmm,' he said.

'Yes, so silly of us to forget to cash in our chips. We were sooo distracted by these electric wheelchairs,' said Brains.

'We're not used to them, you see, and we were fully concentrating on steering them,' Anna-Greta added and for the sake of appearances steered her wheelchair straight into the wall so that her hat fell off. One of the security guards picked it up.

'Thank you, darling,' cackled Anna-Greta. 'It's always difficult to swing,' she added in her broken English.

But the guards did not allow themselves to be distracted.

'Would you please get up? We want to examine the baskets.'

Then the lady in the cash desk stuck out her head and said in a loud voice: 'I can vouch for them! These people are regular gamblers who tend to win. They've come in with just as many chips before. They are on a winning streak!'

The guards looked confused but backed away a little and Rake gave the cash-desk lady a grateful wink. She started to count the betting chips under the penetrating gaze of the security guards. Brains noticed they didn't seem to be giving up, and he gave Martha a questioning look.

Was it time now?

Martha nodded and then he discreetly pressed the remote that activated the radio transmitter in the bathroom. The pre-recorded message started up straight away and the very next moment the older of the two security guards pushed his earphone a bit farther into his ear. He widened his eyes and grabbed his colleague.

'Alarm! Let's go!'

The two men rushed off towards the gambling floor, and Brains looked pleased with himself.

'The radio transmitter worked perfectly. As soon as people get an order they lose all their common sense!'

Martha smiled. It had been complicated recording the order to the guards, and there was no way of knowing whether or not someone might discover the transmitter in the men's room and take it away. But everything had worked according to plan. She gave Brains a wink.

'Brains, you are a genius. You can't imagine how much I appreciate you!'

Despite the fact that they were busy carrying out a complicated crime, Brains blushed right up to his hairline.

While the lady behind the desk changed their betting chips for cash, Martha and her friends pushed the bundles of dollars into their wheelchair baskets, wrapping them in the shawls and covering them over well. Then Rake bowed deeply, smiled his most charming smile and thanked the woman for her help. Then they all left the building as quickly as they possibly could.

Once outside, they picked up speed. When they pushed the joysticks to max, they shot away on their improved wheelchairs towards the hotel. Back in suite 831 again, they congratulated themselves on their success. But there was still more to do before their robbery was complete. Brains and Rake hid the cash boxes while the others took the dollar bundles to the bank so that Anna-Greta, as usual, could transfer the money from the League of Pensioners' Las Vegas account to various accounts in Sweden. Once all this had been done, they took a taxi straight to the airport.

* * *

The next day was exceptionally hot. A steaming, nasty-smelling smoke billowed out from the tar machine as the four road workers smoothed out the surface. They had been putting down gravel and tar all day long and were beginning to get tired. Some had tied kerchiefs around their hair to avoid getting drops of sweat in their eyes; others had their caps pulled low over their faces. Some way away, a steamroller with enormous wheels was rolling back and forth over the sticky black road surface. The men had already tarred quite a lot but they still had a fair bit left to do. The road up to the Hotel Orleans had to be ready by evening, and they had about one third left. Then, suddenly, they heard a strange sound. At first nobody bothered about it, but then the tar-machine driver put on the brakes and jumped down from the cabin. He carefully avoided getting tar under his shoes and reached the pothole his colleagues were busy filling. He bent down and started poking around in the gravel. At the edge of the new pavement he caught sight of a bit of grey metal. He pushed some of the gravel aside and saw that at the end of the bit of metal there was a little lock. His curiosity aroused, he dug a bit deeper in the gravel and soon could pull up a buckled, box-like bit of scrap metal. He turned it this way and that in his hands and then held it up for all to see.

'Just look at this. The remains of a cash box. What the hell's it doing here?'

4

In the brick-red police headquarters at Kronoberg in Stockholm, Chief Inspector Ernst Blomberg sat with his hands behind his neck and his feet up on the desk. The computer screen in front of him was lit up and seemed to challenge him to use it, but it was after 6 p.m. and he didn't feel like working overtime. Soon he would be retiring and it was high time for him to take things a bit easier. And as for his pension . . . He sat up straight, keyed in the password and accessed the internal police database. The Police Pension Fund, yes. He would work out how much money he would get when he retired. He had some big tax debts from the days he had been an entrepreneur and had concocted some sticky face creams in his garage. His products sold like hotcakes but he had been careless with his bookkeeping. He had to pay for that, but if he had a good pension things might turn out okay. He entered his password and accessed the amount in his pension account. This was private business during working hours, but what the hell. Just think of all those weekends he'd stepped in to help when his colleagues had refused! He looked at the various funds where his pension money was invested and worked out the total value. He groaned. It was a pitifully small amount. But who actually paid money into the funds, and what did the payouts look like? The police department had sent him on a special IT course so he ought to be able to check that information. He stretched out to the bowl of candy on the desk and took a handful. At the same moment the screen started fluttering. Some money had just been transferred into the account, increasing his total balance. Mysterious . . . surely nobody worked in the bank at this time of the day? But if it meant more money for retired chief inspectors like himself, that was fine with him. He personally would need every extra krona. The rent for his apartment had suddenly been raised, and he still had that old tax debt to pay off. He thought about the economic criminals he had investigated over the years. They had all had pots of money with their luxury penthouses, big yachts, Porsches and all the rest of it, while he – the leading IT specialist in the police force – was only going to get a few measly thousand kronor a month. Nobody else knew how to sneak a look into people's e-mail or bank accounts without them knowing. Yet he hadn't been given a raise. Blomberg muttered to himself and was just about to take some more candy when the screen started flickering again. Another few hundred thousand kronor had been added to the pension fund. Who on earth wanted to support retired policemen with almost half a million? He must trace the donor. If somebody was so keen to support the pension fund, then maybe they might be persuaded to give *even more* money? Yes, perhaps he could start a charitable organization. Transfer all the money to . . . No, no, he mustn't think along those lines. That would be like committing a crime!

Suddenly he felt afraid, got up and turned off the computer. Best to go home and feed the cat. He had bought some beer and chips for the evening's hockey match as well, so he might as well go and enjoy it.

The following evening Blomberg stayed late in his office, muttering that he must do overtime. At nine o'clock, when all of his colleagues had gone home, he logged into the Police Pension Fund again and found a new figure – four hundred thousand kronor. Where did the money come from? His fingers danced over the keyboard and, after a while, he found what he wanted. He leaned back in his chair and rocked back and forth while he tried to digest the information. The Police Pension Fund had received the money from a bank in Las Vegas. But the Swedish police didn't have an office out there, did they? Chief Inspector Blomberg got up and went to fetch a cup of coffee – a double espresso. Because he understood at least this much: he would be spending quite a few hours in front of the computer. He keyed in his secret alias and logged into the pension fund account again. From there it shouldn't be too difficult to trace the account in Las Vegas where the money had come from. Why not create an account for a charitable foundation and reroute the money into that? Nobody would ever check it. He smiled a little to himself, and immediately felt very affluent. At last he had found a good use for his IT skills. And with a bit of luck there might be a few more payments from Las Vegas during the night.

5

'Do you really want me to collapse in a heap on the conveyer belt? That sounds silly,' said Anna-Greta, looking grumpy. 'Every time we do something suspicious, I have to fall down. Is that all I'm good for?'

It was early in the morning when the League of Pensioners arrived at Stockholm Arlanda airport. It felt strange to be home again, and the long journey had exhausted them. Martha and the others winked at one another but they couldn't relax yet. The plane from Copenhagen had just landed and soon their luggage from America would arrive on the conveyer belt. They knew that the customs officials searched baggage from the US but weren't so concerned about luggage that came from neighbouring Nordic countries. So the League of Pensioners needed to acquire some luggage tags from the Copenhagen flight.

'Nobody can fall over like you, Anna-Greta, but if you don't want to then I can fall instead and you can take care of the rest,' said Martha.

'We'll manage that fine, my dear,' Brains said, voicing his opinion.

Martha nodded and went and stood right next to the

opening of belt three. She peered in between the big rubber strips hanging down over the opening, and through the gap she watched the baggage come in on a cart and observed the airport workers as they started to unload it. The belt was set in motion and the first baggage items came into view. When there was a little space between some of the bags, she saw her chance. Now, she thought, and pretended to stumble, falling right across the belt. Martha landed on her tummy with her hat askew and baggage on both sides of her. No fractured thighs here, she thought proudly, but, mind you, she had done all those gymnastics lessons as a girl. She was swept along the belt between all the bags, flailing her feet and arms as she went. The sight was so remarkable that nobody actually did anything. And while the belt moved along with Martha on it, the attention of the other passengers was transfixed on the strange predicament of the elderly woman. As this was going on, Brains surreptitiously stood in front of the emergency stop button and Rake, Anna-Greta and Christina quickly stole baggage labels off the passing bags – which had arrived from Copenhagen. When the friends had snatched five labels, Brains nodded to Martha, who quickly, and with surprisingly good balance, hoisted herself off the conveyer belt all by herself. All around her, horrified spectators breathed a sigh of relief.

'One shouldn't go too close to the belt; it says so on the sign. I ought to have paid attention,' Martha said sententiously as she tidied up her tangled hair. The travellers around her stared with mouths agape, but Martha didn't care. Her job was done. She followed her friends to luggage belt number five, where the baggage from Chicago was expected. To be on the safe side, the League of Pensioners hadn't flown directly to Stockholm from Las Vegas. Instead they had changed planes in Chicago – as they were of the opinion that anything that might make them more difficult to trace was a good thing.

That same moment, the sign announcing the baggage from Chicago lit up and the first bags appeared. Martha and her friends went closer to the conveyer belt and as their baggage came along, various people around them helped them load the luggage onto two carts. Their baggage included their sturdy suitcases on wheels, their Carl Oscar walkers and, of course, the golf bag containing the walking sticks. Martha and Anna-Greta each took a cart into the ladies' room. There they quickly switched their baggage labels with the ones from Copenhagen and flushed the old ones down the toilet. They then went back to the others.

'What about the golf bag? Shouldn't that have a label?' Anna-Greta asked.

'Oops. We're one short. But I'm sure nobody'll notice there's a baggage tag missing, with all our suitcases,' said Martha, trying to sound convincing.

'We could abandon one of the suitcases, couldn't we?' said Brains.

'Yes, Anna-Greta's for example. After all, her clothes aren't much to—' Rake started.

'Over my dead body! There's my hat and my clothes, and what about my orthopaedic shoes?'

'Oh!' moaned Rake.

'But it's only one golf bag among other baggage. Nobody is going to care. We'll just walk past quickly,' Martha suggested.

'That's how smugglers usually think,' said Christina. 'And you know what happens to them?'

'And just remember what we've got in the walking sticks,' Brains added.

'We'd better get moving, otherwise we'll look suspicious.' Martha hurried them along and took the lead towards the customs checkout desk, closely followed by the others. One after the other they passed the customs officers without any problem and Martha was just on her way out through the doors when she heard a voice behind her.

'Excuse me, madam. Could you please come in here? That golf bag.'

A light-haired, middle-aged customs officer indicated to her to come across to the counter, and at first she pretended she hadn't seen or heard him, but when he came up to her and put his hand on her shoulder, she didn't have much choice. The man lifted the golf bag up onto a marble-like counter and started to look at the contents.

'Hardly what I'd call golf clubs, these,' he said and held up their walking sticks. Brains's stick with its reflectors stuck out a mile.

'Well, I'm afraid we aren't quite the golf-playing kind.' Martha blushed.

'Why have you got walking sticks in a golf bag?'

Martha swallowed and thought about the diamonds.

'Where else can you store your walking sticks?'

The customs officer scratched his neck and looked confused. He weighed at least twenty, perhaps thirty pounds too much, but had a very trendy haircut and was wearing a fashionable leather bracelet on his wrist.

'We're going to have to scan it.'

Now Christina and Anna-Greta noticed that something was amiss; they turned round and joined Martha. She saw their worried faces and took a deep breath.

'Scan? You mean one of those apparatuses that look inside you when you go to the doctor's? Oh how exciting!' she started off. 'You see, I've had a bad tummy and the doctor has X-rayed it several times. And my ankles, dear me! You should see those X-ray images. The bones inside my foot look like spindles. No, it isn't easy being old. You can X-ray my diamonds so I can see what they look like. I know what gold looks like because I used to smuggle that.'

'Yes, um, yes, I see.' The customs officer continued to look deeper into the golf bag, clearly not wanting to engage in conversation with the senile old woman.

'But with gold in, the walking sticks became far too heavy,' Martha rambled on. 'That was why we switched to diamonds. Or are they called emeralds when the gems are green? Unless they are glass, of course, because they were translucent when I put them in there. Unless they are blue, that is. Oh dearie me, now I can't really remember. Do you remember everything, young man? The X-ray doctors are so clever. I've got pictures of my gallstones too. And they were big ones. Do you want to see? But of course that was before I started smuggling plutonium in my navel. I think I've got some photos of that too.'

Martha gabbled on and on, the words just pouring out; Christina found it hard to stay serious and Anna-Greta burst out with such a loud, dry laugh that she almost blew the customs officer over.

'Yes, you scan our walking sticks. That'll be something to tell your colleagues on your coffee break,' Martha went on. 'But to go back to my visit to the doctor's – when he found the plutonium in my tummy he said—'

Anna-Greta's cackling got all the louder and the customs officer looked helplessly around for his colleagues. But they were busy with other travellers so there was no help available from them. The customs officer stood still for a few moments, pondering what to do, and then put the canes back in the golf bag.

'Thank you, that's all for now.'

'But what about the diamonds in my navel?'

The customs officer bowed and Martha couldn't get away quick enough, again closely followed by the others. Once outside the arrivals hall, Martha immediately hailed a taxi and when she turned to her friends in the back seat, her face was full of lines of laughter.

'People are so uncomfortable when they talk to the elderly nowadays, so you can lay it on as thick as you want! You should have seen his expression; I almost felt like consoling him. But now it's probably best we leave quickly. Next stop Stockholm! Let us disappear in the big city.'

'Disappear? How can we disappear?' mumbled Rake in the back of the taxi.

'Clarion Hotel, that will do nicely, don't you think?' she went on, without waiting for an answer. 'They are international there, that's for sure, and they will know all about coordination numbers. They will know that they are temporary personal identity numbers for people like us, who are coming as immigrants to Sweden.'

'Our new identity, yes,' Anna-Greta boasted with satisfaction. 'I thought we'd need new ones to be on the safe side. Our old crimes are still unsolved and I bet the police are still looking for us. It took me a few months to arrange it all, but now we'll have these new coordination numbers. But we can keep our old first names all the same – they're so common anyway.'

After almost an hour in the heavy traffic they reached the hotel and checked in. The porter helped them into the elevator with their baggage but it wasn't until they had got up to their rooms that Martha noticed that something felt wrong – very wrong. They didn't have the golf bag with them. Martha had forgotten it. It must still be at the customs checkpoint.

The large dining room was virtually deserted, with only a very few guests. A waiter was stacking cups and saucers beside the coffee machine and an elderly couple were sitting at a table by the window reading the newspapers. Some businessmen had just finished breakfast. They pushed their plates away, wiped their mouths and got up to hurry on their way. Martha and her friends were late, and they only wanted something light to eat before they could go and take a nap. Martha calmed down with a cup of coffee and some sandwiches and made sure all the others had something to eat before she dared tell them the bad news.

'In the customs hall? It can't be true, oh nooo, the golf bag with all our private capital?' whined Anna-Greta.

'You don't mean . . .' mumbled Christina, opening her handbag and searching for her blood-pressure pills.

'It can't be bloody true!' Rake hissed. 'Are the diamonds gone?'

Martha put her hands over her face and started to sniffle. Brains moved in a little closer.

'Now, now, Martha dear, it isn't all your fault. We weren't thinking either,' he said, and put his arm round her. 'We were so tired, all of us. Things like that can happen so easily. And after such a long journey. You wait and see, it'll sort itself out, my dear!'

'But the diamonds are worth at least . . .' groaned Anna-Greta and started to count in her head. She had grown up in posh and very affluent Djursholm and was used to a certain standard of living, but now things were looking bad.

'We seem to succeed with the crime, but then lose the booty. Perhaps we should cooperate with the mafia so there is a bit of order!' Brains joked.

'Goodness me, no, certainly not!' Anna-Greta exclaimed and dropped her teabag into Martha's coffee cup.

'In detective stories they never go losing all their money,' said Christina, who sounded a bit bolder now that she had taken her blood-pressure medicine.

'I'm sure we'll manage to get hold of the golf bag again

and if we have a little rest it'll probably all seem much better,' Martha said, trying to smooth things over.

'You go and have a rest and dream about Lost Property,' Rake muttered.

Martha gave him an angry look and tried to hold back her tears. Then Brains got up suddenly, causing the porcelain on the table to rattle.

'Some people put all their eggs in one basket. I don't. We're going to manage nicely for quite a while longer, at any rate.' He pulled up his wrinkled shirt – vintage 1950s – and exposed his round belly. Among the greyish-white hairs around his navel you could see a strip of surgical tape right over the hole. He looked a little mischievous.

'The good thing about diamonds is that they aren't so big. There was room for three in my navel.'

6

Customs Officer Carlsson yawned widely and let a colleague take over at the end of his shift. It had been an arduous night and of the two hundred and sixty passengers on the last plane, several had tried to smuggle in cannabis and happy pills. Although the most troublesome traveller by far was that old lady with the golf bag. She had gabbled on like an earthquake. And that talk of having plutonium in her navel! There were some really crazy people around. Now he could at last go home and sleep.

He put his pen away, nodded to his colleagues and was on his way out when he caught sight of the golf bag. Oh yes, of course, he had completely forgotten that. Best to hand it in.

'I'll take this to the destruction container,' he said and lifted it up so that the sticks rattled.

'But that old lady didn't have anything to declare,' his colleague protested. 'So it can't be sent for destruction, surely? She just forgot her golf bag. Take it to the storeroom instead.'

'Oh yeah, damn it!' muttered Carlsson. 'Okay, I'll dump it there.'

He yawned yet again. It was no joke working the night shift. Sleepily he walked off with the golf bag under his arm and stopped outside the storeroom.

'Oh hell!'

The door was locked. He put down the bag, fumbled with his keys and tried some of them. None fitted. He looked around and didn't feel like going back again. But he couldn't leave the bag here, could he? Perhaps he could just take it home with him, even though it was against the rules. He could put it in the hall for the time being and then take it back to work the next day. Or if the bag was good for keeping walking sticks in, then it would do just as well as an umbrella stand. Pleased with his brilliant idea, he whistled to himself all the way to the garage. Now he would drive home to Sollentuna and get some sleep. And why not report in sick tomorrow? He was, in fact, really tired – indeed, completely worn out. Best to have a large whisky and some sandwiches and take it easy.

The next morning Customs Officer Carlsson woke with a heavy hangover and stumbled out into the hall. Hardly looking at what he was doing, he fumbled for the morning paper in the mailbox until he realized that his wife had taken it out hours ago. He yawned and tried to swerve round a pair of children's rainboots on the floor; instead he tripped and fell right onto the golf bag. A crunching sound from inside the bag indicated that something had broken, and he got up somewhat shaken. A golf bag? But he didn't play golf. Then he remembered that silly old lady, and he stood the bag up. The chrome handle on one of the walking sticks had broken off. He looked inside and discovered something shiny. Curious as to what it was, he shook the handle and a whole lot of tiny stones fell onto the floor. Granite, bits of gravel, quartz crystal and some bits of polished glass. The old lady had talked about diamonds – could she have been telling the truth? He shook the other walking sticks. There was nothing special about them other than the fact that all the handles could be unscrewed. Inside them, too, were stones of various sizes and colours. Ah, now he understood: it was a way of giving the handle a bit of weight so that the walking sticks acquired the right stability and balance. Cheap and practical. And that old monster had teased him and said it was diamonds! Hadn't she said something about having gemstones in her navel too? He looked at the broken handle and realized it would be hard to repair. How could he explain that he'd taken home something from the customs hall – which was strictly forbidden – and then, to cap it off, had happened to break it? Perhaps it would be for the best to forget all about it and keep his mouth shut.

Still sleepy, he went to fetch the broom and dustpan but then he changed his mind. No, breakfast first. He slouched into the kitchen, turned the espresso machine on, made some cheese sandwiches and sat down with the morning paper. He read awhile and ate his breakfast and was just going to get another sandwich when his eye fell on the dog's empty food bowl. Oh yes, of course, he must give the dog something to eat, and he ought to feed the fish too. Yesterday he had bought a tin of powdered fish food and some dog food. Carlsson got up, went past the aquarium and out into the hall, where he'd left his brief-case. When he saw the gravel and tiny stones on the floor he had an idea. Hadn't his son said something about want-ing some fancier stones in his aquarium? Carlsson whistled, fetched the broom and dustpan and carefully swept up all the small stones. Then he tipped them into the water and carefully smoothed the stones out on the bottom of the tank. Having done that, he took the packet of fish food and sprinkled some into the water. Satisfied, he took a step back. Pretty little stones they were. The aquarium really glimmered.

7

The large old country house out in the Stockholm archipelago stood on a slope with a view across the sea and, even on a grey, windy day, the place was indescribably beautiful. In the summer the jetty would bask in the evening sunlight, and just above the shoreline was a well-tended yard with a terrace to sit on, a large storage shed, a cellar and a greenhouse.

'Just the thing!' Martha exclaimed, looking happily at the others. She and the rest of the League of Pensioners were walking around the yard, delighting in its features. Rake pictured what he could grow in the greenhouse while Christina inhaled the cold smell of the cellar and thought about all the good food she could store here. In two large sections in the cellar there was plenty of room for potatoes, plums, apples and other fruit, and the previous owner had put up wide shelves along the walls where you could keep everything from milk and mead to wine. A brown-stained door led from the earth cellar to the storage shed, where you could keep all the tools and other things necessary to look after the garden. Next to that sat a large old-fashioned woodworking shed with a carpenter's bench and a lathe. Brains noted with delight that the previous owner had left a set of tools, and he enthusiastically stroked the bench, dreaming of everything he could make there. He smiled happily and took Martha by the hand.

'Old girl, I believe this will suit us very nicely,' he said. 'I think we should buy this house.'

The real estate agent carried on with the viewing and said in a loud voice:

'Norra Lagnö here on Värmdö is a peaceful and select environment with beautiful old country houses. It is estimated to have been built at the end of the nineteenth century. This would suit you well, surely?'

'Thank you, but we aren't quite that old,' answered Martha, looking up at the big old house. It looked exactly like the picture they had seen advertised in the local paper. The house did look very old and had seen better days, but so had they, so it didn't matter, she thought.

'Look! Apple trees and redcurrant bushes,' the real estate agent went on, pointing at some trees and bushes that framed the path that led up to the house. 'And when it gets warmer you can drink your coffee in the lilac arbour if you wish.' He pointed to where some outdoor furniture could be seen under a tarpaulin. Then he took the outside steps two at a time, unlocked the front door and showed Martha and her friends into the front hall.

The old house smelled of wood and of days gone by and the floor creaked. But there was an air of coziness already in the hall.

'What are the neighbours like?' Christina asked.

'Very pleasant. Some bachelors live higher up the slope and a single middle-aged woman opposite.'

'Single? Well now!' said Rake.

The old pensioners hung up their overcoats but kept their shoes on. None of them had been indoctrinated in a nursery school.

'Just look at the view!' the real estate agent went on, and opened the doors to the glassed-in veranda. Out in the bay you could see two giant ferries from Finland on their way towards Stockholm. A little boat with an outboard motor looked like a tiny shell next to them.

'Yes, a superb view, but what about the house?' Martha asked. The diamonds in Brains's navel had given them only a few million, and their budget was still more limited than expected. Despite having gone out to Arlanda airport several times, they still hadn't found the golf bag. Martha and Anna-Greta had asked at Customs, been in touch with Lost Property and gone back to Customs again. Rake and Brains had tried too, but in vain. It wasn't easy when they didn't have a proper baggage tag, let alone a label on the bag. And besides, they had to be careful when they went nosing around. The police must not get wind of the fact that the League of Pensioners were back in Sweden.

'It feels as if the staircase wobbles a bit,' said Martha on her way up to the second floor.

'Yes, it does creak a little, but wood is a living material. A newly built house can't compare with a fine old country house. This is vintage.'

'Vintage?'

'Old and valuable,' said the real estate agent and showed them one of the bedrooms. Brains rocked the floorboards to see how much they moved.

'Carpenter ants, are they vintage too?' he said, and pointed at some ants that had emerged from the cracks.

The real estate agent pretended not to hear, and opened the French windows on to a large balcony. Before them lay the open bay. The sea glistened, seagulls flew over the ice and the two giant ferries from Finland were now silhouettes on the horizon.

'Completely irresistible, isn't it?'

'They're only small boats. Not like when I sailed on the Indian Ocean,' said Rake.

'That was in the old days,' Anna-Greta interposed. '*Pretend* that this is the Big Ocean.'

'Pretend!?' Rake snorted. 'The Indian Ocean doesn't freeze over!'

'But it's all water,' mumbled Christina, although she immediately regretted the remark when she saw his horrified look. As a young man, Rake had sailed the high seas, and he was very proud of it too. Who went on such long voyages nowadays? From now on, he deserved more appreciation and praise, she decided. Christina did rather like him, after all, and was even a bit in love with him, so she ought to show him that. They spent every day together so it was easy to take each other for granted. But Rake could also show a little appreciation – a bunch of flowers would have been wonderful. On the way down to the first floor, she took hold of his arm, stood on tiptoe and gave him a little light kiss on the cheek.

'A lot of roof tiles are broken, the gutters are full of rotten leaves and the chimney is cracked. This isn't for us. You should never buy a house in poor repair,' said Brains after they had looked at everything.

'Yes, you'll have to sell this rambling old place to somebody else,' Rake added.

'But it's the *setting* you pay for,' the real estate agent emphasized.

'Could you phone for a taxi – seniors' rate?' Martha went on, all according to the plan they had decided upon before the viewing. With their pretended lack of interest, they were hoping to save many hundreds of thousands of kronor. Perhaps even millions. The elderly bunch nagged on and on. It wasn't until the real estate agent had lowered the price by almost two million that the League of Pensioners relented and finally clinched the deal. They were surprised at just how much they had managed to lower the price by.

Two weeks later, they moved in. For help with the practicalities of running the house, they were going to employ Christina's out-of-work son, Anders, who was a man in his fifth decade with two children, and his younger sister, Emma, who was on maternity leave.

Emma had nothing against someone else looking after the baby. Life as a stay-at-home mum with a baby was not for her, and she was pleased that she had married a younger man. He was quite happy to look after Malin, and actually liked doing so. Of course, Emma loved her daughter but she was always going on about how a child shouldn't become too attached to her mother – something she had read in a newspaper. Emma had a weakness for all the fashionable ideas and always followed new diets and weight-loss programs.

One grey day in November, Emma and Anders drove out to Myrstigen to take a look at the new home their mother had moved into with her old choir friends. Anders parked his old Volvo outside the rambling country house, scratched his beard stubble and looked up at the building, which had definitely seen better days.

'I don't think we want to get involved with all the maintenance work,' he said, making a face. His sister nodded.

'We'll help them with the everyday things; they'll have to get professionals to do the big jobs.'

'Of course, we'll give them a hand so that they'll at least have some sort of order,' Anders said. 'And since they pay in cash, perhaps me and the wife can still afford to live in the city centre. People with ordinary incomes can't afford that any longer.'

While the brother and sister carried furniture and boxes, furnished the rooms and ran various errands, Anna-Greta bought everything the League of Pensioners needed on the Internet. She loudly and joyfully provided a running commentary as she bought everything from furniture and household equipment to gardening tools and books on Blocket.se. Anders, who knew lots about cars, helped her to purchase an old Volkswagen minibus in good condition, a spacious vehicle which would serve as their private seniors' transportation.

For several days, the gang were busy getting the house into order, and with lots of laughter they furnished the big living room on the ground floor and their own bedrooms. Brains and Rake had both fallen for the same spacious bedroom. It had striped wallpaper and a view of the sea. When Brains realized that it was the only room from which you could see the ships out at sea, he let Rake have it. But it didn't really matter so much because he got an even bigger room that was next door to Martha's.

The beige country house with its white window frames and many mullioned windows was a miracle of fancy carpentry details and it suited them perfectly. Besides a hall and the bedrooms on the second floor, there was a library, a dining room, a kitchen and a lovely glassed-in veranda on the ground floor. Long ago it would have been the summer residence of a rich family from the city. There would have been lots of children there and household staff too. Now it all belonged to the League of Pensioners.

'I think Mum will be comfortable here,' said Anders when they were all installed.

'As long as she keeps calm and doesn't end up behind bars, of course,' Emma answered.

'You don't think they're going to commit more crimes, do you?' Anders asked his sister.

Emma shrugged her shoulders and grinned.

'I couldn't possibly say.'

* * *

The old country house started to feel more like a proper home, and the League of Pensioners did indeed feel at home there. The bedrooms were cozy. Martha loved her flowery wallpaper, and Anna-Greta and Christina were very pleased with the wooden floors and the light colours of the walls. The library looked like a scene from a Carl Larsson painting. The wooden panelling and the baseboards were painted in pale pastel shades and up by the ceiling was a ribbon of flowers and twigs.

'This is almost too good to be true,' said Anna-Greta. 'Not having to live in an institution. This is even better than the Grand Hotel.'

'I'm so pleased that Anders and Emma came to help. I heard on the radio about the home-help services paid for by the council,' Christina told them. 'One woman had seventy different home-helpers in six months!'

'It's a disgrace, it can't go on like that,' Rake muttered and clenched his fist. 'You shouldn't be allowed to treat people like that!'

'Exactly. That's why we should go on working, so that we can help more people so they get to have it as good as us,' said Martha.

And then they all smiled and imagined all the joy their donations could bring. Their deceptions and robberies had indeed paid very well so far.

Despite their successful stay in Las Vegas they still hadn't amassed the five hundred million they wanted. So they couldn't start taking it easy yet, in Martha's opinion.

They must get some more money in. Perhaps they could carry out a new robbery, a little innocent one, something that would provide some money but not be too demanding of them.

All five of them had, however, been a bit careless about their physical condition, so now they would have to make sure they got back into shape before they could even begin to think up any new crimes. Martha looked on Blocket.se and eventually found some cheap equipment from a gym that had closed. An exercise treadmill, dumbbells, ropes and rowing machines were stored in the garden shed until a gym was ready in part of the cellar. She rubbed her hands in delight and looked forward to becoming fitter again.

At their new house, Christina often sat in the library or on the veranda. She had bought a whole lot of classics as well as a big box of English detective stories. While she organized them on the shelves, she hummed to herself or quoted lines from well-known poems. She hadn't felt so good for ages.

Brains was happy with life too. He had got hold of an old motorcycle, which he worked on out in the yard. What he had really wanted was a Harley-Davidson but that was too expensive, so he'd had to settle for a bike from the First World War.

Rake inspected the greenhouse and thought about what he would like to grow in there. Tomatoes were a must, but perhaps cucumbers and grapes too. Then he wandered around in the garden, had a good look at the fruit bushes and started planning what he would sow in the spring. Now and then he glanced up at the neighbouring house. The woman he had glimpsed behind the curtains seemed exciting. She had jet-black hair.

Anna-Greta had been checking an online auction site and finally had found a fancy record player together with fifteen large boxes of vinyl records. Her friends had grumbled at first, but after she had agreed that she wouldn't play her favourite religious song and her accordion music more than once a day, they went along with it. The collection also included a lot of choral music, and that was practical, of course, if they wanted to learn some new songs for their repertoire. Admittedly, they didn't sing quite so often nowadays, as they couldn't perform with their old choir The Vocal Chord now that they were on the run, but they couldn't drop music completely.

Every time Anna-Greta put on a record, she thought of her old love, Gunnar. She had met him on a cruise ship when the League of Pensioners were midway through their first major robbery. He had come to visit her while she was in prison for her part in the art heist, and her criminal activity hadn't seemed to bother him. In those moments when she thought of him, she wandered around the room or stared absentmindedly out a window. Anna-Greta had phoned him several times but had only got through to an answering service. Now she regretted not keeping in better touch with him while she was living in Las Vegas. Even though she was surrounded by her friends, she actually felt a bit lonely.

When they had all settled down in their new home, Martha gathered the friends together in the library for an important meeting.

'We can't call ourselves the League of Pensioners any longer because that name is notorious in Sweden. We must give ourselves a new name,' she said.

'I think we should go with a name that sounds more international,' mused Rake, who had travelled the most in his younger days.

They discussed Halloween, Angel Birds, Grey Oldies, Hidden Diamonds and a whole lot of other titles before finally settling on Outlaw Oldies.

'It's got a contemporary feel to it,' Martha said enthusiastically, and then she and Brains went down to the newly purchased mailbox by the road and glued on the name in big black letters. From now on, all the mail was to be sent to Outlaw Oldies, Myrstigen 2, Norra Lagnö, Värmdö. The five pensioners had acquired a new home and a new life. And a new, dangerous, challenging name.

8

The lights were on upstairs in the eighteenth-century house farther up the slope, where the group of bachelors lived. The old wooden building had white mullioned windows, a very solid-looking front door and brown-stained wooden front steps. But the decorative banisters on the steps were painted black and resembled wings, and the handrails had been painted white and red. The colours were no coincidence, as the people who lived in the house were in fact a proud gang of bikers who had climbed quite high in the biker hierarchy. The Bandangels had their sights set on being part of the Mad Angels. If they did as they were told, they would be admitted as members of the respected club – according to the Yellow Villa, the greatest club around.

'It's time to collect our bloody money!' said Tompa as he got up from the armchair and went into the hall. His trousers sounded like an old leather sofa, and his heavy boots made the floor creak. Tompa Eriksson and Jörgen Smäck, two beefy bikers dressed in black, put on their leather jackets and pulled on steel-capped boots. From the hat rail they took their knuckledusters, gloves and helmets.

Then they looked for their scarves and pulled their hoods on before leaving the house.

It was a cold day and they wrapped the scarves a few extra times round their necks. Then they carefully put on their helmets before kick-starting their motorcycles. The engines came to life with a roar and the two men rolled down the slope. Down by the row of mailboxes at the road, Tompa stopped to see if they'd received any mail. He was just about to unlock the mailbox when he glanced at the box next to it.

'Just look at this! *Outlaw Oldies*, what the fuck!?'

The two men looked at each other and Tompa nervously revved his engine a few times.

'Who the hell are these outsiders? They don't belong here.'

'No, damn it, they must be sent packing!'

'We'll have to check up on them. But not just now . . .' Tompa revved his engine and he and Jörgen disappeared with a roar down the road.

When they reached the pizzeria in the Östermalm district of central Stockholm, Tompa felt an irritating sense of discomfort. Something was bugging him, but he tried to repress the feeling as best he could. He had a job to do and this wasn't the time to start mulling over things. He took off his helmet and strode into the pizzeria, closely followed by his friend. When he'd first joined the gang, he had hated this type of task, but after a while he had got used to it. People who didn't pay only had themselves to blame.

The two men walked quickly through the dining area and straight into the office. The owner, who sat in front of his desk with a half-eaten pizza, a can of beer and a pile of papers, gave a start. Tompa stood in front of him with his hands by his sides.

'The money!'

'It's on its way.'

'You said that last week, too.'

The owner took out a bunch of keys, unlocked a desk drawer and, with trembling hands, opened a little metal cash box. There were a few five-hundred-kronor bills inside.

'Look for yourselves. This is all I've got at the moment.'

'You'll have to cough up the money NOW!'

'I promise.'

'You said that last time, too!'

Jörgen directed some hard, well-aimed punches at the man's face, causing him to fall to the floor. He continued to punch the pizzeria man until he huddled up whining.

'Tomorrow, I promise, you'll get your money after lunch.'

'And we'd bloody well better get it, do you understand?' said Tompa, kicking the man in the stomach. In a rage he also kicked the cash box so that the banknotes flew off in all directions. Then the two bikers left the premises as if nothing had happened.

In the evening, Tompa couldn't stop thinking about the mailbox. A rival gang as neighbours – that was all he needed! The huge LCD television was set on the highest volume and there were some empty beer cans on the coffee table. Next to them were a bowl of nuts and an opened packet of potato chips. Shrieking American voices, shrill film music and the sound of people shooting wildly around them filled the room. Jörgen was half-asleep in the armchair with the remote in his hand. Tompa took a handful of nuts.

'What sort of neighbours are they? Outlaw Oldies?' Tompa asked out loud to the room. Jörgen Smäck pushed himself up out of the armchair.

'Yes, who are they? They moved in and, since then, we haven't seen them.'

'Perhaps they're keeping a low profile after their latest raid.'

'Or they're busy with some protection racket.'

'Feels a threat to have them so close.'

Jörgen Smäck lit a cigarette and inhaled deeply. The gang down there had dumbbells, rowing machines, a bench press and a load of other gym equipment – he had seen the equipment in their yard before they had hidden it all in the cellar. So these new neighbours were clearly strong-arm giants who didn't want to show themselves at a gym but did want to keep fit. And then there had been a hell of a lot of traffic with vans unloading washing machines and dryers, sofas, chairs, a table saw, a die cutter, a grinder, chandeliers, heaps of books, paintings . . . indeed, there was no end to it. Must all be stolen property. But the worst of it all was that these shady types seemed to have moved in for good.

'They never show themselves. Just sit inside waiting.

Believe me, there is something suspicious about them,' said Tompa.

'Yeah, the whole thing is bloody fishy, besides that Super-Grandpa with the wheeled walker, of course. Have you seen the old geezer with the cloth cap? The guy who does his repairs and mechanical stuff outside? Now he has attached two horns, headlights, a plow and an engine to his walker.'

'What a guy! You shouldn't count out old guys. When it comes to old-fashioned technology, that sort of Super-Grandpa is unbeatable!'

The two friends walked across to the window and looked down at the big house. The lights were on upstairs but everything seemed to be shrouded in peace and quiet. The newcomers obviously didn't want to reveal that people were living there, but you could see their shadows on the wallpaper inside the curtains. Jörgen used his beer can as an ashtray and started coughing.

'Perhaps they're wannabes?'

'Wannabes for the Grandidos gang? Hmm. We ought to have a closer look. I don't want to get a bullet in my neck.'

'We've got the gang to help us if things get hot. The Mad Angels never back down.' Jörgen threw the beer can away, opened the fridge and took out two new cans. Tompa shook his head.

'We can't ask the Mad Angels for help on this, we aren't full members yet. No, we'll have to take a closer look first. You know, knock on the door and discuss where the property line is or something like that.'

'Okay, then, and we'll take the knuckledusters.'

'And the chains?'

'No need, they'll see our tattoos.'

'But I'm wearing a bulletproof vest and leather pants at any rate.'

'That sounds wise. And steel-capped boots.'

It was a grey morning and a damp mist lay over the bay. Martha had to use her asthma puffer several times and now and then she coughed a little. She had woken up early and, to get started for the day, she had brewed coffee for herself and the others. An hour later, Christina came and joined her and now she looked out of the window at the overcast morning.

'Usch, such weather! Some wafers and freshly baked buns would brighten things up,' Christina said, getting out some milk, butter, yeast and flour. Then she looked for the salt, found the sugar and cinnamon in the larder, and set to work. There was baking to do!

Martha got out a packet of Fazer Lakritsi sticks and the Finnish lemon licorice that was Brains's favourite candy. When he started nibbling on that, he simply couldn't stop. With some expertise, she poured the black sticks into a glass bowl on the kitchen table. Licorice usually put Brains in a good mood, and she loved to see him happy. More and more often she found herself doing something that she hoped would please him. Since they had left the Diamond House retirement home, they had become much closer friends and planned many crimes together. They worked perfectly together in mutual understanding, almost like an older and kinder variety of Bonnie and Clyde – but without any guns, of course.

Footsteps could be heard from the stairs as Brains came down. His eyes lit up when he caught sight of the bowl of licorice sticks. He gave Martha a wink and took a handful.

'If only you knew how much I adore lemon licorice!' he said and sat down beside her. And although that was exactly what she did know, she felt warm all over and pleased with herself. She leaned a little closer to him.

When the others came down, Martha got up and laid the table for their usual breakfast of tea, coffee, eggs, soured milk, ham and sandwiches. Then she added some liqueur glasses, a bowl of wafers and a bottle of Lapponia cloudberry liqueur. They all sat and waited for the lovely aroma from the first batch of cinnamon buns that would soon come from the oven. Martha thought over all that had happened. Despite everybody having been so mortified after losing the diamonds, the mood in the house was good. After living in a retirement home, they now appreciated every day in which they could do their own thing. Here there was nobody to tell them what to do and when, and they could run their own lives.

Since it was dark and there was slushy snow outside, they preferred to stay indoors. Martha had read that you should lie low after a robbery, so it suited them well. Las Vegas was, of course, very far away, but nowadays the world had become global.

The passivity made them lethargic, and every time Martha had asked Brains to get their gym equipment in the cellar into good working order, he had found excuses. Instead, he drank coffee, played cards, and watched a whole lot of cooking shows on TV. Martha sighed. All of Sweden seemed to be cooking on TV nowadays. They made soup on one TV channel and served casserole on another. What was the point of it if the viewers couldn't be invited to eat, but were simply expected to watch while others ate?

Brains and Rake had just recently discovered computer games and had become far more enthusiastic than was good for them. They stared at their computer screens like compulsive gamblers and even claimed that it was much more exciting than reading books. Christina had then called them uneducated, after which the two friends had withdrawn to Brains's room and played in private.

Sometimes Anders and Emma came to visit, but after having tasted Martha's fish and potato au gratin – when Martha had forgotten to turn the page in the cookbook and therefore only included half the ingredients – they avoided her cooking days. The brother and sister did, however, continue to fill the freezer and pantry with meat, fish, berries and vegetables every time they came to visit.

The aroma of cinnamon buns became all the more intense and when two trays were ready, Martha thought it was high time to summon a meeting. They must continue to search for the golf bag and get some order into their everyday income. Not least, they ought to find out how their money from the Robbery Fund had been used. Martha wanted to see the retirement homes with her own eyes to make sure things had got better. And then, of course, there were their contributions to culture. She thought about their anonymous donation to the National Museum, along with which they had suggested the purchase of more paintings by the French Impressionists. Perhaps the museum had even purchased a new Renoir? It would be exciting to follow up what had happened. And they must also decide what they would do with the remaining capital in the Robbery Fund. None of the five friends liked *passive* riches. Money should promote culture, create jobs or be given to people in less fortunate circumstances in society – not left lying around in a bank account. Martha looked around the room. Her friends had already started on the buns and were now on their second cup of coffee. It was high time to get going.

'Now, everybody, I think it's time we got down to business,' she said in a firm voice, but was interrupted by a creaking sound from the gate. They heard steps on the gravel path and, with an irritated wrinkle between her eyebrows, she went up to the kitchen window. Two big men wearing bulky leather jackets were approaching the door. The men were very beefy and walked with their legs apart and their arms out, rather like little children who have wet themselves. They wore black leather pants and vests, and clumsy black boots. It was a grim sight and they looked threatening.

'They aren't the police, but it doesn't look good,' said Martha, taking some hesitant steps into the hall. She stopped and opened the front door a little. The very next second it was pushed wide open and a damp, icy cold swept into the house. Martha saw the steel-capped boots and instinctively drew back, but still tried to manage a smile.

'Visitors, how nice, please come in! Can I offer you some breakfast?'

The men gave a start, but collected their wits when they smelled the aroma of freshly baked buns.

'Jörgen Smäck, neighbour,' said the man with the most muscles and long rat-coloured hair. He held out a large hand.

'Tompa Eriksson, also neighbour,' said the giant with the shaved head and a tattoo on his neck. He nodded in greeting.

'I'm Martha,' she said, and tried to sound unconcerned.

'We would like to have a chat with the gang who live here.' The giant put his hands by his sides.

'Yes, that's fine. Take a seat,' Martha answered. The men sat down at the kitchen table wearing their leather vests and black T-shirts. Their forearms were covered in tattoos. Christina got out two coffee cups but her hands shook when she put them down on the table. With a forced smile she offered them a basket of freshly baked cinnamon buns.

'Please, help yourselves!'

The men each dug a hand into the basket and put several buns on the table. Anna-Greta said hello to them somewhat hesitantly. Christina backed away.

'The boys, will they be coming soon?' Tompa asked with his mouth full of bun.

'Here we are!' Rake and Brains held out their hands as they introduced themselves. 'Boys, well, it isn't every day we get called that. Thank you.'

The two bikers looked uncomprehendingly at each other. Martha fetched two more glasses.

'Some cloudberry liqueur, perhaps? It goes nicely with wafers.'

Yet another nervous shudder crossed the men's faces before they gathered their wits together.

'Cloudberry liqueur? Booze is booze, I guess. So why not,' said Beefy and he filled his coffee cup. 'We thought we'd say hello to our new neighbours, but perhaps they've gone away for the weekend?'

'No, we're sitting here,' snorted Anna-Greta. 'We are the people who bought the house; this is our new retirement home.'

'Retirement home!' Beefy and the Hulk glared at them. The bikers put their elbows down with a bang and exposed their thick lower arms. On the skin you could see fire-breathing dragons next to skulls and wings.

'You've got some fancy tattoos there, boys,' said Martha, leaning forward. She prodded Hulk on his elbow. 'But doesn't it hurt when they stick a needle in you to do that?'

The giant knocked back the cloudberry liqueur in one go, and coughed.

'It just pricks your skin a little. I'm not an old lady. But that gym equipment out in the yard, we thought—'

'It's important to keep fit,' said Martha. 'Even if you're old, you have to exercise regularly. Don't you do that too?'

Beefy and the Hulk exchanged embarrassed looks and each took another wafer.

'Don't have time. Business, motorcycles and such.'

Brains lit up.

'Could those be Harley-Davidsons?'

'Of course!'

Brains's eyes glistened and a dreamy expression appeared on his face.

'It would be fun to—'

'Some more ginger cookies?' Anna-Greta cut him off.

'No, we're off now,' replied Tompa, the one with the tattoos on his neck. He coughed and in a sheepish voice mumbled, 'Well, thanks for the juice.'

'Booze,' Beefy corrected him.

The two bikers got up, took their jackets and made their way towards the door. Martha grabbed a paper bag and filled it with ginger cookies. When she handed it over, she saw that the one called Tompa had 'Helena' tattooed on his wrist. There wasn't an arrow, nor was there a little heart, but nevertheless. She smiled to herself.

'Here's something to nibble on,' she said.

The men exchanged glances, raised their hands as a farewell and went out. Not until they heard the creak from the gate did any of the five in the kitchen dare open their mouths.

'Help! The real estate agent didn't say anything about that motorcycle gang,' said Christina.

'Now I understand why it was so easy to bargain the price down,' Anna-Greta commented.

'So what do we do now?' Rake wondered out loud.

'Keep on good terms with them,' Martha answered.

'But don't you get it? They're members of a motorcycle gang,' Anna-Greta protested.

'Yes, that's why I invited them in. They are our neighbours, so we must be nice to them. You should always keep on good terms with your neighbours.'

'You must be crazy,' muttered Rake. 'What if they wring our necks?'

'Who knows, one day we might have some use for them,' said Martha and the smell of adventure spread through the room. 'I've learned at least one thing about life. You never know what awaits you.'

Up in the neighbours' house the lights were on long into the night, and there too they had a meeting. The members of the Bandangels MC club had lots of projects going on, shady projects that they didn't want anybody to know about.

'But what shall we do about the old people, then? Just think what would happen if they discover what we're doing,' said Jörgen Smäck, scratching himself on his balloon of a stomach.

'We don't need to worry about those slugs. They've got their hands full with baking cakes and playing cards. They won't be causing us any trouble. But I do have another idea. Why don't we use them as front men? They can be our tools. A drunkard can squeal, but nobody would suspect those oldies of anything, would they? We can fill with them with all sorts of tall tales.'

'And?'

'Don't you get it? We'll shovel a bit of snow for them and help with some heavy lifting. Then when we've gained their confidence, we'll have them sign some papers for us . . .'

'That's a good idea, Jörgen, you're not stupid, you.'

The bikers guffawed, and with much laughter and delight, they ended the evening with a sauna and a crate of beer. That night they slept like logs.

The days passed, but the five old friends couldn't stop thinking about the diamonds. It wasn't just because they were fantastically beautiful. The friends knew that they could get pots of money for them, and they could donate that money to people who needed it.

'It's high time we went on a golf safari,' Martha announced. 'It is late in the season and any day now the courses will be closed for the winter. Who knows, the golf bag might be out there somewhere.'

Brains was the only one who supported her on this. He and Martha dressed up in the latest style of golfwear and bought an ultra-light golf bag on wheels. Then they were ready. Admittedly, they only had one wedge club, but they didn't want to end up with aching shoulders and knees from having to pull along anything too heavy.

So that they would elegantly fit in and not arouse suspicion, Martha had bought a black polo sweater, a knitted cap, a pair of thermal pants, a windbreaker and a pair of thermal socks. For his part, Brains put on a pair of nylon rainpants to cover his old grey flannels. On the upper part of his body, he had a windbreaker and, on top of everything, a black rain jacket. But he had stubbornly refused to wear a cap. It was hard enough going around in those plastic clothes as it was.

They started looking for their missing golf bag out on the Värmdö course. Their special minibus stayed in the garage and instead they borrowed Anders' less noticeable Volvo. Martha turned on the GPS and even though she thought that the loud mechanical voice ought to shut up when she spoke, both she and Brains thoroughly enjoyed the drive out to the golf courses. They started at Wermdö Golf & Country Club and looked to see if there were any golf bags outside the clubhouse and the restaurant.

'A five wood, scorecard and seven iron,' Martha mumbled.

'What did you say?'

'Just a few golf terms, in case anybody wonders what we're doing here. Golf clubs want you to be members.'

Most of the golf bags had wheels and looked both expensive and elegant. Their own old-fashioned model with walking sticks in it was nowhere to be seen. Then Martha and Brains drove on to the next courses, first Ingarö and then Nacka, but they didn't strike lucky at either of them.

Tired, they had a break for lunch and then continued to the clubs to the south and north of Stockholm. Here too, they wandered around a long time and peered at lots of golf bags – but without any luck. After having visited the Lidingö and Danderyd golf clubs, they finally ended up out at Drottningholm. But by then they were so exhausted that they almost forgot why they were there. Instead they walked hand in hand across the soft green lawns and discussed life. In the end, Martha said:

'This feels hopeless but we've had a nice day! Can't we

plan some new robberies so we can go out on day trips again?'

'You don't think we can go on day trips anyway?' Brains asked.

'Perhaps, but planning crimes helps keep our brains in good shape. And a new coup would give us more money than just the diamonds.'

'Indeed. But you can do brain gymnastics too. There are courses.'

'That's true of course,' said Martha. 'But first and foremost we should find the diamonds and see what has happened with our Las Vegas money.'

'Yes, we must ensure that the money has been put to good use,' Brains agreed. 'But how shall we do that? You haven't forgotten that we are all on the Wanted list?'

A chilling wind blew across the course and Martha found herself shivering. Brains put his arm around her shoulders to warm her.

'Our old raid in Täby? That was easy as pie. Things will turn out, just you wait and see. And I've actually got an idea!'

And all the way back from Drottningholm to their new home on Värmdö, they sat in the car and planned. The first thing they would do would be check that their money had been used in the way they wanted. Because money – and they knew this from their own experiences – could easily go astray.

9

'Martha, are you really sure this is such a brilliant idea?' Rake touched his pointed cap for the tenth time and looked decidedly grumpy. The upside-down cone was a part of the traditional costume for the Lucia procession. 'So I've got to have this on, then?'

'If we're going to have a Lucia procession, everybody must do their bit.' Martha had made up her mind and her tone of voice signalled that any further discussion was ruled out. They were on their way to their former retirement home, Diamond House, to see what had been done with the big donation they had made. On St. Lucia Day they had simply decided to do a Wallraff undercover project of their very own. Perhaps their idea of how an undercover investigation should take place was somewhat original, but investigative journalists and people in the secret services had to put up with a lot. The five of them had disguised themselves with suitable wigs and flowing Lucia gowns and then had squeezed into their newly purchased vintage Volkswagen minibus. It was one of those minibuses with a hydraulic ramp at the back so you could transport people sitting in wheelchairs and the like.

Now the five of them were sitting there practising scales. Anders drove while Martha, who sat next to him, didn't bother with the scales. Instead she hummed the 'Sankta Lucia' song and 'Silent Night' in rotation.

'We must hold the key when we sing "Sankta Lucia". Luciaaaaaa, it should be. It doesn't sound right if you make it too short,' she said.

'And we must disguise our voices so that nobody will recognize us,' Christina added.

'Yes, of course. Good, Christina!' Anna-Greta said in praise.

'But, Martha, listen now. Have you thought of something? We are almost five hundred years old altogether and a Lucia procession is usually made up of young girls. Have you completely lost your marbles?' sighed Rake, always quick to criticize.

'But however else are we going to get into Diamond House without being recognized? Don't forget that we are on the Wanted list!'

'But I look utterly daft in a cone cap! And anyway, that's what the boys wear!' Anna-Greta complained.

'Calm down now, it's a good disguise. Now let's sing "Sankta Lucia".' Martha started but no one was deterred from the conversation.

'Do I have to wear a boy's cone just because I'm tall?' Anna-Greta persisted. 'That's discrimination. I want to be Lucia.'

It was doubtful whether they could pull this off with a Lucia who was as tall as a drainpipe and came complete with a distinctive horse's neigh, Martha thought to herself, but instead she expressed herself in as gentle a tone as possible:

'But, Anna-Greta, you didn't want to be Lucia earlier, because you didn't like the idea of everybody staring at you. So there wasn't much else to choose from. But if you've changed your mind, then I can wear the boy's hat instead.'

Silence now settled inside the minibus while the lights of the city passed by. Lit-up shop windows and Christmas street decorations in red and silver glistened outside the bus windows.

' "The cold of the mid-winter night is stern, the stars glisten and glow",' Christina declaimed from the back seat, overwhelmed by the atmosphere around them. 'That's a quote from Viktor Rydberg; isn't he good?' As usual, her head was full of quotes from her favourite authors, the Swedish classics, but nobody listened. They were all fully engaged again in the debate.

'No, I'd rather be one of the girls in the procession, because with a boy's conical hat I'll look taller than usual,' Anna-Greta said decisively. She thought about Gunnar, who she had met on the ferry to Finland the previous year. He could have been a boy in a Lucia procession. He was tall and wiry and actually looked like the former Liberal politician Gunnar Helén. A pity he couldn't be with them now. His sense of humour and warm smile always put her in a good mood and he would certainly have thought that this was fun. Besides, he shared her interest in vinyl records and music, and they used to listen to the golden oldies together. But he still hadn't been in touch, even though she had left new messages on his answering service. She really did hope that nothing untoward had happened to him.

'Righto. You can be one of the girls,' Martha decided. 'But don't forget why we're doing this. We want to get inside without anybody suspecting anything. Okay? We're going to check that the money from the Robbery Fund is being used for good purposes. So remember: this time we are NOT going to steal anything.'

'NOT steal anything!' came the refrain from the back of the bus.

'You don't think that we're going to attract attention to ourselves, then? In Lucia processions, the girls are usually beautiful and young,' said Christina with a touch of envy in her voice.

'You know what, almost no ordinary person can fulfill ideals of beauty like that. Let's create a new ideal!' Martha retorted.

'A Lucia procession of old tigresses? Not for me – I'd rather look at beautiful girls,' Rake grumbled.

'Yes, a nice thought,' Brains chipped in, but said no more when he saw Martha's keen glance.

'Pah, those stylized Lucia girls you see on TV, nobody really looks like that,' said Anna-Greta.

'My point exactly,' Martha said. 'Besides, we have an important mission. Who will ever suspect that a gang of Lucia singers are out doing an undercover investigation? Nobody! We'll surprise them all.'

'Yes, you can be sure of that,' Rake muttered.

'But it is important to ensure that the money has ended

up in the right place,' said Anna-Greta. 'All charity contributions and foreign aid must be followed up, even if the money has been stolen before it has been donated!'

'Yes, yes, but now we must practise the "Sankta Lucia" song,' said Martha, and she started singing again.

'It's important to keep in tune.'

The League of Pensioners sang their way through not only the Lucia song but also their entire choir repertoire, and didn't stop until Anders turned in to the entrance to Diamond House Retirement Home. The dark glassed-in porch looked rather uninviting, there was no Christmas tree by the door and the outside lamp was not working. There were a few lights on in the windows, but there wasn't a traditional Advent light with four lamps to be seen anywhere.

'Hmmm,' said Martha, when they all stood outside.

'How do we get in? It seems to be locked,' said Christina, feeling the door handle.

'If I can get into cash boxes at one of the largest casinos in Las Vegas, then I can get into a retirement home,' Brains thought out loud.

'Right, get your picklock out, then – that's probably the quickest way in,' Martha replied.

A few moments later they were all standing inside the old building with its asbestos-cement cladding from the 1940s, and they took the elevator up to their former floor. Anna-Greta led the way, Christina, who was the Lucia, came after her and they were followed by Rake and Brains.

Then Martha realized that their Lucia procession wasn't entirely well thought out. Now they had a Lucia, a maiden, and all of three page boys. She should at least have stuck to her original intention of being a maiden herself.

'First we'll sing "Sankta Lucia", then "Prepare the Way for the Lord", and after that we'll finish off with "Christmas, Christmas, Brilliant Christmas". On our way out, we shall sing "Sankta Lucia" again,' said Martha and she took out her tuning fork. 'Everybody ready?'

An expectant murmur was heard. Martha struck her fork, raised her arms and they all hummed an A. Then she rang the doorbell of their floor. They had liked it here before the cuts had resulted in them feeling forced to seek out other accommodation. But now the management ought to have received some of their Las Vegas money and so everything should have become much better. Martha peeped in expectantly as the door was opened. A young girl stood in front of them as they started to sing their choral version of "Sankta Lucia". In a solemn procession they then made their way into the lounge with lighted candles while Rake and Brains, at the rear of the procession, handed out ginger cookies. The residents of Diamond House, who sat half-asleep around the dining tables, were disturbed from their dreams and at first thought they had found themselves in another world, but when they heard the choir they smiled happily and keenly accepted the Christmas cookies. Other than the young girl who had opened the door, no members of staff were to be seen, and although it was December 13, there wasn't a Christmas tree, nor were there any Christmas decorations in sight. And the room needed cleaning. Hadn't they received the money from the Robbery Fund?

'The second verse is the same as the first,' Martha whispered in English to her friends when they had sung their first round of songs. They hadn't practised very many tunes. They continued down the corridor, Anna-Greta opened door after door and they sang for the people inside. But the residents were all very drowsy. With each new room they looked into, the friends became all the more dispirited. This wasn't a home, but simply a shameless way of putting people in *storage*! How could it have got as bad as this? The rooms were shabby and the only one that looked to be in better condition than when they had lived there themselves was Brains's old room. But he'd always lived in such a mess that nobody could really say what his room had actually looked like beforehand. His belongings had hidden the floor and the walls.

All the more concerned, the League of Pensioners continued their procession through the so-called home and, even though Martha tried to keep up appearances, she found it hard to hold back her tears. The unfortunate people who lived here had it even worse than they themselves had suffered in their day. What had happened? Had the money disappeared somewhere between Las Vegas and Stockholm? If Anita, ninety-one years old, hadn't gripped her arm and looked at her with a smile all over her face, Martha would indeed have burst into tears. But Anita beamed with joy.

'What a lovely Lucia procession,' she said and took a little bite of a large ginger cookie. 'The Lucia and her maidens are just like us. That was the best Lucia procession I've ever seen!'

And Dolores, in her nineties, who went around with a shopping bag on wheels that was crammed full with blankets, held out some five-hundred-kronor banknotes that she wanted to give to them.

'This is for singing so nicely,' she said and tried to give some of them to Brains. 'Usually I buy some decent food with my money, but I'm happy to share. Everybody ought to be able to live and eat well.'

Brains didn't know what to do, but Martha nodded to him to accept the money and thank her. He understood, and on their way out he discreetly put the notes in the coffee-money tin.

They spilled out onto the street, where Anders was waiting to pick them up in their minibus. They drove on to Raspberry Garden Home, Flower Courtyard Home, Bush Terrace Home and two other residential homes they had donated money to. But none of the residents had any better conditions at any of these care homes either. Martha noted all this down in a red book and swore out loud.

'Who the hell has laid their hands on our donations!'

Soon they were all in a really miserable mood.

'We'll go to the National Museum and see which paintings they've bought. We donated millions to the museum too, didn't we?' Martha suggested, wanting to end the day on a positive note.

Even though they were now all yawning widely, they decided to take a look at the grand old building. They went up in the elevator, stepped out into the exhibit rooms and had a good look around them. But when they came to the French Impressionists, they couldn't see any new paintings in the section where they had recommended that their donation was to be used. There were only the same old paintings that had always hung there. With long faces, they marched through the rooms and were finally stopped by some security guards.

'We haven't booked in a Lucia procession,' said the oldest.

'Lucia procession? Goodness me no, this is an art installation!' Martha exclaimed indignantly. And then the friends took the elevator back down again and returned to their minibus. On their way home, the mood in the bus was sombre. They were all asking themselves the same question: Where on earth had all their money gone?

10

There was a humming sound from the computer, and a beaming Anna-Greta snuck a look at Gunnar. He had forgotten to disconnect his old answering machine and hadn't heard her messages. But when she finally did get hold of him, he had wanted to meet her straight away. She had seen him park his car, and when he came in through the gate and walked up towards the house, she felt so happy, she was warm all over. She had missed him so! It was amazing how some people made you feel good just by being there.

He greeted her with a big bear hug and after a cup of tea, with a drop of cloudberry liqueur, they went up to her room and listened to her new vinyl record, a recording of somebody called Bruce Spring— something. She had wanted to try something new, but was completely astonished to find such modern music on vinyl. And the record had been so expensive too! In fact, she had grumbled quite a lot about that, until Gunnar put on one of their old favourites – Jokkmokks-Jokke – and managed to steer the conversation to other subjects. He was very keen to know what she had been up to, but he soon noticed that something was weighing on her mind.

'What's the matter, Anna-Greta? You look as though something's troubling you,' he said, and stroked her on the cheek. Then Anna-Greta couldn't hold back any longer.

'I transferred all our millions from Las Vegas, but now it looks as if they didn't arrive,' she sniffled.

'I'm sure we can sort that out too,' he said comfortingly and he took her by the hand. 'I'll find your money!'

They walked hand in hand down to the library, where the others were sitting and reading, all except Brains, who was drowsing in his armchair. Anna-Greta and Gunnar went straight up to the computer, and then Martha realized that Gunnar knew what had happened.

'It's absolutely dreadful,' said Martha. 'We transferred money to retirement homes but the money seems to have disappeared.'

'I heard that; almost two hundred million kronor, right?' said Gunnar, staring at the computer screen. He screwed his eyes up under his bushy eyebrows and shook his head. His bangs hung down over his eyes and his long, thin fingers moved quickly across the keyboard. The others got up and gathered around him to look. In the background a wall clock ticked away.

'If so much money hasn't reached its destination, there must be something fishy behind it,' he added.

'Oh, Gunnar, this feels so dreadful. Of course, I was stressed, but everything seemed to be working as usual. I sent the money over the Internet. I wasn't worried at all that it would get lost,' Anna-Greta sobbed.

'We'll sort this out, just you wait and see . . .' he said to console her, but his body language said something else.

After all, Gunnar wasn't exactly a hacker, even though he had been passionately interested in computers and had done his best to keep up with developments. After his wife died, he had completely immersed himself in the world of computers, and his grandson Ola kept him up to date with the latest technology. It was Ola, too, who had encouraged his grandpa to go on a cruise to Helsinki, the weekend trip where he met Anna-Greta.

'A bit tricky getting inside these systems. Bank confidentiality is well guarded,' he muttered. 'You can see that the money left your account but then what happened? That's the difficult bit.'

A murmur of agreement went round the room.

'That's what is so weird about transferring money on the Internet. One moment it's there, and the next moment it's gone. Vanished quick as a flash,' said Martha, staring at the computer screen with its columns of figures. From the outside she looked calm, but inside she was so upset that she had to clench her fists hard so as not to thump the table.

'I can't understand it at all. I transferred the money to the retirement homes and cultural institutions. Several millions. The banks guarantee that it works properly, after all,' said Anna-Greta. She had lost a hair slide and some of her hair had fallen onto her shoulders. Her lower lip quivered.

'Don't worry, I'm sure we can sort this out,' said Gunnar to calm them, and silence again settled round the table. Anna-Greta found her hair slide and put her hair up again. Thank God for Gunnar! His optimism was one of the qualities that she had fallen for first of all. And he didn't keep his computer skills to himself – he had taught her a lot of things too. When he sat there in front of the computer and tried to help them, a warm shiver went right through her. Gunnar was somebody you could rely on, and he didn't help just her, he was ready to help them all. When they had first met, he had explained that most women bored him, but not her because she was different. For him she was an exciting tornado, and the fact that she was involved in criminal activity didn't bother him at all. She was doing it for the sake of society and so that others would have a better life.

'You know, this is going to take some time,' said Gunnar after a while, and he pushed his glasses up onto his forehead. 'Give me an hour or so and I'll see what I can dig out. You can play cards or do something nice in the meantime.'

Everyone except Anna-Greta left the library, and soon loud dance-band music blared from the loudspeakers next to the record player. Gunnar had evidently brought some of his records with him. He was from the west of Sweden, from Värmland, and people from there were well known for trying to create a cozy feeling around them, but now, of course, he was faced with a real challenge. Two hundred missing millions made it hard to build a cozy atmosphere!

Time passed and Martha, who was sitting in the kitchen, started getting worried. Vinyl record after vinyl record revolved on the turntable without anything happening. It seemed to be a very difficult task and was taking an awfully long time. When finally Anna-Greta emerged to fetch her friends, she seemed to have been crying in despair, but had obviously also been consoled, because her cheeks were red and she had a little kiss mark on her throat.

Martha took a bottle of whisky, six glasses and a bowl of salted nuts into the library with her. Cloudberry liqueur was too mild for such a serious situation. Their proceeds from almost a whole year's worth of robberies and fraud seemed to have vanished into cyberspace, so something much stronger than cloudberry liqueur was called for. In fact, the loss was so great she simply wasn't sure if she could take it in.

'Well, then, let's see what's happened to our money,' Martha said as she poured out the whisky. 'Those millions must be out there somewhere.'

Gunnar reached out for a whisky glass and took a large gulp.

'Whisky is just what we need.'

Then he described how he had found the payments going out from the Robbery Fund and had succeeded in identifying the account numbers of five retirement homes, the National Library and the National Museum in Stockholm.

'But the mysterious thing is that—' Gunnar started to explain.

'The National Museum, yes, exactly,' Martha said, cutting him off. 'I thought they were going to buy a Renoir, or at any rate a French Impressionist.'

'And the money to the National Library is a self-evident donation. We must support literature,' said Christina.

'Yes, and you have sent some money to the Museum of Technology too, I see . . .' Gunnar went on, and looked up from the screen. 'But—'

'Yes, of course; they need money to document old-fashioned technology,' said Brains. 'There aren't many people who can take a car to pieces nowadays.'

'You have transferred money to those accounts, but when I hack into them I can see that the money never arrived at its destination,' said Gunnar, taking a handful of nuts and washing them down with a little more whisky. 'It looks as though the money disappeared en route, so to say.'

'What do you mean, "en route"?!' Martha objected. 'Anna-Greta knows about computers. There must be something wrong somewhere, unless a hacker has been at work.'

Anna-Greta raised her head and looked a little more satisfied.

'Perhaps the money has been listed wrongly in the bookkeeping?' Brains suggested.

'Hardly,' said Gunnar.

'What about the Police Pension Fund, then? Can you see the payments into that?' Martha asked when she remembered that they had omitted to mention those transfers. It had been after a party with lots of champagne, and in their joyful tipsiness they had decided to donate some money to that cause. It was only a few hundred thousand kronor, but they could at least have a bit of fun. They had given those poor detectives enough work recently. Perhaps the money might pay for a few golf tournaments or a trip to the Canary Islands.

'The police, hmm, you didn't mention that. Let's have a look,' said Gunnar, and he started looking for the pension-fund account. 'Hmm, hard to open this, hang on a moment.'

He eagerly pressed the keys and tried various passwords. Then suddenly he whistled.

'Here it is. I can see a donation of four hundred thousand kronor. So the money reached that account.'

Anna-Greta put her hands up to her face and moaned.

'We were doing our best to help people who really needed assistance, and the only ones who actually received the money were elderly police officers!'

'But they could surely do with a bit of help too,' Gunnar said.

Martha went into the kitchen and got out a bottle of cloudberry liqueur and a bowl of chocolate wafers. Whisky wasn't going to suffice here after all.

Gunnar continued his efforts to trace the movements of the money. After a while he stopped and stared at the screen.

'I don't get this. There are transfers here of several millions to the Police Pension Fund.'

'Well now, Martha, you did think it would be fun to give some money to pensioned-off constables. Lots of fun, right?' Rake grumbled.

'But they only got four hundred thousand – the rest of the money was to go to retirement homes.' Anna-Greta blew her nose and leaned over Gunnar's shoulder.

'And look at this, the day after the money arrived, it disappeared again from the account. It just vanishes,' Gunnar went on.

'Somebody is pinching our stolen money. What nerve!' Christina exclaimed.

'But if the money ended up in the wrong place, can't we just grab it back?' Brains suggested, trying to sound like a man of the world even though he didn't know much about computers. 'What I mean is, can't we just press Control plus Z, for example. On the computer, that usually works.'

Gunnar quickly looked down at the table so that Brains wouldn't see that he was smiling.

'Regrettably, you can't just alter something like this by simply pressing a button. Besides, the Police Pension Fund is protected with passwords. We can't go in there and mess around without leaving tracks behind us.'

'Numbers on a screen, no – what I like best is solid gold,' said Martha, and without thinking poured some cloudberry liqueur into the whisky.

'The boys who live up the road might be able to hack their way into something like this. I can go and ask them?' Brains offered, being keen to have an excuse to visit the neighbours and have a closer look at their motorcycles.

'No way! We are not going to mix with them!' Christina exclaimed. 'You must have seen the tattoos!'

'Gracious me, we have made a mess of things.' Anna-Greta sighed, stretched for her whisky glass and knocked back almost all of the contents in one gulp. The others gave a start. Their friend was usually very restrained when it came to liquor.

'But listen now, look at this: a transfer of thirteen million,' Gunnar suddenly said and pointed at the screen.

'That's the same amount we donated to the National Museum!' exclaimed Anna-Greta. 'How could that be?'

'I don't know, but when I trace the course of the money I get to Beylings Legal Firm. Perhaps the rest of the money has gone there too?'

'Beylings Legal Firm,' they all repeated in unison, and felt decidedly uncomfortable. Lawyers always made them feel like criminals.

'But then all we have to do is go and fetch the money, right?' Martha maintained, even though deep inside she realized it would be difficult.

'No, I can't get in any further,' Gunnar mumbled. 'At this point the money disappears into a myriad of accounts. And there are firewalls left, right and centre! Like a Berlin Wall.'

'Firewalls or Berlin walls' – Anna-Greta slurred her words and her breath smelled of Glenfield's – 'what difference does it make? We still can't prove the money is ours. And if we start digging around, they'll be able to trace us and then we'll end up in prison. Remember that we're still on the Wanted list.'

The truth sank in and they fell silent. All the work they had done to gather in money for the Robbery Fund, and then somebody had pinched it and redirected the whole lot to a legal firm. It was just too much! And nobody could make the effort to comment upon it. Silence, save for the clinking whisky glasses, descended on the room.

'We rob and we rob, and want to do a good job . . .'

Christina started to compose a poem but became silent when she couldn't find any more words rhyming with *rob*. After such enormous losses, she was quite simply in poor shape. As were the others. Feelings of anger and despair were mumbled, along with various suggestions as to how they should move on. In the end, Anna-Greta spoke up:

'There is no way we can just drop this. Whatever we do, we must get that money back!'

'Absolutely! I'm certainly not going to give up,' said Gunnar.

'Nor are we,' agreed the others and felt a little bolder for having Gunnar's support.

'Yes, my dears. We shall get those millions back, but for now . . .' Martha shut her eyes. 'Whisky and cloudberry liqueur in the same glass isn't to be recommended. I'm going to retire to my room.'

And without waiting for an answer, she put her cardigan over her shoulders and said goodnight. But when she reached the top of the stairs the others could hear her humming a tune. A song that just happened to be about a bank robbery.

11

Martha sat on the edge of her bed, looked at the floral wallpaper and pulled her nightdress over her head. Exhausted, she slipped in between the sheets. All the money that the League of Pensioners had worked so hard to rob was now gone! How in heaven's name would they be able to get the missing millions that had travelled all the way from Las Vegas? Bandits who stole several hundred million by computer hacking were not amateurs. Perhaps they were even mafia types. And challenging that sort was dangerous. For that matter, perhaps the bikers in the neighbouring house were dangerous too. The new name on their own mailbox, Outlaw Oldies, could attract more biker gangs. She must remember to remove it.

Martha raised herself on her elbow and adjusted the covers and pillows. She didn't want to be involved with dangerous people. Would it not be better to start all over again with new crimes? They couldn't just sit here and play bridge and fill in sudokus while the old and poor were in need. No, it was high time that the League of Pensioners struck again. And why not try a proper bank robbery, like the professionals? In fact, those institutions ought to get a prize for the smartest business in the world, she thought half-asleep, putting her hand over her mouth and yawning. The bank officials said that you should deposit your capital in their bank accounts, but as soon as you walked there to get your money out, *then you couldn't!*

'Because we have stopped handling large sums of cash,' a smiling bank official had explained to Martha one day. And perhaps they had to do that at the banks nowadays, when they lent out money they didn't really have – with gold reserves and the like. And Martha thought that it was even more outrageous that *they charged interest on that make-believe money!*

Admittedly, the League of Pensioners would find it hard to conjure up such a brilliant scam, and – in comparison – a little bank robbery was nothing. Wasn't it high time that somebody challenged the banks? And why not, in that case, a gang of pensioners? Martha puffed up the pillows, lay on her side and pulled the covers up to her chin. After a few moments a peaceful smile appeared on her wrinkled face. Her eyelids drooped and soon she was deeply immersed in an exciting dream where she robbed ten banks on the same day.

The next morning, Martha went down to the cellar and looked at their future gym. Next to the boiler room there was a space that at some time in the past must have been used as storage for logs and coal. Brains had promised to clean the place up, but since computer games had entered his life he found it very easy to forget everything else.

Martha couldn't wait any longer. So she got hold of a housecleaning service, and roped Anders and Emma in to give her a hand too. They painted the walls white, put up exercise bars and laid down linoleum. Then, when it had all dried, they managed to get all the gym equipment down into the cellar. They even put up those big rings in the ceiling, but Martha saw those as more of a decorative feature. None of them could jump up that high – no way.

A few days later, everything was ready and Martha wrung her hands with delight. Now they would get back into shape! From today on, there wouldn't be so many cakes and buns, and in their place would be more greens and fruit. The others reluctantly went along with this for the sake of their friendship, but deep inside they suspected that new plans were being laid. When Martha started talking about fitness and greens, a bank robbery tended to be in the offing.

And they weren't wrong, as the very next day she started up. The cellar gym wasn't very large, and already after thirty minutes there was a smell of sweat. Martha was a hard taskmaster and her poor friends had to suffer the consequences.

'One. Two. One. Two. Full speed ahead! Up with your arm and up with your knee – a little higher. That's it. Don't cheat! What are you up to, Rake? Up, stretch, switch and up again, twist and bend down! That's the way!' Martha shouted out the instructions and waved her arms. 'Lower your head a little, lean in, and continue for a while like that . . .'

She kept a good lookout so that nobody skipped anything, but she could hear from their heavy breathing that the others were beginning to tire. Just a little bit more, a little more effort. She thought about Anders and Emma, and was grateful that they had helped her with the gym. They had realized that she was cooking up some new robbery plans and they understood how stupid it would be if somebody was to fall and fracture their thigh right in front of the police. Suddenly the music stopped.

'Oh dear, the music system evidently isn't entirely synchronized yet,' said Martha and she went up to the apparatus. The others relaxed and started to gather their things together. 'Hold it there, we must go on. With a bit of gymnastics we will all be a lot fitter—'

'—to carry out new bank robberies,' Brains finished for her.

'I didn't know you needed wall bars, rowing machines and treadmills to commit crimes,' Rake muttered.

'Exercise strengthens your arms and legs, and it will be helpful if we have to carry cases full of banknotes,' Martha went on, panting while she checked the cables. But the music system had conked out. It had been tampered with and didn't seem to want to play CDs. So instead they tried to connect it to the record player – which pleased Anna-Greta.

'It can be a bit tricky connecting a record player to this music system,' said Brains and he went and stood next to Martha. 'Let me have a look.'

He fiddled around with the cables and before long the music started up again. Martha gave him an appreciative look and went back to her place.

'Ready? Up, stretch, switch and up again, twist and bend down! That's the way! And one more time!' she called out.

'Stuff this, I've had enough,' said Rake, stopping in the middle of a move.

'But, my dear, you who are so fond of women. And they like a nice body to look at, don't they? Not everybody is in as good shape as you,' said Martha.

Rake changed his mind and returned to his place. But before long Brains, too, protested.

'I think we've done enough gymnastics now,' Brains panted, and pointed at his sodden T-shirt.

Martha lowered her arms. Perhaps she was too demanding. But if you were going to rob a bank, you couldn't just fall over and end up lying on the floor with bundles of banknotes around you. However, if the others were tired, then she would have to adapt to that.

'Okay, we'll say that's enough for today,' said Martha. 'After a shower we can get together and have a drink. It's time to go through our plan.'

'*Your* plan,' Rake pointed out, and he picked up a towel and went on his way. Christina watched him a long time.

'I don't know what's the matter with Rake. He's become so sensitive lately.'

'It's probably my fault,' Martha sighed. 'I decide too much. Men don't like that.'

'No, it isn't that. He's been so difficult recently, it's as though we're not on the same wavelength. It feels like he doesn't care about me anymore.'

'But, Christina, you know he is very fond of you. You are his best friend.'

'Friend – but that's just it. We have been more than that, but now it feels as if he just isn't here, so to speak.'

'Men live in their own world, and women in ours. Now and then they collide, but that can't happen all the time,' Martha said to console her. 'And here I am bossing and ordering people about all the time. That's a sensitive issue, I can tell you.'

'Don't worry about it, because if you hadn't organized us we would never have achieved anything at all,' said Christina.

Then Martha, warm and sweaty though she was, went right up to her friend and gave her a big hug.

'You know what?' Martha said in a warm voice. 'I think it will all sort itself out, the love bit as well as the money. It always seems to work out in the end.'

'Like hell it does!' said Rake, who happened to pass them just then.

12

A few hours later when they had all had a drink and were relaxing in the billiard room down in the cellar, they suddenly heard the sound of motorcycles. The sound came nearer and a happy expression spread across Brains's face.

'Harley-Davidsons. And more than one of them!'

'A whole biker gang. What if they're coming for us?' Christina shrieked and turned pale. Martha rolled up the blueprints of the Handelsbanken premises, and got up. She quickly went across to a white plastic pipe which hung among the other PVC pipes up by the ceiling. She unscrewed the lid and put the blueprints inside. Then Martha closed the pipe again and had a quick look through the window.

'The gang must be on their way to the Bandangels. Come and have a look! They've got some weird wings on their backs – you know, ones with skulls. Perhaps it's best we go to bed,' Martha suggested, and she moved towards the stairs. The others gathered their things together and followed her. They had hardly got upstairs to their rooms and combed their hair before the doorbell rang. They came out and stared at each other, then took some hesitant steps down the stairs again. They stopped in the kitchen, but were uncertain as to what to do. In the end, Christina couldn't keep quiet.

'Shall we open the door?' she wondered out loud, in a pathetic voice.

'I'll do it,' Rake exclaimed heroically and strode up to the front door. He glanced quickly in the mirror and then stood in front of the door handle for quite a while and expanded his chest. Then he pushed the handle down as hard as he could.

'Hello, I'm Lillemor. Neighbour. I'm the person who lives in the brick house on the other side of the road,' said a deep woman's voice.

'Oh, yes, right,' said Rake.

Martha went to the hall to have a look.

'Thought I'd see if I could come and get acquainted.' The woman had bushy eyebrows, jet-black hair and bright red lips. Without waiting for an answer, she stepped right in.

'Yes, why not,' came a mumbled response from Rake. 'We're sitting in the kitchen.' Like a gentleman he helped her off with her coat and showed her in. Martha and the others cautiously said hello, while Rake straightened his tie and felt in his pocket for his comb.

'What about a cup of tea?' Rake offered.

'A quick cup,' Martha added, and thought about the meeting that they still hadn't finished. She had just been about to describe how they could get into the bank vault, and she wanted some feedback from the others. Now, however, Rake's thoughts were very far from bank robberies.

On his way to fetch the teapot, he brushed past Martha.

'Didn't you say that we should be on good terms with our neighbours?'

Martha thought about a doormat that Anna-Greta had made. It had the slogan 'If you're beautiful, rich and unmarried, then I'm at home'. And this raven-haired woman didn't have a ring on her finger and looked very unmarried – and as if she could devour a man in one big gulp. There was nothing wrong with her self-confidence either: she had already sat down at the kitchen table and dipped her long fingers into the bowl of chocolate wafers. With an elegant movement she fished up a wafer between her red-painted nails and popped it into her mouth. She looked around her in the kitchen with curiosity and even peered into the library as if she wanted to memorize every little detail. When she had finished the wafer and got a cup of tea from Rake, she pulled out a pack of cards.

'I can tell your fortunes, if you like,' Lillemor said with a dazzling white smile.

'Our fortunes?' Rake raised his eyebrows.

'Yes, I work with Tarot cards. I can foretell the future.' Before Martha could stop her, she had laid out two rows of Tarot cards in a cross. She turned towards Rake and said in a veiled voice: 'Tell me your personal identity number!'

Rake tugged at his tie. 'Well, now, that isn't the sort of thing you hand out indiscriminately,' he said and looked as if there was nothing he would like better than to reveal the exact date of his birth, right down to the hour and minute.

'I must have those numbers to be able to judge your

potentials in life. Let us begin by looking at the challenges waiting for you this year.'

'Challenges? Yes, we men are always facing difficult tasks,' said Rake, his cheeks beginning to redden slightly.

The fortune-teller lowered her eyelids and nodded.

'When I sailed out on the oceans, there were often storms and once—' Rake went on.

'What about the Arcana?' the fortune-teller cut in and put her hand over his. 'Your date of birth!'

Rake looked at the others, embarrassed, then leaned forward and whispered something. The special personal identity number that Anna-Greta had arranged for them when they returned to Sweden would hardly do. He must use his own, or at least one pretty close to it. He decided on the same year but a date earlier than his own birthday.

'Well, if you need it for your prophecies . . . '

'The Arcana, yes. You see, I add up the year, the month and the days, and that gives me a number. Then I see a pattern. But I don't think we will bother about the Minor Arcana, which deal with the small events in life, because I can see something big here. Let us go directly to the Major Arcana.'

'That will probably be for the best.' Rake nodded.

Lillemor turned the top card over. 'Yes,' she said, 'it's just as I thought,' and she looked up with an overflowing smile. 'You are enlightenment, warmth, riches, success, joy and harmony . . .'

'Yes, perhaps I am,' said Rake, now with his cheeks glowing bright red.

'But, of course, you are not a high priest.'

'Oh no, that's Martha,' Rake let slip rather too quickly.

Lillemor picked up a new card.

'Here I can see a lot of exciting things that are going to happen to you during the coming year.'

Rake gave a start. What could she actually see in the cards? Surely she couldn't predict bank robberies, could she?

'Life is waiting for you. I can see a new relationship. Yes, I see—'

'A new woman?' Rake asked.

'If you are ready. Love is the strongest force in the universe. We Tarot interpreters have signed an oath of confidentiality so you can tell us everything,' she went on, and she angled her head to one side and leaned forward so that her cleavage was visible. At that point Martha got up.

'I realize you have interesting things to talk about, but you'll have to do that later. We were going to have a meeting.'

Martha felt a hard kick to her shins and Rake glared at her.

'Now I haven't had time to tell you *your* fortune, but we can do that another time,' Lillemor proposed and then gathered together the cards without taking her eyes off the stylish man with the tie. 'I live in the brick house, below the Bandangels boys.'

'Ah, I see. But perhaps we can do that fortune-telling another time?' Martha decided and gestured to Rake to show their neighbour out. Not until the front door had shut again did Christina open her mouth.

'Fortune-tellers are not experts on robbing banks, so we don't have any use for her. The best thing to do is to return to our meeting!'

She sounded so decisive that nobody thought of saying otherwise out of pure surprise. But Rake had gone up to the window and was looking down towards the brick house.

13

Martha sat in the kitchen sipping a cup of tea with lemon. The day of the great bank robbery was approaching. There was no going back. The League of Pensioners must get hold of some more money.

'Now things are warming up, it is best to be prepared,' mumbled Martha, reaching out to pick up the brochure she had got hold of at the security seminar the previous week. You can learn a lot at Stockholm University, she thought, and couldn't help but smile. She had gone out to Frescati, the modern campus on the edge of the city, and then found the right lecture theatre and sat down right at the back. Then she had listened to the experts' advice about security and how to react in the event of a robbery. For Martha, it was a question of 'know your enemy'. In this case, the enemy was the general public, who would try to sound the alarm and stop presumptive bank robbers. The instructions were clear:

Remain calm
Do not try to stop them
Do as the robbers say (that sounded good)

Observe, try to remember what you see (less good)

Sound the alarm when you can do so without risk

In other words, it shouldn't be so very difficult to rob a bank. Pleased with what she read, Martha closed the brochure and glanced towards the library. The dry needles from the Christmas tree had formed a soft, brown carpet under the spiny branches, and the mulled wine and ginger cookies of the festive season had long since been finished. The robbery was to take place after Twelfth Night, when the workers were busy building Citybanan, the new subway line. In Stockholm they had decided to make a six-kilometre-long tunnel under the city centre to improve transit. They would be detonating charges for the new train tunnel and, what was even better, the city council had advertised the exact times of the explosions.

Martha got up from the kitchen table, rolled up the blueprints and put them back into the hiding place in the pipe in the cellar. As she passed the Christmas tree again, she was reminded of the times she had celebrated Christmas with her son. Her baby's father had left her when the little boy was only two years old. She had grown very close to her only son. Today he would have been forty years old if he had been able to grow up. She felt a sudden pain in her chest. Even though it was so long ago, she still mourned him. The loss of a child never really healed. Perhaps it was the greatest sorrow there was. That was why she must always keep herself occupied – so that she wouldn't remember; indeed, quite simply so that she wouldn't have time to remember. Her son had drowned when he was only five years old, when his life had hardly begun. How could anyone else ever be able to understand how much it hurt and that the sorrow never seemed to leave her? Martha pulled out her hanky and blew her nose. Then she sat in silence for a long time and stared out through the window before she went down to the front hall. She put on her boots and winter coat, picked up her bag, and went outside. Although she had been in other relationships, she had never remarried. There didn't seem to be much point when she was too old to have children.

The sinking moon cast a blue-white light over the snow as she walked across to the workshop. A bit farther away she could see the lights from some of the huge ferries that went to Finland, and from up the slope she could hear the bellowing sound of the bikers' music, of a type she thought was called heavy metal. Brains and Rake had been busy in the carpentry shed all day, secretly preparing the equipment that was needed for the bank coup. Now Martha couldn't restrain her curiosity any longer – she simply had to see what they were doing. In the evening, she and Brains had gone through the robbery plans before presenting them to the others. Martha and Brains were very close and shared most of their thoughts. But for once, Brains had been secretive and had insisted that he wanted to surprise her.

'You shouldn't always have to be thinking of everything, my friend. Now it's high time that you let the rest of us give you a hand,' Brains had said, and he'd stroked Martha on the cheek.

'Bank robberies, Martha dear, are not always so easy.

The banks have so many alarms installed all over the place, and the police react immediately to them. So we must be smarter than them, do you see?' Brains had said that morning and given her a wink. That was spot on. Martha had a weakness for uncomplicated solutions: they fooled lots of people. If something was sufficiently simple, nobody suspected anything. Not least engineers and policemen. With something really ingenious you could win time and avoid getting caught. Martha stamped the snow off her boots and pushed the shed door open. It smelt of sawdust and glue, and the machines all seemed to be running at maximum capacity. There were planks on the floor, metal sheeting and tarred roofing shingles, and on a shelf she could see a pointed, tube-formed thingamajig she didn't recognize. It reminded her of an old-fashioned artificial leg made of metal. There was so much noise in the carpentry shed that she got right up to the milling machine before Brains noticed her. He turned the machine off, smiled proudly and nodded towards the adjacent room.

'We will be finished soon. We're just going to make one more as a reserve, and polish the others.'

Martha stared and, without thinking, took a step back. On the workbench lay several fake pistols, and over by the wall Rake was pretending to shoot with them.

'Bang, bang,' Rake shouted as he cocked the trigger.

'But what in heaven's name are you cooking up?' Martha gasped.

'We're preparing the robbery, of course,' said Brains. 'Don't they look good? Absolutely convincing.'

'Bang, bang, bang,' Rake continued.

Martha picked up one of the black-painted fake guns as if it was a poisonous snake.

'But, Brains, dear, what on earth are you thinking of? We don't want to get ourselves killed, do we?'

'They're only made of wood.'

'*Hands up!*' The classic English words came from Rake as he approached them with a smile and a black gun in his hand. 'That frightened you, right? They look really good, don't they? I painted them with metallic black paint so they look just like the real thing.'

'Why do men always want to shoot? Dear me, no!' sighed Martha, taking the guns and dropping them into her big flowery bag. 'Besides, the police can start shooting at you.'

'But what are you doing? We haven't finished them yet,' Rake protested.

'No fake guns! There won't be any shooting here, no way! Now it's high time that you stopped playing those computer games. After just a few weeks, they've influenced you. What about reading a book instead?'

Martha did a quick about-turn and left the carpentry shed. And completely forgot what she had put in her bag.

14

The taxi turned off at Stureplan, went up Sturegatan and passed the corner of Handelsbanken before turning into Karlavägen. Martha was now right in the city centre.

'I wonder, perhaps . . .' she muttered to herself.

'Are you sure you can't see the entrance you're looking for? Now we've driven round the same block several times.'

The taxi driver glanced impatiently in the rear-view mirror and sighed while crawling along so slowly that the cars behind started to honk their horns. Martha had asked him to drive slowly enough for her to scrutinize the surroundings. How else would they know which escape routes they should choose? They had taken a taxi instead of their minibus because Christina had told them about all the surveillance cameras in the city centre. They were everywhere, and after a robbery the police went through all the recordings from the cameras close to the scene of the crime. It would definitely look suspicious if a minibus with a wheelchair ramp on the back was seen slowly driving past the bank again and again.

'My cousin lives somewhere round here. The address was Karlavägen something and as soon as I see the front door then I'll know where I am. So silly of me not to bring his telephone number along. He's invited us to a party, you see.'

'Just one more time round the block, but then I've got to end my work day. The wife's waiting at home.'

'Well, then,' said Martha, 'I think the big door over there looks familiar. Just drop us off a bit farther down the street, and we'll find our way.'

'Good luck!' mumbled the taxi driver, and he pulled up to the curb and stopped. The meter stood at 888 kronor.

Martha picked up her handbag, opened it and screamed.

In her bag were the fake guns! She had intended to burn them, but they had got completely mixed up among the powders and makeup that filled her bag. For a fraction of a second she had thought they were real and had reacted. The taxi driver jumped out and pulled open the door to the back seat.

'What's the matter?'

'My heart is a bit wonky sometimes,' Martha complained, and put her left hand over her chest. She could hardly tell him about the guns. But it seemed as though she didn't have to as, the very next second, Martha felt two moist lips pressed against her mouth, accompanied by an overpowering smell of garlic.

'Bbb . . . whaa . . . whaa!' could be heard from Martha before Brains decisively pushed the kiss-of-life taxi driver away and held Martha in his arms.

'It's all right. She does scream like that sometimes, but it isn't as bad as it sounds,' Brains reassured the driver while at the same time managing to get Martha out of the vehicle.

'But shouldn't we take her to hospital?' the concerned driver asked.

'No, no. You know women, they always exaggerate things.' Brains smiled as he paid for the ride. The others climbed out, rather confused, and when the taxi driver drove off they asked what had really happened.

'This is what!' said Martha, and she opened her bag so that the guns were visible again. Then Christina crumpled up in a faint.

It took a while to revive her, but after two candies she was back on her feet. Martha regretted that they were making such a display of themselves. They had dressed in dark grey coats they'd bought from a charity shop and had left their walkers at home specifically so that they would melt into the crowd – and cause as *little* attention as possible.

'How are you feeling, Martha?' Brains asked. 'You really frightened me. And then that taxi driver too—' He abruptly stopped at that point because he realized that, for a brief moment, he had felt something that resembled jealousy. The taxi driver had almost kissed his . . . *his* woman!

'Everything's okay with me,' said Martha. 'Just as long as he doesn't remember us,' she added, but she realized at the same time that the chances of that were poor.

'Was it really such a good idea, this taxi ride? How many times have we slowed down right outside Handelsbanken? What if they suspected something?' sighed Rake.

'Before a bank robbery, you must always check the escape routes and iron out all the details,' said Christina, who had now livened up. 'This was absolutely necessary. That fortune-teller can spout on all she wants about ominous events in the future, but it doesn't mean she is right.'

Rake opened his mouth to protest, but managed to restrain himself. Lillemor had become a sensitive topic of conversation. Over the last week she had knocked on the door almost every day with new predictions about Rake's future. Of course he wanted to hear what she had to say. But now Christina had become grumpy and thought that enough was enough. He had maintained that he wanted to sort out certain things in his life, and also excused his interest by saying that it was best to know what might happen to you if you really were going to rob a bank. But since he couldn't breathe a word about the actual robbery, none of the others thought this was an acceptable explanation. The fact that he blushed in a suspicious manner every time anyone mentioned Lillemor was much more telling.

When the taxi had disappeared round the corner, the five friends walked up Flora's Rise in Humlegården Park, where they had a good view of the bank and its immediate vicinity. They had the park behind them, with the National Library, the tree-lined paths and the lawns, and, on the other side of Sturegatan, you could see the entrance to Handelsbanken. They had a good look around, crossed the street to the other side and went past the bank door one last time before Martha thought it was time to head for home. For their return journey they first took the subway to Slussen, and then a taxi out to Värmdö. It had been a trying day and they needed some rest.

However, the minute they opened the front door, Martha said: 'It will soon be time to do this for real!'

They all looked at each other and immediately became serious. Talking about and playing at bank robberies was one thing, but doing it for real was another matter entirely.

Martha saw her friends' nervous faces and so launched into a pep talk: 'And don't forget that this is all for a good cause. Since the state doesn't do things properly, we must do our bit. So we're doing this as a friend and protector of the poor – we are the twenty-first century's version of Robin Hood.'

Robin Hood, Rake reflected, would no doubt have been very angry if he'd known that an old lady some hundreds of years later compared herself to him.

15

Christina had fallen asleep on the veranda with a camelhair rug over her legs and warm socks on her feet. She snored loudly, because in the afternoons she never used her false teeth and, besides, she had a cold. Rake glanced quickly at the sleeping figure. Admittedly, he did have a bit of a bad conscience as he crept up beside Christina to check that she really was fast asleep. He also felt a bit guilty because of the relief he felt when he discovered that indeed she was. But he simply had to go and visit Lillemor. He couldn't help it. That charming woman was so beautiful, so unpredictable and exciting; she was like a stormy voyage in uncharted waters. Curiosity drove him towards her as if he'd been aquaplaning. A man like him, who had sailed the seven seas and seen so many countries, couldn't just sit still in an old wooden house and do nothing. No, he must get out and about. He must see this fascinating woman again.

Lillemor had such interesting eyes, Rake thought as he put his overcoat on. She looked at him in that special way that some woman had, and despite being about sixty years old, she was still extremely sexy. He combed his hair, made sure his coat was buttoned up and walked off towards the brick house where she lived. It was one of those modernist-style buildings and it didn't fit in with the surroundings at all, but in some way it was right for her. Lillemor was not like other people. He rang the doorbell.

'Well, now, is it you, Rake? What a nice surprise. In the name of Light and Love, welcome!'

Rake rather lost his composure as a result of this unusual greeting, and he felt his entire body warming up. What a fantastic welcome! He immediately felt very, very wanted. She held out a clothes hanger and he fumbled quite a long time before he finally managed to get his overcoat on it. Out of the corner of his eye he saw that she was wearing a bright red silk blouse, a short black skirt, red leg-warmers and high-heeled shoes.

'Would you like a cup of tea?'

'Err, yes, please,' Rake answered and breathed in the sweet smell of incense in the room. He smiled like an idiot and felt as though he was at a school dance and was just about to ask the prettiest girl in class to dance. They went into the living room, and when Lillemor asked him to sit down at the dining table, his clumsiness abated. He straightened his tie, ran his fingers through his hair and said:

'What a nice blouse you're wearing.'

'Oh goodness, this? I always wear it when I tell fortunes.'

He could see that she was blushing. 'It's nice having you as a neighbour,' Rake went on. 'I've thought a great deal about what you said. About my future, that is.'

'Ah yes, your future,' Lillemor said, and fetched the

teapot. She put two teacups on the table and brushed against his hand as she did so. It seemed to Rake that she had done it on purpose, but he wasn't really certain. Somewhat absentmindedly, he sipped his tea, wondering why it tasted a bit funny. She must have noticed.

'Ginger. It does you the world of good,' Lillemore explained. 'Ginger, a bit of milk and cinnamon. I always have that in the tea when I want to cozy up.'

'Cozy up?' Rake repeated, with a hopeful note in his voice.

'Yes, when you huddle up on the sofa, read a book and feel really good.'

'A book, yes, right, of course. I play computer games . . .' Rake started saying, but stopped himself at the last moment. Instead he tried to recall the title of the last book he had read, but couldn't think of it. It was such a long time ago.

'Now, Rake, do you want me to tell your fortune again?' Lillemor asked and put her hand over his. Rake shuffled his feet and hardly dared look at her. He had thought for a long while about what excuse he could have to be able to visit her – not just this once, but often – and in the end settled on the idea that he was seeking guidance in the world of the Tarot cards.

'I know that it's mainly women who read Tarot cards, but I'm so curious. Can you teach me to tell fortunes?'

'To tell fortunes? But, Rake, my dear, you must have the gift.'

'It might come to me.'

'But I can tell your fortune. Isn't that enough? It takes a

long time to learn how to interpret the Tarot cards.' Lillemor went and got something out of the desk drawer and returned with a leather pouch. She carefully untied it, and pulled out a deck of cards wrapped in a black silk cloth.

'You know, the cards don't have any power in themselves, but they feel your energies,' Lillemor said, making eyes at him. 'To succeed, you must have a well-developed intuition and learn all about the cards.'

'I've got intuition, that's for sure,' Rake assured her cockily. 'When I was out at sea I could feel when a storm was brewing, and I can predict when it's going to rain.'

'No, that's not really what I meant. Every card means something special, and can be laid in different combinations.'

'No problem.' Rake reached out to pick up the deck of cards.

'No, stop! This deck of cards is mine. It is not good for them to be influenced by another person. I'll get another deck for you,' said Lillemor, and she got up.

What the Dickens is she going on about? Rake wondered. Couldn't she just sit down so that, well, he could cozy up with her? When she came back, he moved his chair a little closer.

'Can't you do that volcano for me?' he asked, and let his hand fall onto her knee.

'The Arcana, you mean? But then I need to know which sign of the Zodiac you were born under,' she said, removing his hand. 'Now, tell me your date of birth again.'

'I'm a Capricorn,' he mumbled. He'd completely forgotten the date he had given her last time. He didn't dare give her his real personal identity number. That number was the key to all manner of information about somebody, and what if she was in cahoots with the biker gang up the slope? He tried to remember what he had said – was it perhaps the day before his real birthday? He took January 3, 1931.

'Ah, right,' said Lillemor, and she gave him that smile that sent a tingle of heat all through his body. 'The Capricorn tempts us, and takes over our common sense. We lose our self-control and start thinking things we don't want to do, or ought not to.'

'Oh,' he mumbled, and gave her leg a squeeze.

'The Devil stands for selfishness, manipulation, greed, ill-will, envy and—'

'Can't you take another card?'

'The Capricorn will not allow himself to be guided by lower impulses.'

It's really more a question of male impulses, Rake thought, and moved his hand up her leg a little.

'The card symbolizes what has been preordained,' Lillemor went on, without removing his hand. 'As a Capricorn you might feel that you're not really capable, or that others haven't discovered just how capable you are.'

'I can agree with you about that last bit,' said Rake and he moved even closer to her.

'Perhaps you feel dependent upon the person you love, but at the same time experience the feeling that perhaps you are not good enough.'

'Pah,' he muttered, because by now he had tired of her talk. Instead he did what he always did when he had an attractive woman right next to him. He put his arm around her waist and kissed her. Lillemor came to an abrupt halt, closed her eyes and leaned back.

'You know what, Rake, I can teach you a lot of other things too,' she breathed, and put her hand with the red nails around his neck.

A little later, Rake left the red-brick house feeling exhilarated and happy. He almost felt like dancing for joy where he stood, but then he remembered Christina. Best to lie low awhile. His Christina was quite wonderful and he didn't want to ruin their fine relationship. No, this was just a little adventure, something to spice up his life, and nobody need know about it. He opened the gate and whistled to himself as he walked home. When he passed through the veranda on the way in, he said hello to Christina as naturally as he could before sneaking upstairs. But he caught a glimpse of her face. And what an ice-cold look she gave him!

Martha had seen Rake sneaking upstairs, and had shaken her head. It was bad enough that Rake had gone to visit that fortune-teller woman, but it was almost worse that he then spent his time staring longingly out the window or busying himself with his cards. Christina had cried herself to sleep and Martha sincerely hoped that her friend would have the strength to put up with this until the day when Rake finally realized that Lillemor was simply a gold-digger. Then he would surely apologize and beg Christina to take him back. Sometimes you had to let men do their thing, Martha thought; it was best in the long run.

The next day, Christina settled down in the library with her camelhair rug over her legs, a much-read book and a steaming cup of tea on the table. A pile of crumpled tissues lay there too. She had been crying – again. Brains came in through the door and saw her withering figure. He went across to her.

'Is that book so very sad?' he asked.

'I don't know about that,' said Christina almost inaudibly, and hid it under the rug.

'What is it?'

'The book?' She took one of the last tissues from the Kleenex box and tried to say something, but couldn't find the words. Then Brains's curiosity got the better of him and he tickled her arms until she let go of the book. He fished it out from under the rug. It was pink and the title bluntly announced: *How to Get Them Where You Want Them. All about Men: A Manual for Women.*

'But my God, Christina, what on earth are you reading? If anybody can take care of men in this world, then it's you,' said Brains, sitting down next to her.

'Rake doesn't think so. I believe he is enthralled by Lillemor.'

'I'm not so sure about that. I think he rather fancies himself, that's what this is about.'

'That's nothing new, but just watch how he runs over to Lillemor. I'm jolly well going to outwit him.' Now

Christina's voice sounded a little bolder. 'Because in this book I'll find out how to read men's signals.'

'Signals?' Brains couldn't follow her. Signals reminded him of telegraphy and mysterious radio signals in the atmosphere. 'What do you mean by that?'

'Well, those subtle signals that men send out unconsciously,' Christina explained. 'It says here that you should listen to your man, talk to him and study the inside of his brain.'

'But, Christina, my dear, is Rake really worth all that effort? Can't you just be your usual self? You are really nice exactly as you are,' said Brains.

'Do you think so?' asked Christina and she started to cry again. Brains picked up the manual and started to thumb through it.

'It says here that the way to a man's heart is via your nose,' he said. 'What sort of hocus-pocus is that?'

'Nothing strange about it at all. It's an important book. There is so much about men that women don't know.'

'But via your nose? That sounds like a detour to me,' said Brains. 'Usch, just have a bit of patience with Rake. I'll see if I can have a word with him.'

16

There was total silence. *Postpone the bank robbery?* What had Rake said? He couldn't be serious, surely? And on an evening that had begun so well.

As always, Martha thought it was important to make the evening before a big job a really special occasion. Faithful to her habits, she claimed that you ought to celebrate both before and after an event, because if something should go wrong then at least you would have had a bit of a party. So the evening had begun with a glass of champagne, which happened to turn into two, and everyone was slightly tipsy even before dinner. While they ate the delicious shellfish salad, Christina had quoted her favourite lines from a Swedish classic, *Karlfeldt and Heidenstam*, and they all listened contentedly. But when they got to the lamb fillet with herbs and Parmesan cheese, Christina switched to detective stories, which included tales of murder by poison. The stories got worse and worse in their descriptions of sudden, violent deaths. It wasn't really her style and everyone realized that things still weren't as they should be between her and Rake. Martha tried to lighten the mood by suggesting that they sing something by Evert Taube, but even though she filled the wine glasses, their usual high-spiritedness didn't materialize. Something was wrong – you could feel it in the air. And Rake had been unusually withdrawn and quiet, not saying much during the meal at all. In the end, he wiped his mouth, pushed his plate away and, after a long hmmmm, he cleared his throat.

'Lillemor has said that it isn't the right time to do anything adventurous just now. The moon is on the wane, so you shouldn't involve yourself in anything new and demanding,' he said in a loud voice. 'All my energy should go to developing things on a personal level, and I shouldn't waste time on other things. I think we should postpone the robbery.'

'You can't be serious!' said Martha.

'Well, if that's what Lillemor said,' Christina replied in a cutting voice, 'then we must of course cancel the whole thing.'

Total silence followed, and Rake fidgeted with his tie. His gaze was firmly fixed on his plate and he didn't dare look anyone in the eye.

'It would be dreadful to end up in prison without you, Christina,' Rake mumbled.

'Enough of your silly talk, you fool!' Christina responded with glowing cheeks. She had seen with her own eyes how Rake had gone across to the brick house earlier in the day. 'You know perfectly well that men and women don't end up in the same prison,' she hissed.

'Perhaps we should sing something,' Martha said to distract them. '"Gulli-Gullan" might not be appropriate, but—'

'What about a sweet little song about how you can get lady fortune-tellers to go up in smoke.' Christina lost her temper, pushed her chair back with a crash and rushed out of the room with her hands over her face. Martha looked appealingly at Rake.

'Please, try to get her back in a good mood. Otherwise it will all go to pot tomorrow.'

'I think we ought to postpone—' Rake tried again.

'No, we aren't changing any plans.' Martha cut him off in such a decisive tone that Rake didn't know what to say. 'Go upstairs and console Christina,' she ordered.

'Well, I don't understand why she got so angry. She has been completely out of sorts recently.'

'Of course she's angry. You have ignored her, as you must know!' said Martha. 'You have been paying attention only to Lillemor.'

The conversation was interrupted by a shrill ring of the doorbell. Oh, not her again, Martha thought angrily, and she marched across to the hall. There she took a deep breath and stood up tall, ready to refuse admittance to the fortune-teller who had destroyed the good atmosphere among the gang. She pulled the door open wide.

'Now, you just listen to me, you hocus-pocus hag, be on your way!' she said.

'What the hell!' Tompa, in a black leather jacket and heavy-duty boots, moved back so quickly that he came close to tumbling down the steps.

'Oh, dear, I thought . . .' Martha muttered.

'I wonder if I could borrow a carton of milk?' asked Tompa, scratching the tattoo on the back of his neck. 'It's bloody typical, we've run out.'

'Ah yes, come in, come in!' said Martha, thinking that it wasn't every day you were relieved to get a visit from a member of a biker gang. She led the way into the kitchen.

'Here you are.' Martha handed over a carton of milk.

'Nice place you've got here,' said Tompa, nodding towards the rest of the house. 'Perhaps we could have a look round? Last time we only saw the kitchen.'

Martha quickly worked out the pros and cons, and came to the conclusion that a quick tour might be good for neighbourly relations.

'Yes, happy to oblige,' she answered, and when she walked past the others she winked and pointed into the interior.

'I'll just show him round a little,' she explained with a smile, the giant of a man behind her. Rake got up to protest, but Brains put his hand on his shoulder.

'Martha knows what she's doing, don't worry,' Brains whispered and smiled at Tompa as he passed.

'The bedrooms upstairs aren't much to look at, but down here we have the dining room and the lounge,' said Martha. She proudly displayed the large rooms with their wooden floors and antique wallpaper and let Tompa see the view from the veranda. Finally they stopped in the library.

'Piles and piles of books!' exclaimed Tompa reverently and pointed at the book spines. Slowly and deliberately he looked at the authors' names and read out Strindberg, Heidenstam and Lagerlöf before stopping when he reached the big collection of crime fiction. Then he caught sight of something on the side and took a few steps to the right. Martha hadn't had time to see Christina's most recent purchases, but as soon as she saw Tompa's expression, she regretted the tour. His eyes grew darker as he picked up book after book with titles such as *The Swedish Godfather*, *Mafia War*, *The Swedish Mafia* and *Hell from Inside*. The last one was about a member of a dangerous biker club. When Tompa looked up, his facial features had tightened up and his shoulders were tense.

'Well, well, I never . . .' he said and when she asked what he meant, she didn't get an answer. He just shook his head, pushed the books away as if they were carrying the plague, and muttered something about being in a hurry. In two quick strides he was out in the hall and in one swift movement he had slammed the door and was gone.

'Goodness me, he was suddenly in rather a hurry,' said Martha.

'Next time why not suggest that the Mad Angels have their annual general meeting here when the house is full of stolen goods?' snorted Rake.

'You know what, soon I'll start thinking it was calmer at the retirement home,' said Anna-Greta with a quick glance out into the yard. 'That Tompa is a fishy character and he must have been suspicious when he saw the books. A criminal can smell out another criminal.'

'We're not criminals, we are simply generous pensioners,' Martha protested.

'Who are going to carry out a bank robbery tomorrow,' sighed Brains. 'But seriously, I think we can probably talk with Tompa. It's one thing reading about crime, but committing a crime is something quite different. I don't think he could have the slightest suspicion of what we are doing.'

'Don't be too sure. You should never say never,' said Martha and she sank down onto a kitchen chair. Her hands shook. During the tour, Tompa had hinted that the Bandangels might soon be admitted as members of the real Mad Angels. And even though they hadn't got that far yet, she had seen the look in Tompa's face. She had sensed a bottomless cold in those dark eyes. And from that moment, she knew: this man was dangerous.

When Tompa had taken off his jacket and come into the sitting room, the widescreen TV was blaring at full volume as usual. Jörgen had fallen asleep with the remote in his hand. He snored loudly but gave a start when Tompa came in.

'Urrgh,' Jörgen said by way of a greeting.

Tompa nodded, went into the kitchen and opened the fridge. There he put the milk carton next to the two others they already had.

'There's some more beer on the bottom shelf,' mumbled Jörgen in the direction of the kitchen. He sat up and rubbed his eyes and looked sleepy when his friend came back with two cans of beer in his hand. 'Well, what was it like?'

'The milk trick worked fine. I got to see the house. Seems okay down there – except for the piles and piles of crime books.'

'So they like crime, then?'

'Looks like it. And they had mafia books and a book about the Mad Angels.'

Jörgen burst out laughing and Tompa joined in. He opened a can of beer and flopped down on the sofa. While he drank, he glanced absentmindedly at the movie on the TV.

'But it makes you wonder. On the way past the garage I saw that Super-Grandpa had put two new seats in that minibus they have,' he went on. 'What if more old people are going to live there? If they like crime, they might start nosing around. They might fancy themselves detectives.'

'No, not a chance. They spend all their time indoors, right? I can't really see why they even need their own minibus. Don't they usually phone for taxis?'

'Perhaps they don't want to travel with others or to have to wait for buses that never come on time. They are entrepreneurial types, that lot.'

'Maybe we ought to keep an eye on them. The calmest of waters can suddenly turn stormy, you know.'

'Take it easy, man. They are harmless old people.'

Tompa took a few big gulps of the beer, put his feet up on the coffee table again and turned up the volume on the TV with the remote. Then he changed his mind and lowered it. 'You know what? The club premises – now we've put a floor in and painted it, we must fix it up so we can bring the rest of the gang here.'

'All it needs is a few pictures on the walls and for us to get some nice furniture.' Jörgen burped and put his feet up on the coffee table too.

'And then we've got to clean out the garage and sheds so there'll be room for everything.'

'But what if our over-the-hill neighbours cotton on to what we're up to?'

'They won't have a clue!'

Jörgen turned the volume of the TV up even further just as the baddie and his gang broke into a bank. The machine guns smattered. A bank robbery. It seemed that this kind of crime had become popular again.

17

Brains looked up towards the grey facade with SVENSKA HANDELSBANKEN written on it in large letters. Soon it would be time. He wandered around suspiciously close to the entrance and glanced at the double glass doors. It ought to work. The equipment in the walker was ready and he had prepared himself well. Nevertheless, a bank robbery was still a bank robbery. Martha always managed to make their activities sound so harmless, but they were, in fact, criminal acts. And his walker might attract attention. It didn't look like your run-of-the-mill kind as it had a much stronger construction. If anyone went up to it and lifted up the empty box in the basket, he could be found out. On the other hand, who would do that? No, in a society designed for thirty-five-year-olds, he could safely feel forgotten – and that was something that suited him perfectly just now.

Just a few more steps. He looked around him. No rain, no snow. You could see the stars and the moon on the wane over Humlegården Park. For a moment he worried about Rake and sincerely hoped that the fortune-teller's nonsense hadn't got a permanent hold on his friend, but then he consoled himself with the thought that they had, after all, managed to persuade Rake to join them. Rake had apologized and said that of course he would do his bit for the gang, and after a glass of cloudberry liqueur he was back to his old self again.

A Porsche swooshed past with the radio on at full volume and an old lady walked slowly and laboriously round the corner onto Karlavägen. Brains waited until the coast was clear. He most certainly didn't want any unnecessary witnesses. The street was empty again. Right, then, now it was time at last! There was a mat on the floor in the entrance lobby of Handelsbanken announcing that you were welcome inside. And he was going to go inside, but absolutely not in the way that the bank management had intended. His wrinkled hand inside his mitten felt for the button on the walker handle and then pressed it. With a thud, a homemade battering ram shot out from underneath the walker and went straight into the door of the bank.

The prosthesis, reinforced with steel, met its target and made a hole in the door. Brains took a few unsteady steps forward to catch the hard-to-steer walking aid. But the engine didn't turn off like it should have; instead it was so strong that the walker spun round a few times before the alarm in the bank went off. The racket gave Brains a jolt. And that's supposed to be bulletproof glass, he mused when he saw the size of the hole in the glass door and the bits of broken glass below it. He hastily pressed the walker handle again and the prosthesis quickly retracted back under the basket, parking itself with a click. Brains was really proud of his new invention, which had been inspired by a computer game about sea battles during antiquity. In those days, the ships had a pointed battering ram right at the front and they rowed at full speed into the enemy boats and tried to sink them. Of course his invention wasn't quite in that class, but he was pretty sure it would confound the police. No unnecessary fingerprints here, no way. Or as Martha had put it, an artificial leg is a lot more effective than fake guns.

Brains raised his hat and set off down the street in the direction of Stureplan, before turning towards Humlegården Park again. The alarm made such a shockingly loud noise that just then he was happy he wasn't a professional criminal – you could get tinnitus for less!

Some distance away, Martha had noted when Brains raised his hat and she pulled out her cellphone. She quickly punched in 112. When it was answered, she shouted into the phone as loud as she could.

'The alarm has gone off at Handelsbanken on the corner of Sturegatan and Karlavägen. It's a bank robbery, Constable. Come at once!'

She put the phone back in her bag and followed Brains into the park. At the other end of the park, outside the National Library, stood a regular ambulance along with a military vehicle with a large red cross on it – an ambulance bus. Anders was waiting for them there.

'Nobody saw me borrow this,' he said with a wide grin as he patted the military vehicle on the hood. 'The security at Karlberg Palace isn't very efficient. The army is not as attentive as it ought to be,' Anders added as he opened the back doors.

'Suits us fine,' said Brains and he rolled his walker in. When he had done that, Anders handed over a small Christmas tree. The needles had all dropped off but somehow it still had its decorations. With the tree in one hand and Martha in the other, Brains set off back through the park towards the bank. He stood up on Flora's Rise with Martha by his side so they would have a good view of what was happening. Not far away, Rake, Christina and Anna-Greta had already taken up positions, pretending to be scared observers. Now and then they looked at each other while they waited, but they were careful not to stand too near to one another. Even though the five-member League of Pensioners now jokingly called themselves Outlaw Oldies to try to disguise their identities, they hadn't forgotten that they were still on the Wanted list.

Meanwhile, Anders locked the military ambulance bus and went into the smaller ambulance, where Emma was already sitting behind the wheel.

'Well, then, now we only have to wait,' said Emma and she felt in her pocket for her packet of cigarettes. Luckily, she had managed to get a babysitter and didn't have to worry about little Malin. Emma couldn't reach her cigarettes. Then she remembered that she shouldn't have any cigarettes, nor should she smoke now. Why hadn't she thought of bringing along nicotine chewing gum? The activities of her mother and her friends did make her rather nervous.

Up on Flora's Rise the atmosphere was charged too.

'So far, not a sign of Securitas or the police. It's like we thought. Five minutes ought to be enough for the robbery,'

Martha noted. Six minutes after the alarm had sounded, a police car arrived on the scene. It came up Sturegatan, turned right into Karlavägen and stopped outside Handelsbanken. Martha put her hand on Brains's arm.

'Oh, isn't it exciting! Just like in a film,' she said. 'But, of course, this is for real.'

Equally enthusiastic, Brains took her hand. It felt so nice and cozy here in the cold. Yes, with Martha by his side he always felt so much stronger.

A police constable got out of the car and went up to the broken door. The uniformed officer leaned down and examined the hole in the double glass. Then he spoke into his cellphone.

'He'll be telling them that somebody has kicked a hole in the door,' said Brains with a low, cackling laugh. 'If only he knew that it was an artificial leg!'

'Made of steel!' Martha added.

The next moment, a Securitas van drove up and two guards got out, unlocked the door and entered the bank. They turned off the alarm and the two men and the policeman talked for a while. They were shaking their heads as if to indicate that there was nothing to be concerned about, then returned to their vehicles and drove away.

'Perfect,' Martha muttered and she raised her hat twice, before putting it back on her head again. Anna-Greta noticed the signal and waited another six minutes before she came out from among the trees. Calm and composed, she crossed over Sturegatan to the sidewalk on the other side. Christina quickly looked all around her, and just as she passed the bank she pretended to slip on a patch of ice and fell helplessly backwards against the door. Christina had, of course, protested at having to fall down again, but they had all insisted that nobody could fall down better than her, and in the end she had given in. She landed elegantly on her back, propped up by one arm. Martha had coached both her and the others in several different balancing exercises, so Christina was able to get back onto her feet quickly. When Anna-Greta got hold of the door, the alarm went off again, and with her hands on the bottom of her spine, she shuffled round the corner and disappeared down the street. Martha fished out her cellphone and punched in 112 again.

'Is this the police? You must come at once! The alarm is going at full blast here at Handelsbanken on Karlavägen. I think they are robbing the bank,' she shouted into the phone. Then she put it back in her pocket and with a smile looked at Brains.

'Now we'll see how long it takes them this time.'

The League of Pensioners waited a while before they caught sight of a Securitas van heading at high speed towards the bank. Martha looked at her watch. Five minutes and thirty seconds. Then a police car slowed down outside the bank. A constable lowered a side window and stuck his head out. The policeman briefly spoke to the Securitas man, not even bothering to get out, before he drove off again. Shortly afterwards, the alarm stopped and the Securitas van disappeared again too. Everything was as before, and the few curious people who had come to look at what was happening just shrugged their shoulders and hurried on. Martha glanced at her watch.

'So far, so good,' she said, but even she could hear that her voice sounded more tense than usual. 'Now we only have to wait another fifteen minutes. Then bingo!'

It was beginning to feel really cold, and the following minutes were the longest Martha had ever experienced. Time after time, she looked at her watch and found herself thinking too much about all the trouble she had caused. And now she had got her friends involved in something fishy once more. What if they ended up in prison again and couldn't see each other for several years? And even if prison was a great deal better than a retirement home, they really were very comfortable in their big old house. Besides, Martha had heard that prisons were lowering their standards now too. She looked at her watch again. Sixty seconds to go. She took a firm grip of her wide-brimmed hat and started counting to herself. Then she nodded at Brains. He moved his head slightly in answer and took a firm grip of the little Christmas tree with its decorations and crackers still hanging on.

'Well, then, Happy Christmas!' Brains said cheerily and, dragging the Christmas tree behind him, he walked towards the entrance to Handelsbanken. Martha, Rake and Christina followed him but kept their distance. Just as he reached the entrance, he pretended to get his breath back while he leaned the decorated tree close to the hole that the artificial leg had made. He discreetly loosened the specially prepared Christmas crackers and dropped them one after the other into the hole in the broken glass door. The Christmas decorations with their pictures of lit candles and smiling Santa Claus figures rolled around for a moment and then detonated in muffled explosions, followed by the sound of broken glass. Yet again, the alarm started up and even Anna-Greta, who was somewhat hard of hearing, could clearly hear it.

Upon hearing the shrieking alarm, Anna-Greta immediately pressed the quick-dial button to Anders and Emma after which she took a few steps towards the door, fell again, then put her hand to her chest, screaming. When she saw the first onlooker approaching, Anna-Greta squeezed a prepared bag of blood under her sweater and let the blood slowly seep out between her fingers. Then Martha phoned the police. She used the same pay-as-you-go SIM card again, to make sure the police would disregard the call. She knew only too well that after the third phone call of the day, they would not be interested in what she had to say.

'I bet one thousand kronor that the police won't come this time,' she mumbled to herself, but fell silent when the police switchboard answered the call.

'The alarm has gone off at Handelsbanken on the corner of Karlavägen and Sturegatan. You must come immediately,' said Martha. 'It's a real bank robbery, the sort you see on the TV, you see, Constable.'

She elaborated about all the villains who must have forced their way into the bank and how much money they could get their hands on with such a crime, and then she ended the call and fast-dialled Securitas.

'This is Clara Johansson from the Internal Accounting department at Handelsbanken on the corner of Karlavägen and Sturegatan,' said Martha with a superior voice.

'My code is 543JKL14 – yes, you've got that among your papers. Now the alarm has gone off again, the third time in a short period. This is a false alarm, I must inform you. You've already been here several times. Securitas is really ripping us off. Just because somebody has damaged the door, it shouldn't mean that we have to pay thousands of kronor for you to come and switch the alarm off every time it goes off. We're not going to pay for yet another visit. I'm going to personally turn the alarm off!'

Martha didn't know if it would work; it was simply an extra security measure. Regardless, they would have at least five minutes and that should suffice.

'Right, let's go,' said Martha. She took Brains's hand in hers and squeezed it hard. 'Now don't get nervous, we're going to manage this. Nobody in the history of the world has committed a crime like this. The police won't have a clue as to what's happened!'

'Well, my dear, let's hope so,' said Brains. He tried to sound bold but his voice was shaky.

He had hardly said the words before they heard an ambulance approaching with its sirens wailing. Anders and Emma were on their way. The sound came closer and soon the ambulance screeched to a halt just outside the bank entrance. Martha and Brains went to meet it, and a few steps behind them came Rake and the others. Anders and Emma, disguised as ambulance paramedics, hurried out with stretchers and blankets, and with Brains's help they discreetly picked the lock of the entrance door.

The stretchers looked just like any old ambulance stretcher, but if anyone had decided to take a closer look, they would have discovered the slight mounds in the middle. Under the carefully folded blankets lay two fully dressed shop-window mannequins, with overcoats, boots and all. Anders and Emma hurried inside the bank, and Martha just had time to notice the doormat with its message WEL-COME TO HANDELSBANKEN. She smiled, muttered a 'So nice of them indeed!' and hurried in the direction of the bank vault. The alarm was still deafeningly loud, but not loud enough to block out the sound of detonations from the train-tunnel builders somewhere underneath them. At that very same moment, there was also a series of powerful explosions down in the vault, where Brains had lit a smoke bomb and some very large Christmas crackers. Grinning red Santa Claus figures, blackened candles and bits of paper flew in every direction while the smoke slowly spread out. Brains wasn't as good at pyrotechnics as he was at mechanics, but he could read technical drawings and the charges inside the Christmas crackers did the trick. The iron bars and the door with its steel hinges fell to the ground with a crash. Martha, Rake and Christina – coughing somewhat – made their way down the stairs and into the vault. Without wasting any time, they quickly collected the money from the security boxes which lay broken on the floor.

Outside the bank, Anna-Greta lay with blood on her hands and waited for Gunnar – who was an honorary recruit for the League of Pensioners. Could she rely on him? Would he understand just how important he was for the success of the whole coup? She jerked a little for the sake of appearances, and with a hairpin put another hole in the bag of blood inside her sweater. At last she saw him running down the sidewalk. She closed her eyes and hoped he would do mouth-to-mouth on her. Instead he arrived and gave her a brisk thump on her chest, using both hands to press on her ribcage, which was the latest thing they taught you in First Aid courses. The bag of blood split and her ribs got some quite rough treatment but that didn't stop him. Gunnar wasn't being romantic at all – he could have resuscitated an Egyptian mummy.

'Gunnar, take it easy,' she gurgled. 'I'm still alive!'

But her beloved didn't hear her – he was focused on his task. He had clearly been watching too many of those catastrophe films on TV. When she couldn't take it any longer, Anna-Greta threw out her arms and hissed in her most cutting voice:

'You men always have to take things too far. Simple mouth-to-mouth would have been sufficient.'

More spectators now gathered outside the bank in tight groups. This has to work, Anna-Greta thought to herself. She groaned a little – partly because her ribs now ached, and partly for appearances – but she stopped immediately when Gunnar finally pressed his mouth against hers in a new resuscitation attempt.

Inside the back vault, the others were toiling away as best they could. Martha had pulled the blankets off the stretchers and uncovered the mannequins. She quickly unscrewed their heads so that Brains and Rake could fill the dummies with money. They all worked quickly and knew exactly what they should do because they had practised this several times back at their house, although the real thing was a lot more difficult.

Their progress was slower than expected, and Martha became all the more nervous. The smoke made their eyes smart, and outside things were getting increasingly chaotic. Finally, Brains and Rake pushed the last of the banknotes down the mannequins and screwed the heads back on again.

'Next stop – Emergency!' instructed Martha and she nodded to Anders. He quickly put the first mannequin on the stretcher, covered it with the blanket again and then, together with Emma, carried it out to the ambulance. When Emma and Anders came back in to fetch the second mannequin, the head fell off. They were running out of time. Martha screwed the head back on again, which still left a bit of a gap, and Rake lent her his tie to cover it. Then Anders and Emma covered that mannequin with a blanket as well and hurried out of the bank with the stretcher.

'Make way! Make way!' Anders shouted out when he and Emma pushed through to the ambulance, but in the rush they carelessly let a corner of the stretcher bang against the ambulance door and one of the mannequin's shoes fell to the ground. Emma quickly bent down and picked it up, threw it inside the ambulance and slammed the door. Martha, Brains and Rake, who were now also pretending to be injured, struggled across to the ambulance but were turned away by Emma.

'Wait here, there isn't room for you, I'll fetch the ambulance bus,' she said and rushed off across to the National Library, where they had parked it. While Emma fetched the big vehicle, the crowd grew bigger. Anna-Greta whimpered a little more in front of these spectators, and Martha and Brains moaned and groaned loudly too. Rake, however, kept on nagging about how he must get his tie back, but just as he was about to protest even more, they heard three quick toots from a car horn. Emma hadn't bothered driving on the gravel paths. She had gone straight over the park lawn and now the military vehicle was right opposite the bank on the other side of the street.

Anna-Greta struggled onto her feet and, supported by Gunnar, she tottered across the road and into the big vehicle, closely followed by Martha, Brains and Rake. Gunnar, who wasn't injured at all, pretended to be a close relative and entered the ambulance, closing the doors before he sat with the others. When Anders drove past in the ambulance with its wailing siren, Emma pulled out behind him with the military ambulance bus. A large cloud of black diesel exhaust followed in her wake. Then both vehicles drove at great speed towards Huddinge Hospital. It was a bit farther away than Karolinska, and there wasn't so much security there.

18

'Here it is!' Anders shouted out, as he turned into the Huddinge Hospital entrance. His hands were clammy and he was breathing rather heavily but he forced himself to drive calmly and carefully, as if he was a proper ambulance driver and not a villain fleeing a crime scene. In the parking garage he spotted the minibus belonging to the League of Pensioners which he and Emma had driven there earlier in the day. He slowed down and parked right next to it. Soon afterwards the ambulance bus pulled up too. Emma got out, opened the back doors to both vehicles and signalled to the others to keep quiet. Under the cover of darkness, Emma and Anders then unloaded their 'stretcher cases'. Inside the minibus, Martha and Christina helped to seat the mannequins on the two extra seats that had been specially installed. They fastened their seat belts and patted them on the cheek for appearances. One of the mannequins had again lost a boot, but Martha quickly put it back on again. They mustn't risk the success of the entire coup by being careless about details.

In the ambulance bus they were all busy too. Anna-Greta wiped off most of the blood that she and Martha had collected in plastic bags at a Värmdö slaughterhouse. Despite being in a hurry, she couldn't help smiling at the thought of the confusion at the Forensics Lab if they tried to do a DNA test. The blood came from lame racehorses that had been slaughtered during the week and, however thorough the tests were, they would all show the same result: the DNA samples from the badly bleeding lady on the pavement outside the bank came from a horse. So Anna-Greta felt calm; she might laugh like a horse, but the police wouldn't be able to trace her.

Martha and the others cleaned the ambulance as best they could before Anders finally drove it back to the parking area for the hospital's emergency vehicles. It was a bit more complicated to deal with the military ambulance bus, but the League of Pensioners had a plan for that too. When they were all seated in their minibus together with the mannequins, Martha happily steered out onto the 222 towards Värmdö, while Anders and Emma took the ambulance bus and drove back into the city again. At a well-chosen place under the Essinge highway they stopped, tidied things up and changed their clothes. When they had finished, they even had time for a short nap. The alarm clock on Anders' cellphone rang at 4:45 and he got into the driver's seat again.

The stars were clearly visible in the night sky as they drove the ambulance bus back to the barracks at Karlberg Palace. Anders had done his military training there, and it was easy for him to find his way around. At Ekelund Bridge he paused at the barrier and then turned into the park. The engine ticked over as Emma jumped out and quickly opened the gate with a demagnetized old credit card. Then she got back in next to Anders, who calmly put the vehicle into first gear and drove up to the parking lot. He parked the bus at an angle, as if he had been a bit drunk, turned the engine off and left the keys in the ignition. Before the two of them got out, they looked back inside the bus.

'Does it look convincing?' Anders asked, taking his gloves off.

'Perfect. I bet you anything that the army's ambulance vehicles really do look like this sometimes.' Emma looked at the beer cans and whisky bottles on the floor, some empty and some still half-full. Emma had spiced up the scene with some mascara and lipstick on the front seat and a pair of knickers under one of the other seats. Anders and Emma smiled, pulled their hats down over their ears and ran off towards the commuter-rail station.

19

It was now quite late, and Jörgen and Tompa had already downed six beers each. During the evening they had painted the bar stools in the club premises, fried some juicy steaks, heated up some frozen fries in the oven, watched TV, challenged each other at various video games, and talked about chicks. Now they were getting rather sleepy and weren't entirely sober either. A sweaty Tompa opened the doors to the balcony to let in some fresh air. With a can of beer in one hand and a cigarette in the corner of his mouth, he looked out across the moonlit landscape. The trees looked black and abandoned sticking up out of the blueish white snow, and the sea looked like an endless field that disappeared in a grey horizon. He was just thinking how fantastic the archipelago was at this time of the year when the sound of a car startled him. A Volkswagen minibus! He heard voices and slamming car doors. He withdrew into the house and closed the balcony doors. Then he walked across to the window and looked out. Well now, it was the group of old people coming home, but at this time of night? And what on earth were they doing? It looked as if they were carrying something. Tompa pressed his nose against the window.

'They're taking corpses into the earth cellar.'

'Cool it, man! You shouldn't have had that last beer,' Jörgen called out from inside the room. He yawned and continued to play his video game.

'Have a look yourself! This is just unbelievable!'

Jörgen Smäck grudgingly got up, put his controller down and went and stood next to Tompa.

'It'll be nothing to get worked up about,' he started saying, but soon changed his mind. 'What the hell are they carrying?'

'Yeah, right, do you see what I mean now?'

Outside their neighbours' house, the old lady called Martha could be seen helping two of her friends carry a stiff corpse wearing a coat and boots, its legs dragging along the ground. Suddenly they dropped the corpse and the man the bikers had nicknamed 'Super-Grandpa' started gesticulating wildly. He then went and fetched his walker. When he got back, they all helped to push the torso of the corpse over the basket on the walker which they then pushed across to the cellar. When the corpse had finally been stuffed away inside the cellar, Super-Grandpa closed the door and locked it, and then they all went inside the house.

Tompa put his hand on his forehead and gasped for breath. 'Have they murdered someone? Maybe with poison – how else could they do it? But if they . . .'

'You didn't drink any of their milk?'

'No! It's still in the fridge. But seriously, what are they up to? What if there are more bodies down there?'

Tompa looked down at the big old house. At first, he had been pleased to have a gang of harmless pensioners as neighbours, but now he was feeling uneasy. As soon as they could, they ought to go down there and take a look inside the cellar to see what those idiots were up to. With determined steps, Tompa went into the kitchen, opened the fridge and took out the carton of milk. He opened it, sniffed at the contents and then poured it all down the sink. You could never be too careful.

Martha and the gang had taken off their coats and hung up the keys in the key box. They were all a little shaky and high on adrenaline. They had succeeded again!

'Let's celebrate!' Christina chirped happily. And even though they were all tired, they took each other by the hand and carried out a sort of improvised dance in a ring around the kitchen table. Then Christina started to sing the song of the robbers in Kamomilla town, after which they all cheered. In an atmosphere of great jollity they sat down at the kitchen table.

'We pulled it off!' Anna-Greta proclaimed. 'Soon we'll have so much money that we can open our own bank.'

'Not another bank, my dear,' said Martha and she fetched a bottle of champagne and six glasses. 'There are more than enough banks already.'

'Yes, but it is such an incredibly profitable business. When things are going well, you take all the money yourself, and when they aren't going well, you demand that the state forks out. Well, we can do that too.' Anna-Greta neighed in pleasure. 'Then we can open lots of investment funds and ask people to invest their savings there. It is so wonderful to watch the capital grow. Let's see now, something connected with the environment and climate . . .' Anna-Greta was talking faster and faster as she became more and more carried away by her idea.

'No, no! We shall make do with the money we have. We are not going to become like those finance sharks who just want to see their capital grow. We are going to do something sensible with the money!'

'Like what?' Rake wondered. 'Think about our millions in that drainpipe. They're still there, getting mouldy.'

He was referring to a ransom that the League of Pensioners had demanded in exchange for some paintings from the National Museum. When they had found themselves in a precarious position, they had hidden the money in a drainpipe at the Grand Hotel, and before they had fled Sweden they had tipped off the police about the hidden booty. But as the authorities had taken it to be a bad joke and had not done anything, all the money was probably still there. The League of Pensioners had talked about hiring a scissor lift in order to retrieve the money from the drainpipe, but Anna-Greta, who was a careful spender, had said that sooner or later the hotel would be renovated and then all they would need to do would be to pick the old drainpipe up from a container, and that wouldn't cost anything. So for the time being they had not done anything about it. Besides, as Martha said: It is better to have money in a drainpipe than in a bank.

'To get back to the question of the money from the

bank robbery. I think we should donate it straight away so that there is no risk of us losing it,' said Brains.

'Exactly!' Martha exclaimed in delight, and she downed the contents of her champagne glass so quickly that she started choking. Not until Brains had thumped her back a few times could she carry on. 'I know what. Do you remember von Rosen's bombing raids over Ethiopia? When he bombed them with food from his airplane, to make sure that the people who were really starving would actually get help? Well, we can do the same. Except we could drop banknotes!'

'Excellent idea, and that way we avoid all the go-betweens,' said Christina, who had learned how they do things in the world of finance.

'Yes, that's it; if we invest our cash in shares or investment funds or ask the bank to look after it, it will only cost us lots of money,' Gunnar said.

'Great idea, and we wouldn't have any storage costs either,' Anna-Greta chipped in. 'You're a genius, Martha.'

The room was filled with such genuine appreciation that Martha found herself blushing. Brains held her hand under the table and she couldn't resist leaning her head against his shoulder. It immediately felt like a delight to be alive.

'Mind you, we can't rent a plane and shower old people's homes with banknotes. We must think up another way,' said Gunnar and he sipped his champagne.

'We can compete with the ice-cream trucks,' Brains suggested. 'Then we can play jingles and drive out to where the people who need the money are.'

'Or why not pretend to be the official bailiffs? We can say we are from the National Enforcement Agency. They can get in anywhere,' said Anna-Greta.

'Or perhaps Jehovah's Witnesses?' Christina thought out loud, remembering what things had been like in her Nonconformist church childhood back home in Jönköping.

'Usch, we don't have to make things so complicated. Can't we just be our usual pensioners' choir, visiting the old and poor and singing songs?' Martha suggested.

'And leave behind a shopping cart of banknotes that have the same numbers as the ones stolen from Handelsbanken? Then they would trace us straight away,' Rake warned.

'There, you see, there are disadvantages to being rich. And there are advantages to being poor too,' Martha said. 'Then you never need to worry about what to do with your money.'

'That was the silliest thing I've heard,' the others said with one voice. 'And you say that now, after all the work we've put in!'

Silence followed. It was obvious that they were all very tired and that the lack of brilliant ideas was because they had more bubbly in their heads than good suggestions.

'Champagne straight after a bank robbery does make you a bit lethargic,' Martha said after a while, and she smothered a yawn. 'We've got our millions that we want to give away, but the banknotes are numbered and they mustn't be traced back to us. It is more complicated to be a criminal than you might think.'

The others nodded sleepily.

'Let's talk about it tomorrow,' Anna-Greta muttered, and she had hardly finished saying that before the chairs could be heard scraping as they all got up. Yawning, but in good spirits, they navigated towards the stairs. Christina stopped next to the bottom step and clapped her hands. Her eyes were sparkling.

'Isn't it just fantastic! Several newly stolen millions. Now we're really back in action!'

The morning after the big Handelsbanken robbery, Anders felt absolutely exhausted, but he still had things to do. Reluctantly he opened the back door and got the new tires out. Martha had told him that it was best to change the tires on their minibus so that the tire tracks couldn't be traced. He shivered, and got out the jack, the rim wrench and his work gloves. He sighed as he looked at the back wheel. The rims looked rusty and they needed changing too but, of course, he didn't have to do that now. He yawned and started to jack up the back wheel. The jack squeaked. That too had seen better days and needed oiling at any rate. Everything was getting old nowadays. And that included him. He still hadn't found a new job; when you were in your fifties it evidently wasn't so easy. Did you have to be thirty or thirty-five nowadays to get a job? He unscrewed the four bolts, changed the wheel and then tightened the bolts with the rim wrench. Then he fetched the next wheel. He had been sacked from his job at the Employment Office, and that still smarted. The reorganization, the talk of how some of the staff were superfluous,

the way his boss told him that he no longer had a job . . .
Anders remembered everything from that afternoon meeting. And since then he had applied for several jobs. He had
been asked to attend a couple of interviews, but nothing
ever came of them. You could almost say that was even
more humiliating. Having worked in the Employment
Office, he of all people ought to know how to get a job.
*Try to find out what type of personality you have, see which sort
of job would suit you best and test your capacity* . . . He
thought about all those empty phrases he had used in his
pep talks to people who came to the Employment Office
during his years there. One year had passed, and he was
just as unemployed as the day his boss had given him a
parting gift – a bottle of wine and a plant in a pot.

He walked round the minibus and set to work on the
wheel on the driver's side. For some reason, the bolts here
were even rustier and he had to really exert himself to
loosen them. He panted. No, never again would he set his
foot inside the Employment Office – he was too proud for
that. He must get a job some other way. But there was no
need to panic: he was fully occupied with doing little jobs
for his mum. And Christina gave him a handful of
thousand-kronor bills now and then as if they were merely
a carton of tissues. He couldn't deny that it was hard to
explain to his wife and friends what he actually did, and he
was afraid that the bubble would burst. If only he could
get a bit more cash, he could perhaps start a private home-
care service. Nowadays the local councils used consultants
who taught the municipal home-care departments how to
cut down on service for local clients. Yes, indeed, that was

what they called them nowadays – people who needed care were called clients. But with his own home-care service he could give friendly and generous care. He certainly wouldn't turn it all into a question of trying to cut costs as much as possible, like the councils did now. But until he had gathered together enough capital to start up, he would have to go on helping with crimes. Anders got up and rubbed his back. Two wheels to go. The next time, he would take the minibus to a garage.

The lamp on the desk next to the computer was still turned on, but Chief Inspector Blomberg was sleeping deeply. During the night he had done so many searches on the Internet that he had eventually nodded off to sleep at his desk. His cat, Einstein, had then jumped up from his basket and laid down on the keyboard, where he had spent the rest of the night. Now the black-and-white cat arched his back and stretched out so that yet another row of Zs showed up on the screen. After many hours of delightful sleep and licking of paws and fur, there were also several hundred Xs, Qs and semicolons, although Z was, for some reason, the letter that occurred the most. Einstein's favourite position was to lie down with his tummy on all the letters, including the period and semi-colon, and comfortably park his tail on Enter. This could cause a lot of problems for the chief inspector, but Blomberg had such a soft spot for the animal that he allowed it to keep him company while he worked. Blomberg was usually very careful to keep the cat away from the desk and to close the computer room before he went to bed, something he had made a habit of since the cat on one occasion had put his left paw on the letter Ö and then, purring, pressed the key thousands of times. But that evening, the cat had been free to do what it wanted. Einstein yawned widely, stretched out so that the letters Å, Ä and Ö were all pressed at the same time, and jumped down onto the chief inspector's stomach and then to the floor. Blomberg woke up with a start.

With wide-open eyes he stared at the computer screen and tried to interpret the secret codes before he figured out that it was Einstein who was responsible. Swearing, he got up, let the cat out and then spent a long while tidying up before he could get back to his own notes. Blomberg rubbed his eyes. Now, what had he been busy doing? Yes, some time ago he had of course transferred money from the Police Pension Fund to his own shadow Environment and Senior Service Fund. There was almost two hundred million in his fund now, but even so he wanted more. The trouble was that there had been no activity at all for quite a while in that Las Vegas account. Could it be an organized crime account that was only activated after they carried out a crime? Something that the mafia used? He must have stumbled across some sort of criminal activity. After all, who could lay their hands on so much money?

Blomberg started to sweat. What would happen when they started to look for their missing money? They would, of course, trace it to his computer, seek him out and then . . . Bang! He must get rid of his MacBook immediately and transform the stolen, black money into white money as quickly as possible – because white money was legal, while black money was dirty, even though it kept the economy running. Blomberg shuddered at his own thoughts. He was heading at high speed straight into the shady underworld.

Blomberg thought about it. As soon as possible, he ought to place those stolen millions somewhere sensible. Shares or horses? He had already sent some of the millions to Beylings, the lawyers, to get help with his tax debts. But the rest? The chief inspector got up and started to walk round the room, stopped at the bookcase and ran his fingers over the files. This was where he kept secret copies of the criminal cases he had been involved in. He saw the investigations as trophies from his successful life fighting crime. Absentmindedly, he picked up one of the files and started thumbing through it. Without thinking he sifted through all the old reports, letters and invitations. There were the stylish invitation cards that invited him to parties and fancy dinners at Beylings. Yes, the legal firm's logo with the star and the scales of justice turned up several times. His tired brain tried to make the connection. Of course, he had often been invited there during the years he worked on economic crime. They had tried to bribe him many times. The legal firm didn't just work with tax questions – they also stretched the law and helped finance sharks turn black and grey money white. How many swindlers had the Beylings lawyers helped to escape justice? The firm now had even more work as the state had sold off the taxpayers' assets – housing, retirement homes, schools, pharmacies and so on. Cunning mercenary types had bought up some state-run facility for 600,000 or 800,000 kronor and then in turn resold it for millions more. The profit had to be hidden away so that it wasn't too blatant. The lawyers knew how to do that.

Blomberg immediately felt much brighter. His Las Vegas money would not be a problem for the Beylings specialists. He got up, fetched a tin of cat food and called to Einstein. His life as a pensioner would perhaps not be so lonely and boring as he had feared.

The entire day, everybody at the Karlberg barracks was very angry. Even though the ambulance bus looked its usual self on the outside, the fuel tank was almost empty and inside was a dreadful mess. Not only were there lots of empty bottles everywhere, the drunken idiots hadn't even tried to cover their tracks. The officers interrogated people, but, despite their efforts, didn't manage to get any confessions. None of the cadets would admit to having been drunk and borrowing the army ambulance bus to use for purposes that it was most definitely not intended for. At a quickly convened meeting, it was decided to punish all the recruits: fifty extra push-ups and confinement to barracks for one week.

20

A real Harley-Davidson! Of course he ought to be more careful, but Brains was attracted by the Bandangels' motorcycles in the same way that a gang of businessmen were attracted by a red-light district. The Bandangels gang kept their brightly polished Harley-Davidsons inside the big old shed over by the neighbouring house, and Brains longed to be there. The bank robbery was over and the 'girls' had bossed him around long enough. It was high time for him to think about himself.

Brains put on his knitted cap and gloves and walked up the slope, fully determined to get a look at the motorcycles. He was going to ring the doorbell, ask if could borrow a screwdriver and then start talking about the bikes. But when nobody answered the doorbell, he was disappointed. It had been an effort to walk all the way up the slope. Mind you, as he was already here . . . Brains was a man who liked to improvise and follow his own impulses. He glanced up at the house to make sure there was no sign of either of the bikers, but the whole house was as dead as before. Then he went up to the shed and felt the door. It was locked, but there was nothing special about the lock, he noted. He pushed in the blade of his Swiss knife and carefully opened the door.

Four brightly polished Harley-Davidson motorcycles were parked by the wall and a bit farther in he glimpsed a half-open door to another room. His heart was pounding, but he simply must go inside and touch the beauties. There was a Street Glider. He took a deep breath and caressed the shining metal. His gaze wandered over the engine, the back axel and the handlebars, bringing a sparkle to his eyes. And there was a Sportster 1200 with its engine suspended by rubber, and a Harley-Davidson Fatboy – not to mention that motorcycle that Marlon Brando had in *The Wild One*. Tears welled up in Brains's eyes. He closed them and remembered the wind in his face when he had driven around on his Harley-Davidson in his youth. Devotedly he patted the motorcycles as if they were dear pets. No doubt about it, beauty was not only lovely women and sunsets.

For quite a while he looked at the highly polished bikes and completely forgot that he was trespassing. Perhaps there was more to see farther in, in the next room? To quell his curiosity he pushed open the door, and as he did the smell of paint filled his nostrils. My God, the boys had their own club premises in here! The walls were painted red and the long bar was made of polished black oak. The floor wasn't wood or linoleum, but had light grey quarry tiles. There was a bunch of barstools in the middle of the room and framed photos of old superbikes were spread out below the bar. He gave a start. In a broken frame with cracked glass discarded by a garbage can there was a picture of a genuine Harley Rider – his absolute favourite. The bike he had when he'd met Lisbeth, the first love of his life. He remembered that particular summer as one of the best of his life, and no bike he had owned since then came anywhere near it. For ages he had wished for a picture of that bike, but had never managed to get hold of one. Now here it was, in a broken frame and about to be thrown away. He kept on looking at the photo and was soon lost in a reverie. There were lots of photos here. Nobody would notice if he borrowed this particular one. He battled with his conscience for a moment, but then his emotions got the upper hand and he let the photo disappear inside his overcoat.

Then he moved farther into the room. In the far corner he caught sight of empty paint cans. The bikers were evidently busy decorating. For a moment, Brains recalled his youth at the bar in Sundbyberg. They were a great gang that met there. Those were the days. They had worked on their bikes and dreamed of the fanciest superbikes and women. Brains would have liked to have a beer with the boys in the bar now too, but perhaps two men wanting to join the Mad Angels were not really his type. A lot of them were involved in extortion and black market stuff, and he'd even heard that they were into drugs too. No, it was probably best to get out of here before the boys caught sight of him. Brains backed up, closed the door and hurried out the same way that he had come in. On his way home, the thoughts whirled around inside his head. If the Bandangels fitted out a new clubhouse, then they would soon attract the Mad Angels and lots of other biker gangs. The quiet and peaceful pensioner's life he had imagined was evidently about to turn into something very different.

21

'I've latched on to Martha's money-bombing idea.' Anna-Greta spoke so loudly that they all gave a start and found themselves thinking about exploding bombs instead of giving to charity.

'I think we should call our latest idea the Gift Drop Project,' she went on and nodded to Gunnar to start up the computer. The League of Pensioners were gathered in the library and they were now curious to see what Anna-Greta and Gunnar had concocted. Ever since the pair had been reunited, Gunnar had come to visit them several times a week. Recently he had even spent the night in the guest room. And now he was involved in the Gift Drop Project. Gunnar pressed an icon on the computer labelled 'Gift Drop' and an aerial image of Stockholm, complete with street names and the locations of various retirement homes, appeared.

For several days, Anna-Greta and Gunnar had been sitting in front of the computer, planning. In Gunnar's company, Anna-Greta had picked up even more computer skills, and the others had been able to hear her chuckles of contentment as she worked with Gunnar. Now she was standing in front of the screen with a pointer in her hand, waiting for her friends to be quiet.

'It's one thing to rob a bank, but quite another to deal with the loot,' Anna-Greta explained, as though she was giving a lecture. 'We must ensure that the money doesn't end up in the wrong hands.'

'Well, I've thought that for a long time,' Rake said with a grin on his face.

Anna-Greta pretended not to hear him.

'Internet shopping has progressed so enormously lately that we can order anything we want,' she went on and pointed at pictures of cellphones, cameras and furniture.

'We pay over the Internet, store the goods here and then we can hand out the gifts after that. When we want to deliver something we simply use the services of a transport firm. And some suppliers will even deliver goods directly to the customer; it's amazing how modern it has become.'

'But the stolen money is in banknotes and those numbers will be known. How can we pay with that?' Christina wondered.

'Now listen! There is something called laundering money,' said Anna-Greta with burning cheeks, her gazed fixed upon the floor. For her, former bank employee that she was, it didn't feel right to say this, but needs must.

'Launder money? I know. The race tracks and casinos . . .' began Rake, sounding like a man of the world.

'Not exactly; in fact, it is better to use exchange bureaus. The staff have a duty to find out where the money comes from and what it is going to be used for. But that doesn't happen in practice. Nobody cares. If we set our minds to it, we ought to be able to deposit around two hundred thousand kronor a day.'

'Deposit?' Brains asked.

'Yes; we've got those fake personal identity numbers – you know, the temporary numbers that all people who move to Sweden get. I have opened some new accounts,' said Anna-Greta, slapping her pointer against her hand like a real teacher. That is, like the teachers used to do in the old days.

'It's fantastic. You've done a really good job there. That sounds excellent,' said Martha as she got up. She returned a few moments later with the gang's newly purchased dining cart. On it were a coffee pot, coffee cups and a bowl of wafers. While the precocious pensioner-villains drank their coffee, they concocted their very special laundering plans, which had nothing to do with dirty clothes.

The next day, the League of Pensioners travelled into Stockholm to change the stolen money into foreign currency. They split up and went to different parts of the city. Martha chose the Forex exchange office in Östermalm, Rake went to an office on Söder Island, Christina to an office in Vasastan, and Brains walked to Kungsholmen with two paper bags full of banknotes. Anna-Greta took the Roslag local train out to the fancy suburb of Djursholm to exchange her stolen money there. It was a setting in which she knew how to behave, and with a proud posture, an elegant fur coat and an authoritative voice, she asked to exchange her money for dollars, but it wasn't so easy. The rules were a lot stricter than she remembered and it wasn't until she told them about her imminent journey to Florida and her plan to buy a plot of land in Gran Canaria that finally they relented and agreed to exchange the money.

In the days that followed, they went to a whole lot of exchange offices, but their plan wasn't working. The staff had been given newer, stricter instructions. So in the end, Anna-Greta decided that they would have to go to the Solvalla horse races after all.

Anna-Greta really wanted to go on her own and fly under the radar as much as possible because, with her professional background, she was slightly ashamed of being seen at such a place. But when she told Gunnar, he looked at her with such sad eyes that she understood: being in a relationship, or, at any rate, almost in a relationship, meant certain commitments – and if she didn't take him with her, he would be deeply offended.

One late sunny afternoon, Anna-Greta and Gunnar set off for the Solvalla racecourse. They took the subway to Rissne and decided to walk the last bit. Anna-Greta pushed the walker in front of her. They had Martha's floral cloth bag filled with cash so Gunnar kept a watchful eye on the treasure in the basket.

'The old guys with the hottest tips are the ones sitting over there, I've heard,' said Gunnar, nodding in the direction of a cluster of men standing outside the racecourse.

'But the basket is full of money. I don't know if we dare go over there.' Anna-Greta hesitated.

Betting on the horses and handling large amounts of cash was actually a bit scary. The banknotes from the Handelsbanken robbery were red-hot in the floral bag. Now that she thought about it, they ought to have hidden the money in a simple sports bag, or indeed anything other than Martha's floral cloth bag. It attracted too much attention. Her hands squeezed the handles of the walker. Gunnar noticed and stretched out a hand.

'You know what? This is nothing compared to our Internet transfers. Now we're dealing in small change.'

'But how can you say that? When I worked in the bank we saved kronor in coins. Two hundred thousand in cash is not just a bit of pocket money.'

'Of course, but if we spend these banknotes it'll be nothing compared to what we lost on the Internet.'

Anna-Greta realized that Gunnar only wanted to calm her. Having company when you are out on an adventure wasn't such a bad idea after all, she thought. Besides, Gunnar's father had been a big-time gambler and taught him quite a lot about racehorses. That felt reassuring.

Quickly, they walked on, and after they had got their tickets they deliberately took a wrong turn and went into the Stallbacken – the stable area. This was restricted to trainers, jockeys and other people directly connected to the horses, but Anna-Greta and Gunnar had decided that they wanted to check on the condition of the horses themselves. Above all, they were hoping to find somebody who was doing shady business, because today they were going to be buying betting slips. Anna-Greta liked the sound of the words 'betting slips': it made her feel adventurous. The plan was that if somebody won one hundred thousand on one of the horses, she would offer to buy the winning betting slip for one hundred and twenty-five thousand kronor in cash. Then, when she went to the betting counter with the slip, she would get one hundred thousand that nobody could trace. Not bad. But decidedly shady . . .

The horses were warming up in the Stallbacken. Anna-Greta and Gunnar took a good look at them all. Anna-Greta was now feeling confidently eager. They were going to launder money, and lots of it!

'Fighter Gull is going to win,' an elderly man confided in her beside the entrance to one of the stable buildings.

'But what about that one there?' Anna-Greta wondered and pointed at a black horse with small ears, but without horseshoes.

'Joker Ride? That one's going to break into a gallop and will come in last.'

Anna-Greta and Gunnar walked on and went into the main building. They took the elevator up to the restaurant, from which they had a magnificent view of the racecourse. They sat down at one of the tables and ordered beer and some shrimp sandwiches. Anna-Greta looked around her and tried to find someone who might want to sell a winning slip – someone who looked a bit suspicious. Here, at any rate, was where the big-time gamblers congregated. If a gang of middle-aged women, for example, had backed a winner, then they would celebrate with lots of noise, but the professionals kept a straight face. So she and Gunnar had to be very attentive.

Leaning back, she listened to the talk all around her and watched as the horses gathered, ready for the start of the next race. Three minutes to go. Gunnar got up.

'I'm betting five hundred. It would be fun to gamble a bit too.'

'Yes, we all need a bit of pocket money,' agreed Anna-Greta.

When Gunnar came back, the start car had already pulled away at high speed, and the race was underway. Goodness, how fast those horses run, Anna-Greta thought as they whooshed past. 'How clever they are, our bow-legged friends!' she exclaimed in a loud voice.

'Four-legged friends.' An elegant man in a brown suit on a neighbouring table corrected her.

'Magical Star has a jockey with a firm hand,' Anna-Greta went on, to compensate for her faux pas. She was sure the jockey's skill was a decisive factor.

'The driver, you mean?' the brown suit said. 'Yes, Magical Star has a good driver.'

'Driver? Were the jockeys called drivers?' Anna-Greta mumbled to herself.

The voice on the speaker got louder and more rattled the closer the horses got to the finish, and then she heard a gang cheer just a few tables away. It was a little group of middle-aged ladies; they certainly weren't shady big-time gamblers. A man got up and walked towards the elevator. Nothing in his face expressed joy. Now was the time.

Anna-Greta got up so quickly that her beer glass

started to wobble. She wobbled too and realized that the beer she had been drinking was much stronger than she'd thought, but she was in a hurry, so, with the aid of her walker, she sped along as fast as she could towards the elevator. Once she was down on the ground floor she caught sight of the man, who was walking straight towards the men's room. Typical, she thought. What would she do if he carried out his business transactions in there? She waited for what felt like the longest time ever and then spotted him exiting the bathroom, still holding the winning betting slip in his hand. She approached him cautiously.

'Err, got summat to sell?' Anna-Greta slurred. The beer really had been very strong.

The man looked up in surprise.

'You've won ninety thousand, haven't you? I saw the odds,' Anna-Greta went on, and then gave him a knowing wink, just like she'd seen in the movies.

The man stared at her.

'Okay, I'll give you one hundred and ten thousand for the betting slip. Cash,' said Anna-Greta and reached down for the bag.

'But this isn't a betting slip. This is a prescription for horse medicine.'

'I was just joking,' Anna-Greta stuttered and she fled back to Gunnar. Thankfully, as the evening wore on, their 'deals' started to go better. After the evening's most important race, Anna-Greta and Gunnar managed to buy two winning betting slips. They had been able to go about their business undisturbed. Neither of the big-time gamblers had the slightest inkling that the two charming pensioners that evening had laundered banknotes from the Handelsbanken robbery. Then they took a taxi home. They didn't dare walk through the park again with real, untraceable money.

22

It felt safer now that all of the five million in 'Hugin', the larger of the two mannequins, had been changed into bills that couldn't be traced back to the robbery. The remaining five million, in 'Munin', would have to be exchanged at another time. The League of Pensioners didn't want to shuttle back and forth to the Solvalla racecourse or the Forex exchange offices anymore. So, after Anna-Greta had deposited their arduously 'laundered' money in the League's newly opened accounts, they all gathered together on the veranda to discuss further plans. Instead of coffee, they had switched to tea, and instead of wafers they had scones. Martha thought they needed a bit of variety and, besides, it was wise to show that nothing was set in stone and that even their most routine arrangements could be changed. They must not stagnate; they must always be in top form.

The meeting started and, refreshed by the tea, they were indeed all in very good form. The day had come when at last they could start their Gift Drop Project. The friends had already drawn up a list of retirement homes that would be targeted; now they only had to decide what they would gift to them.

'First, we'll do the retirement homes, then the City Mission Charity and then the museums that have had to cut back the most,' Martha started off. 'What do you think we should give them?'

'We must find out what people really need so that we don't spend money unnecessarily,' Anna-Greta stated, keen to make her opinion known.

'Easy as pie,' said Rake. 'Beautiful young women, a glass of the hard stuff and some good food . . . and perhaps a visit to—'

'Dirty old man!' Christina hissed, and she threw out her hand so that her cup fell to the ground.

'I was only joking,' Rake attempted, but he didn't look especially credible.

'What about a car or another kind of vehicle?' Brains wondered out loud. 'Or a motorcycle with a sidecar?'

'I think we should give away "electronic tablets" instead,' Gunnar put in. 'Then you can read books and newspapers or play computer games and do all sorts of interesting things.'

'Good idea! And what about a subscription for regular deliveries of nourishing food? Various shops and companies offer that service nowadays – Lina's Shopping Basket or whatever they call themselves,' Martha went on.

'Good food needs to be accompanied by good drinks too,' Brains stated authoritatively. 'At the state alcohol shop we can buy bottles of wine by the carton, champagne and whisky too, for every retirement home in the country.'

'But the alcohol shops can't deliver to other addresses – it would all have to go via us,' Anna-Greta pointed out.

'I don't see that being much of a problem,' Rake said – and he didn't expect anyone would notice if he took a few bottles for himself at the same time. They might well come into use if he went across to visit Lillemor and wanted to treat her to a drink or two.

The discussion went back and forth and after a little break the meeting got going again. The mood was quite joyful – to put it mildly. Now Brains wanted to give away sports cars and Harley-Davidsons to all the retirement homes in the country; Rake was keen on yachts and cruise tickets, while Martha and the other ladies were dreaming of providing gyms and health centres, before they finally returned to earth and settled for season passes for gyms and spas.

By the time they got to the end of their list, Anna-Greta's notebook was full. Then Martha opened her mouth to add walking sticks to the list, but she suddenly remembered the sticks with the missing diamonds and kept quiet. Instead, she was relieved to hear Anna-Greta proposing folding walking sticks and everyone was happy. After that, they helped to put together an address list.

'Right, let's order these items!' cried Martha.

'But, Martha, dear, shouldn't we get some sleep first?' said Brains.

'Nonsense, this won't take long!' she answered and then they gathered together in front of the computer, cheering and commenting loudly at every purchase made. When nobody was looking, Rake took the chance to add their own address to the impressive delivery list, because he thought they didn't have to give everything away. They could have a bit of fun themselves, surely?

When Anders and Emma came to visit that evening, they found the whole gang snoring on their beds. In the library there was an open bottle of vodka as well as a bottle of cloudberry liqueur that was almost empty. They looked at each other in horror.

'This criminal life doesn't exactly seem to be very healthy,' Emma sighed. 'Every day they seem to have to *celebrate* something.' She gathered together the glasses and put them in the sink, where she gave the unwashed cups a disapproving look. 'Has it occurred to you that we have turned into a home-help service?'

'That's true. We clean, take clothes to the dry cleaners, do the weekly shopping and fill the fridge and freezer. Today I'd thought of going to a soccer game, but instead . . .' Anders made a face.

'But they do pay well, and we don't need to have any other job.'

'I'll grant you that,' Anders mumbled and thought about his financial circumstances. He didn't get much in the way of unemployment benefits, but managed okay now, thanks to the thousand-kronor banknotes that Christina gave him now and then.

'But just look at what a mess they've made here,' Emma groaned and she pointed at the half-full glasses and the unwashed cups. She picked up one of the cups and sniffed at it suspiciously.

'Oh my God, even the cups smell of vodka!'

'What of it? That's not our business. Mother has her life, and we have ours, don't we?'

'Yes, but the idea of having a boozing criminal as a parent!'

'Let her do what she wants. The most important thing is that she is happy and comfortable,' said Anders as he started filling the dishwasher. 'And don't forget that we, too, are criminals now. We have assisted in crimes . . .'

Hearing those words, Emma raised her eyebrows and dug a packet of cigarettes out of her bag. She lit a cigarette and inhaled deeply twice, but stopped when she heard footsteps on the stairs. Martha!

'Well, well, how nice to see you! What about a little champagne? We have a lot to celebrate, you can be sure of that!' Martha beamed.

Rake, too, was on his way down. He was looking a bit the worse for wear and he wrinkled his eyebrows when he caught sight of them. Emma could guess what he was thinking. Christina was always getting visitors, but Rake hadn't heard from his son in the last few months. He pretended not to care, but Emma knew otherwise. She liked Rake, and thought that his absent son could at least phone now and then.

The stairs creaked again, and Christina came into the kitchen. She brightened up when she saw them. Their mother was neither red-eyed nor angry, as she had been recently. Now she looked very much in control of things. Her two children looked at each other, relieved, because they had noticed that things weren't as they should be, but they had not really understood what had been wrong. But anyway, when their mother hugged them, everything seemed to be all right again.

'Well, well, this is nice. I hoped it would be you. And Anders, dear, I need a bit of help with something.'

Oh no, not again, he thought but had no time to protest before Christina resolutely took him by the arm and went off with him to the veranda. The two of them talked a long while out there, and when they came back in, Christina was giggling while Anders just shook his head.

'What is it?' Emma whispered to him when she saw her brother's shocked look.

'Mother has lost her marbles. It's all beyond my comprehension,' he sighed. 'But I've promised not to say a word.'

23

The days passed, and Rake couldn't forget Lillemor. He had seen how Tompa went into her house sometimes and he wondered what those two were up to together. The fellow was admittedly younger, but neither as intelligent nor as well-groomed as he himself was. Nor had he travelled as much. No, Tompa was nothing to worry about. Rake straightened his back. Bandangel or not, he didn't care. That biker was no match for Rake!

As soon as the League of Pensioners had laundered the money, and got some safe cash to spend, Rake saw his chance. He must do something to impress Lillemor. He pondered this for several days and then came up with an idea.

'The path needs fixing,' Rake declared brightly, and with a bit of help from Gunnar ordered a truckload of gravel and stone slabs from the Internet. At first everyone was surprised, but then they agreed that it was probably best to let him do his own thing. If Rake could be in charge of his own little project, then it might put him in a better mood – there had been problems on that front lately. Above all, there was still tension between him and Christina, and that affected all of them.

'There are enough slabs there to build a cathedral. Rake always has to go over the top,' sighed Martha two days later when she saw the heaps of slabs and gravel beside the gate. This wasn't going to be an ordinary gravel path; no, Rake had decided to lay stone slabs using various sorts of granite. He had had a summer job laying slabs when he was a teenager, but that hardly qualified him, and to take on a designed path when he was over the age of eighty was perhaps a bit too bold.

'Now I'll show them, those so-called experts on TV!' Rake said when he pulled on his overalls. 'They wouldn't even have dreamed of a path like this. You can forget those fancy landscape-gardeners – here comes Rake!'

So out into the yard he went. He measured and planned, his enthusiasm clear for all to see. They all understood how serious he was the following morning when they woke to the sound of a roaring backhoe which seemed to have gone berserk in the yard. Between the gate and the lilac arbour, Kalle's Mini Excavator AB was busy digging up a strip with Rake standing close by, gesticulating frantically. When he came into the house half an hour later, he had a satisfied smile all over his face, and didn't seem to be tired in the slightest.

'What are you up to, Rake? Do you want to make an impression on her across the street?' Christina asked, and she pouted.

Rake's face changed colour. 'No, no. This is something called landscape design,' he announced solemnly and pointed at a sketch with stone slabs laid in various patterns. 'You can see it here, a path which talks with nature.'

Rake had heard that phrase on TV and thought it sounded impressive. He held up the sketch. 'The path will go from the gate to the garden and every five metres there will be a design feature.'

'And what do you have in mind for those?' Christina asked. 'Stone slabs laid out like Tarot cards, perhaps?'

'Now, now, Christina,' Martha mumbled.

'Just you wait! I'll lay rectangular patterns like the sails of a full-rigged ship. This will really be something, mark my words!' Rake shouted and hurried outside again.

From up on the veranda they could see Rake go up to the man driving the backhoe, show him the sketch and then point at the heap of stone slabs. The man manoeuvred his excavator, lowered the bucket and lifted up a few slabs at a time, which he then placed next to the path.

'Rake thinks he can manage the rest by himself,' Christina sighed.

'Let him be. He'll discover soon enough that he won't be able to do it,' Brains reassured her.

'But he is so obsessed by all those do-it-yourself programs on TV. Yesterday there was a smiling man who built, painted, furnished and then cooked all in the very same program. Rake muttered that the idiot gave all of Sweden's male population a complex, and then he went out, put a half-hitch on one of the stone slabs and dragged it off towards the garden. I thought he would have a heart attack!'

'Best we go out and help him, then,' Anna-Greta said, and Gunnar nodded in agreement. But Christina shook her head.

'I don't think he wants any help. Since Rake started hobnobbing with Lillemor, you can't talk to him. I bet you he's doing this to impress her,' she sighed.

'It'll blow over,' Brains said to console her, and he put his hand under her arm. 'Guys can be like that sometimes. Now let's go outside. Be careful on the steps.'

When they got out into the yard they saw that Kalle's Mini Excavator AB had left and Rake now stood there on his own. He looked at the heaps of slabs, bent down and tried to move one of them. He couldn't. Christina rushed forward.

'No, Rake, please, take it easy. You can hurt your back, fracture your thigh and—'

'Not me, no way. You should have seen how I climbed up past the topsail on the big sailing ships. Right up to the crosstrees of the topgallant, I'll have you know. Ropes and agility, that's my thing. I know how to do this. But we need a block and tackle.'

Rake went off to find the equipment he needed, and that same moment caught sight of Tompa. The giant stopped next to the gate and looked at the heaps of stones.

'Ah, yardwork, is it?'

'That's right,' said Rake nonchalantly, reaching out to the rope and tying an elegant knot around the biggest slab.

'Listen, man, at your age, you should be relaxing. Me and Jörgen, we'll sort this out in no time. We've done this before.' Tompa flexed his biceps, pulled out his phone and called his friend. Rake didn't know what to do; it looked as if Tompa was going to get all the glory. That wasn't the idea.

'But you shouldn't have to . . .' Rake protested.

'Now listen, we'll fix this!' Tompa declared and he nodded up the hill to where Jörgen could now be seen wandering down. Whether Rake wanted them to help or not, the two Bandangels members had taken over his project.

They fetched a wheelbarrow, Rake took the lead, and then the two bikers laid the stone slabs where he pointed. Now and then Rake glanced across to the brick house, but, thank goodness, Lillemor didn't seem to be at home. After less than two hours, everything was done and a satisfied Rake came back into the house.

'Clever boys, those two!'

'Rake, there'll be a price to pay . . .' Martha groaned.

'But Christina, it looks nice, doesn't it?' Rake asked. Christina had no option but to nod and give praise, after which calm settled over the old house once again. And that lasted exactly two days.

It was late in the evening and really cold and dark outside when Tompa and Jörgen knocked on the door. This time they didn't have boots with steel toecaps on, but they didn't seem any the less intimidating. Martha felt a cold shiver go deep into her soul.

'Hello, one and all. Bit chilly outside, isn't it? Anyway, we'd like to have a word about something,' said Tompa with a bundle of papers in his hand. He was just about to cross the threshold.

'Of course, of course,' said Brains, who wanted to hear if they'd got any new motorcycles lately.

'Hello, guys,' Rake greeted them. 'Thanks for helping with the slabs. A nice job, boys!'

'A little cup of coffee, perhaps?' said Martha with a forced smile. She had a lump in her tummy. She always did when she got bad vibes. The giants nodded and sat down at the kitchen table. Martha made some coffee and put out Christina's newly baked cinnamon buns. Tompa took a big bite and put the bun down.

'Yes, the pathway looks very nice indeed,' Tompa started saying with his mouth full.

They all nodded. Waited.

'But that's not why we're here.'

'No, we realize that,' Martha mumbled.

'Yes, well, you see, we buy and sell properties. We drew up a new contract and got it signed but now our colleagues have gone home. We just need to have the document witnessed. So we need some signatures.'

'Yes, that's right. It usually requires two witnesses,' Anna-Greta recalled from her bank days.

'No problem,' said Rake.

'Let's have a look,' said Martha, reaching out to pick up the contract. The lump in her tummy was now the size of a Pilates ball. Documents, bikers and signatures did not mix well together.

'Yes, you only need to sign down there.' Jörgen pointed at the last page of the bundle of papers.

'Yes, right,' said Martha, trying to play for time. Shady types and contracts – she had read time and time again about how naïve people got swindled. The theme came up a lot in crime novels and books about the mafia. Unscrupulous villains could buy a property, do no repairs, triple the rents and squeeze all they could out of it. When the mismanagement was reported and the authorities were alerted, it was too late. By then, the crooks had already transferred the property to a 'goalkeeper' – usually a drunk or a homeless person who didn't have any money anyway. But what if Tompa and Jörgen had decided that their elderly neighbours would be good as goalkeepers? Martha's nose could smell out anything fishy and she thought things were starting to smell rather bad. She tried to produce a smile.

'Well, you see, I usually never sign anything without actually reading what I'm signing first,' she explained.

'That isn't necessary. We've had our lawyer check it all,' said Tompa, in a slightly more decisive voice.

'Of course we'll sign. Give me the documents,' said Anna-Greta, who wanted to get rid of the bikers as quickly as possible.

'Wait,' said Martha.

'But witnessing something isn't a problem,' said Anna-Greta, who had retired from the bank long before all these shady goalkeepers became common in Sweden. And before Martha could stop her, Anna-Greta had signed with a flourish and then handed the document to Gunnar, who signed without even looking. Tompa nodded, thanked them and quickly snatched the document back.

Martha felt a cold shiver run down her spine. The bikers must not be allowed to leave the house with her friends' signatures.

'Thanks very much, we'll be off now,' said Tompa.

'Oh what a pity! Perhaps I can just borrow the document a moment so I can make a photocopy. It's my memory, you know. An old person like me doesn't remember anything. Nothing at all.' Martha got up and stretched out her hand.

The bikers looked at each other, and she could see what they were thinking.

'I'll just make a little copy for myself, and if you change your mind, then I promise I'll rip it up.' Martha made her decision and quickly snatched the little bundle of papers from them.

Tompa shrugged his shoulders while Martha disappeared into the library.

The others could hear the machinery starting up and then making a rattling sound. After a while, Martha came back in, bright red in the face.

'So sorry, boys, now don't you go getting all angry at me. We've got a new photocopying machine and . . . I think I did it wrong. I should have asked for your help, but—'

'Do you need help?' Tompa interrupted.

'Err, it's a bit late now,' said Martha and she pulled some paper out of her floral bag.

'To think it could go so wrong! I'm not so familiar with these apparatuses. I think I must have put the piece of paper in the shredder,' she said, and she held up the strips.

It suddenly felt bitterly cold in the room, and Tompa jumped up.

'You did WHAT? We'll be back, you can be sure of that! Jörgen, come on, we're off!'

The two bikers stormed out and no one dared say a word until they had vanished up the slope.

'Why did you have to go and do that?' Anna-Greta wondered out loud.

'They wanted to involve us in their criminal activities,' answered Martha. She went and threw the shredded paper into the fireplace, then piled up some logs before reaching out for the matches. But when she lit the fire, her hands were shaking so much she could hardly manage it.

'Are you all right, Martha dear?' said Brains, putting his arm around her shoulders.

'I'm frightened. For the first time in my life, I am really frightened.'

24

Perhaps the Bandangels were just biding their time. Either that, or they were planning something dreadful. Days passed and the League of Pensioners worried about what the bikers would get up to.

'We can't exactly lower our guard,' said Martha. 'Before we know it, they'll be back with some new trick.' The League of Pensioners gathered in the library while they listened to Beethoven's Fifth, the Victory Symphony, over and over again.

Finally, Rake shrugged his shoulders and said: 'I'd best go and see Lillemor and find out what she has to say about the future!'

Christina, who was busy reading a play by Lars Norén, stiffened and glared at him. As soon as Rake had gone out, she phoned Anders.

'Now, my boy, it's time to do it! I can't stick this out any longer. It is time to carry out the plan.'

'But Mother, are you really going to go through with this?' Anders replied. 'I thought you were joking.'

'Now you'll do as I say, or else you can forget any inheritance,' Christina replied firmly.

* * *

The next day, Anders drove into town and, a few hours later, came out to the big old house with a large box. When the others asked what was in it, he answered somewhat evasively – but Christina looked pleased.

'Are you really sure that you want me to do this?' Anders asked his mother after dinner when they sat in the basket chairs on the veranda. The oil lamps were burning, and the sea lay black and still before them. The lights from the city lit up the evening sky and the smell of the oil lamps spread across the veranda. The others had gone into the library to play bridge, but Christina had stayed on outside because she wanted to talk to Anders.

'Lillemor isn't at home, so you can put the carton on her porch,' Christina said and she lowered the wick of the oil lamp, which had started to smoke. 'Make sure the carton is damaged in one corner to arouse her curiosity, so she can't resist looking inside. And don't forget to address the parcel to Bertil "Rake" Engström.'

'So you want it to look as if the delivery has gone to the wrong address?'

'Yes, like I've said all the time,' said Christina, and her tone of voice was so sharp that Anders gave a start.

'Okay, but I refuse to do anything like this again.'

'Now, now. Let's hope there won't be any more times,' said Christina.

At eleven that evening, when Lillemor came home on her bicycle from a meeting with her Tarot friends, she found a large parcel outside her front door. She leaned her bicycle against the railings and quickly went up the front steps. Feeling a little sleepy, she opened the door and took the parcel into the kitchen. After she had taken her coat off and turned the coffee machine on, she lit a cigarette. Then she looked at the parcel, but was disappointed when she saw the label. It was addressed not to her, but to Bertil 'Rake' Engström. There was no sender and the box had been damaged in one corner. The lid was now crooked and the contents were almost spilling out. She fetched a roll of sticky tape but couldn't manage to get her nail under the edge of the tape on the roll. What could be inside Rake's parcel? No sender – that in itself seemed strange. Her curiosity increased. Lillemor put the tape aside and got the lid off the carton. There was a large, soft package inside. She prodded it first, but then couldn't resist opening a corner. The colour of her face changed from light pink to darkest red and she pressed her lips together. When Rake rang the doorbell the next day, she had spent all morning getting more and more angry.

'I think you shall have to go to somebody else with your questions about the future,' Lillemore said, without letting him over the threshold.

'But can't you tell my fortune and then we can sit on the sofa?' Rake replied and made an attempt to give her a hug. 'You can't imagine how well I've been getting on with the Tarot cards.'

'Sit on the sofa with you, you dirty old man! Over my

dead body!' She pointed at the opened parcel. 'That parcel seems to have come to the wrong address.'

'What parcel?'

'Don't play all innocent! I'll make one thing damned clear to you: you can keep your Inflatable Barbara for yourself! The front gate is over there. Be off with you!'

She kicked the carton so that Inflatable Barbara fell out and flopped onto her side with what sounded like a sigh.

'But I had no idea . . .'

'Be off with you!'

Christina saw Rake return from the brick house across the road, and had the greatest difficulty keeping a straight face. God punishes some people straight away, the saying goes. But if God doesn't do his bit, then you must take care of things yourself, Christina thought, and she sent a thought of gratitude to Anders too. This should have taught Rake a lesson.

During the following week, Rake hardly responded when people talked to him; he just didn't seem to hear. They had never seen him with such an absent look on his face before, and the only person who wasn't worried about it was Christina. Everybody thought that was a bit strange, but when they realized that Rake had stopped visiting Lillemor, they started to put two and two together. Something had happened.

The weekend passed, and on Monday Rake asked if he could get a ride with Emma into town. He was away all day and when he came home late in the afternoon, he had a large parcel under his arm. He just said a brief hello, told them he needed to rest a little, and then he stayed in his room until suppertime.

'I'm beginning to be rather worried about Rake. I just hope he isn't ill or something,' Martha sighed.

'Rake?' Christina snorted. 'There's nothing ailing him, believe me.'

After supper Rake went and fetched a handful of birch logs and laid a fire in the grate in the library. With nimble, practised hands he laid a bed of firewood on some crumpled paper, put the logs on top in a criss-cross pattern and then lit it. It immediately started burning brightly, and the others smiled in relief. Rake always saw it as a challenge to try to light a log fire with only one match, and he was just as pleased every time he succeeded.

During the evening they played a hand of bridge, but when Rake didn't try to cheat, they got a little worried again. No, he still wasn't his real self, and when they asked how he was feeling, he just grunted. Soon they all felt so tired that they thought it was time to go to bed, so they got up and bid one another goodnight.

Christina went up to her room, put her volume of Gustav Fröding's poems on the bedside table, and was just about to get undressed when there was a knock on the door. She recognized the knock. It was Rake.

'Come in!' Christina called out.

Rake stood in the doorway, plucking up the courage to start speaking. He had combed his hair and smelled of aftershave.

'This is not exactly an original gift, but you do like

him,' Rake mumbled and he handed over the rectangular packet he had brought with him from town earlier.

'Goodness me, Rake!' said Christina, surprised, and she ripped off the wrapping.

'A reproduction, of course, but Anders Zorn's *Summer Delight* is a beautiful watercolour.'

Rake looked pleased but left the room. When he came back, he had a bunch of flowers in his hand. He put them down, fidgeted a great deal with his tie, and not until Christina opened her arms did he dare go forward and give her a hug.

'I apologize,' Rake said. 'I'm very sorry, I wasn't thinking. Can you forgive me?'

And then Christina smiled and gave him a really, really big hug.

25

Martha paced back and forth in front of the entrance to Diamond House retirement home. She looked expectantly down the hill. At last it was time for Operation Gift Drop. It was cold and the sun shone from a deep blue sky, but Martha was so excited that she hardly felt the chill in the air. A delivery van approached and she smiled to herself. The delivery seemed to be working. The van came to a halt by the retirement home.

'I'm Inspector Siv Petterson from the Ministry of Health's control unit for standards in retirement homes,' said Martha, walking briskly up to the driver as he opened the van door. She held up her official identity card, which Christina had produced, with her name and photo.

'You what?' The driver, a man in his thirties, stopped abruptly.

Martha now stood in his way, pulled out a binder and thumbed through the papers.

'This concerns the goods to be delivered to Diamond House. We must check the delivery system is working correctly,' Martha said in a friendly manner.

'Then you'll have to be quick about it. I'm in a hurry!'

the driver muttered. He looked at his delivery list, opened the back doors and pulled out the cart.

'Can I look at the order?' said Martha in an authoritative tone. She pulled out a copy of the order from her cloth bag, took the list from the driver and checked that they contained the same items, which she ticked off.

'This has got nothing to do with you. The goods are for Diamond House,' the driver grumbled.

'That is correct, but so many strange things happen today, and in this case the people who made the order have asked us to check the delivery. Things can disappear en route, there are hijackings and so on.'

'Hijackings?'

'Yes, it is really dreadful,' Martha complained. 'You must have read about how all those eighteen-wheelers lose their trailers, vehicles are stolen, packages get lost in the mail. So those of us at the control unit have a very important part to play. Now let's see, it all seems to be in order. I only have to check that the goods in the packages are the same as what is listed on the order. I'll come into the retirement home with you.'

The driver swore in Finnish. Martha remained calm and watched closely while the disgruntled man went to fetch the packages. When he had put all the parcels in the service elevator, Martha followed and walked up to Diamond House with him. She discreetly pulled her hat over her wig, adjusted the elegantly shaded glasses and put her gloves on. As long as she didn't give herself away by reverting to her childhood accent from the south of Sweden – something she tended to do when she got really excited

. . . No, she must concentrate on her task. The driver rang the bell, the door was opened and Martha recognized the young dark-haired girl from the St. Lucia Day celebration.

'I'm Inspector Siv Petterson,' said Martha and they shook hands.

'I'm Nurse Anja. What can I help you with?'

Martha described the purpose of her visit, showed her identity card and, after Anja had signed the delivery list, they went into the large sitting room. Martha looked around the familiar surroundings. The stuffy smell and the same old furniture from when she and her friends had lived in the home were still there. Diamond House was just about as appealing as an old, run-down school. I must remember to send some new furniture, Martha thought, and jotted it down on her notepad. The driver rolled in the goods while Anja went round and gathered the residents. It took a while, but eventually about twenty people clustered around the big ornate table in the dining room. They looked sleepy and confused and Martha wrinkled her eyebrows.

'Have you given them anything? They seem so sleepy.'

'Just some tranquillizers,' said Anja.

'If you take care of old people, they don't need tranquillizers, do they?' Martha muttered. 'What about gym exercises?'

'Gym exercises? I don't know anything about that,' Anja answered.

'And the kitchen? Have you got a new kitchen yet?'

'We've got the microwave ovens . . .'

'There should at least be a new kitchen here! Don't you communicate with Director Mattson?'

'Director Mattson and Nurse Barbara? They own so many retirement homes now, and most of the time they are away on business trips.'

'I want to get hold of them.'

'That won't be so easy.' Anja gave a little laugh. 'We've tried to present them with our complaints, but we never get any answers. They have an address in New Jersey.'

Martha felt a burning anger and the knuckles around her notebook turned white. The money that she and her friends had sent from Las Vegas might have disappeared, but she had learned that the management of Diamond House Enterprises had made a profit of more than seventy million kronor last year. Martha had hoped that they had reinvested some of the money in the retirement homes. But no. She opened her big cloth bag.

'My friends!' Martha said, pulling out a bundle of gift cards for a company that Anna-Greta had found on the Internet that stocked and delivered all sorts of equipment.

'These gift cards are valid for a whole year and I'll mail copies of them to Diamond House Enterprises. Now you can buy ovens, stovetops, sink units, dishwashing machines, yes, all the kitchen equipment you need. In two months, our control unit will return and check that everything is installed.' Martha signed the delivery list and put her pen back in her bag. 'Surely you realize, Nurse Anja, that conditions should be as nice as possible when you are old.'

The girl turned red in the face and was just about to say something when they heard a strange noise from the big sitting room. They all rushed in. Dolores had lent her

Rippy all-round knife to Henrik, also in his nineties. To the accompaniment of jolly cheers, he cut through the tape around the parcels. Anja had never been in a situation like this before. She hadn't read a word in the regulations about what you should do in the event of gifts and contributions from outsiders.

'Ooooh!' could be heard from the residents at Diamond House. Like children at Christmas, they ripped off the wrapping paper and threw it aside. With exclamations of joy, the residents pulled out iPads, iPhones, books and movie DVDs. Some Belgian chocolates fell onto the floor and Martha realized that Christina must have been responsible for that particular order. She herself had ordered yoga mats, stretching bands, dumbbells and lots of other exercise equipment, while Rake had wanted to bring joy to the residents with computer games, model boats and garden tools. Brains, for his part, had ordered workshop tools as well as anti-slip mats, magnifying glasses, talking watches and walking-stick holders to attach to walkers. Right at the bottom of one of the packages lay a packet wrapped in gold paper. Everyone fell silent.

'What's this?' the driver wondered out loud, and he looked on the back of the packet. 'It says here that this package shall be opened in the presence of the Ministry of Health's control unit for standards in retirement homes.'

'Yes, that's correct,' said Martha and ticked an item in her notebook. Henrik, the man whom Dolores was evidently rather fond of, offered to open it. He untied the string, slowly and carefully took off the paper wrapping, and opened the packet.

'It's full of envelopes,' he mumbled, pushing his glasses up to the top of his nose and looking more closely.

'Good, that's as it should be. The box contains an envelope for each and every one of you,' said Martha. She picked up a bundle and handed them out. The rustle of envelopes being opened could be heard, and then Henrik exclaimed:

'I can't believe this. An electric scooter! I've got an electric scooter!'

'Right. The same present for everyone,' said Martha. 'The scooter is for walks in the vicinity and there is also a voucher for a package tour to Gran Canaria.' She again dipped her hand into her floral bag, pulled out a brown envelope and handed it over to Anja. 'This is for the management. It's a list of all the things that have been donated to you today. The donor wishes to remain anonymous. And in addition . . .' Martha took a deep breath, because what she was now going to say was extremely important. 'In addition,' she said again, 'to enable these gifts to be made proper use of, here is a special cheque to pay for two new members of staff who will assist in looking after the residents here. The money is specifically for that purpose. We at the Ministry of Health's control unit for standards in retirement homes will return to check that the donation has been used for the purposes stipulated.'

Anja's eyes were like saucers, and several of the residents started to shed tears of joy. Martha, too, found it hard to hold back the tears and for quite a while couldn't find any words at all. But the driver, who was getting impatient, broke the silence.

'Right, that was the lot. Thank you and goodbye.' He walked towards the door. Martha stopped him.

'I know you have a lot of other deliveries today. I just happen to have been told to check those deliveries too. If I can follow along with you in your van, it will be quicker.'

'What?'

'Yes, mark my words. Our control unit often checks deliveries. When it comes to money, it is *always* necessary to check where it goes.'

26

Ever since Tompa and Jörgen had seen their elderly neighbours carry those bodies into the earth cellar, they had been extremely worried. They didn't want the police to come to the neighbourhood, and if there really were dead bodies, they would be facing a serious sanitary problem as soon as the spring thaw set in. Then it wouldn't be long before that nosey fortune-teller down the hill called the police. No, they had to deal with this themselves. Jörgen and Tompa kept a watch on the big old house and waited impatiently for an opportunity when all five of the elderly occupants were out at the same time. They waited and waited and, finally, early one Monday morning, the whole gang climbed into their old Volkswagen minibus, with the wheelchair ramp on the back, and set off from the house. When the sound of the engine faded away, Tompa realized that this was the chance they had been waiting for. Excellent!

'They've gone. The coast is clear,' he called out into the room. 'Come along, let's go straight there.'

Jörgen Smäck peered out of the window. His hair stuck out at all angles, and he had dark rings under his eyes. He had been busy doing woodwork in the club premises long into the night.

'Let's go! Have you got the headlamps?'

Tompa nodded.

'I just hope there aren't any corpses down there. We'd better put our gardening gloves on.'

The men went down into the hall, put on scarves and jackets and pulled on their heavy boots. The cold air hit them when they left the house, and Tompa wished he had a wool cap on too. But of course, bikers weren't known for going around in wool hats, so he would just have to suffer the cold. Even motorcycle helmets were frowned upon in the club. And now he suddenly regretted having shaved his scalp. A mop of hair did at least give you a *bit* of warmth.

'It's locked!' said Jörgen when they got to the cellar. There was a gap in the door and it would be easy to force it open, so Jörgen looked around for an iron bar, but then remembered that they shouldn't leave any trace of their activities. 'Okay, we'll have to lift the door off.'

Together they managed to bend the door a little so that they could get a good grip, which enabled them to lift the door off its hinges. They carefully leaned it against the wall and went inside. There was a smell of earth and potatoes, and when they got a bit farther inside, their nostrils were filled with the smell of alcohol. Somebody must have dropped a whole box of vodka bottles, Tompa thought, as he adjusted his headlamp and let the ray of light illuminate the wall. Or rather the boxes. Postal packages, unopened boxes, IKEA packets, and carton upon carton of whisky and champagne had been stacked up against the walls. Furniture too, garden tools, reading lamps and various other boxes of goods were lined up along the cellar wall.

'When did all this stuff arrive?' Jörgen wondered out loud.

'Must have been when we were having a nap. It looks like a damned department store in here!'

'No, more like a booze shop,' said Jörgen and he kept his headlamp pointed at the cartons of bottles. 'But what have we got here? Cloudberry liqueur?'

'Just look at the whisky and all that other stuff. These oldies are criminals – isn't that what I said? They must have been out on a burglary tour again. They're a crafty lot!'

'That must be why they wouldn't sign those papers for us. That Martha, she's a cunning one. Perhaps we ought to set her up!'

'Yeah, or keep tabs on the whole gang.'

The two bikers looked around and behind some boxes of whisky and a treadmill they caught sight of two manne-quins dressed in winter coats, dresses and boots.

'Well, that's a surprise. Are they going to open a fash-ion boutique too?'

Jörgen lifted up one of the mannequins and held it up so that Tompa could see too. 'So they weren't dead bodies, they were shop-window dummies! Talk about false alarms – this was nothing to worry about, then. No wonder they could manage to carry them.'

'But what are they going to do with all this stuff?'

'They must be a bunch of kleptomaniacs, the whole lot of them. Can't be any other explanation.'

Tompa and Jörgen looked at the other boxes and then passed the mannequins again on their way out.

'Hey, you know what? Wouldn't it be fun if we had one of these dummies in our club room? We can dress it in a jacket with our logo on it, and then put it next to the bar,' Tompa suggested.

'Yeah, that'd be fucking cool! We'll do it!'

That evening, some Mad Angels members and the rest of the guys from the Bandangels were coming for a party. And the club room needed to be ready by then. The shop dummy would be perfect. The two bikers nodded to each other in agreement and set to work. They quickly took the coat and boots off one of the dummies and set them up to make it look as if the dummy was still lying there. With a bit of luck, the old folks wouldn't even notice that the dummy was missing. When they had finished, they turned off their headlamps and put them in their pockets. It was time they were on their way. They quickly put the door back onto its hinges, checked nobody had seen them and then hurried down the path to the gate – with the mannequin in Tompa's arms. As they did so, they heard an engine and saw a delivery truck on its way up the hill.

Tompa quickly looked for a hiding place for the dummy, but didn't have time to hide it before the truck came to a halt just outside the gate.

'We'll have to pretend we live here,' Tompa whispered to Jörgen as the driver jumped out of the truck.

'Ah, here come the goods we ordered,' Jörgen improvised and the two of them exchanged glances. Tompa was reminded of all the booze and other stuff in the cellar. The evening's party was to celebrate the fifth anniversary of the Bandangels and to inaugurate their new club room. The pensioners probably wouldn't even remember half of what they had ordered. So they might as well borrow a few boxes of booze and arrange a prize-giving to reward the guys who had done a good job. Tompa walked up to the driver, looking as though he owned the place.

'You can unload the goods here beside the gate. We'll sort it out.'

The driver, who was in his fifties, glanced quickly at Tompa.

'Andersson, Myrstigen Two?'

'Yepp, Andersson, that's me. Myrstigen Two.'

'Right you are, sign here!'

The driver held out his order pad, and Tompa scribbled something illegible.

'Do you want it all here by the gate?' The driver went round to the back of the truck and opened the doors.

'Here will do fine. We'll put it all in the cellar afterwards.'

The driver looked at Tompa's leather vest and seemed to be weighing up how to react. But then he shrugged and lowered the ramp at the back of the truck, got out the cart and started to pile up the boxes. He unloaded them at the gate, and then went and fetched some more. Looking rather stressed, he thumbed through his delivery instructions and checked the boxes still in the truck. Some boxes were to be delivered to a retirement home too, he noticed, and he fumbled with the lists. Then he put another three boxes on his cart, stopped and checked through the lists again, then changed his mind and replaced the three boxes with four others. Then he ticked off the items on his list and wheeled the boxes to the gate.

'Right, then. That's the lot,' he said, at the same moment catching sight of the shop dummy. The dress hung down crookedly. 'Ah, you're in the fashion branch, right?'

'Not exactly.' Tompa blushed.

'Oh I see. Nowadays lots of guys like women's clothes. You don't have to be ashamed of something like that . . .'

'What the . . .' Tompa raised his hand to hit the driver but managed to restrain himself. 'No, no, it's for my girl-friend, you know. A surprise . . .'

The driver broke into a wide smile, closed the back doors of his truck and climbed up into the cab.

'Don't be shy, guys. I know what it's like. I like dressing up sometimes. You can actually find really lovely clothes second-hand. Lots of lace, frills and the like.' He laughed, put the truck into first gear and drove off with the wheels spinning.

'Idiot!' Tompa muttered. 'Take it easy. Drop it, and come and check out the boxes instead.'

'There'll be loads of stuff here for our party. What about having a raffle?'

'A raffle? We're not having an afternoon tea for house-wives, okay?'

'Well, what about giving prizes?'

Tompa didn't get any further than that before they heard the sound of an engine again and a delivery van from a well-known wine merchant approached at full speed. It slowed down and finally came to a halt right in front of the old house. Jörgen prodded Tompa in his side.

'This is our lucky day, no doubt about it!'

Tompa nodded and signalled to the driver to lower his side window.

'Is this Andersson, Myrstigen Two?'

'That's right. You can put the boxes next to the others,' directed Tompa authoritatively and he pointed to the pile next to the gate. 'We've got a party this evening!'

The driver glanced at Tompa's tattoos and hesitated.

'Gimme the paper so I can scribble on it!' Tompa roared and grabbed the delivery list. With a grand gesture he wrote his illegible signature, and then gave the driver a hearty thump on his back. He talked a bit about the weather and watched as the stressed-out delivery driver unloaded more boxes of booze from his van. Perfect – just what they wanted! He followed after him and helped to unload the cartons while Jörgen stacked them next to the others.

'Cloudberry liqueur? Who drinks that?' the driver asked when they had finished.

'The girls, you know,' said Tompa.

The driver rolled his eyes and climbed back into the cab.

'And that shop dummy, what's that for?' the driver asked, pointing at the mannequin, which leaned at an angle next to the gate.

'Drunk as hell! Cloudberry liqueur is potent stuff,' Tompa smirked.

The driver guffawed, started the van, raised his hand in a wave, and set off.

'He didn't check very carefully. Just because we were here by the gate he thought it was our booze.' Tompa laughed.

'He just wanted to be on his way as soon as he saw us. But what shall we do about the oldies?'

'They'll think the goods haven't arrived yet or they'll forget the whole order. Short-term memory and all that. That's what happens when you get old. We can simply take the lot.'

'But if they make a fuss, what then?'

'We'll soon sort it out.'

'Okay, but we'd better take the shop dummy first before anybody else catches sight of it.'

Tompa fetched their big cart from the yard and quickly loaded all the boxes. Then they took the lot up to their shed, unloaded it all and returned with the snow blower. They still had time to cover the tracks of the deliveries.

27

The glassed-in veranda was really cozy and they were all happily occupied with something. Anna-Greta and Gunnar were solving sudoku puzzles, Martha was knitting, Christina was reading and Rake looked longingly out across to where a big ship was passing by. Brains put his feet up on the sheepskin stool in front of him and hummed in contentment.

'We haven't ended up in prison yet,' Brains said. 'Now we've fooled the police again. We're getting good at this.'

Prison? They all gave a start and it was as if the light from the oil lamps fluttered in fright. The unease could be seen in everyone's eyes. As with health care and schools, things had gone downhill for the country's prisons recently. No member of the League of Pensioners wanted to end up behind bars again.

The gang had eaten a good dinner and the coffee cups had been emptied. 'We've committed a crime and mustn't get too cocky – that would be dreadfully dangerous. The police might be on our tracks without us having a clue about it,' said Martha, putting her knitting down on her lap. She was busy knitting a scarf for Brains and discovered to her horror that she had made it striped black and white, so that it reminded her of prison clothes. It might be best to dye it another colour perhaps? The week had passed by quickly, it was Friday evening and they really ought to do something. After all, the art of living a good life was to brighten up grey everyday life with tiny treats. That was what made life worth living. She looked around her. Anna-Greta and Gunnar were still busy with their sudoku, Brains had started to dismantle an old radio and Rake had got out his Tarot cards. Christina looked up from her book and snuck a look at him. Now that he didn't visit Lillemor any longer, he interpreted his future in the Tarot cards all by himself. He had laid the cards out in a circle on the veranda table and tried to work out if he could see any sort of pattern. Christina gave him a stern look, put her book to one side and pulled out her nail file. Then she started to file her nails with rapid, sweeping movements. Rake hadn't actually been over to Lillemor for a long time; perhaps everything would work out in the end. Martha looked at the wall clock and put her knitting aside.

'We ought to see if they mention the bank robbery on the news this evening. It's been unusually quiet for a while.' Martha got up and went into the library. The others looked at each other, picked up their things and hesitantly followed after her. Rake extinguished the oil lamps and looked out across the bay again. Now the water was dark and still. Rake gathered up his Tarot cards and thought about his son, Nils, who was out at sea for the majority of the year. It occurred to Rake that it would be nice if he could invite him to the house, then they could rent a yacht and sail around for a few days. The islands here might not be a match for those outside Göteborg over on the west coast, but Nils ought to see a bit of them anyway. Rake recalled how they had often visited the Maritime Museum together. Now that his son was grown up they hardly ever saw each other. But this coming summer perhaps things could be different. Rake nodded silently to himself and steered his steps towards the library. Martha had already turned the TV on.

'Yes, it's weird that they haven't said any more about the bank robbery,' commented Brains. 'That must mean they don't have any leads.'

'Pity for them! Ten million kronor are missing and the police don't have a clue about the perpetrators.' Anna-Greta smiled and squeezed Gunnar's hand. The others quickly exchanged glances. Nowadays Gunnar almost never went home; he spent most of his time here in the old house. He and Anna-Greta were always sitting in front of the computer, and after supper one of them would sneak into the other's room when they thought nobody was watching.

The opening jingle of the TV news could be heard and Martha now turned up the volume so that Anna-Greta could hear. Her friend still refused to use a hearing aid.

'Perhaps it was rather rash of us to hand out the money so soon after the robbery. What if the police link the bank robbery with all the gifts to the retirement homes?' Rake said.

'Oh no, nobody cares at all what goes on in retirement homes – we don't need to worry,' Martha said.

'Besides, we haven't handed everything out yet; we've got lots more in the cellar and other orders are awaiting delivery. I've sent off for some more stuff,' Anna-Greta pointed out. 'It should arrive any day now.'

'Quiet, now they're interviewing the police.' Christina hushed everybody so that she could hear. She poured out a cup of coffee and listened attentively. The reporter interviewed a Chief Inspector Blomberg, who looked most concerned, and when he started to talk about a professional international gang being involved in a bank robbery, the friends burst out laughing. The reporter asked whether the police had any leads, but the chief inspector just shook his head and said: 'No comment!' However, he did want to get in touch with shoe shops that sold Oldvan boots.

'Martha, couldn't you have tied the laces a bit better?' Rake complained.

'For goodness' sake, a stiff on a stretcher can't rob a bank, even a policeman must understand that,' Martha hissed in answer.

'We would like the public to get in touch with any information they might have,' Chief Inspector Blomberg went on. 'We would gratefully welcome any observations made in the vicinity of the bank.' The reporter nodded enthusiastically and Blomberg twice cleared his throat before going on: 'After the explosive was detonated inside the bank vault, we can see on the CCTV two badly injured people being carried out on stretchers and taken to an ambulance. But the strange thing is that nobody has seen them since.'

'No, quite right,' Christina joyfully exclaimed. 'We've fooled the lot of you! Haha!'

'We are hoping for the injured parties to get in contact with the police,' Blomberg went on.

'Right you are, I shall immediately ask the mannequins to phone you,' Rake joked.

'But the casualties must have been taken to hospital,' the reporter pointed out. 'Can't you trace them there?'

'Of course, but, like I said, we don't want to make all the details public yet. We would, however, welcome more tips.'

Then the news program moved on to the latest news about the bad working conditions and pay for women and Rake thought it was time to turn the TV off.

'Nobody seems to suspect us yet,' Martha summarized and took a chocolate wafer. She ought to be a bit more careful about her weight, but she wasn't going to worry about that just now, not on a Friday evening. 'Perhaps we could phone in some misleading anonymous tips, such as that two injured people have been seen at a camping site or something like that?'

'No, it's best to lie low. Remember the boot.'

'But that isn't a problem, is it? We've still got it.'

'But when it fell onto the sidewalk it might have left a footprint,' Brains pointed out.

'Oh dear, oh dear!' Martha groaned. 'So stupid of me not to tie the laces better, but it isn't so easy. Mannequins nowadays are so slim that they look like famine victims, the lot of them, just like the fashion models. I did tie the laces as tightly as I could.'

She blushed a little, because suddenly she realized how silly she had been. The boots were, of course, her own. But as they had been on the mannequin it simply hadn't occurred to her that they could leave footprints. And they wouldn't have done if one hadn't fallen off. Perhaps she should burn the pair of boots now, to be on the safe side. Martha had taken a deep breath to propose doing just that when suddenly they heard a weird noise from down the hill. At first it sounded like an approaching hail storm, but then it turned into a loud rumble.

'What is it?' she exclaimed and sat up straight in the armchair. 'Motorcycles! It must be an entire biker gang!'

'They must be having a meeting – they have clubs for that,' said Brains, who had read about the Grandidos and Mad Angels over the years.

'On a Friday evening? No, more like a party. They've been running around all day up there, shifting crates of beer and all sorts of stuff,' said Rake, who had noticed what they had been busy doing when he had walked slowly past Lillemor's house earlier in the day. Through the window he had seen Tompa inside and that worried him. Did she hang out with the Bandangels boss? He hadn't dared tell the others that he had often seen Tompa at Lillemor's house. Now his conscience was troubling him. Might he have said too much to her about himself and his friends? He couldn't remember.

The sound of the engines got louder and became a roar when more and more motorcycles zoomed up the hill and into the yard of the yellow house. Martha and the others snuck up to the window.

'Just look at that!' Christina whispered when a gang of beefy men dressed in black got off their bikes, stretched and then adjusted their leather vests. 'They look like Mad Angels. At any rate, they've all got a skull with wings on their backs.'

'Uff, that gives me the creeps,' Anna-Greta exclaimed.

'What shall we do?' Christina asked anxiously, dropping her nail file.

'You can relax, Christina my dear. Those sorts of people don't want any bother where they live. We should be happy to have them as neighbours,' Rake said to console her.

'But they don't *live* here, they're just going to have a *party* here. And how peaceful is it going to be with twenty souped-up motorcycles?' Christina sighed.

'But just look at those machines,' said Brains with a glisten in his eyes as he pressed his whole face against the window. Another two bikes, three cars and an Opel mini-bus came up the hill and stopped outside the Bandangels' house. It said KENTHA'S HEAVY METAL BAND on the minibus, and some long-haired young men stepped out. They each lit a cigarette and then started to unload a set of drums, some guitars and a few amplifiers, which they somehow managed to carry into the shed.

'Oh my God, there'll be no sleep tonight,' Rake sighed.

'I know!' Martha cut him off. 'If the Bandangels are having a party night, then I think we should have a party too. Then we won't be disturbed by all their noise.'

'Aha, female logic,' said Rake.

218

'That's a great idea!' Brains nodded enthusiastically. 'We've got lots of wine in the cellar.'

'And don't forget the champagne. We must celebrate the fact that so much time has passed since the robbery and we haven't been found out,' Christina chirped.

'That's right, you'd better watch out, Mad Angels, here we come!' snorted Anna-Greta, clapping her hands in delight. 'Hold on tight, it's party time!'

28

Kentha's Heavy Metal Band were playing, and a hit from Iron Maiden was blaring out at top volume inside the club room. The lights had been turned off, and in front of the tables covered with empty beer cans, lit up by red and white candles, was a gang of half-drunk bikers and their girls. Drums and guitars were accompanied by loud roars and the in-unison clapping of hands when the Mad Angels bellowed in time to the music. Along the length of the bar, leather-clad types rocked back and forth grasping beer cans or with a stiff drink in their hands. Tompa, with his arm around the mannequin, was more drunk than sober. He had an empty whisky glass in his hand and talked and laughed at the same time as he hammered the beat with his left foot. With hazy eyes, he looked across the room with a happy smile on his lips. The place was jam-packed! The Mad Angels had arrived with ten men, and fourteen of the Bandangels were there as well as a whole bunch of real knockout babes. All of them had come to celebrate the Bandangels' fifth anniversary in their new club rooms, and he and Jörgen had already received lots of praise for the set-up. The president of the Mad Angels had said that at the next Mad Angels meeting the committee would recommend the Bandangels as full members. Tompa hadn't felt so good since he got his first motorcycle. He winked at a sexy blonde at one of the tables, and raised his glass. The girls they had invited were really dishy! Some of them belonged to the Mad Angels gang and you couldn't touch them, but many of them were single. Tompa felt hopeful for the night ahead. That blonde one with the long hair and the high heels looked promising. He raised his whisky glass and winked at her again. The next second, a heavy fist landed on his shoulder.

'I saw that. Don't lay a hand on my woman!' shouted a two-hundred-pound giant in jeans and a black leather vest. Tompa swivelled round and gasped for breath when he saw the silver logo on the guy's chest. It was the vice-president of the Mad Angels – Lennart Möre! The guy nodded towards the blonde girl and held up his fist so that Tompa felt the knuckledusters with the Mad Angels emblem against his nostrils. He swallowed and tried to look cool.

'No, no, take it easy. I've got a girl,' Tompa lied. 'I was only thinking about the prize-giving.'

'The prize-giving? What prize-giving? Have you got permission from us?' the vice-president asked.

'Did I say prize-giving? No, I mean the raffle, of course. We need someone who can draw the raffle tickets, you know, and so I wanted to ask one of the guests.' Tompa tried to wriggle out of it as best he could.

'A raffle? Tombola and all that stuff? Well, if you want to. But just so you know, if you so much as look at my woman again, I'll smash your nose.'

'Take it easy, I promise. And the raffle is going to be good. You can win booze, iPads and we've even got some biker gear,' he ventured to add.

'Well, make this one of the prizes too. I want to win it!' said the vice-president and he thumped the shop dummy so hard that her head became crooked and the helmet fell to the floor.

'The dummy! Yeah, sure. We'll include that,' said Tompa, picking up the helmet and putting it back on the dummy's head again. His hands shook and he tried to think about what to do. Jörgen had been against the raffle so Tompa had shelved the idea, but now he had spouted on with all this raffle talk so as not to get his face smashed in. So he must arrange something anyway. And why not? They had all those boxes of booze from the oldies as well as all the boxes they had carried in from the delivery truck. Tompa felt a bit bolder.

'You know what, we'll start selling raffle tickets in half an hour and then we'll pick the winning tickets,' he said, leaning the dummy against the bar and hurrying across to the house. He had helped his mum with her charity bazaar just before Christmas and they had had lots of those raffle-ticket rings left over. He just needed to find them.

Brains and Rake were rummaging around inside the cellar looking for something good to drink, while Christina shone her flashlight on the labels and suggested this and that. In a happy mood, they chose a few bottles of Rhine wine and sang as loud as they could while they were at it.

Christina wanted to put some bottles of red wine in the basket of her walker too and had decided on a fine Bordeaux. She was just about to do so when something startled her.

'Oh dear, someone's knocked over the mannequin.' She bent down to lift it up again, but immediately realized that there was only a heap of clothes there. 'Oh my God! Where's our "Munin" mannequin? Have you hidden it?'

Brains and Rake shook their heads.

'It must be here somewhere,' said Brains, looking around him. 'The cellar has been locked.'

They searched and searched, but only 'Hugin' was still there. However hard they looked, there was no sign whatsoever of 'Munin'. The mannequin with half of the money from the Handelsbanken robbery had disappeared.

'Five million vanished into thin air. This is just too much,' Christina stuttered.

'Good thing it wasn't all ten million,' Brains sighed.

Rake, for his part, didn't manage to articulate a sensible word, just a load of angry sounds. Then he blurted out a rapid stream of all the swear words he had learned during his years at sea, and finished by saying: 'How the hell could this have happened? We can't just steal lots of money and then lose it again all the time. We must bloody well make sure we get it back!'

'Preferably not lose anything at all,' Christina mumbled.

'This is VERY hard to explain,' Brains moaned, and he took off his cap and put it back on again several times. 'We'd better go out and have a look around to see if there are any tracks. The mannequin can't just have flown away!'

The three friends left the cellar and shone their flashlights on the ground outside, but they couldn't find any tracks at all. Dejected, they shuffled back to the house to tell the others.

Tompa searched among the boxes in the shed. Now it was a matter of quickly putting together some prizes. The first prize ought to be a whole box of whisky, and they could raffle some goodies from the other boxes too. But first he must check what they contained. Some of the boxes were clearly labelled, but on others there was just a company name. Tompa thought about all the fancy stuff the neighbours had in their cellar: lamps, cellphones, household equipment, iPads, rugs and lots of other stuff. There must be a lot of valuable things in these boxes too, so why not simply have one or two of the bigger boxes as prizes? It was their fifth anniversary after all! He quickly fetched the cart and loaded some of the boxes together with the cartons of booze. Now the Mad Angels would have an evening they would never forget.

When Tompa returned to the clubhouse, Kentha's Heavy Metal Band was going full steam. Drunk bikers were dancing while the vice-president was rocking with the mannequin, trying to get it to drink beer. Tompa wheeled in the goodies and waited until they had finished dancing. Then he piled the boxes up on the stage and got hold of Kentha's mike.

'We've got an anniversary here today and we're going to have a raffle with some bitchin' prizes! Each ticket costs only ten kronor, and here are the prizes.' He patted the boxes and pointed at the labels. 'The first prize is a box of Glenfield's prime whisky and then we've got champagne, cellphones and a few surprise boxes. But no more than ten raffle tickets per person. Okay?'

The announcement was met with drunken bellowing and applause, and Tompa had to shout into the microphone several times to quieten everyone down.

'Anybody like to help sell the raffle tickets?' He held up his mum's rings of tickets.

'A raffle! Soon you'll be getting us to do a ring dance and a sing-song,' Jörgen muttered in disgust.

'Of course we'll help, Tompa,' said Jörgen's girl, Elisabeth, and she got hold of her boyfriend. 'Now we're going to sell these raffle tickets!'

Jörgen raised his hand in a dismissive gesture but changed his mind when he saw her face. Reluctantly, he did as he was told and started to sell the tickets to those in the clubhouse. Tompa looked at them and felt happy. What a great evening!

29

When Rake rushed into the library and told the others that the mannequin had disappeared, they all laughed and clapped their knees in delight at the amusing joke. It wasn't until Christina and Brains loudly shouted that it was actually true that everyone fell quiet.

'Has the money gone? It can't be true! HAS THE MONEY GONE?' Martha found it hard to breathe and had to reach out for her asthma medicine.

'Have we lost our loot again? We really do seem incapable of keeping track of anything!' Anna-Greta exclaimed. 'If this had been at the bank, then we would all have been fired. No, next time it'd be best if we stole money on the Internet.'

'Not sure you're the right person to suggest that, exactly,' Rake pointed out. 'Or perhaps you've found the missing Las Vegas money . . .'

'That was a mean thing to say! Not even the United States can protect itself against Internet pirates,' Anna-Greta quickly retorted and then started snivelling. Gunnar laid a consoling arm around her.

'I'm sorry, I should have thought before opening my

mouth,' Rake hurried to say. 'But you know what? I could see if Lillemor knows anything. Perhaps she can see in her Tarot cards – I mean, see where the mannequin has gone?'

'You certainly won't contact her!' Christina shouted in a high, piping tone. 'And, for that matter, perhaps she is the one who has taken it.'

'No, Christina, she's a fine woman is Lillemor, and she would never do that.'

'Isn't today the day they pick up the garbage? The garbage men might have taken the mannequin by mistake,' Martha ventured to suggest.

'But we don't keep the bins in the cellar any longer, Martha, we keep them out by the road. No, I don't think that explains it,' said Anna-Greta.

'Well, all we've got to do is go out and see if they've emptied the bins,' Brains said and he got up. Brains went out into the hall, put on his overcoat and disappeared outside. He was so quick that Anna-Greta didn't have time to stop him. The mannequin had disappeared from the cellar, not from the garbage.

Brains was outside quite a while, and he came back in with a cloud of cold air around him.

'No, nobody has emptied the garbage,' he said, and blew his nose. 'Yesterday I saw both mannequins, and today "Munin" has gone. But, despite that, I couldn't find any tracks in the snow. None by the road, and none by the cellar.'

'Fishy business. Did you find anything at all?' Gunnar asked.

'Not really, just a wool sock that somebody must have lost.' He went out into the hall for a moment, dipped into the pockets of his overcoat and pulled out the black sock he'd found by the gate. He returned and held it up so that everyone could see it. 'Anybody's?'

'Give it to me,' said Martha, and she examined it more closely. 'This is a man's sock, a large size, too; it isn't much of a clue.' She looked at it from toe to heel and then handed it to Christina. Each one studied the sock in turn, and shook their head before passing it on to the next person. Brains gave it a particularly thorough examination, finally even sniffing at it.

'Hmm, none of us has lost this. It smells of motor oil.'

'Perhaps it belongs to one of the bikers?' Anna-Greta suggested.

'Do you think they've been looking through our cellar?' Christina turned pale. 'Perhaps they want to steal something as a sort of revenge for our not signing those papers?'

They all went completely silent and Christina got the jitters just at the thought of one of those leather-clad two-hundred-pound giants being in their yard.

'Is there anything else missing beside the mannequin?' Christina asked.

'I thought that there were a few less boxes in there. We'll have to check that. But "Munin" is the most important thing. We've got to find the mannequin straight away, so this doesn't end up the same way as the golf bag,' said Martha.

'After a crime you should get rid of any evidence as soon as possible,' said Christina.

'Why not ask the neighbours,' Rake garbled. 'I can nip across to Lillemor and —'

'You will most certainly NOT nip over there!' Christina cut in.

'No, we'll go straight up to the Bandangels. They're having a party and are bound to be in a good mood. I can go up there and have a look,' Brains offered, enthralled by the thought of seeing all those motorcycles again.

'If you can get the mannequin back, then that's okay,' said Martha. 'They've just opened their new clubhouse and perhaps they needed a shop dummy for something?'

'Next you'll be claiming that they've got Barbie dolls too!' Rake snorted.

'No, now listen,' said Brains, and his voice had acquired a nostalgic ring. 'In my youth our biker club in Sundby-berg had the best clubhouse you could possibly imagine. The inside was painted yellow and black and on the wall hung everything from saddles and handlebars to exhaust pipes. In the middle of the room was a black-painted show-case and inside that on a cushion we'd put a biker helmet, a worn leather jacket, leather leggings and boots. So a mannequin for decoration, why not?'

'You're right. It's worth checking,' Anna-Greta conceded.

'But it's dangerous going up there, isn't it?' Christina sounded worried.

'Wait, I've got an idea,' said Martha. And then she started giggling, which quickly turned into laughter and soon she was laughing so loud she almost choked. They all looked at her.

'Martha, what have you thought up now?' Brains queried, looking horrified.

It was cold and there was a full moon, which made the bay shimmer light blue and crystal. Brains and Rake panted in the cold air as they slowly and cautiously made their way up the slippery slope. While they were walking along they could hear the thumping beat and they understood that the party was still in full swing. Slightly nervous, they continued to struggle up the icy road in their far-too-tight leather gear with the Mad Angels emblem sewn onto the back of their vests. Not only were the clothes tight, but they were also ticklish! In her hurry, Martha had forgotten to sew in the threads on the inside.

'What if we get beaten up?' said Brains as he supported himself on Rake.

'No risk. Bikers can be really nice; you just have to treat them with respect.'

'But if they start fighting, what then?'

'You just do this, you say: "Oh, you dropped your knife!" and then, when they bend over to look, you just head-butt them,' said Rake, who was used to fights from his days as a seaman.

'But I'm not as strong as I used to be,' Brains pointed out.

'In that case, just kick them hard where it hurts.'

Brains could just see himself going round kicking two-hundred-pound giants between their legs and he didn't think it was such a good idea.

'Won't we do better with friendliness and respect? They can't kill us just for knocking on the door.'

'But we're pretending to be Mad Angels veterans. What if they find out we're just bluffing?'

'No way, they're too drunk for that.'

Brains took a deep breath and thought about what Martha had said. She had encouraged them to go up to the Bandangels and claim they were old members of the Mad Angels, scarred warriors who wanted to have a beer with the guys. Who would refuse entrance to a couple of over-age veteran bikers? And once they were inside the clubhouse, they would start looking for the mannequin.

'If you find "Munin", then you've only got to bring the dummy back down here so we can hide it,' she had said. It was that *only* word, Brains thought. Nothing is *only*; most of the time *only* is something extremely difficult. Catching sight of the mannequin and taking it away with them – they weren't exactly the same thing. No, this wasn't going to be easy. Brains and Rake reached the top of the slope, went into the yard and stopped a few moments in front of some beautiful Harley-Davidson bikes before they went up the steps and rang the bell. After a while they heard some steps and one of the Bandangels members opened the door. Brains, who had learned that it was better to have the first word rather than let someone else have it, took a deep breath:

'A bit of whisky to help things along. Cool party!' he said and offered the biker a large bottle of Glenfield's.

'Errh, but the party is for members only.'

'Come off it! Don't you recognize us? Hell, man, we're veteran Mad Angels! We are the ones who started the club down in Skåne. Now listen, boy, you must be new! Here's the man himself, the first vice-president!' Brains gave him a friendly punch to the stomach.

'And we've met before – don't you remember the Fixer? Nice of you to invite us.' Rake tried to sound self-assured.

The guy hesitated but Brains pushed the bottle of whisky into his arms and simply walked in with all the confidence he could muster. The biker backed up and Rake even allowed himself a big grin.

'We're a bit late, but I'm sure you've got some grub left.'

The guy opened his mouth to say something but by then Brains and Rake were already inside the clubhouse. Brains almost slipped.

They went farther inside the premises and Brains came to a halt, nostalgic at the sight of the bar and the fancy decorations. Best of all he liked the group photos of several Bandangels members and some framed photographs of Harley-Davidson bikes. He took a few steps forward. There were those framed photos he had seen on the floor earlier; they had now been hung up on the wall. They were all there except the picture he had managed to sneak off with. Nobody had noticed that it was missing.

Before Rake and Brains had reached the bar to get a beer each, they caught sight of a lanky youth who carefully lifted down one of the group photos and put it on the counter. He put it with the picture facing down, and Brains and Rake exchanged looks of surprise. They saw how he loosened the back of the frame, took out the cardboard and then passed the framed photo from man to man at the bar. As it passed, each person picked up a tiny bag of white powder, which quickly disappeared inside a pocket. The photo they had back at home, what if that contained white powder too? He suddenly felt afraid. Drugs! They had better get the hell out of there, and quickly too. He grabbed Rake's arm and nodded meaningfully towards the bikers leaning over the tables with their rolled banknotes.

'Rake, we'd best get out of here now.'

'Not without the mannequin. Look over there.'

Brains turned around. A two-hundred-pound tattooed giant was dancing with 'Munin' and a whisky glass. Now and then he tried to get the mannequin to take a gulp, while singing as loud as he could. When he saw his snorting mates, he stopped beside the bar, put his glass down and asked for a mirror. Brains froze. Perhaps they could go up to the mannequin now, pretend to ask for the next dance and then dance out with it through the door? If the giant could play around, then surely they could too. The biker asked the bartender for a bag of white and then rolled a banknote.

'Why not simply ask if we can borrow the mannequin. Surely the guy isn't going to dance with it all evening?' Brains whispered.

'No, I know what, we'll ask a girl to ask him to dance.'

'Right, you do that.'

Rake immediately felt uncertain.

'Well, we could wait too,' he muttered.

'Now look, the guy is going to the bathroom. Now we can take the mannequin and dance off!'

'Dance? In these tight leather pants! I can hardly walk, let alone dance! But, I know, we'll pretend that we're offering it some drugs.' Rake plucked up his courage again and grinned. He had never done it himself, but he'd seen others with drugs.

'Right you are, let's strike!' said Brains and he went across to the counter. The bartender beamed at them.

'A beer?'

'Yeah, what else!' Rake tried to look like a man of the world. The bartender filled a glass and Rake took a deep gulp. But when he put the glass down, he happened to bump into 'Munin' so that the mannequin slid down towards the floor. He quickly straightened it up again. Pure luck that the head hadn't fallen off. They'd better take the mannequin right now, before the other biker came back. Rake's hand was shaking as he grasped the beer glass.

'Brains, cover me. Let's go,' Rake whispered and took a firm hold of 'Munin'. They snuck away and had almost got out of the room when there was an enormous roaring:

'Don't try that, you've got to pay too!'

'Oh yes, of course,' Rake muttered, and he fished up a hundred-kronor note, which he gave to the bartender. 'Keep the change.' Then he moved off towards the main door, protected by Brains.

'Hey, you two old guys there, who are you?' An enormous fist landed on Rake's shoulder and he would have fallen over if Brains hadn't been standing right next to him.

'Errhhmm,' Brains murmured but was cut off by a drumroll and a spotlight up on the stage. He and Rake backed towards the front door with the mannequin but people were pushing behind them and they didn't get very far. They exchanged a pained glance. Here they were, carrying a fortune, but they couldn't move. The heavy metal band's dark-haired drummer hit the drum skin all the harder, ending in a deafening crescendo when Tompa ran up onto the stage and got hold of the mike.

'Right, boys, now it's time!' Tompa shouted as he looked around the room beaming with joy. Tompa had borrowed the dummy's helmet and asked Jörgen and his girl to dump the raffle tickets into it. He was actually really pleased with himself, because all the raffle tickets had been sold. All he had to do now was to ask somebody to draw the winning tickets. He looked at the assembled company, but was interrupted by Jörgen, who came towards him on unsteady legs. He pressed his index finger against Tompa's forehead.

'Raffles are for little kids. And just because you like presents, you don't have to go and make a fool of all of us,' Jörgen slurred and he grabbed hold of the microphone stand.

'Sssh, Jörgen, cool off, man, we're having a party!' Tompa hissed. He signalled to the lighting technician to start up the disco ball in the ceiling. The spotlight went on, and red, blue and green cascades of colour swirled around the room. Jörgen swayed a little, burped and dropped his can of beer onto the floor, before speaking into the mike. 'Your mum said how thrilled you were when you opened presents on Christmas Eve.'

'Shut your face!'

'You've always said how much you love your mum and how dependent you have been on her . . .'

Tompa took a threatening step forward when Lennart, the vice-president, strode up onto the stage.

'What are you playing at? Aren't we going to have the raffle draw soon?'

'Yes, of course,' Tompa murmured, and he shook the helmet so that the raffle tickets were mixed up. 'Right, now all you have to do is pick a ticket.' He held out the helmet and Lennart took one.

'Number twenty-two, who has number twenty-two?'

A short guy with an enormous girth made a victory sign while he waddled up to the stage.

'I'll take the box, of course,' he said and pointed at the box with ten bottles of whisky.

The next number to be picked out was thirty-four, and the winner chose a box of champagne.

'Are they all going to choose the booze?' the vice-president muttered darkly. 'Those who are drawn first will take the best prizes straight away. Why not put a cover over all the prize boxes and only allow people to point?'

'Point at a shape and then discover what you've won?' Tompa asked.

'Yes, then there'll be a bit of excitement.' By the tone of his voice, Lennart made it clear that he wanted this to happen.

'Yeah, right, let's do that!' Tompa agreed.

Lennart grabbed the tablecloth from the closest table so that glasses and plates went flying in all directions.

'This'll do nicely,' he said and handed it to Tompa, who enthusiastically went up to the mike and explained the new system.

Brains and Rake tried again to back out with the mannequin but then came to a halt once more. The drummer produced another loud roll of the drums and when he finished, Tompa went across and put the cloth over the prize boxes. The atmosphere grew all the more tense because everybody knew that there were several boxes of booze, but also lots of other prizes that they hadn't a clue about.

Now things heated up in the clubhouse. As soon as a winning number was called out, a drunken biker tottered up to the stage, pointed out his prize and, to the accompaniment of loud cheering, opened the box. Every bottle of booze was applauded, and the guests were singing and jeering at full volume. After a while, more and more prizes turned up from the other boxes too, cellphones, an iPad, a gift voucher for an electric scooter and lots of other stuff. The party revellers could hardly restrain themselves. A clean-shaven guy with a ponytail pointed to a large rectangular shape under the cloth, pulled out the box, and ripped off the tape.

'What the . . .? Support stockings!'

'Yeah, right, have you no sense of humour?' Tompa said, smoothing it over. Laughter and jeers continued to fill the clubhouse while he wondered what he should do. Where did that come from? The next moment there was a violent roar and he twisted round. Lennart, the vice-president, had won a box too and now stood with a folding walking stick in his hand, and it had a flower pattern on it too.

'Is this meant to be funny?' Lennart shouted.

Tompa went up to the drummer and asked him to end the raffle draw, but the president of the Mad Angels, Olle Marling, had already got a winning number. He shouted out:

'I won, I won!'

'It depends on which number you've got,' said Tompa, and he tried to calm him.

'The winning number, of course,' said Olle Marling, ripping the wrapping paper off the largest box that he had found under the cloth.

Rake and Brains looked at each other, and with the mannequin under their arms they moved a little farther towards the door. Out of the corners of their eyes they saw the Mad Angels leader dip into the box and pull out the contents. There wasn't so much light on the stage and the flashes from the disco ball made it hard to see what he had won. But then came the first restrained giggles, which gradually grew louder. Then the cheers erupted. He had won five hundred incontinence pads. For men.

'Oh, I see, you've been to your urologist,' came the comment from a heavily made-up girl who stood close by. She was a nurse and had long been pissed off because Olle, the Mad Angels leader, had dumped her.

'What did you say?' he roared out and delved into the box once more. He pulled out a fistful of Lady Wings, incontinence pads for women. The crowd couldn't restrain themselves any longer. The roars of laughter echoed throughout the clubhouse. Never had any member of the Mad Angels been so ridiculed. Tompa turned pale, and brought the raffle to an end. What had they actually stolen?

'What are you laughing at?' Olle Marling bellowed.

'It was just a little practical joke.' Tompa tried to smooth things over. Then the ex-girlfriend leaned forward and whispered something in Olle's ear. Suddenly, the Mad Angels president understood what a fool they had made of him. His entire body was shaking in anger, and, blinded by fury, he rushed down from the stage. Tompa backed away but Rake didn't have time.

'You idiots and your raffle! Is this meant to be funny? Give me the dummy! I'm going to take something with me!' he roared, grabbing the mannequin and storming out of the building. He almost knocked Brains and Rake over on his way out, and it took them a while to compose themselves and regain their balance.

'Err, that's our mannequin . . . !' they shouted as loud as they could.

But Olle Marling didn't hear them. He was already on the way to his bike with the dummy in his arms.

Brains and Rake hurried after him. They got to the front steps just in time to see the Mad Angels president accelerate away on his bike down the hill. 'Munin' was tied on in a sitting position, without a helmet and with the red shawl blowing in the wind.

Olle Marling drove at full throttle in the direction of the town with the mannequin on the back of his bike. Not far from the clubhouse in Orminge, he forgot the speed limit. When he turned off from the main road he was doing at least a hundred kilometres an hour. The police radar check was hidden out of sight and he discovered it too late. A well-built, uniformed police officer waved him onto the shoulder and Olle had no choice but to stop. He swore and tried to keep his face turned away so as not to blow alcohol fumes right in the face of the authorities. The policeman lit up his face with a flashlight.

'How fast were you going then?'

'About fifty, no more.'

'Lucky for you that our radar apparatus is a bit wonky, otherwise you'd be fined for speeding. That must have been at least a hundred. Right, blow into this!' The policeman was holding a breathalyzer tube.

'No, I'm stone-cold sober,' Olle protested.

'And you expect me to believe that? Blow!'

He held out the breathalyzer. Olle's lips tensed. He didn't know how he could get out of this. Should he fill his mouth with tobacco, chew some Vicks throat lozenges? But he didn't have anything with him that could fool the apparatus.

'What a lot of midges!' exclaimed Olle, swearing and waving his hands.

The policeman looked around and, somewhat confused, started waving his hand too. Then Olle leaned forward and made sure the policeman's hand hit him.

Olle exclaimed and dropped the breathalyzer, which landed on the road. He swiftly allowed his bike's front wheel to roll over it.

'What happened?' said the policeman. 'You hit it so it went flying,' replied Olle, rolling the front wheel back and picking up the squashed apparatus. 'Sorry, not my fault,' he went on, handing over the broken bits.

'Then it will have to be a blood test! And hello, what

have we got here? Your friend hasn't got a helmet on. That'll be a fine.'

'It's just a—'

The policeman pulled his report pad out.

'Have a look for yourself!' Olle snapped as he unscrewed the head. The policeman almost fainted.

'Not easy to see that in the dark,' he mumbled and put his report pad back in his pocket. And now he had completely forgotten the blood test. Olle grinned widely, put the head back on, raised his hand in farewell and set off again.

30

In police headquarters at Kungsholmen, rapid steps could be heard and a door was roughly pulled open with unnecessary force. Chief Inspector Blomberg swore like a trooper and slammed the door behind him. Had the people at the forensics lab been out in the sun too long? He had been waiting for the analysis of the blood stains outside the Handelsbanken branch and was hoping for a breakthrough in the investigation. But now? To start with, they'd taken a very long time to test the samples, and now, when finally they sent an answer, it was ludicrous. His hand shook as he held the telephone.

'DNA from a horse! What are you playing at, you nitwits! We want the lab reports on the blood from the Handelsbanken robbery, not from the Solvalla racecourse!' he shouted.

A friendly female voice asked him to behave like a gentleman when he spoke to her. Then she described the blood samples, the reliability of the tests and all the work they had put in when doing the analysis. She stubbornly maintained that the blood had come from the sidewalk outside the bank, and his protests got him nowhere.

Before the end of the call he was absolutely convinced that somebody was playing a joke on him. An old, grey-haired policeman, on the wrong side of his sixtieth birthday, was somebody you could make a bit of fun of. They would be sitting there doubled over in laughter when they had their coffee break at the lab. At least he would soon be retiring!

In a rage, Blomberg sat down in front of his computer and pushed aside a heap of binders. He had intended to sneak off early from the office but on his way out he had bumped into the head of the crime squad, Superintendent Strömqvist. He had given him some extra tasks and even had the audacity to ask him to do overtime. That superintendent had also withdrawn his earlier promise to Blomberg about being able to retire early, blaming the change on the recent complicated cases and heavy workload at the office.

'We need every man we've got,' he had said. 'When the bank robbery has been solved we'll look at your application again.'

Blomberg had been thinking that he'd soon be a pensioner, but now he wasn't even going to be allowed to work reduced hours. No, he was still stuck working full time – and overtime. All their resources were to be concentrated on the Handelsbanken robbery. They seemed to be just treading water in the investigation, and even after questioning all their contacts they had no leads. Blomberg had been asked to interview people working in stores that sold fireworks. Blomberg felt like a fool going around asking such questions. He remembered the conversation he had had in one store in Karlaplan. He had, admittedly, forgotten to show his warrant card, but nevertheless . . .

'Have you got any fireworks?'

'Not at this time of the year. But we do have bags of seeds that you can hang in the trees for the birds . . .'

That was the stupid sort of conversation that his investigation resulted in, and, considering that millions of fireworks had been sold in Sweden for the New Year's celebrations, the task felt hopeless. There were no other leads except for a single footprint in the snow. That was really strange. A bank robber couldn't be one-legged, could he? In addition to this, the police hadn't been able to cordon off the crime scene soon enough, so virtually every Stockholmer who had passed the bank had left footprints. He took a chocolate and tried to calm his nerves. The greatest mystery was those two victims who had disappeared after the explosion. The witnesses had seen two wounded people who were carried away on stretchers and put into the ambulance, but none of the Emergency departments of the hospitals in the Stockholm area had admitted any such patients at that time. At least they had managed to secure some blood samples from the scene, and, if only the lab stopped muddling up the test results, that ought to provide some clues.

In every investigation there are always so many false alarms. Blomberg sighed again. He was getting nowhere; he needed help. He would ask his boss for reinforcement: he needed an experienced detective; he had more important things to do. All those millions he had fished up from the account in Las Vegas must be used. He was not going to postpone the meeting with Birgerson, the expert at Beylings Legal Firm.

It had stopped raining and now a cold wind blew in from the water down at the docks. The containers were still wet and the pavement shone. Blomberg shivered and pulled up his collar. It was always so cold in Sweden. Weather like this ought to be against the law – yes, it should be a criminal offence! Blomberg gave a start; he seemed to think of nothing but crime nowadays.

'This is where your goods end up. Nice, isn't it?'

The lawyer, Birgerson, pointed at the former workshop down by the harbour. He had driven Blomberg to the old area where they used to look after island boats. Now it had been converted into a storage area where you could rent space. Beylings had rented a large unit. Blomberg was reminded of the old Eriksberg shipyard in Göteborg with huge hanger-like premises where large diesel engines and boats had once been built. This was something similar. These halls were enormous.

'Most of this will have been moved on within a month, and then you can rent this space,' said Birgerson, gesturing with his hand towards the sailing boats on their stands, and a row of trucks. 'As soon as you've acquired your stuff, we can take over ownership on paper so that nothing can be traced to you. Then, when everything is quiet, you can sell.'

'But more than two hundred million – that'll be a lot of goods.'

'It's okay. We'll buy a Beneteau Swift Trawler, a few motorized sailing vessels, some vintage boats and yachts. That will add up to quite a lot. Then we can put in some bids for Rolls-Royces, mobile homes and Porsches too. But all that takes up a lot of space. Why not invest in art and diamonds? We've got special storage units for that, with the right temperature and humidity. And then there is property, of course, but there can always be problems with tenants, so we charge quite a large fee to administer that.'

Chief Inspector Blomberg leaned against the wall, pulled out his handkerchief and wiped his brow several times. This almost made him dizzy. Birgerson was talking about millions as if they were popcorn; indeed, the lawyer seemed to have lost contact with reality. Perhaps that was what happened when you only thought about money. Money, money, money.

'Apart from the luxury boats, could we perhaps buy some Bentleys and Porsches?' Blomberg stuttered. 'And then, of course, the big spring art auction has one or two nice things.'

'Quite right. Art is the way to go!'

'But what happens if there's a break-in or the whole warehouse burns down?' Blomberg asked, thinking that a fire in this oily hall could destroy not only all the stuff stored here, but also all his dreams of a comfortable retirement. Birgerson unlocked the doors to the heated units deep inside the warehouse, turned on the light and smiled.

'A break-in? Do you mean one that has been arranged, or an ordinary one?'

Blomberg moistened his lips.

'Err, an ordinary break-in. What if somebody comes and steals stuff?'

Birgerson nodded, and with a light touch of his finger on a control panel, the storage shelves and rows of paintings started to move on the grey-painted rails on the floor.

'Fire and theft? We're insured. We are Folksam's best customer.' He laughed. 'Some people are busy with insurance fraud . . .'

Blomberg felt a shiver go down his back. This was a different world, one which he didn't fit into. But having gone this far, he must go on.

'We take twenty-five percent as a commission, and that includes administration and storage costs,' Birgerson churned on. 'On the other hand, you avoid tax and detailed questions from nosey authorities, and we take care of everything. Like I said, it's good business for both of us. And anything you store here will be safe. We have security staff and the whole area is wired up with alarms.'

When Blomberg drove home that afternoon, he had the car radio on full volume. He sang along with Frank Sinatra's 'My Way' while he drummed his fingers on the steering wheel in time with the music. His meeting with Birgerson had gone well despite everything, and after their visit to the harbour they had gone through everything once again in the legal firm's office and he had been given some insider tips about suitable cars and boats to buy, and also advised to invest in established artists whose paintings were steadily increasing in value. When he sold his investments, the firm would put the money into various accounts in New Jersey and the West Indies. So this was how the big boys did it. Blomberg's face was one big smile. He would never again have to worry about money. Those IT courses he had gone on had finally turned out to be very profitable!

By the time he had stepped into his apartment, and was met by a meowing Einstein, other thoughts began to make themselves felt. Seeing as he had so much money now, perhaps he could share some of it? He could donate to the homeless too. He got out a tin of cat food but stopped when he saw the red label announcing a special price. He always bought food and cat litter when it was on sale, but on these tins he saw that the best-before date had passed. He hoped Einstein wouldn't notice. He put some spoonfuls of Whiskas in a dish and poured some water into the bowl next to it. The cat trotted expectantly up to the dish with his tail in the air, but once he sniffed at the old food he turned his back on it and demonstrated his dissatisfaction by going and lying down on Blomberg's bed. Damned cat! Blomberg thought. How the hell could the creature read the labels?

He returned to his ponderings. Why should he give his money away? After all, he had struggled his whole life. No, no way! Now he was going to have some fun, see his capital grow, and be successful.

Pleased with his decision, he went into his bedroom and looked forward to a night's well-earned sleep. Einstein wasn't on the bed any longer; he had moved into the cat basket. Blomberg yawned, put on his pyjamas and got ready to slip between the sheets. But just as he was about to do so, he stopped abruptly. Yesterday's cat food had also been a bargain buy and Einstein had got his revenge.

31

It was now high time to do something. The League of Pensioners had no money left and things were looking really bad for many retirement homes. The moment had come when Martha would have to inform everybody about their precarious situation. To lessen the shock she had chosen one of Stockholm's best coffee shops, Delselius in Gustavsberg. Failures and disappointments must be presented when people have their stomachs full. Even Julius Caesar had operated that way.

Cheesecake with a base made from dinkel flour, Dutch chocolate layer cake, a classic Schwarzwald, and, to top it all off, some large portions of sumptuous strawberry cream cake. Martha looked longingly at all the tasty offerings, but she had no appetite at all. Her tummy seemed to be tying itself into knots, as if she was getting a bug. She looked on as the others drank their coffee and enjoyed their cakes; she couldn't manage even a crumb. In the end, she had to speak out. She put her coffee cup down and, forcing herself to be calm, said:

'I realize that this is going to come as a shock, but

we've no money left in the kitty. There's nothing there, nothing at all,' she said with an uncharacteristically shaky voice.

'What are you saying? Nothing in the kitty? That can't be true.' Rake shook his head and pointedly pushed his plate aside, with half of the strawberry cream cake uneaten. 'Nobody has stolen so much in such a short time as we have. No, the money can't be all gone, that's simply not possible!'

'Sssh!' Christina hissed and looked around anxiously.

Martha managed to produce a little smile, and fidgeted with her napkin.

'I'm terribly sorry, but it doesn't look good at all. We won't, of course, give up looking for the golf bag or the money that disappeared on the Internet, no indeed not. We'll make sure we get that capital back one way or the other, but what we need now is cash.'

Yes, it really was as bad as that. Not only was the mannequin missing, but the Las Vegas money was also lost. And during her outings as an inspector from the Ministry of Health's control unit for standards in retirement homes, Martha had seen even more cutbacks in spending in the places she had visited. To save electricity, the managers had turned off every other light in the corridors and now the old people could hardly see where they were going. That had made Martha so furious that she had immediately asked Anna-Greta to put in an order for ten boxes of one-hundred-watt light bulbs, which Emma then delivered to the various homes. But, of course, just ordering new light bulbs wasn't enough. There was so much else to be done. Martha plucked up courage to say:

'It's high time we struck again! The money that we put so much hard work into collecting – that is all gone and we can't wait until we have traced it. We must fill the kitty now!'

So far everyone except Martha and Rake had been eating their fill, but suddenly the others, too, seemed to lose all their enthusiasm for the pastries and cakes.

'We do actually have some other problems too,' said Brains, who thought that he should use this opportunity. He told them about the powder that had been hidden behind the photographs.

'White powder?' Martha almost choked. 'So the Mad Angels haven't just gone off with our five million. You've been stealing drugs from them by mistake too.'

'Yes, I suppose you could put it like that,' said Brains and he became bright red in the face. 'Mind you, I didn't steal it; I just couldn't resist that fantastic picture of my old motorcycle.'

'You must give it back to them immediately. Thou shall not steal!' said Martha as though she really meant it.

'I'm not sure we ought to have an opinion on that,' Rake muttered.

'Pah, we only steal from the rich to give to the poor,' said Martha. 'And we don't charge anything for it, unlike the banks.'

'And we don't lend money either,' Brains added in the same vein, but stopped himself abruptly when he remembered the money in the mannequin.

'Besides, we only occupy ourselves with *real* money and not those immaterial loans. If only we could learn how to keep it as well, though,' said Anna-Greta with a deep sigh.

Martha nodded, reached for the coffee pot, and filled their cups. Even though there were certain risks in them being seen out together so soon after the bank robbery, they must enjoy themselves too. Martha had also come to realize that she did rather push the others, so the least one could expect was that she would arrange some nice get-togethers. It was just a pity that she had such bad news. However, she tried never to serve bad news without adding something hopeful at the end. Something which pointed towards a solution. She and Brains had actually discussed this. They had sat up late the previous evening and sketched various ideas that might provide a way out from this precarious situation. They had put together a plan. Although, as for that powder that Brains had acquired by mistake, well, she couldn't face thinking about that at all. Perhaps she ought to be sensitive and diplomatic and say something like, 'Dear friends, you've worked hard but unfortunately we must carry out another robbery. The biggest we've ever done.' But she didn't dare say that. Not yet. She put her napkin to one side and cleared her throat.

'Now the thing is, as I said earlier, we don't have much cash left and that rather restricts us.'

'No wonder! We either lose it or it gets stolen,' Christina stated. 'Our local fortune-teller, Lillemor, could perhaps find out where it's all gone?'

Rake pretended not to hear.

'And, in fact, we've lost more than you think. That stuff that the Bandangels had in their raffle was from our latest order,' said Anna-Greta. But instead of being angry, they all smiled. Rake and Brains had told them about the prizes and all that had happened with the bikers.

'It's strange that the driver muddled up our delivery with the one that should have gone to Diamond House. You should have seen when one of their leaders held up his Lady Wings and thought they were motorcycle gloves!'

A certain merriment spread round the table.

'Considering how many of our millions have disappeared, a few boxes are neither here nor there,' Martha said. 'But the mannequin is quite another matter.'

'Quite unbelievable! We were just on our way out when a guy grabbed it off us. I've no idea how we can get it back now,' Brains said, bemoaning the situation.

Anna-Greta had been silent for a while, but couldn't restrain herself any longer. She put her cup of hot chocolate down.

'Never in all my days at the bank did I experience losses like this.'

'But listen, during economic crises ten million times as much vanishes. What we've lost is nothing in comparison,' Gunnar chipped in.

'Yes, and banknotes have a tendency to fly off, while gold . . .' began Martha, who was discreetly preparing them mentally for the next robbery.

'Unless the money goes off on a motorcycle, of course,' Brains added.

'Perhaps we should borrow some money?' Anna-Greta suggested, her many years of service in the bank having left their mark. 'With a low interest rate . . .'

'*Borrow!* Are you out of your mind?' Rake exclaimed. 'That is pure ROBBERY! We could do with our own gold reserve!'

'Exactly! And gold doesn't go astray as easily as diamonds or money,' said Martha and she glanced at the others to see their reaction. 'I thought that—'

'You've never thought of trading with oil, have you?' Rake cut her off. 'Then at least there's time to relax between deliveries.'

'Gold or oil. Same difference. Before we can retire properly, we must have five hundred million for the Robbery Fund. We all agreed on that. We'll simply have to exert ourselves again. Ever since the bank robbery, I've actually been thinking about a new coup. And one that would outshine all others.'

'Weren't we going to sit here and relax?' Christina interrupted, licking a bit of whipped cream off the corners of her mouth.

'Exactly! We can't bloody well carry out a robbery every week!' Rake added to the criticism.

'Shush!' Christina hissed anxiously, looking around, but luckily nobody had heard.

'We still have money stuffed down the drainpipe at the Grand Hotel. Can't we try to get at that?' Anna-Greta queried, being of the opinion that it was unforgivable to lose things through carelessness.

'We'll rescue that money when the time is right, but

now we need much more than that. Several hundred million – and I have a brilliant idea.'

'Oh no, not again!' moaned Rake. Martha lowered her voice.

'If we can pull this off, then we can relax permanently afterwards, and we will have helped society too.'

'Don't you think you take too much upon yourself, Martha dear?' said Brains, patting her tenderly on the back of her hand. 'I mean with all this social welfare . . .'

'When the state forgets about people, then we must do our bit and intercede,' Martha answered in a decisive tone. 'We can actually help people in need, if only we put a bit of effort into it. And you know what? This new coup is going to be great fun to carry out too!'

'I can only echo the words of Margaret Thatcher,' said Christina. 'Money doesn't fall down from heaven: you have to earn it here on Earth. You're quite right, Martha, we must keep on working.'

'Absolutely. Nobody feels good if they have too little to do, and since we will have to carry something heavy, we must increase our training sessions in the gym,' Martha went on. 'Besides, a bit of gymnastics will perk us up.'

'A bit of whisky would, too,' muttered Rake.

'Oh goodness, you are a bit of a slave-driver, my dear,' said Brains and he pointedly put his hands on his tummy. 'Gymnastics again. We're all a bit tired you know.'

'But, Brains, we talked about this only yesterday,' Martha argued. She looked from one person to the other. They were observing her closely and she noticed a dangerous feeling of rebellion in the air. She must not let it go any further.

'We don't have to do gymnastics and eat salad every day; we can come here and enjoy pastries a bit more often.'

'Yes!' they responded in unison and they each took yet another cake. Calm returned to the League of Pensioners. Martha looked thoughtfully down into her coffee cup and realized that from now on she must proceed very, very carefully if she was going to get them to go along with her. Because she was never going to give up. She must do her bit. Just when Martha had relaxed and was thinking of the journey home and a relaxing evening which included a hot bath followed by a little rest on the sofa with a good book, Rake cleared his throat.

'I'm going on robbery strike! Before I do anything else at all robbery related, I want to check that drainpipe,' he said.

The following day, it was windy and it rained hard too, but, even so, the whole gang travelled to the Grand Hotel in Stockholm. Rake was really keen on following up the drainpipe money, so they all went along with it as, when he was in a bad mood, everybody was affected. Christina phoned for a taxi and asked to be taken straight to the Grand Hotel. However, when they reached the Old Town, they encountered problems straight away. The driver slowed down.

'Sorry, we can't go any farther,' he told them.

'What do you mean? Drive up to the entrance!' Rake ordered.

'I'm afraid I can't get any closer. They have cordoned it off,' said the driver, and he stopped at Karl XII Square.

'But surely you can get a bit closer than this, can't you? We don't want to take part in a Stockholm Marathon just now,' Rake barked.

'Like I said, they've cordoned it off. State visit. But why not walk over to the hotel? A bit of exercise, perhaps?'

'Exercise? No, not again!' Rake climbed out of the taxi swearing loudly and clearly. He was not in a good mood. 'Exercise freaks everywhere! Can we never have a bit of peace and quiet?'

They started to walk in the direction of the hotel but didn't get very far. When they approached the quayside, they noticed patrolling guards with bulletproof vests and walkie-talkies.

'What if one of those tough-looking guards finds the money?' Christina said in a rather nervous tone.

'And my tights,' whispered Anna-Greta. She remembered how she'd had to sacrifice a pair of good tights when they needed something to stuff the money into.

Somewhat hesitantly, they walked a little closer and looked for a way to get round the taped-off area. But just as they plucked up the courage and worked out how to get past the guards, the entire facade of the building lit up. White spotlights illuminated the whole hotel and beams of light went from the top of the roof right down to the sidewalk, and even covered some of the building next door – the National Museum.

'Oops! Doesn't look like this is a good day to go climbing up drainpipes,' said Martha.

'And we won't be able to do it in secret, either,' Christina pointed out.

'Rake, you know what? I've bought a new computer game. Wouldn't it be more fun if we went home and played that instead?' Brains tried.

None of the ladies protested against this uncultural suggestion. They wanted to get Rake home. And Martha had to concentrate on the next robbery. The biggest ever.

32

Jörgen Smäck went out to the path with his garden shears. He wanted to trim the lilac hedge around the yard so that it would fill out nicely by the summer. Then it would prevent people from looking in, and that might well be necessary. Just as he was lifting the shears, he caught sight of Tompa, who looked cautiously in both directions before he hurriedly left Lillemor's house and went out onto the road. Jörgen wrinkled his brow. What on earth was the nutter doing? He had been to see that fortune-teller several times lately and he always came out with a smile on his lips. But he had never mentioned these visits, not a word. No, lately he had been really weird.

Jörgen thought about that crazy raffle and how Tompa had made a fool of the Mad Angels' president, Olle Marling. The shop dummy had saved the day. For some bizarre reason Olle had taken a liking to it, and if he hadn't taken it with him, that would probably have been the end of the Bandangels' chances of becoming full members. They still had a shot. But if they succeeded, then Tompa would have to look sharp and forget his fortune-teller lady. Jörgen went up to the gate.

'Tompa! What the hell are you up to?'

His friend came to an abrupt halt and his neck turned dark red. 'What's the matter?'

'You're always over at that fortune-teller's.'

'So? She's all right.'

'Have you forgotten we're Bandangels?'

Tompa tried to look dignified but he felt as if he'd been caught out. Lillemor had tempted him into the mysterious world of Tarot cards. She listened to him, was friendly and attentive, and seemed to care about him. That meant a lot for somebody who had always had complicated relationships with women. He thought about Helena. He'd been so in love with her that he'd even had her name tattooed on his wrist, but the ink had hardly dried before she went off with some other guy. Sure, he liked girls, but they made him feel insecure. He got on best of all with older women like Lillemor. But of course he didn't dare say that, he, a member of the Bandangels, got on so well with a sixty-year-old woman. She was old enough to be his mother. She had invited him in for coffee and cakes several times, laid out her cards and told his fortune, and it was so exciting to hear what she had to say about his future. She had even knitted him a pair of wool gloves and given him small presents. But he couldn't tell Jörgen any of this. Tompa scratched his neck and hummed a few times before finally he knew what he could say.

'Jörgen, don't you get it? At the party, Olle Marling said that the Mad Angels needed more land for their stuff. You know, extortion and so on. If we can offer them a plot of land, then it will be easier for us to be accepted as members.

So I've been trying to get on really good terms with Lillemor, since her plot could be divided.'

'So that's what you've been up to?'

Tompa nodded. He had always been good at lying.

'Of course. Thought it might be good if we show we're ambitious.'

'So how much would she want for the land, then?'

'We should reckon on about seven million. If everyone in the gang coughs up a bit of dough, it could work.'

Jörgen worked back and forth with his garden shears. At the party, Olle Marling had made it clear that the Bandangels must do a whole lot of work before they could count on becoming members of the Mad Angels. Then he had asked for help. Some promised protection money hadn't been paid, and now it was time to make up for it. Jörgen knew what that meant. Yet another extortion job alongside the ones that were already waiting for them. At least it was smart of Tompa to think ahead.

'We could buy out Lillemor, and the oldies in that big rambling house too? That might be even better,' Tompa went on. 'A bit of pressure on Super-Grandpa and his gang, and they'd soon sell. Jörgen, all of this area could be ours, do you see?'

'Yeah, that's real smart. Let's start with the oldies. They have a much bigger plot of land. And we can con them.'

They were both silent for a few moments, then they looked at each other and grinned.

33

'Oh Jesus no, not somebody from Customs & Excise! I asked for reinforcement, not some ignorant bastard I'll have to teach the job to.' Chief Inspector Blomberg groaned and swept out his hands.

'This will work out fine, just you wait and see,' answered Strömqvist, his boss, and he disappeared out of the room. The door slammed shut behind him and Blomberg swore out loud. He had been so looking forward to getting help with the Handelsbanken robbery, and then they had gone and sent an out-of-work customs officer. An incompetent idiot who had been kicked out of Arlanda Airport Customs & Excise after having stolen stuff that was meant for destruction. Strömqvist thought that the former customs officer could help them with new approaches to the investigation. This was a major bank robbery, not kids shoplifting candy from a corner store! Blomberg's train of thought was interrupted by a firm knock on the door, and before he had had the chance to say 'Come in', the door was opened. A well-dressed, slightly overweight middle-aged man with curly hair, a high nose and rosy cheeks entered the room.

'Chief Inspector Blomberg, I understand. Sven Carlsson at your service!' He then produced a high, jolly laugh.

'Yes, right. We are going to work together, I believe.' Blomberg nodded towards the empty chair on the other side of his desk and waited until Carlsson had sat down. 'So you have applied to join the police?'

'Yes, indeed. I wanted to develop my skills. At Arlanda Airport I saw everything from smugglers and drug pushers to fraudsters, and, well, I thought you might have a use for my knowledge.'

'So you think *we* might have a use for *your* knowledge?'

'Exactly, and since we're going to share an office, I thought—'

'Are we going to share an office?' Blomberg's face turned bright red. Would he not have an office to himself any longer? What would he do about all his private financial affairs? Admittedly, no more money had come in from Las Vegas, but he still had all his dealings with Beylings. Blomberg pursed his lips.

'Well, then, you'll have to ask for your own computer and furniture and so on.'

'Already done. It'll be delightful to work together. Your superior said that you can teach me about police work.'

'Oh, he did, did he?' Blomberg was close to exploding. Not only had his early retirement been prevented, but now he would also be forced to teach police work. The intruder! There was only one thing to do. Give the guy a case to work on. He opened his file.

'The bank robbery on Karlavägen, you know . . .'

Carlsson lit up.

'The Handelsbanken robbery, oh yes, that's hot. Suits me fine.'

'Read all the case notes. We need to know which types of fireworks the shops in Stockholm sold at New Year's.'

'Types of fireworks, no problem!'

'Write a report about it. When you've finished that, I've got something else for you.'

'Lovely!'

Blomberg raised his eyebrows. Carlsson seemed to be as energetic as he was stupid. Perhaps even more of the dreary work could be passed on to him?

'Oh yes, another thing, we want to know how many Oldvan shoes were sold in Stockholm in the last six months.'

'Lovely! I'll sort that out!'

'So you think it's looovely?'

'Yes, indeed it is. Don't you?'

Blomberg leaned back in his chair and pressed his fingertips together. Perhaps it wouldn't be so bad to have this plump guy assisting him after all. The customs man could do all the boring work. Then he could devote his time to more important things, such as filling Beylings' storage facility at the docks.

'Oh another thing, Carlsson, perhaps you'd like to make a cup of coffee? Then you can read the reports in peace and quiet before you do a round of the hardware stores.'

When Blomberg came to work the next day, he stumbled in and hung up his coat and hat. He wasn't really properly awake. He had had a sleepless night during which he had tried to fathom how the bank robbery had been carried out, without success. Now he rubbed his eyes, yawned and, with his thoughts elsewhere, made his way to his office. He stopped in the doorway and opened and closed his eyes several times. At first he thought he was hallucinating. But no, this was real.

Blomberg supported himself against the door frame and made a rather pathetic gasping sound. His office had been refurnished. What had previously been an ordinary Swedish bureaucrat's office had been transformed beyond recognition. His desk, his office chair and his simple visitor's chair had been moved to the corner of the room, while that bumbler Carlsson had spread himself out over the rest of the space. The customs official sat there smiling in a comfortable purple armchair with a footstool under a pipe-shaped turquoise reading lamp. Next to him was a modern adjustable desk with a dark blue top, and above that hung a white rice-paper lamp. There was a grey and black mat with a blue tulip pattern on the floor, and in the window hung curtains with a pattern of flowers and leaves in the same colours. Virtually every other surface was filled with plant pots.

'Nice, isn't it? I thought we'd make it a bit cozy in here. It cheers one up,' said Carlsson.

'I don't think "cheers one up" is quite the right expression,' muttered Blomberg.

'Ah, perhaps you'd like some flowers in vases on the desks too?'

'No!'

'Do you like the colour scheme?' Carlsson went on.

'The colour scheme?'

'Yes, perhaps you would rather we had everything in red?'

'Carlsson, here at the office, what counts is work.'

'Goes without saying. I found it hard to sleep last night so I took the opportunity to go through the lists of the number of fireworks and Oldvan shoes sold in Sweden.' Carlsson started to thumb through his papers.

'Oh, did you really?' Blomberg sat down. 'And?'

'I think we've got some leads. It's so exciting. We're bound to catch the robbers soon.'

'And what makes you think that?'

'Well, if you really want something to work out, then it usually does, don't you think?' The customs official grinned widely and brushed away a crumb from the corner of his mouth. 'But Blomberg, first I want to ask you a favour. I brought an aquarium with me. It's a bit heavy to carry up here on my own without it splashing, so—'

'We are going to have fish here too?'

'Oh yes, you wouldn't believe how soothing they can be.'

'*Soothing?*' Blomberg sighed deeply and was about to retort but then he just felt tired and couldn't be bothered to explain.

'Okay, then. We'll bring the goldfish tank in.'

34

The plans for the great gold robbery were becoming all the more tangible and, in keeping with tradition, the League of Pensioners went out on an expedition. The National Historical Museum was a large building with lots of halls and exhibits, and it was important that they didn't get lost. Besides, they must know exactly what they would have to do. Martha and Brains exchanged glances. They weren't actually nervous at all, because if a gang of pensioners go into a room full of gold treasure, then the guards most probably don't immediately think: 'Hello, here we've got some prospective villains.' No, indeed not – the guards wouldn't be bothered at all, just as long as nobody behaved suspiciously. Martha was certain they would be left in peace.

In a joyful and enthusiastic mood, the League of Pensioners and Gunnar bought their tickets at the entrance to the Historical Museum and immediately navigated their way to the Gold Room. They stopped before going down the stairs and solemnly breathed in the magnificent atmosphere, then they took a firm grip of the handrail and began their descent. The stairwell leading to the room with the treasure was bathed in a red, almost sacred light and, for a brief moment, Martha thought that she didn't want to commit a crime here. But then she pulled herself together. As a villain you sometimes have to do things which you don't really approve of. And they had, of course, failed to retrieve their money from the drainpipe so they must make up for it.

Martha couldn't forget the scenes from the retirement home where she had seen the grey, miserable life that the people led there. She knew what it was like if you didn't live in cozy, pleasant surroundings and couldn't eat good, nourishing food. The people who lived in the retirement homes and the staff who worked there – they all suffered. She and her friends were going to put a stop to that. If possible, all those who were in need should get help, even the poor who sat on the streets begging. Sweden's cultural heritage was priceless and Martha had high hopes. If they could only steal the nation's gold treasures, then they ought to be able to get enough money to help those in need. But it wouldn't be easy.

'Oh, look, isn't that lovely! It makes one so happy to see something as beautiful as this. The architects have really succeeded here,' said Anna-Greta halfway down the stairs. She had studied art history in her youth and delighted in what she saw.

'Not all architects were born inside a rectangle,' said Martha.

'Today's unimaginative builders should to stick to Lego instead; they'd cause less damage,' Gunnar sighed.

'Or they could design tiny, tiny postage stamps,' said Rake.

When they had reached the bottom of the stairs, Anna-Greta hung onto the railing awhile.

'Oh my goodness, how will we manage all these steps with the gold and everything?'

'Easy as pie – there's an elevator for the disabled,' said Christina.

'And every public space must have an evacuation plan clearly visible,' Brains added, pointing at a map on one of the walls. He pulled out his cellphone and took a photograph. 'By the way, are we going to have electric wheelchairs again? I mean, this time I could perhaps improve them even more.'

'We have no need to exit the museum like rockets, surely?' muttered Rake.

'There're more than a hundred and ten pounds of gold and a hundred and thirty-six pounds of silver here. Let me see, gold costs about five hundred and fifty thousand a pound, or perhaps more at the moment. That would mean fifteen million straight off, and then there's the silver too,' said Anna-Greta in a satisfied tone. 'But really we need more; this isn't going to go far when it comes to caring for the elderly.'

'No, but I had thought about extortion. I vote for a ransom of, say, five hundred million. The Swedish state can't simply ignore the value of the country's ancient past,' Martha chuckled.

'Oh yes, you wouldn't believe what they can ignore!' said Rake.

'But how are we going to lay our hands on the gold?' Christina butted in. 'First things first: we must carry out a successful robbery.'

Her question seemed to hover in the air while the five of them wandered around in the basement exhibit area. Inside the display cases lay large, fat rings, exquisitely decorated bracelets and jewellery of the finest gold.

'Just look at that!' Rake burst out, pointing at a well-preserved helmet that had been found at Vendel Church in Uppland. A stylish bronze comb ran from the neckpiece right up over the top and slightly below the eyeholes, while some dragon-like creatures slithered up towards the forehead.

'Magnificent!' Brains agreed.

Rake stood there with his nose pressed against the display window for a long time and just sighed, and the others had to drag him away. They walked around inside the Gold Room and read about farmers who had plowed their fields and found gold in the earth, and it wasn't long before they were all in really high spirits. Martha thought about the fields of canola down in Österlen, where she ran around when she was a little girl, and she wondered whether there had been gold there too. Christina tried to work out how much gold had come from her home district in the Jönköping area. For a while, Rake went on about how they should buy a metal detector and fetch silver and gold themselves from graves on Gotland, but then the others shushed him and said that that was illegal and he always had ridiculous ideas.

When they had done a last round of all the exhibits in

271

the room and were on their way up to the cafeteria, Martha suddenly emitted a roar, one of those happy aha-roars that made them all turn round. She waited until an elderly gentleman had gone past and then she gathered her friends together around the museum's large stone from Gotland. It was a high stone from the Viking era, from Ardre, with several images carved on the front. You could see Odin's eight-legged horse Sleipnir, a Viking ship with a sail, and something that looked like Volund's smithy. Martha stood with her hands on her stomach and emitted the strangest of sounds. They all looked at her. What was wrong?

'What's the matter, Martha dear?' Brains asked.

'I hope you haven't done yourself an injury. Do you feel ill?' Anna-Greta asked.

'No, no,' Martha sobbed with laughter. 'I've got it. Now I know exactly what we should do! Brains, can you take a photo of us all together here beside the image stone?'

Brains obediently raised his iPhone, pulled a few faces to get the others to laugh, and then took the picture.

'But why do you want me to take a photo just here?' he asked.

'Where else, when we are going to commit the boldest robbery of the century?' Martha answered.

After visiting the museum they took a taxi to the House of Culture in the city centre and sat down in the café up on the fifth floor. From up there they had a great view of all the stressed city-dwellers and a never-ending stream of cars that drove round the fountain with Edvin Öhrströms' glass obelisk in the middle. It felt really good to be surrounded by culture without having to steal it; indeed, spending a little time in the House of Culture was almost like a mini-holiday. But, regrettably, the café could offer neither wafers nor cloudberry liqueur.

'Are we really going to steal that gold?' Christina wondered out loud as she stared absentmindedly out through the panoramic windows while looking for her lipstick and powder compact in her handbag. 'Isn't that rather a pity?'

'But, my dear, six hundred and sixty pounds of the very finest precious metal is worth the effort,' Martha answered. 'The state ought to pay a lot of money for our national heritage!'

'But the Gold Room is like a bunker. We can't break in just like that,' said Brains.

'Who said we should break in? No, this must be carried out in an elegant and sophisticated manner,' Martha explained.

'Glad to hear that – no explosives, then; I was beginning to get worried,' Brains said.

'No, they're absolutely out of the question. Don't forget that we are dealing with cultural artefacts,' Martha pointed out.

'But how will we be able to get any money for them?' Anna-Greta asked. 'Is it really worth all the trouble?'

'Of course it is. Please remember: we must fill the coffers of the Robbery Fund, otherwise our charity project will just completely collapse. The old people must not be ill treated one single day more.'

'Or we could simply abandon the idea of saving everything and everyone, Martha. You want to save the whole world . . .' Rake sighed.

'Until we've sorted this out, we really can't retire,' Brains said. 'Martha is right.'

'But I don't want to end up in prison,' said Christina in a serious tone. 'What if they put us on a diet of bread and water among a load of scary prisoners? Now that the state has started to make cuts, where will it all end?'

'Well, prison would at least be better than a retirement home,' Rake argued.

'And we wouldn't be plied with sedatives.'

'Pah, we will go back neither to prison nor to a retirement home. The plan is watertight, I promise,' Martha said in her best reassuring voice.

'It sounds exciting. I'm on board,' Gunnar said politely, a little excited to be involved in another crime.

'In that case, and if you are with us, then I can go along with another coup,' said Anna-Greta.

'Gunnar, how nice that you want to join us. We need all the keen minds we can get. Besides, my dear friends,' said Martha as she rummaged around in her big cloth handbag for a pen and a notepad. 'Have a look here. This plan is really quite something. We're going to have lots of fun and I bet you a million that we won't get caught.'

Emma turned her cellphone off and looked at the bed where her daughter lay asleep. Goodness, what a grandmother little Malin had. An elderly, elegant woman who carried out bank robberies and quoted literary masters. And now Christina had phoned to say that she couldn't be a babysitter this week. Something had cropped up and she couldn't do it. Emma couldn't help but smile. Her mother, who at one time had been a rather subservient housewife in the posh district of Östermalm, had developed into a more confident and decisive woman. Perhaps she could learn something from that? Emma was far too weedy and ought to do something with her life. Emma lit a cigarette, but stubbed it out again when she saw Malin. She mustn't smoke anywhere near the child, no, and she didn't feel like going out onto the balcony while it was raining. A pity that Anders' children weren't the same age as Malin, now that he and she got together so often. It was delightful to get on so well with her brother. And absolutely necessary. She herself was little and looked frail but was tough inside, while Anders was handy and strong but lacked patience. Yes, they were both needed as assistants for the League of Pensioners – it was actually a full-time job!

Emma slowly combed her blond, fluffy hair. Christina was always so neat and well groomed, while Emma didn't really care about her appearance – more or less in protest. She was now on maternity leave and also had her hands full with the League of Pensioners. Makeup and nice clothes would have to wait until she was back at her old job again. She was just about to put a load of dirty clothes in the washing macine when Malin started to scream. It was time to feed her again, and change her diaper. Did babies do anything else besides eat and defecate? Emma made a face. She'd better see to Malin right away. Then she mustn't forget to arrange a sitter for the end of the month. The League of Pensioners evidently had a new crime in the offing.

35

The gate squeaked and steps could be heard outside. Somebody was on their way down the path to the house. Martha put the Gold Room evacuation plan aside and looked quickly around her to ensure that nothing else of a revealing nature was visible. This particular morning she was alone at home and unprepared for a visit. Christina had gone to Emma's, and the others were out shopping. Martha hadn't had the energy to go along with them, but now she regretted it. Just as long as it wasn't Tompa and Jörgen, she thought and felt her stomach tighten. She did what she could to look her usual unconcerned self, but deep inside she was afraid of them. The sound of the doorbell cut through the house and she didn't even have to look through the window to know who was there. Despite the new stones on the path, she had recognized the footsteps. The bikers were after something. She knew they didn't want to borrow some milk. Martha swallowed, put her knitting aside and went towards the door. In the hall she quickly combed her hair, threw a glance at her tense face in the mirror, and opened the front door.

'What a surprise, visitors today! Please come in!' Martha said as boldly as she could muster, but her voice was thin. She held open the door and Tompa and Jörgen entered and walked right into the living room without taking their boots off. They looked around.

'Where are all your friends?' Tompa asked.

'They've just gone out shopping. I was too tired to go along. You don't have so much energy when you get older. Coffee?' Martha attempted a smile.

'Yeah, why not?' Tompa and Jörgen nodded and followed Martha into the kitchen. She prepared some coffee and put out a plate of wafers too.

'A little cloudberry liqueur to go with it, perhaps?'

Without waiting for an answer, she put out three glasses and started to pour.

'Thanks, but I don't think—'

'Pah, don't be shy, boys.' Martha raised her glass. '*Skål*, dear neighbours!'

'Yes, right, *skål*, *skål*,' Tompa and Jörgen mumbled and tried to drink without making a face.

'Well now, have you got any new tattoos today then, boys?' Martha said and glanced at their forearms. Tompa scratched himself on his neck, embarrassed, but obediently rolled up his sleeve.

'Only these.'

'Oh, so fancy! A skull. Perhaps I should get one. No, I've probably got too many wrinkles.'

'To have a tattoo?' Tompa laughed out loud, but this time it sounded scornful.

'Yes, I think so. Although, won't your skulls look

weird when you get older?' Martha asked as innocently as possible.

'Errr,' mumbled Jörgen.

'They might even turn into smiling skulls.' Martha giggled nervously and put down her glass more clumsily than usual. She cleared her throat. 'Well now, boys, what's on your mind?'

'It's about the land here. We'd like to lease your plot.'

'Our plot? Oh, I'm terribly sorry, but that's out of the question. Rake has his garden and we like to sit in the lilac arbour and enjoy our afternoon coffee and the lovely view. No, we need all our land ourselves, quite simply. Sorry.'

'But at the right price?' Jörgen asked.

'Nothing less than five hundred million.'

Tompa's and Jörgen's ingratiating smiles vanished and their eyes darkened. They moved a little closer to Martha.

'Perhaps you should ask your wise friends, because we need this land,' said Jörgen, now in quite another tone of voice.

'Like I said, five hundred million.'

'Then we'll have to solve it some other way.'

They moved even closer, and Tompa discreetly rubbed his finger on his ring with the skull motif.

'Solve it some other way?' Martha tried to sound indifferent but there was a bit of a flutter to her voice. She shouldn't have stayed at home all alone – she should have known better. She could hardly engage the two men in close combat! Martha sipped the hot coffee and tried to think of some way to get the two giants out of the house. Her hand holding the coffee cup shook and when she put the cup down she knocked it against her bag out of nervousness. Oh yes, of course, she had the remote control in there. Now how did it work? Brains had said that if you put the remote against your throat you could use yourself as an aerial and open car door locks from a distance – indeed, from up to one hundred metres. Would that work for other apparatuses? Brains had modernized most of the things inside the house. Martha pulled out the remote and pressed it against her throat, pressing one of the buttons as she did so.

'What's that?' Tompa asked, suspicious.

'Instead of heart medicine,' Martha answered. 'Everything is so modern nowadays.'

Tompa and Jörgen moved a bit closer.

'We must have that land,' Tompa said again, this time so roughly that Martha was really scared and backed into her chair. She put the remote back in her bag and at the same time took out a fruit lozenge. Candy calmed her when she was nervous.

'A candy, boys?'

Tompa and Jörgen shook their heads and quickly exchanged looks. All sorts of thoughts were racing through Martha's mind. What if Brains was wrong, if he was just boasting like men do? Perhaps the remote didn't work at all. Then at last she heard 'John', the robot vacuum cleaner, start up in the library, rattle across the wooden floor, and collide into the sofa with a bump.

'What? What was that?' Tompa said and quickly got up.

'Empty the dust bag, empty the dust bag,' John announced in his English robot voice, slightly distorted after all the collisions with the furniture.

'What?' Jörgen exclaimed and looked worried.

'Such a lot of dust here, such a lot of dust here!' John went on in his Oxford English accent.

'Who's that?' Tompa said.

'Oh, that's only my darling John,' Martha answered. 'We're such good friends.'

'But you said you were on your own.' Tompa looked nervously around.

'On my own? I just forgot to say he was here.' Martha gave them a wink and tried to look innocent. 'Well, you see, you know what it's like, you have to make use of your opportunities. But, please, don't tell! Men are always so jealous.'

'So you've got—' Tompa started to say, but he was immediately cut off by the voice from the library.

'There's a mess here, it must be cleaned. There's a mess here, it must be cleaned. Have you had an orgy?' John asked in his robot voice from the other room – the voice sounded more distant now. Why on earth had Brains reprogrammed the vacuum cleaner so that it said a whole lot of unsuitable things?

'Have you had an orgy? Empty the dust bag!' could be heard from the library.

'Shut up!' Jörgen exclaimed – he couldn't speak English and had no idea what John was saying. He got up and strode towards the door to silence him.

'Stop!' Martha shouted. 'John is ill. He's got German measles. You'll catch it!'

'Oh!' Jörgen stopped in his tracks.

'Clean the brushes, clean the brushes,' came the muted

voice. The battery was running out. Martha realized the danger.

'Please, the others will be back soon. John and I can't meet often.' She nodded towards the library. 'I must go to him.'

'All right, all right, we'll be off, but don't forget that we want to buy or lease your land. We'll be back.'

The bikers adjusted their leather vests and hurried on their way. When they had gone, Martha opened her bag and turned John off with the remote. Then she went out onto the veranda and sank down in the wicker chair. Her heart was thumping and she was all sweaty. She stared out across the water and tried to calm down, but she was shaking all over. When the others came back, she couldn't even manage to get up from the chair; she remained sitting there and it took quite a while before her friends got a word out of her. Even then she didn't say very much. She didn't want to frighten them too.

The next day, when Christina threw a glance at the thermometer outside the window, she saw Tompa walking around in the garden.

'Listen everybody, the Bandangels are snooping round here,' Christina said and she waved Rake and the others across to the window. Tompa had a measuring tape. He had fastened one end to a branch and was now walking along the fence measuring the length of it. When he reached the bushes by the water, he turned straight in towards the lilac arbour.

'What in heaven's name is he up to?' Rake asked.

'They're cooking up something,' Martha replied, as she reluctantly realized that she must tell them about her unpleasant meeting with Jörgen and Tompa. 'The Bandangels want to lease our land.'

'But they can't do that, can they?' Christina moaned.

'I said that we wouldn't go along with that.'

'The worst thing with biker gangs is that they have their own laws,' Rake said. 'They don't care very much about what we say.'

'But they've got fancy motorcycles,' Brains said, trying to calm things down.

'We'll have to keep an eye on them. I don't think we can continue to keep our stuff in the cellar. They've already been there snooping, so we can't take the risk. We'll have to get some new storage space.'

'Ah, you want us to go out working again,' Rake sighed.

'Take it easy. Brains and I can manage this on our own, can't we?' said Martha and she held out her hand. Brains took it and squeezed so hard that Martha felt such a warm sensation spread through her body, suddenly she was lost for words.

'Yes, quite right, Martha, we'll manage this. We'll certainly find some good storage facilities on the Internet,' Brains added, actually feeling rather proud that he had at last started to understand how the Internet worked.

'Why not try Stockholm Docks?' Christina suggested. 'They have lots of storage there. Our stuff will just vanish in the mass.'

Everyone thought Christina's idea was good, and a little later they went onto Google Maps and zoomed in on the dock warehouses. They studied the fencing, the guard boxes and the gates, and settled on the older part of the harbour where they used to repair boats in bygone days.

'That would do us nicely. Let's drive there and have a look,' said Martha, getting up. 'We'd best go straight away before the rush-hour traffic starts.'

Martha and Brains drove in towards the city, turned off towards the free port area and finally reached a high fence with a guard box and an entry with a lowered barrier.

'I wonder that they'll say when they see a minibus with a wheelchair ramp on the back?' Martha said when they drove up to the barrier.

'I don't think the guard over there would have reacted even if we'd come in an army tank with caterpillar tracks,' said Brains, nodding towards the guard box. Inside sat a young man who must have been about twenty-five years old, with a cellphone pressed against one ear, rocking on his chair. He hadn't even noticed that they had driven up. It wasn't until Martha and Brains knocked on the window a few times that he turned towards them, yawned widely and reluctantly put his phone down.

'Err?' he said. It was presumably a question.

'We want to rent a storage space,' said Martha. 'The best you have. It must have an alarm and be guarded but it doesn't have to be too big.'

The man with the phone thumbed through some papers.

'Everything is full. All that we have is a small storage unit right at the far end of the old ship-building hall.'

'Right, we'll drive there.'

The security guard opened the barrier and let Martha and Brains through. Then he closed it again, picked up the phone and, with his iPhone pressed against his ear, walked in front of the minibus in the direction of the old ship-building area. When they reached a red-brick building with a large wide door facing the water, he stopped, dug into his pocket and pulled out a plastic card. He fed that into a little thingamajig next to the door, keyed in some numbers and turned the alarm off. Then he opened the door with the same card. Martha and Brains got out of the bus and followed him into the warehouse. They entered a large storage area which smelled of garage, sea and diesel oil. The concrete floor looked as if it had been cast just a few years earlier, but the high red-brick walls must have been about a hundred years old. All around were shiny luxury yachts, sports cars and motorcycles of the latest models, and there were storage shelves farther inside as well. When Brains caught sight of a Harley-Davidson, he got out his phone and started taking photos.

'No, you can't take pictures in here!' The security guard waved his hand disapprovingly.

'Why not?' said Martha.

'Well, there are things here that people might not want everyone to see.'

The security guard grinned and continued towards the door right at the end. Martha's curiosity had been aroused; she discreetly pulled out her own phone and dropped back a bit behind the men before taking pictures of everything that looked exciting. Brains realized what she was doing, broke into a wide smile and gave her a wink. When they reached the door, the man pulled out his plastic card again and, after a click, he opened the door and showed them inside the final storage area.

'This is a bit too small for the big players, unless, of course, they've got expensive art,' he said and laughed. 'The city needs larger units.'

'The city?' Martha wasn't sure what he meant.

'Yes, the city council. Everybody knows that. They are selling everything nowadays, and the people who are involved don't want to know how much money they earn from that.'

Martha restrained herself, angled her head to one side and played stupid.

'I'm sorry, I don't understand at all.'

The security guard hesitated, turned off his phone and put it into his pocket. Then he pulled it out again and started to enter a number. Martha stopped him.

'Ah, I see, you don't really know anything, you're just pretending, right?' Martha cajoled. To question and challenge men was not a bad idea. Martha had often found in the past that they just wanted to show how much they knew.

'I know how this works. This is just a part-time job for me, a bit of extra money, otherwise I'm a student at Handels.'

'Handels? You mean the School of Economics?'

'Yeah, right. And there you get to hear one thing and another. About how they're selling council property such as retirement homes, daycares and schools. There's lots of money involved in that.'

'Really?'

'Yes, and then there's the home-care services and all the council-owned housing too.'

'What is that about?'

'It's worth a lot of money. So when they sold it off, lots of people got very rich.'

'How? What do you mean?'

'Smart city business types got to know the people responsible and said that they'd give a bonus and a percentage of the future profits if they could buy certain things.'

'But you can't do that. That's bribery.'

Now the security guard smiled widely and patted Martha condescendingly on her shoulder. 'Business is business. At Handels we use our brains!' The security guard pointed at his forehead. 'This is what we use when we do business. I know somebody who bought a nursery school building for a hundred and fifty thousand kronor. The council official who handled the sale got twenty thousand for his trouble. But the man who bought it then went and sold it again for many a million just a few years later. A good business transaction, don't you think?'

'Goodness, to think that you boys at Handels know all about things like that,' said Martha with false admiration in her voice.

'The profits end up in the West Indies, so you don't have to pay tax. It's as easy as pie for the big players in the branch – but the people who get the bribes have got a problem. They can't have all that money visible in a bank account.'

'Oh, I see, so they buy a luxury yacht or a Porsche?' said Martha.

'You've got it. But it's a boat or a car that, on paper, is owned by somebody else – for example, a firm of lawyers.'

'And then, of course, that firm of lawyers needs some space where they can store the goods,' Martha added.

The security guard nodded.

'Pretty smart, isn't it?'

'I'm beginning to understand,' said Brains. 'So they store the stuff here for a while until they can sell it without arousing attention?'

'Yes. Everyone is happy and satisfied and makes a profit.'

'Except, of course, us ordinary taxpayers,' Martha pointed out. 'The things that we have paid for with our taxes are sold off cheap and then somebody makes a profit from that. Oh, that's so immoral!'

'Ah, everybody cheats and, as long as I get my salary, I don't care. Anyway, what are you going to store here?'

Stolen goods, Martha came close to saying, but managed to restrain herself at the last moment.

'Oh, just a few knick-knacks,' she said and blushed.

'Knick-knacks?'

'We've had a break-in and we want to store our stuff somewhere safe,' she said.

'No problem. There are alarms here everywhere and the whole place is guarded,' assured the security guard.

'Excellent,' said Martha and Brains in unison. Then they trooped back towards the guard box at the entrance. As usual, Martha didn't use her real name or personal identity number but instead used the fake coordination number and her new identity. When they had paid the deposit, and received keys and their codes, Martha couldn't restrain herself any longer.

'But if a firm of lawyers owns all the stuff in there, how can you know who is actually the real owner?'

'Of course there are names. You'd have to hack into some computer or other, madam.' The security guard grinned and patted her again on the shoulder.

'Yes, I suppose that's exactly what we'd have to do,' Martha mumbled, while realizing that he had said too much. So there were names to look for. Strange how much somebody could reveal when they were talking to old people. It was as if they thought that the elderly had stopped thinking. For youth and politicians, the elderly just didn't seem to count. Not at all.

On their way home in the minibus, Martha and Brains couldn't help thinking about what they had just heard, because they had sufficient experience to realize that some very fishy things were going on in those storage areas.

'Strange that we could walk through a storage unit that was rented by somebody else,' Brains said, sharing his thoughts with the group.

'But perhaps it was the only space not already rented out,' Martha suggested.

'Or perhaps that security guard rented it out to us on the side. I think he needed some extra money for his studies and he thought that we weren't a risk, so he could rent the space inside.' It was the same attitude that they encountered again and again. People regarded you as completely incompetent just because you were older.

'Exactly, you are right. We never even got a copy of the contract. But, in fact, that's rather a good thing. If he doesn't do as we say, we can threaten to reveal his shady deals.'

'Goodness, Martha, what an idea! Although that wasn't a kind thought,' teased Brains as he leaned forward and gave her a little kiss on the mouth. Martha suddenly fell silent and let herself be filled with a completely different feeling – a really nice one.

36

Feeling quite exhilarated, with her hair a bit dishevelled and her cheeks rosy, Martha was on her way to Riddarholmen in the Old Town with Brains. The Gold Room robbery must be prepared for thoroughly and they must go over their plan. A completely crazy plan, which required them to make a few things. They drove slowly along the quayside and stopped at a little doorway that faced the water.

'It must be here.'

Brains adjusted his glasses and looked up. Yes, indeed, that was it: CONSERVATION AND RESTORATION, it said on a large brass plate to the left of the entrance. Martha parked and nodded towards the building.

'It's in there that they make copies of runic stones. I think we can learn a lot here, just you wait and see.'

'You're so full of ideas, Martha. There's never a quiet moment with you. But it is rather exhilarating,' chortled Brains.

'I do like you, you know that?' Martha answered, closing her eyes and leaning against his shoulder. 'But it isn't me who's turned us into criminals. It's society. If only they'd taken a bit better care of their citizens.'

'Yes, but then we wouldn't have had as much fun, would we, Martha?' He stroked her cheek and suddenly looked very serious.

Martha became shy and embarrassed, fumbled for the door handle and quickly opened the bus door. They got out, and Brains opened the back door and took out a little plaster statue that they had bought at a garage sale – a figure of David with a damaged head and a broken arm. Brains rang the doorbell. They had come to see a restorer and, after announcing the reason for their visit, they were let in. In the entrance they were met by an assistant who smiled a welcome. They went into an enormous open room which had stuff all over the place, and wherever they looked, they saw something that needed repairing: statues in bronze or plaster, paintings and old furniture. Right at the far end there were some copies of image stones made in PVC plastic which were marked as belonging to the Swedish Exhibition Agency. Martha gave Brains a little prod in the side.

'Just as I thought – they still make copies in PVC plastic here.'

'I'm sorry?' said the restorer as he entered the room.

'I was just saying that you have such beautiful picture stones here,' said Martha. 'They look just like the real ones.'

'Yes, they'll be going out in a travelling exhibit. Handy, aren't they? And they weigh almost nothing,' answered the restorer, a bald overweight man wearing a stained coat.

'Fantastic! The man I've got here was also fantastic before I dropped him on the floor,' said Martha, stroking the little statue of David. 'Poor David fell off the table and, well, you can see for yourself what that resulted in.'

Martha described in detail everything that needed to be repaired, while Brains quietly stepped aside and sneakily photographed all the image stones and runestones inside the studio on his phone. He even took pictures of the cans of PVC plastic, hardener and other products used in the studio that he saw on the floor. When he had finished, Martha picked up her plaster statue, stroked David's broken arm and said:

'I've got several statues at home that also need repairing. If I bring them in too, perhaps we can get a good price for doing them all?'

'Yes, of course. I'll estimate a price for the whole lot,' said the restorer.

'Then we shall come back later.'

'What about the plaster statue?'

'I'll bring that with me next time. I am so fond of looking at it,' said Martha, patting David so hard that another little bit of plaster loosened. Then she smiled the widest smile she could, nodded to Brains, and together they left the restoration workshop.

On their way home, they stopped at Byggmax in Nacka and purchased boat varnish, PVC plastic and various paints in shades of red, black and grey. With heavily loaded shopping carts, they then returned to the minibus absolutely exhausted, and sat there with their arms around each other for quite a while to get their breath back before they could manage to drive off again. To be on the safe side, they stopped at the Delselius coffee shop for something to restore their energy, and they both had a coffee and a shrimp sandwich before driving on. It was lucky they did because, when they got home, they found the rest of the League of Pensioners full of energy and gathered around the computer. Gunnar and Anna-Greta were explaining something to the others.

'Oh good, you've come just in time,' said Anna-Greta in a jolly tone when she caught sight of them. 'We're busy setting up our secret archives for planning robberies: Stasi Senior.'

'Stasi Senior? What a fine name. I assume it is about the preparations for the gold robbery?'

'Yes, indeed. We've got the photos that Brains took in the Gold Room, and I hope that you got some good pictures today too. We'll put them straight into the archives.'

Brains handed over his phone so that Anna-Greta could transfer the pictures to the computer.

'I think we've got what we need,' said Brains. 'I took pictures of all the image stones in the workshop, and also of the hardener and other materials they use for their plastic copies.'

'It's amazing how handy it is to store things on the computer. You can get everything in order,' said Anna-Greta, delighted, and she created a new Stasi folder with the day's date. 'Right, let's have a look.'

She clicked her way to the photos from the docks, and the rows of luxury boats and Rolls-Royces and other cars appeared on the screen.

'Goodness me!' Anna-Greta exclaimed. 'What on earth are these doing here?'

'A secret storage place for bribes. Utterly crazy. They store things worth millions and millions,' said Martha.

'But why are they all stored there and not being used?' Gunnar asked.

Martha told them what the part-time security guard had said and they all sighed and shook their heads.

'What a swindle! At least we're working for the common good,' said Christina. 'Fraudulent use of taxpayers' money is a serious crime.'

Anna-Greta pulled out the desk drawer and took out a magnifying glass. 'You can see the registration plates . . .' she pointed out.

'That's what I thought. We must check with the national vehicle registry,' advised Martha.

Gunnar did some searches on his laptop. After a few minutes he stopped.

'Mysterious. Most of them belong to a firm of lawyers, Beylings.'

'Then that security guard with the cellphone was right,' said Brains. 'The firm can't own all that themselves. Those luxury goods are simply registered under their name.'

'But who actually owns the cars and boats? We can't just let go of this.' Christina was curious now. 'Those owners must have something to hide: tax evasion, fraud or perhaps even theft.'

'Yes, you're quite right, we must investigate this further. But first we must rob the Gold Room. Now we must concentrate on that,' Martha reminded them.

'Indeed we must,' Brains agreed. 'Anna-Greta, can you zoom in on those pictures from the restoration workshop?'

While Anna-Greta clicked her way through the day's images, Martha fetched some tea and scones. She had also bought some tasty cinnamon buns at Delselius', which she put on the dish, together with some oatmeal cookies and candy. It was important to keep everyone happy with an afternoon tea. However, nobody bothered to sit down and relax; instead, they each took a cinnamon bun and then gathered around the screen, where they looked at the fantastic full-scale image-stone copies that Brains had photographed. Thanks to the fact that he had put a box of matches next to each object in the photos, you could work out exactly how high and wide the image stones were. You only had to measure the matchbox and then you had the scale. Brains had thought of everything. After they had looked at all the pictures, the whole gang felt so tired that they decided to rest for a while. Then, after a little snooze and a good meal, Brains and Rake went straight out to the workshop. First they covered the windows with a piece of black cardboard, and then they put on their work overalls. After that they got out the compass saw and sawed out a full-scale template of one of the pictorial stones. It was very hard work and they had to take several breaks for a beer and to get their breath back. Every stage of the job gave them cause to have another drink, so, in the end, the wooden image stone was not as precise as it could have been. 'We're not quite as strong as we used to be,' protested Brains.

'Mind you, we do have experience, and that makes up

for a lot,' said Rake. After a bit of discussion they realized that some stages of the work would need young strong muscles. They returned to the house and, after they had explained, Christina nodded and went to phone for Anders and Emma.

The next day, the workshop was a hive of activity and Anders, who was a bit of a handyman himself, took charge. Admittedly, he was middle-aged and not quite as strong and supple as once he had been, but he had held a hammer and saw enough times to think he knew it all. With the help of a bit of masonite and particle board he managed to put together an image stone with the same measurements as the museum's large stone from Gotland. Then the girls took over and used a file and sandpaper until they got something reminiscent of rough stone.

It was like a really weather-beaten picture stone, Rake thought after Christina had worked on it awhile. 'You're really rather clever, you know!' he told her.

'Thank you, Rake. Well, as you'll realize, this is not something a fortune-teller could do. And I can paint it, too,' said Christina proudly with glowing cheeks.

It wasn't until the following day that the League of Pensioners had the energy to continue with their home made picture-stone model. Brains mumbled something about casting in plastic not being one of his strong points, but he had at least learned enough for their little home project, so he greased the model and, together with Rake and Anders, put it into an enormous open tank in the workshop. Then he and Rake mixed together some hardener and the PVC plastic in a large bucket and got ready to pour.

'Stand by! Now you'll have to give us a hand, girls,' he called out while the sweat dripped over his face and nose. 'Right, tip the bucket now!'

They all helped to pour the dough-like mixture into the tank while Brains and Rake mixed some more new dough until finally the whole image stone was covered. Satisfied with their work, they stood there and looked down at the enormous stone buried in the plastic.

Suddenly Christina cried out. 'You know what? I think we've forgotten something.'

'Oh no, I don't think we have,' said Brains confidently with his hands on his hips, but, nevertheless, he looked at his friend with some consternation.

'When you cast something, you use a clay form and then smash the clay so that you can get at the cast object afterwards. But what do we do here?'

They all stared at the picture stone, which was completely buried and was in the process of being stuck forever to the PVC plastic.

'Perhaps we've made a blunder here,' said Brains.

'We? You mean you?' Rake sneered.

And so it came about that the Great Gold Robbery at the Historical Museum had to be delayed for a couple of weeks.

37

Customs Officer Carlsson hummed to himself while he checked the CCTV images from outside Handelsbanken. Mozart's *'Eine kleine Nachtmusik'* was playing in the background and he was in the best of moods. This was quite different from the extremely boring CCTV images at the airport. Here people were going back and forth on the sidewalk, sometimes a cyclist passed, sometimes a dog, or people hurrying past with their briefcases, lattes or smartphones. Now and then someone tripped on a loose brick or stood there arguing, which looked absolutely hilarious. He zoomed in on the passers-by and, to be on the safe side, he had even got hold of the images from the week before the robbery. Suddenly, he thought he saw someone he recognized. Carlsson backed up the tape and looked at the scene again. On the sidewalk next to Handelsbanken stood an elderly lady with a hat and overcoat, talking on her cellphone. Her appearance seemed familiar but he simply couldn't recall where he had seen her before. He made a note and then continued to look through the footage. There she was again, talking on her phone. He leaned forward and zoomed in on her. Indeed, the face was certainly familiar, but however hard he tried, he couldn't remember who she was. One thing was certain: she was of interest for the investigation. She had been in the same place the week before. That could hardly just be a coincidence.

Spring was in the air and all the members of the League of Pensioners had sauntered down to the bay with the intention of having a swim. If the wind hadn't just started to blow, Rake probably would have dived in head first, but instead he did an elegant about-turn when he reached the edge of the water and mumbled some complicated explanation for why he wasn't having a dip just this particular day. Instead, he went back to his sun chair on the veranda. The others followed his lead and they all sat in their white bathrobes and lapped up the sun. From a bowl of ice, Martha fished up some juice, beer and cider, which she shared out. She looked out across the water and felt that familiar tingle in her tummy that always cropped up when she was slightly nervous. It often happened the day before something big was going to happen. Something criminal. The picture stones were ready, the plans had all been finalized and they only had to go through a final briefing.

'My dear friends, tomorrow is the big day,' Martha announced. 'Just remember to handle the stolen articles carefully. We're talking about Sweden's national heritage here.'

'Indeed,' Anna-Greta agreed with a loud voice. 'We're only going to borrow the gold and it must be in just as good a condition when we give it back.'

The others nodded in solemn unity. Everyone was pleased that finally they would be getting back into action. The preparations had taken longer than intended and the making of the image stones had been much stickier and more difficult than they had thought it would be. In the end, Brains and Rake had managed to do the casting, and then the girls had taken over with the finishing flourishes. Thanks to Anna-Greta's collection of history books, and under the guidance of Christina, they had been able to copy the image stones exactly. The end products looked so natural, with the boats and the figures, that Rake had become really interested in history. However, some details did differ from the genuine articles. On the back there was a door so that you could go inside the image stone, but since the shell was of Styrofoam and the PVC plastic had been much heavier than they had imagined, you couldn't hang the stones directly on your shoulders. So Anders had helped Brains to put together a supportive wooden frame on wheels. In addition, the stones had been fitted with numbered hooks so that you could hang the gold treasures inside. Then the five friends, with Gunnar's assistance, rented a trailer, checked out where all the alarms were placed, and studied staff routines at the Historical Museum. Now the only thing left to do, was to actually carry out the *Great Robbery*.

'Yes, my dear friends. Sleep well tonight. Tomorrow evening is the big event.'

Martha raised her glass and they started singing the Swedish national anthem – after all, they were just about to lay their hands on Sweden's national heritage.

38

All morning they had been adding the final touches to the image stones before they fastened them securely on the trailer. Now the League of Pensioner's old minibus trundled along in the Stockholm traffic with Anders at the wheel. He and Emma were on their way to the Historical Museum, as instructed by their mother. He slowed down at Narvavägen and turned left towards the museum. His right hand brushed his unshaven cheeks.

'Like I said, there's no rest and no peace when Mother gets started, dear me, no,' Anders sighed.

Emma nodded, tired too.

'Now Mum and the others are going to commit a crime again. What can we do about it?'

'Sis, there isn't much we can do, but look at it like this. Mum has her friends and is in good spirits. She is so perky that she can even babysit for you sometimes. She doesn't complain about aches and pains and how lonely she is, but instead giggles when she talks about robbery coups and the like.'

'Yes, of course, you're right about that.'

'Since they refuse to live in any type of retirement home, we've simply got to help them as best we can.'

'Yes, sure, but they've only recently committed a crime, so I thought we'd be able to take things easy for a while,' Emma sighed. 'Malin isn't sleeping well nights so I'm actually beginning to get a little tired.'

After the Handelsbanken robbery, both Emma and Anders had intended to live their usual and safe middle-class lives, but now, once again, they had been pulled out of that calm existence – not to help a tired, aging mother but to assist her in crime.

'We can hardly protest. We are already deeply involved in their activities. If Mum gets caught, then we'll go down with them.' Anders scratched his chin.

Emma pulled out some chewing gum and started to chew frantically. How long was the prison sentence for assisting in a robbery? Or stealing antiquities for that matter?

'We are in this up to our necks; we've simply got to keep working. I think they could take things a bit easier. They are wearing us out.'

'Don't let Martha hear you saying that. Then she'll force you to start in the gym too!'

Emma laughed, the typical resigned laugh of an exhausted mother who hasn't slept properly for several nights. 'Right, here we are. Drive into the yard and stop by the steps.'

She and Anders were wearing stained restorers' work overalls and had timed their visit for when people were having their lunch break. At that time there were always a lot of visitors and nobody would bother about them. They parked the minibus, went round to the trailer and lifted off one of the image stones. Thankfully, you couldn't see the wheels because they were retracted; otherwise, they would have been hard to explain.

When the two of them passed the entry hall they cheerfully greeted the staff and continued towards the Gold Room. They put the first image stone down just next to where the stairs started and then went to fetch the other two. Finally they put two notices next to the grand image stones, museum notices which even had some text in English. Brains, who was very good at languages, had wanted to have Italian, Spanish, Russian and Croatian too, but the others had protested. The notices must look just like all the others in the museum. When Anders and Emma were finished, they took a step back. The picture stones, with their images of ships, gods and legends, really did look just like the real thing. Christina had even managed to portray Odin's eight-legged horse Sleipnir.

'To think that Mum can forge things too!' said Anders, sounding rather proud.

'Say she can copy artefacts, not forge them – somebody might hear us,' Emma whispered. 'We'd best be moving!'

Emma and Anders left the museum as quickly as possible so that few people would notice their presence.

In the evening, the League of Pensioners arrived with a large group of people interested in history to listen to the museum's evening lecture about the Vikings. A sprightly curator, who had recently defended his doctoral thesis, which had come to the conclusion that the Vikings had never existed, was talking. All the studies must be done again, he claimed, and Martha quickly stood up to protest, but just as quickly sat down again. This particular evening it was best to keep a low profile. A very low profile.

Later, when the guards had shooed out the last of the visitors after the lecture, Martha, Christina and Anna-Greta stayed on in the ladies' room.

'Couldn't we have found a nicer place to hide ourselves?' Anna-Greta whispered from where she stood squeezed inside one of the cubicles.

'There are no CCTV cameras in here, so get your cleaners' uniforms on,' Martha reminded them.

'Cleaners' uniforms on,' Christina and Anna-Greta repeated in unison and soon you could hear strange sounds from the cubicles accompanied by sighs and groans while the ladies changed. Then they were quiet again.

'Ready?' Martha asked.

An affirmative murmur was heard and Martha's cellphone started to vibrate at the same time. This was the agreed signal. Martha pressed the key to see Rake's text message. She shook her head. Rake had evidently tried to text her with the autocorrect program turned on and all she could see was a row of a strange combination of letters.

'Oh dear me, what a mess,' said Martha, turning pale. Why had Rake needed to show how modern he was just now? Did that mean that the coast was clear? Or that it wasn't? She must make a quick decision.

'Rake has sent a coded message from his Nokia,' she announced. 'It's time to go now.' And with that the three ladies left their temporary residence and set off towards the entrance hall.

Outside the museum, Anders had driven up with the

Volkswagen minibus, now transformed into a van with the name SENIOR CLEANERS on the side. Brains and Rake got out of the van, opened the back doors and took out two cleaners' carts. Then they closed the doors, adjusted their work overalls and made sure they had their mops, cleaning rags and brushes with them. And Martha's handbag. She had insisted that it could come in useful should something unforeseen happen, and must be put next to the elevator. After looking around in all directions, they approached the wheelchair elevator on the street level, put Martha's handbag in, pushed in their cleaners' carts, and then went in too. They pressed the button for the entrance hall and, while the elevator worked its way up, they prepared themselves mentally. The elevator doors opened and they went straight out. Right into the arms of two guards.

'We're turning the alarm on now,' said an officious type in his fifties.

'No, Securitas are going to service the alarm system today. That's why we're doing the cleaning now,' Rake replied and waved his mop.

'I haven't heard anything about that. You'll have to come back tomorrow.'

'No, we're here now. Look for yourselves!' Rake spouted on and fished out a piece of paper from his overalls, a document full of official stamps. Christina had been in top form and there was hardly an empty space on the whole sheet. 'And anyway,' Rake added, 'at Senior Cleaners we always do the cleaning in the evening. You wanted us to be invisible, since you don't like making a show of using cheap labour.'

'Hmm,' said the guard. 'Just a moment, I'll have a word with my colleague.' He went off, but when he came back he arrogantly gestured towards the exit.

'Sorry. You'll have to come another time. I can't take responsibility for this.'

'You don't need to,' Rake replied with a glance at Brains. His friend didn't look happy. At this point he would have to do something he didn't like, which they had planned as an emergency measure if something went wrong. But now the time had come. Rake steered his cart to one side and when the guard turned his back, Brains pushed a wet cleaning rag against his face. Two quick breaths of the ether and the guard sank to the floor. Rake hurried to fetch his colleague.

'Your friend just collapsed.'

The younger colleague saw his comrade lying lifeless on the floor, went pale and rushed up to him. When he bent over, Brains was ready again.

'Welcome to the party,' he said and pressed the rag in the man's face.

'Wha . . . wa . . .' the guard blurted out before he, too, collapsed in a heap on the floor. Then Rake got out his phone to send a new text. But before he could send it off, Martha, Christina and Anna-Greta turned up. They nodded discreetly to their friends and walked determinedly towards the Gold Room. At the top of the stairs they went up to their image stones, looked around, opened the back doors and stepped inside – all except Anna-Greta, who had left her glasses at home and walked right into the real image stone from Gotland.

'Oh my goodness!' she mumbled, somewhat groggy, and quickly switched to the stone next to it, the one made of PVC plastic.

'We ought to have put the image stones a bit closer to the wheelchair elevator,' Martha mumbled in a low voice from inside the cramped space. The plastic felt rough against her neck.

'A good job we've got some breathing holes,' Christina answered in a stressed voice from inside her stone, and she inhaled through the opening in an old Viking sail. 'I hope the carbon dioxide level doesn't get too high.'

'When the police see the picture stones move they'll think there is something wrong with the CCTV cameras,' Anna-Greta guffawed, and for the first time in the history of the museum a picture stone could be heard snorting.

When they had each closed the door on the back of their pictorial stone and lowered the wheels, the three ladies rolled slowly and carefully towards the elevator. They tried to do it with jerky movements like in an old silent film to make it look as if the camera was wonky, so they couldn't move very fast, and Brains and Rake, in their Senior Cleaners caps, had soon caught up with them.

'You can imagine how confounded the police are going to be,' said Rake with a broad grin when he'd managed to squeeze his way into the elevator with his cart. 'Ancient runestones pursued by two cleaning carts . . .'

'They're called image stones, not runestones,' Anna-Greta corrected him, her voice echoing inside the stone copy.

'Shush! Keep your wits about you!' said Christina in a

hollow, half-dampened voice. 'This crime requires concentration!'

Her voice sounded so funny from inside the stone that they all simply had to laugh and it took a good while before they had pulled themselves together to such a degree that Brains could press the 'Down' button in the elevator.

When they reached the basement, Martha's voice could be heard: 'Have you got everything with you?'

'Yes, even the smoke grenades,' said Rake holding up one of the bottles of cleaning fluid with its new contents.

'Excellent, excellent,' could be heard from inside the stones as they navigated on their wooden wheels towards the Wishing Well in the Gold Room.

'Are you ready?' Rake said, with the bottle of cleaning fluid in his hand.

Various sounds emanated from inside the stones and Rake interpreted them as a yes. The next moment, a smoke grenade was on its way down into the Wishing Well.

39

As soon as the smoke started to smart their eyes, Brains regretted having brought the grenades. It would probably have been better to use carbon dioxide snow, or why hadn't they just drilled a few holes in one of the fire extinguishers? Now it was hard to see and it would be tricky to work fast. But of course it was too late to have second thoughts now. They only had a few minutes.

Rake and Brains went behind the display cases. Once there, Brains pulled out his new invention. Christina had pointed out that villains often gave themselves away by using the same modus operandus for every crime. So it was a question of doing something new and Brains had done his best in that respect. In the increasingly dense smog, the two men steered their cleaners' carts in behind the display cases and set to work. Rake pulled out his battery-powered drill from the shaft of his broom, and started to systematically drill holes in the edge of the cases. Then Brains took over with his specially prepared mop. With a slight squeeze of his hand, the compass saw with its laser blade shot out and, to the accompaniment of a squeaking racket, he sawed a large opening into the back of the cases. Then along came Martha, Anna-Greta and Christina, inside their image stones. The magnificent ancient monuments slowly rolled along, turned their backs to the display case, and then doors were opened and flabby arms were exposed. There was very little time, and Martha and her friends didn't waste it. With gloved hands they grabbed the gold and put it inside the black garbage bags with the same number on them as the various display cases. Then they hung up the bags on the numbered hooks inside the stones. Thanks to the fact that the ladies had practised this manoeuvre several times in the workshop at home, it all went very smoothly, but perhaps that also made them a little blasé. They were by no means as attentive as they ought to have been, and they didn't notice the cracks in the PVC plastic. With each bag of gold the strain on the plastic became all the greater, and it started making cracking sounds. However, because the laser saw made such a dreadful racket, none of them heard the mysterious cracking in the plastic. They could hardly hear what they were singing.

'Tiddelipom, tiddelipom,' Martha hummed.

Anna-Greta was singing to herself, a song about gold, and Christina something by Ernst Rolf. Indeed, the mood was good inside the image stones and, thanks to the lowered wheels, the three inside could move very quickly. They emptied the display cases in the Gold Room in seven minutes exactly.

'To the elevator!' Martha directed them in a panting voice from inside her stone, upon which the ladies rolled their stones back, closely followed by Brains and Rake.

This time the ladies carelessly took a shortcut across a slight threshold which resulted in the bags of gold shaking. This was too much for the PVC construction, which cracked all over with a crash so that the stones collapsed.

'Oops, they don't seem to have hardened properly,' said Brains, surrounded by a heap of plastic.

'And I had such faith in you,' Rake grumbled.

'Oh my goodness, this really isn't going according to plan!' Anna-Greta complained in horror and she picked some bits of plastic out of her hair.

'Now listen to me, hurry up! We must pick up the bits. It's a good job we've got the cleaner's carts,' said Martha, spurring them on. 'Don't forget the gold!'

Rake and Brains joined in immediately and with amazing agility managed to fill the cleaners' carts with the remains of the image stones. Finally, Christina rushed up to the nearest fire extinguisher, loosened the catch and started to spray everything around her.

'Christina, dear, we don't need to hide fingerprints. We're taking all the bits with us,' Anna-Greta coughed. But Christina didn't have time to answer, because just as they were putting the last of the bits of plastic in the carts they heard the police sirens.

'The alarm was turned off!' Brains shouted, aghast.

'Pah, there must have been a special alarm on the display cases that was connected directly to the police. Run!' Martha spurred them on and with the cleaners' carts full of gold and plastic they hastened to the elevator. But just as they had managed to squeeze in with the loot, Martha caught sight of something that Rake was holding under his arm.

'Oh my God! The magnificent helmet from Vendel – you can't take that. That is priceless and more than fourteen hundred years old!'

'But it's so incredibly stylish!' Rake protested.

'It makes no difference. Give me that. It's part of our cultural heritage and is absolutely irreplaceable!' Martha insisted, taking the helmet from him. 'Run to the bus, you lot. I'll soon join you,' she went on breathlessly and turned back.

'Just leave it outside the elevator,' said Brains, but Martha had already hurried away. He hesitated and was just about to press the button for the ground floor when he realized they were already there. They must quickly get the cleaners' carts out, and move towards the door instead. He trusted that Martha would come after them. They rushed towards the door but just as they were about to open it, they heard the sirens, which were now very close. Outside, two cars screeched to a halt. Brains peeped out carefully and saw that the police and the men from the Securitas van were already on their way up the steps. When they had disappeared, he nodded to the others, and silently and discreetly the four went out with the carts to their bus, which was parked farther down the street.

'Uff, that was a close one,' said Rake when they loaded in the carts and closed the back doors. 'But where on earth is Martha?'

With the invaluable helmet under her arm, Martha ran into the Gold Room again in a boiling rage. Rake's folly was endangering the entire robbery. They had agreed about the gold, but this was a helmet made of iron and bronze and, besides, it was unique – there was nothing like it anywhere else in the world. She must put it back in the display case so that it didn't get damaged. The first case on the left, there it was; she went in from the rear and put the helmet back. Weird, she thought. Why were men always so fascinated by guns, swords and helmets? Was it because of having done military service, or was it in their genes and in the way they were brought up? Men must have a warrior gene, she concluded, and she rushed back to the elevator where she had left her big bag with the floral pattern. Before she knew it, she was on the ground floor and rushed towards the main door. She wrenched it open, hurried out and ran straight into the arms of two policemen.

40

Oh, this is nice! Martha looked around her in the beautifully furnished room at the police station, where the fittings and colours were well thought out down to the tiniest detail. This sort of nicely designed interior was something you usually only saw on the morning TV programs; indeed, all that was lacking was a few candles. A pity that she had been taken here on account of decidedly compromising circumstances – it would have been more pleasant to sit here and enjoy it all in peace and quiet. She fluffed up her hair and pulled her floral cloth bag closer. It made her feel safer. The police hadn't wanted to give it to her, but then she had said that she must have it with her or else she might die from a sudden heart attack. You shouldn't upset an old lady, she explained, and waved her finger at them. Nobody dared say she was wrong.

The constable had interrogated her for a whole hour but she hadn't revealed anything. She had just talked about the weather and the lovely furnishings in the room and praised Blomberg for his excellent taste. She had commented upon the nice colours and, time after time, pointed to the cozy footstool beside the armchair. Most beautiful of all was the aquarium; she exclaimed now and then with increasingly eager gestures – such nice little stones and plants, and what lovely goldfish! In between she pretended to be confused and she had done this for such a long time that she was absolutely exhausted. Blomberg thumbed through his papers.

'What a lovely aquarium, Constable!' Martha repeated yet again and smiled. She noticed how the gravel in the bottom of the tank glimmered quite incredibly. Just like diamonds.

'Now, listen to me. The aquarium is not mine; it belongs to Carlsson, my colleague. We are talking about gold, not goldfish. Somebody has stolen gold from the Historical Museum.'

'Oh, that's naughty!'

'What were you doing at the Historical Museum in the middle of the night?' Blomberg looked rather grim.

'I was looking for my husband. The alarm went off so I rushed inside to see if he was there.'

'In the middle of the night?'

'That's when women look for their husbands.'

'What?'

'Escort girls! That's all I'm saying. You do know about that, Constable?'

Blomberg found himself blushing but he couldn't prevent it.

'Somebody has broken into the display cases in the Gold Room. How do you explain that?'

'Oh good, did you find my husband there?'

'We're dealing with a crime investigation. This is serious.'

'Love is serious. Always. You have such beautiful eyes, Constable.'

To his great annoyance, Blomberg blushed again.

'That isn't what we were talking about.'

'Don't try to worm your way out. Are you married?'

'You are under suspicion of stealing gold from the display cases in the Gold Room.'

'You don't say, Constable. I'm so pleased – are we going to live there together?'

Chief Inspector Blomberg groaned, wiped the perspiration off his brow and didn't know what he should do. Then Martha got up without warning and went across to the aquarium.

'Well I never, this is really nice. Can I take some fish with me?'

'What are you talking about, woman!'

'But just look – goldfish! Are these the ones that were stolen?'

Martha's ensuing laugh was so shrill that Blomberg simply couldn't take any more. Not another second with this confused old lady. He put his file to one side.

'I think we shall have to do this interview another day.'

'Well, that would be nice indeed. Are we going to meet again? Then I can bring some food for the fish.'

Blomberg smothered a sigh and went across to Martha to say goodbye. She hugged him so suddenly that he fell backwards.

'What a lovely time we've had together!'

'I think it would be best if I phoned for a taxi,' said Blomberg.

'Yes, do that, Constable, but I want to be driven in a racing car,' Martha teased. Blomberg pretended not to hear, and called a colleague, who guided Martha out of the room. Next to the elevator she bumped into a plump, middle-aged policeman with a modern haircut.

'Now who was that?' Martha asked, because she thought she had seen him before somewhere.

'It's that Carlsson,' said the young police officer, who now escorted Martha into the elevator. They went down to the ground floor, and then the officer helped her to go out to the taxi that had been booked by the police.

'Sture Spa in the city centre,' Martha said to the driver. She wasn't going to let a taxi arranged by the police take her home. No, most certainly not. Christina had taught her a lesson or two about leaving a false trail.

Up in his room, Blomberg sighed as he sank back down in his chair. He looked out of the window and wondered what he should do now. He hadn't managed to get a single sensible word out of the old girl. But she was a kind old dear and he couldn't find it in himself to get really angry with her. It couldn't be easy growing old, and she hadn't grumbled and complained. No, she was just happy and confused.

Rapid steps could be heard from the corridor, and Customs Officer Carlsson entered the room. He looked excited.

'Blomberg, you know what? That elderly lady – I've seen her before!'

41

The boss of the Mad Angels, Olle Marling, went into the clubhouse for a beer. He took a can of Carlsberg from the bar, took a few gulps, then put it down on the nearest table. Then he caught sight of the shop dummy. A nice trophy, that, he thought, and took a closer look. Life-sized and with fancy leather gear. But, on closer inspection, he noticed the Bandangels logo. He tried to rip it off, but it was very firmly sewn on. Then he tried to take the dummy's clothes off, but he couldn't manage that either – everything seemed to be glued on. All the more irritated, he looked for something he could use to remove the logo. First he tried a knife, then a fork. It didn't work, and he soon realized that if he kept on that way he would rip all of the dummy's clothes to shreds. He went into the kitchen and saw that the cupboard under the sink was open. Perhaps he could find something there? His eye caught some rags, cleaning liquid, a dustpan and an iron. The iron, of course – that would solve the problem. He went back to the bar, found the nearest socket, plugged in the iron and was soon ironing the logo with a little pressure, back and forth. The glue started to loosen its grip, and, rather pleased with himself, he put the dummy down on the floor so that he could finish the job. He could pull the logo a little, but it wouldn't come completely loose. He turned the iron on again and lit a cigarette. Just as he was about to take his first puff, the dummy suddenly started to burn. He looked around for a fire extinguisher but couldn't find one, so instead he grabbed some bottles from the counter. Quickly he unscrewed the tops and poured Schweppes and lemonade over the fire. As a finishing touch he lifted the floor mat from in front of the bar and put it on top of the dummy. When the fire was extinguished, he picked up the dummy again. The leather jacket was half burned, the trousers were smoke damaged and the whole thing smelled of burned cabbage. Accompanied by a cascade of expletives, he kicked the dummy and then threw it into a corner. The head was knocked out of position and ended up all crooked, but he couldn't be bothered to straighten it. Instead he wiped up the mess on the floor, put the mat back in place and left the room. You should never have a hangover, he thought; it gives you a headache and then you make a mess of things.

The League of Pensioners didn't wait. As soon they'd got home with their loot, they set to work. It was starting to get light out, and they were all very tired but, once you'd started, you had to finish. In a jolly mood, and very pleased with themselves and their own inventiveness, they put the gold inside black garbage bags, filled them up with soil and then planted cute little flowers on top. They had seen the garden experts do that on TV when they prepared things for the summer, and if the pros could do it, then so could they. Afterwards, they allowed themselves a few hours' sleep before the next job. Gunnar kept watch while the others, led by Rake, walked out into the garden to hide the booty. Unfortunately, they hadn't managed to lay their hands on all of the gold, and some of the most valuable treasures were still in the museum, but you had to count on some losses. Or, as Martha said, you can never have everything you want in life, and, anyway, thirty-five kilos of gold wasn't anything to sniff at.

The sun stood high in the sky, and when Martha had safely returned to them, they all walked down to the lilac arbour, and while Martha set out the coffee cups and cakes, Rake and Brains started to plant the gold. Anna-Greta and Christina had gone a bit farther down in the yard to fetch some manure, because Anna-Greta had what she called 'a much better idea' and Christina happened to agree with her. After a while they came back with the wheelbarrow fully loaded with dung.

'Now, boys,' said Anna-Greta with a serious look on her face. 'It would be better to put the gold in a dung heap. Nobody would ever think of looking there.'

'What are you on about?' Rake muttered, leaning on his spade.

'If somebody has seen you shovelling soil here and is wondering what you've got in the garden, then we're in a pickle. Nobody wants to stick their fingers into a dung heap,' Anna-Greta went on.

This was followed by complete silence. Rake looked confused and Brains stopped digging.

'Haven't you noticed how the Bandangels have been keeping an eye on us from up in their house?' said Martha, joining in the conversation. 'I agree with Anna-Greta and vote for the dung heap.'

'Thirty-five kilos of gold in a dung heap.' Christina suddenly started having second thoughts. 'Perhaps that is a little adventurous after all.'

'Yes, but we can put some pine needles and an ants' nest on top,' Rake proposed, and tried to have a positive attitude. Christina had told him that he was forever grumbling and complaining, and now he wanted to show a new side of himself because, with all his heart, he wanted to win her back. The watercolour hadn't been enough, and it had taken longer than he had expected to repair the damage done by those little visits to the brick house. Why did women make such a fuss? A little adventure was nothing to bother about.

'An ants' nest? That's a brilliant idea, Rake!' said Christina and a smile spread right across her face.

'Thank you,' he said in a thick voice, and took her hand in his. Perhaps Christina had forgiven him after all? And he needed that, because Lillemor was a dead loss now. The last few times he had snuck across to the brick house, he had been met with excuses or heard Tompa's voice from inside the house. With Christina it was quite different. She was trustworthy and faithful; you knew you could rely on her.

'But,' Anna-Greta chipped in, 'what if somebody

decides to pinch our manure? Our neighbours, the Bandangels, for example.'

Now there was silence again and they all reflected on what Anna-Greta had said.

'I think we should do what we planned. Bury the gold and then put a bit of manure on top. And an ants' nest,' said Brains.

They all agreed that was a good compromise and finished the digging and put the spades and rakes back in the tool shed.

'Right, then. Now all we need to do is write the letter. Let's sit in the lilac arbour,' Martha suggested. 'That will give us some inspiration.'

'You do know that this is extortion?' said Christina.

'Oh, it isn't so bad,' Brains claimed. 'Really, all we are doing is borrowing the gold for a while. The ransom money will go back to health care, schools, culture and the like. The state will get it all back.'

'Exactly, but it's starting to be too much to keep track of now that they are dismantling the welfare state,' Martha sighed. 'Besides, social attitudes are so strange nowadays. Everybody thinks of themselves, and they don't look after one another like they used to. If it goes on like this, we'll have to work round the clock.'

'Now don't exaggerate, Martha. You don't have to save the whole world,' said Rake. 'You can leave a little for others to take care of.'

They withdrew to the lilac arbour, and Martha served their usual coffee with wafers and cloudberry liqueur. But they were all so tired that they nodded off for a while before finally they started to compose the letter. They discussed various ways of formulating their demands and, as usual, it was Martha who had the pen and notepad. She wrote down their suggestions:

> *We have the treasures from the Gold Room. They can only be saved for the realm of Sweden if you pay a ransom of five hundred million kronor – money that shall go directly to the country's retirement homes, health clinics, hostels for the homeless and schools. Not until the payments have been made in accordance with the accompanying list will you get the gold back. Don't try any tricks: we can hack our way into all bank accounts and check that you have followed our instructions. If you don't do as we say, we can wreak havoc on the finances of the state.*

Martha thought that the last bit sounded youthful and bold and, besides, it was something of a false trail. Then the police would think that some young people had stolen the gold to make things better for the elderly and others who were in strained circumstances. On the other hand, that bit about havoc in the finances of the state perhaps wasn't a threat, because the havoc was already there for all to see, Anna-Greta thought. Then Rake hummed as he thought that over, and said that he hadn't heard from his son for the last six months and perhaps young people today didn't care about others at all, especially the old; no, they only thought about themselves. So, of course, the letter couldn't have been written by somebody young, in his opinion. Then they all protested and said that his forty-year-old son Nils was actually an adult now and as soon as he got his next leave, he would surely come to visit. Nowadays seamen didn't come ashore as often as they used to, and that could make things difficult.

'You don't need to worry. He'll phone you some time. He always does,' Christina concluded, after which they returned to the question of the ransom note. Brains, for his part, thought that the bit about wreaking havoc in the finances of the state sounded rather exaggerated, but Martha was adamant that it was easy to do just that, because the powers-that-be in all countries succeeded in doing it every day. Anna-Greta nodded in agreement and was especially pleased with the phrase 'the realm of Sweden', since it had a cultural ring to it and would indicate that the people who had sent the ransom note weren't just a bunch of idiots but people with education.

'We mustn't forget to include addresses and bank account numbers, so that the money ends up in the right place, and make a point of how music, art and the theatre ought to get at least fifty million,' Martha said.

Martha added the bit about culture and then Gunnar turned on his iPad and they all started to look for addresses and account numbers for retirement homes, hostels, museums, schools and other affected institutions. When the others discovered that Martha had included the Historical Museum among those that would get money, they asked her why.

'First we steal gold from the museum and then you want the state to go in and support it with donations. I can't follow this at all,' said Anna-Greta.

'It's just like with the banks,' Martha answered. 'First they take people's money and then they go to the state and ask for subsidies when they have carelessly lost the money. If you want to know who has inspired me, then guess!'

'The banks, of course,' they said in unison and then fell silent in philosophical pondering.

The League of Pensioners continued to work at gathering account numbers and addresses and when finally they had managed to produce a long list, they were all satisfied except Anna-Greta.

'Aren't we going to keep something for ourselves from that gold robbery? After all, we were the ones who did all the work. We put in so much work casting those image stones too.'

'You can be rich in many ways,' Martha lectured them. 'Giving away money to others is wealth too. An inner happiness. Now let's have a cup of hot tea and print out all the addresses.'

'But seriously, we have worked at the computer and slaved away to find all the information – surely we can have some compensation?' Gunnar interposed. Anna-Greta gave him an appreciative look. She had thought the same, but for the sake of unity she hadn't dared say so.

'Yes, we must have something to live off, too,' Christina agreed.

'Okay, I understand,' said Martha. 'It'll work out. As long as we don't become like the city finance sharks who pile up their money and always want more. Or the people who stretch the law and in the end can no longer see what is right and wrong.'

'You can stretch me this way and that way,' said Rake. 'I don't know if we can regard ourselves as a good role model, exactly, but regardless, we must have money for food.'

'Yes, yes, I know,' said Martha. 'Think about the golf bag and the Las Vegas money. Sooner or later we'll find them and then it'll all be right.'

As they all realized that Martha wouldn't listen to any objections just now, they went back inside the house and started to finalize the ransom note. This time there was no question of cutting out words from old newspapers or anything so old-fashioned. Brains had fetched a fully functioning computer from the recycling centre in Nacka. Using this computer they sent the ransom note in an e-mail and ended the long day by throwing the computer off the jetty and then toasting one another with liqueur.

When Martha went to bed that evening, she was very tired and was soon deep asleep. In the middle of the night she woke up with a start. She had remembered who Carlsson was! He was the Customs & Excise man who had wanted to look inside their golf bag at Arlanda airport. He was actually the last person who had handled the golf bag. What had happened after they had forgotten it on the table? Nobody had been able to confirm that it had been sent for destruction, but neither had anybody seen it in the storeroom or the Lost Property office. And what was it that Blomberg had said about that fish tank? That it wasn't his. Suddenly things were becoming clearer.

* * *

Chief Inspector Blomberg sat in his office, all his thoughts on the museum robbery investigation. Customs Officer Carlsson had received a tip-off about the robbery and had immediately asked the informer to come to the Kronoberg station.

'We must find out more straight away,' said Carlsson, at the same time regretting that he couldn't talk to the informer just now because he had his gym class. 'But you're a real pro, and if you want you can sit in my armchair,' he ended, and hurried off to the sports centre with his sports bag. Blomberg sighed. Customs Officer Carlsson had really made himself at home in their office. The designer plant pots covered almost every available surface, and Blomberg had been lucky to keep one corner of the room for himself, but at least he was next to a beautiful, expensive plant – although he hadn't a clue as to what it was called. The phone rang and reception asked about the visitor.

'Yes, send the informer up!' a resigned Blomberg said.

'Right you are. An old lady called Martha is on her way up now,' came the reply from the reception desk, and as soon as Blomberg heard the name he came to his senses.

'What did you say? No, don't let her in, for God's sake! Not that old girl. What? It's too late; she's on her way up?'

There was a knock on his door and before he had managed to pull himself together, the door swung open wide. This time Martha had on an elegant hat and a fancy two-piece suit and carried a big cloth bag with a floral pattern. She smelled of perfume.

'Well now, Chief Inspector Blomberg, how nice to see you again!' said Martha and she put her bag on the desk. 'I suppose we shall sit here, if you're going to interrogate me, am I right?' she added and went and sat down in the same place as before.

'Interrogate?'

'Yes, I've got a hot tip for you, Constable. And this is very important; it is indeed, so you had better write it all down.'

Blomberg threw a tired glance at Martha and reluctantly sat down on the other side of the table.

'Well?'

'The Historical Museum and the gold that disappeared, you know?'

'Yes, we have talked about that before.'

'I saw a suspicious person when I was there.'

'I thought you were searching for your husband?' Blomberg's voice was dripping with acid.

'Not him, he's dead. No, I saw a police car slow down in front of the museum. I think it was one of those cars with false registration plates that had been painted to look like a police car. One hears so much about that sort of thing nowadays.'

'Yes, of course, a police car with false plates.' Blomberg hadn't bothered to turn the tape recorder on.

'I saw the villains too,' Martha went on. 'They were wearing leather vests with Mad Angels written on them. They went into the Gold Room together with two men from the Grandidos.'

'Yes, of course. They are all such good friends.'

'They hugged one another so sweetly, I can tell you that.'

'Love at first sight,' Blomberg muttered.

'Then they drank beer and paddled in the Wishing Well. It was all so lovely. You ought to have been there! You haven't turned the tape recorder on, Constable. That is naughty!' Martha gave Blomberg such a strict look that he had no choice but to turn the machine on.

'And you know what they said then, the boys?' Martha went on. 'Well, they said that they would share one of their women with each other. Just as if we women were an object to trade. That's a dreadful attitude towards women, don't you think so, Constable? No, that is not something I agree with.'

'I'm not sure anybody would want to use you as an object to trade, so you needn't worry.'

'What did you say? Shame on you, Constable! Just because I'm a bit over sixty, you don't have to rub it in that I don't count as a woman any longer! That was a most offensive comment, I must say! Now you have deeply insulted me. I am certainly not going to reveal who stole the gold now. Good morning to you,' Martha said, and she got up so quickly that her chair fell over.

'Well, I'll say good morning too,' said Blomberg, relieved, turning off the tape recorder, pleased to have dealt with her so quickly.

'Oh yes, I nearly forgot. I've got some food for the fish.' Martha turned round when she was halfway out of the room.

'I'm not sure that is necessary.'

'Oh yes,' said Martha, opening her cloth bag and pulling out a little packet of fish food. Before Blomberg could stop her, she was standing there by the aquarium.

'Come along now, you cute little fish, here's some food for you!'

Blomberg tripped on the fancy rug and, before he could reach Martha, she had poured out so much fish food that the water turned milky and the fish fled in all directions. Then Martha's watch dropped down into the water too.

'Oh gosh, Constable, look what happened. My best wristwatch!' said Martha, and she put her hand into the tank. Then she filled the empty fish-food packet with gravel and stones from the bottom and, to be on the safe side, took an extra handful of gravel before she fished out the watch and put it on top.

'Hallelujah! I managed to rescue it. A good thing my watch is waterproof!' she exclaimed and gave him a damp pat on the cheek. Then she put the packet with the gravel and stones into a supermarket bag and put that into her cloth bag.

'Well, then. I hope the fish are happy now.'

'If they are still alive.'

'Good day to you, Constable. I hope you noted down in detail what I said, so that you'll be able to apprehend those museum thieves. They had such dreadful tattoos. Do you have any, Constable?'

Blomberg took a firm grip of Martha's arm and showed her out of the room.

When she left the police station, she walked along to a minibus parked a bit farther down the street and knocked on the windshield. Anders smiled and opened the door.

'Right, off we go. You should have seen his face! Blomberg

was completely bowled over when he saw me again.' Martha giggled.

'Did you get hold of the diamonds?'

'Oh yes, I did indeed, and a bit of fish food followed along with them.'

42

Brains opened the window, stretched a few times and took a few deep, pleasurable breaths of the mild fragrances of spring. He would spend today with Martha and his friends, drink some strawberry tea with cloudberry liqueur, eat Christina's newly baked buns, play some computer games and then, of course, study the motorcycles that passed on their way up the hill. Those bikers did seem a bit dangerous, but if you were nice to them, then surely nothing nasty would happen, would it?

Brains put on a jacket and went outside to the mailbox to fetch the mail. Then he discovered that the name on the mailbox was now almost unreadable – somebody had scraped it so that it was all buckled and the name was hard to decipher. That was bad luck! Oh well, he could repair it and then put a new nameplate on the box too. Brains went in to fetch his toolbox and returned with it in the basket of his walker. He quickly glanced up the hill to where the Bandangels had their clubhouse and wondered if one of them had deliberately crashed into the mailbox. Deep inside, he was actually slightly afraid. Of course, he loved talking about motorcycles with the bikers, the way men do, but this biker gang did rather give him the shivers. They had more or less threatened Martha when she refused to lease the land to them. What would they do next? You had to be very careful with these sorts of people. It felt as though one of them could knock him down with a little finger. Of course, he most probably wouldn't have been able to defend himself when he was young either. They would have floored him before he had even got his fists up. No, it would be best to keep on good terms with them. Be nice, repair the mailbox as best he could, and then forget about it. You had to make the best of life and not get bogged down in details.

Brains had had a good life and led a comfortable existence, even though Martha perhaps arranged these robberies rather too often. The old girl ought to learn to take things a bit easier. At her age, she was far too energetic for her own good. It would be lovely when finally they got all their millions where they belonged so that they could settle down. Because even though he would rather lie on the sofa or be in his workshop, he had to take part in everything she thought up. He was worried about her, and he didn't want her to get into trouble. Of course, they did have an extremely good time together, and yes, he had become so fond of Martha that it was hard to imagine life without her. Without his realizing how it happened, Martha had become more than just a friend. Indeed, it actually felt as if he had fallen a bit in love with her. A crush on a criminal! He smiled at the thought, and started to laugh to himself. Who was he to talk!

Just as Brains was going to start repairing the mailbox,

he heard the familiar sound of a Harley-Davidson. He quickly got out his cellphone and took a photo. Tompa saw him, slowed down and drove right up to him.

'Did you take a photo? I don't like people taking photos, got it?'

'I wasn't taking a photo of you, but of the bike.'

'Really?!'

'I see you've got a touring model. That's been my dream bike all my life!'

'Yeah, it's a real Road King.'

'That's quite something, almost like a Street model,' said Brains enthusiastically. 'But I saw some even fancier ones at the docks, I can tell you.'

'At the docks?'

'They were mind-blowing. You should have seen 'em, and they were absolutely new too. There was even a shining Electra Glide Ultra that looked as though it had come straight from the factory.'

'You can't fool me. An Electra Glide Ultra at the Stockholm docks? No way.'

'Oh yes it was. An air-cooled twin-cam. Do you want to see it?' Brains browsed through the photos on his phone and opened the image. He held the telephone up for Tompa to look. 'A beauty, isn't she?'

'That she is.'

'There were lots of other good models there too. Have a look!'

Brains clicked image after image, and as the luxury cars and boats appeared on the screen, Tompa leaned closer to get a better look.

'Where in the docks in Stockholm, did you say?'

'Behind the big gates in the old ship-building area. There's simply loads of stuff there.'

Tompa fidgeted with his helmet and asked Brains to show him the photos again. He looked all the more interested, until finally he opened the bag on the side of his bike and pulled out another helmet.

'What about a trip on the bike? Shall we cruise down to the docks?'

A ride on a touring bike? Brains pondered this a few moments. He wondered if he was up to it. But the last time they were in the gym, Martha had said that he had become really quite agile. Yes, there was no harm in trying; he wouldn't get another chance like this.

'Right, let's get on the bike!' said Brains, seizing the opportunity. He took the helmet from Tompa, who put the walker next to the ditch and helped him up onto the second seat.

'You'll be able to get us inside that warehouse so that I can get a look at those fancy things you showed?' Tompa asked. Brains nodded, snorted a little to himself and put on the helmet.

'I can tell you, locks aren't and never have been a problem for me,' he said and smiled one of his most youthful smiles.

Martha hadn't seen Brains all morning and was growing rather worried. He hadn't said anything but had just disappeared. It was unlike Brains, as he always made a point of saying where he was going to be. None of the others knew where he had gone, and Rake simply said that Tompa had taken him for a ride on the motorcycle. Brains would have warned her if he intended to talk with the Bandangels. Martha now felt so worried that she couldn't concentrate on anything at all. What had happened? Surely Tompa wouldn't harm him, would he? What if the motorcycle crashed? Brains could be badly injured!

The very thought horrified her, and she walked back and forth inside the house, going from room to room for a long time before she decided to do some baking. She ought to take better care of him, give him some nice things to eat and make sure they did lots of enjoyable things together. Martha should spend more time with him, quite simply, and not just plan crimes. Oh, do let him come back safe and sound! Then they could go for a walk, pick some berries and flowers and so on. Or, at any rate, pick up all the twigs and pine cones that had fallen onto the lawn.

Martha went into the kitchen and thought about what she should do to bake a tasty cake. She asked Christina for advice, and she turned the whole kitchen upside down in her eagerness to make something delicious. After two attempts, she finally managed to make a cheesecake with a raspberry topping, which was Brains's favourite. It didn't look exactly like it should, but the batter had been very tasty. She took the cake up to her room and laid the table for coffee. Then she got out her knitting and waited. Martha waited and waited long into the afternoon and when finally, after several hours, she heard his steps on the stairs, she was so relieved that she almost started to cry. Quickly she lit the two scented candles and cast a glance at the coffee table, where the cheesecake had the place of honour surrounded by a coffee pot, a dish of wafers and a bottle of egg liqueur. Yes, at the last moment, she had switched the cloudberry liqueur for a bottle of egg liqueur. Egg had a good effect on men, she had read in some advice column or other.

When Brains finally did come into the room, his hair stood on end, his clothes were all wrinkled and his expression was one of pure bliss.

'What a motorcycle, Martha. We ought to buy one,' he said, but fell quiet when he saw the candles. 'Goodness, is there a power cut?'

'Not exactly.' Martha blushed.

'Well, that's lucky, because I really am too tired to get my tools out. You can't imagine what I've been doing today.'

'Well, I've got some idea. Would a Harley-Davidson have anything to do with it?'

'Amazing, you can always read my thoughts!' Brains looked delighted, sat down and pulled Martha towards him. 'Yes, I saw lots of Harley-Davidsons down in the warehouse. And, you know what, a lot of luxury cars and boats, just like last time. I took pictures of the whole lot, and so did Tompa.' He felt in his pocket for the phone. 'I'll show you!'

Martha took his hand in hers.

'Shall we have a cup of coffee first?' she said, and gave him a very serious look. 'You might not believe it, but although you've only been gone a few hours, I missed you really dreadfully.'

'You don't say? By the way, what sort of cake is that?'

'A cheesecake. Well, it might not look so pretty, but it tastes good,' said Martha. 'At least the batter tasted good.'

'Have you made it?' Brains came to life. 'A real cheese-cake, my favourite cake!' He stroked her hair. 'You know what, Martha? Even though I've seen lots of beautiful vintage cars and motorcycles today, I was mainly thinking of you. At one point when we were looking around in the warehouse Tompa got such a hard look in his eyes that I, well, I was terrified and then I thought that, well, I sort of thought that . . .' Brains's voice faded away.

'What did you think?'

'That, well, if I didn't get to see you again . . .'

Brains hummed and cleared his throat a long while because he wanted to, sort of, say something more. In the end he jumped.

'To think that I've met somebody like you, Martha! Yes, you've sort of installed yourself in my brain and heart and you live your own wild life there.'

Then Martha smiled and leaned her head against his chest.

So it turned out that that particular day ended up as one of the most fantastic that Brains had ever experienced. A trip on a Harley-Davidson in the morning, and then a long, delightful time with Martha in the afternoon. Not until the candles had burned out and the coffee was ice cold did they start on the cheesecake, which by then had received a direct hit from a foot or an elbow. But what did it matter on a day like this, because, even though they weren't young any longer, they had made an important decision: they had got engaged.

43

The wall clock ticked away and the pensioners sat in the library and waited for the evening news on TV. They had heard on the radio that the Handelsbanken robbery was as good as solved and that the gold coup at the Historical Museum soon would be too. The police would hold a press conference and this would be broadcast live on the news. Martha and Brains had intended to celebrate their engagement and the retrieval of the diamonds, but now they were at a loss. They realized that things were serious because the Historical Museum had been cordoned off and scene-of-the-crime technicians were busy collecting evidence. Besides, the police had said that the gold robbery would result in long prison sentences. The news on the radio had really given them a scare. Nobody did anything and nobody said anything. They all waited.

Martha remembered the Sollentuna remand centre after their heist at the National Museum the previous year. The little cell with the furniture attached to the wall and a toilet and sink made of metal. She didn't want to find herself there again. Nor did she want to end up in Hinseberg, the women's prison. Admittedly, it was in a nice setting in the countryside and you could be outside, make your own food and do gymnastics, but some of the inmates, oh dear me, no! A shudder went through her body as Martha remembered how difficult that Liza had been, the girl who had threatened her. No, she didn't want to go back there, nor did any of the others.

Never before had the atmosphere been so pressing in the old house. We've just charged along like fools, Martha thought, and realized that they had seen their crimes as a contribution to society; they had wanted to do what was best, and hadn't thought so much about the consequences. What they had done were criminal actions and now the police seemed to be on the tail of the thieves. Before they knew it, the pensioners might be forced to flee abroad again. That was, of course, a good reason to go off travelling in foreign countries, but they couldn't just keep on packing and repacking, could they?

Martha had brought her knitting with her, but even though she was doing her best to finish a jolly, colourful hat for Brains, she kept on dropping stitches and even found herself knitting the wrong pattern. She just couldn't stop thinking that the police might be on their tail. The boys ought not to have used ether, she thought; that might have left some traces. Perhaps it might lead to a few extra years behind bars. But that guard had evidently been something of a know-it-all, and that could make it hard to keep your patience. There ought to be a warning triangle, like they had in cars, for know-it-alls, she thought. Then you could avoid them. The familiar jingle of the news started up and now they all looked at the TV screen.

The gold robbery was not the main item. First came a report about the dreadful financial situation of some European countries. For the time being the problem had been solved by new loans without security, and everyone had gained a little breathing space. Martha didn't think much of that sort of policy; it was like playing Old Maid. No, she thought there should be proper gold reserves and security for all loans.

'At least we have real gold,' Martha said proudly and nodded towards the garden. Brains agreed with her.

'But just because we've got real gold out there doesn't mean we should become arrogant. We have only borrowed that gold,' Anna-Greta said, correcting them.

'But I really do wonder what is going to happen with the world's finances,' Martha sighed. 'Somebody will be stuck with the Old Maid card in the end.'

'Martha, can't you let others deal with the world's economy?' said Rake with a deep sigh. Martha didn't have time to reply because, at that moment, the news about the Historical Museum started. A bearded reporter with a microphone in his hand stood next to a uniformed Blomberg in front of the museum steps.

'Are there still no leads in the hunt for the gold thieves?' the bearded man asked.

'Interpol has been brought in. We have our contacts. Sooner or later the gold will be found.'

'Could you comment upon the ransom demand? Will the Government pay the ransom?'

'The Government will not pay the ransom, as a matter of principle.'

'But it is said at the museum here that the thieves want the ransom to go to the elderly and poor and others in need of support.'

'I don't wish to comment on that. Our job is to find the criminals.'

'The Timboholm treasure and the rest of the gold in the display cases are an irreplaceable part of our cultural heritage. Is the state really not going to save those treasures?'

'That is not something upon which I can comment. Excuse me.'

The interview ended abruptly and the League of Pensioners watched in silence as the camera swept around the Gold Room and zoomed in on the empty display cases. Martha turned the TV off with the remote.

'Well, there's nothing to worry about just now, at any rate,' Martha said. 'But it would be a scandal if they didn't pay.'

'Of course they must pay,' Brains agreed. 'I can't imagine them not doing so.'

'Regardless, we've done a neat job; you can't see any damage to the display cases,' said Christina, who particularly cared about matters of aesthetics.

'Is that so? Well, you came a long way with the right drill and a compass saw,' Brains pointed out.

'The police said that they were on the way to solving the crime, but they don't seem to have any leads at all. I think they've run up against a brick wall,' said Anna-Greta, relieved.

'But it's surprising they haven't got on to us,' Brains mused out loud.

'Yes, but Christina destroyed our tracks with the fire extinguisher,' Martha reminded them.

'Did you, Christina?' Rake came to life and looked at her with admiration. 'Well, that was brilliant, my dear. To think that you had the presence of mind to do that.'

'You learn a lot from reading books,' Christina answered and nonchalantly put on some more lipstick to improve her colour. 'But those are books. I don't know whether computer games can teach you as much.'

Rake fell silent.

'But what should we do? The state has not paid out anything – there's been no money given to the retirement homes or to culture,' Martha sighed.

'And none to our secret account either,' Anna-Greta added. 'Yes, I'm sorry, but Gunnar showed me how to do it, so, well, I did actually set up a little account for ourselves so that we can buy presents when we go to visit retirement homes. The old people were so pleased last time. Besides, we have to pay a lot of rent for the storage space at the docks. That was a really bad deal; we're paying without having a single thing stored there.'

'Okay, okay, we need money and luck has not been on our side. It can't all be perfect,' said Martha, who was feeling more confused than she ought to be. She tried to gather her wits and think about police work, the non-payment of the ransom, and money that had gone astray, but she didn't really have the energy. She wanted to give Brains a kiss instead. 'You know what, when I think about it, the idea of asking the state for money was doomed from the start.' Martha didn't stop there. 'It takes such a long time for them to decide anything, so, before that happens, we'll all be dead. Why not send letters to some venture capitalists instead?'

'Yes, they usually work fast,' said Rake, nodding. 'But they should get something for helping us.'

'A pity we didn't get more gold from the Gold Room. If that hardener hadn't been too old and caused the image stones to break up, then perhaps we could have taken a bit more so that we could give some away,' Brains said.

'Yes, the hardener *was* too old, but it's always difficult to see the expiry date on the packets,' Martha said to console him.

'We can't give the gold away,' Anna-Greta cut in. 'That's state property. It is quite enough with all the other stuff that they have sold off.'

'Can't we create a shell company that those finance sharks can buy?' asked Gunnar as he joined in the discussion. 'Some future dummy company of the sort they think they can earn money with?'

'Yes, perfect!' they called out in unison, but then when they realized that they had no idea how you created a dummy company, their enthusiasm turned into a quiet murmur. They were all feeling a little bit down because, despite their detailed planning of the coup, the gold robbery hadn't given them any money at all. Suddenly Anna-Greta started giggling.

'The gold robbery was a flop, but we have done something new – at least we can be pleased about that. Before, we got the loot but then lost it. Now, we failed to get all the loot and, on top of that, we can't get rid of it.'

She looked at Gunnar and then burst out in such an infectious laugh that the others couldn't help but join in.

'Perhaps it's time to make a new attempt to trace the missing Las Vegas money. Those millions must have ended up somewhere,' Brains added, trying to turn the conversation in a more positive direction.

'You're right. We've taken on too many different things. Perhaps I can make an attempt to hack into that legal firm,' said Gunnar.

'That would be great, because Beylings seems like a shady operation,' said Brains. 'I saw lots of luxury boats and motorcycles when I was in the dock storage area. That warehouse is also full of art and vintage cars.'

'Yes, that's right, I'd completely forgotten that.' Martha looked up so quickly that she dropped her knitting onto the floor. 'When we talked with that security guard, the student with the phone, I jotted down some codes he had next to his computer. Brains, do you remember? It looked like a list.' Martha delved into her big handbag. 'What if we can trace Beylings' clients that way? Why didn't I think of that before?' She rummaged around a few moments, and then fished up a rather crumpled piece of paper, which she handed over to Gunnar. 'Even if Beylings only rent the storage facility, they must have the names of the owners.'

'Yes, of course they must.' Gunnar got up and sat in front of the computer. 'Give me an hour or two, and perhaps I can sort that out.'

Anna-Greta went and sat next to Gunnar and waved to the others to leave. So they went down to the cozily furnished room in the cellar where they had a billiard table, a card table and comfortable armchairs. They played bridge while they waited, as that was something they thought was just as good for your brains as crossword puzzles and sudoku. They found it hard to concentrate and nobody could be bothered to accuse Rake of cheating, even though he dropped several cards onto the floor and, in some mysterious way, kept on winning. Gunnar and Anna-Greta took their time and two hours had passed when finally they came down to the cellar with their report. They had evidently worked really hard because this time Anna-Greta didn't have any kiss marks on her neck.

'Now just listen to this – it's incredible! All those things belong to some city politicians,' said Gunnar, pointing at the printout he held in his hand. 'We found an old list of luxury goods owned by Cornegie and Care Trust AB.'

Brains gave a whistling sound.

'On top of that there are lots of things that belong to somebody called Blomberg,' Anna-Greta went on.

'That's not my Chief Inspector Blomberg, is it?' said Martha, suddenly becoming alert.

'Yes, I think it is, because this Blomberg is a member of the board of the Police Pension Fund. Besides, he will soon be a pensioner himself and he owes the tax people lots of money. So he would have plenty of reasons to do this.'

'I'm beginning to fathom this,' said Christina. 'Our transfers to the Police Pension Fund actually worked, but then something went wrong.'

'Exactly. Because from the Police Pension Fund somebody could trace the money back to our secret account in

Las Vegas. An IT expert or an accomplished hacker has managed to redirect the transfer to himself.'

'And laid his hands on the money,' Anna-Greta added. 'Shameful, don't you think?'

'Blomberg has bought paintings, cars and boats for hundreds of millions recently, and they have all been registered as belonging to Beylings,' Gunnar went on. 'That simply can't be a coincidence.'

'But what has that got to do with us?' Rake wondered, finding it hard to keep up.

'The things that Blomberg has bought, including paintings by Liljefors and Zorn, are worth about two hundred million. So Blomberg has got at our transfers via the pension fund and then redirected the money to his own account.'

'What a villain!' Rake rolled his eyes.

'The swine!' Martha exclaimed. 'Gunnar, let me look at those computer printouts.'

Gunnar handed them over and Martha studied the list carefully for a long time while the furrow between her eyebrows grew all the larger.

'Now listen to this. We're going to get at that Blomberg and all those crooked politicians. We'll get every krona back. I'll see to that.'

'But Martha, my dear, how are you going to do that?' Brains asked, with a worried look on his face. 'We aren't going to commit some more crimes, are we?'

'I've had an idea. We shall delegate,' said Martha.

44

'Good morning, nice weather today!'

Brains had waited a long time before finally he caught sight of Tompa. Then, quick as a flash, he had put on his overcoat and hurried out. When the biker came walking down the slope, Brains pretended he just happened to be on his way to their mailbox. He raised his cap.

'Hello!' Tompa answered.

'You know what? I found this in my desk drawer. I don't think you will ever have seen such a fancy bike,' said Brains, fumbling in his coat pocket and pulling out a wrinkled old photo. 'A beauty, isn't she? This is what I had when I was eighteen and picked up the girls with. The wife fell for it straight away.'

'Yep, girls go mad when they see one of those.' Tompa caressed the photo with his thumb a long while before handing it back.

'But that bike simply doesn't compare with those luxury goods we saw in the warehouse,' said Brains. 'Jesus, that was quite something! That legal firm, Beylings, must be stinking rich.'

'Beylings? Do you know about them?'

'Yeah, I mean they own the stuff we saw.'

Tompa straightened his back and gave Brains a searching look. 'You're right, man. They are smart. And their clients . . . Beylings make those shady types even richer,' he said with an edge in his voice.

'And all the luxury boats, cars and all the art that just stands there collecting dust,' Brains sighed.

'Oh yeah, those guys in fancy suits look very fine on the outside,' Tompa spat onto the gravel. 'Some criminals just look prettier than others, but they're all the same.'

'The thing I was wondering about was that Beylings can't own all that stuff themselves, or what do you figure?' Brains asked. 'Perhaps it's just in their name?'

Tompa looked pensive.

'Yeah, right. Even shady types need good lawyers. I bet you that Beylings are scared this could come out. I've got to go now, see you, man!' Tompa suddenly found himself in a great hurry and rushed off. Brains watched as he hurried on his way, then he checked the mailbox and went back inside the house.

'Well, how did it go?' Martha asked when she met him in the hall.

'According to plan, my dear! I have sown some seeds. He'll soon be going places.'

Tompa didn't need many days to think this over. By the end of the week, he had Jörgen onside and, on Friday, just before lunch, they set off to the city. They roared past Stureplan, and at the Riche restaurant they drove up onto the sidewalk and took off their helmets. Jörgen ran his fingers through his sticky hair and Tompa undid the buttons of his leather vest. It was rather warm to be in leather and heavy boots at this time of year, but sometimes it was necessary. With a well-aimed kick, he sent an empty beer can flying over the road.

'Ready?'

Jörgen nodded and together they strode off in the direction of Beylings. They stopped at the fancy entrance on Birger Jarlsgatan 4E, where a red mat and beautiful oil paintings could be seen inside the lobby. They rang the bell and when a woman's voice asked who it was, Tompa replied in a light voice: 'Flower delivery for Beylings.'

Once inside the lobby they adjusted their leather vests and took the elevator up. They found the lawyers' office on the third floor and rang the doorbell. Tompa paced back and forth impatiently in the hall. Even though he had done this many a time before, he always felt a bit uncomfortable. Now it was high time that the Bandangels showed some results. As yet, the Mad Angels board hadn't voted to admit the gang. So they needed to step up their game. They had to show what they could do.

A secretary opened the door. On the way in, Tompa noticed that the hinges of the security door had had a bit of a knock. Excellent – then the alarm wouldn't work properly.

'We're here to see Mr. Birgerson.'

'His room is down the corridor, but do you have an appointment?'

'We always do.'

Without waiting for an answer, Tompa and Jörgen

went straight down the corridor and looked at the name-plates. When they reached Birgerson's door, they stopped, looked at each other and nodded. With a quick tug Tompa pulled the door open. Birgerson, sitting behind his desk, looked up in surprise.

'Who are you? I don't have any appointments now.'

'We are here to check some things we've been wondering about.'

Birgerson discreetly pressed the button which activated the CCTV camera. Tompa noticed and gave Jörgen a knowing nod. His friend looked quickly around, backed away and silently cut the cable to the camera.

'You must explain yourselves.' Birgerson tried to sound in charge.

'Nice stuff you've got at the docks.'

'I don't know what you're talking about.'

Tompa pulled out his phone and showed the photos from inside the warehouse.

'How in the name of?'

'Motorcycles, boats, vintage cars, art and all that shit. All just been bought. It's amazing that your office "owns" so much stuff.'

There was no mistaking the irony in his voice. Birgerson reached out to the alarm button. Nothing happened. Tompa noticed and smirked. The damaged security door. The technicians must have disconnected the alarm so that they could repair it.

'What are you going to do with all them luxury items? Present for the wife, perhaps?' Tompa teased.

Birgerson didn't answer.

'Ah, I see, you're just middlemen, right. Do they pay you well, those tax-dodgers? You must get paid a lot by them, right? Stinking rich!'

'I have no reason to reveal anything about my clients' business,' Birgerson retorted.

'You are the one who owns this firm. Do the police know about all this? Your shady deals, I mean.'

Birgerson suddenly looked worried, moved some papers on his desk and reached out for his cellphone. Tompa saw the movement and with a quick swipe of his hand the phone was knocked to the floor.

'Get out of here!' Birgerson shouted.

Tompa and Jörgen ran up to him and lifted him out of his chair to his feet. Birgerson's forehead shone and he smelled of fear. They pushed him.

'You know very well what this is about. You have a legal firm that deals with shady business. We want ten million within a week to keep our mouths shut. Otherwise we'll take something as security, yeah, those things in the warehouse will do nicely for that.' Tompa smiled, but it was only his mouth that moved. He pressed a hard elbow into the lawyer's side. 'Have you understood, or should we go to the police right now?'

'But—'

'Economic crime. It would mean a lot of years behind bars!' Jörgen smirked.

'Our firm is not guilty of anything. You have simply imagined—'

Tompa and Jörgen despatched the computer to the floor and kicked the phone into the corner of the room.

'Don't try it. Ten million, we said. We'll be in touch!'

'But—'

'If you don't pay' – Tompa lifted his fist and put it right under Birgerson's nose – 'then we'll have no option but to collect the debt and then you'll be in a right mess. Don't involve the police or it'll be the last thing you do. Your son goes to Östra Secondary College and is a promising member of the Bromma Boys team. You don't want anything to happen to him, do you? As long as you do as we say, then everything will be all right.'

When Birgerson finally retrieved his telephone, the two bikers had already left the offices and disappeared down the street. From below he could hear the sound of two motorcycles starting up and driving off. He went up to the window and looked out. He had too much work, hadn't really had time to deal with all that stuff at the docks, and now some idiot had let those bikers get in. This was looking really bad. The insurance premiums hadn't been paid yet and he certainly didn't have ten million. The firm was not doing well, even though he tried to keep up appearances, and, as if that wasn't enough, this had happened. Birgerson could usually control himself, but he started to weep. He had no idea how he could solve this.

Customs Officer Carlsson stuck his USB into Blomberg's computer and clicked on the icon. This time he had downloaded the CCTV footage from the Historical Museum and the Gold Room. He leaned forward and pointed.

'Here, Blomberg, here's the old lady I told you about. I

recognize her from before, when I worked at the airport. She's on the images from outside the Handelsbanken branch too.' Carlsson put his finger on a shadowy picture of Martha when she was walking round and round the Wishing Well with something bulky over her shoulder, perhaps a large handbag. Now and then she leaned over the railings and studied the money in the water; sometimes she spoke to some other elderly people. 'Surely that's the same old woman you interviewed?'

'Oh my God, it's her. No, please, not her again!' Blomberg moaned and put his hand on his forehead.

'Did you arrest her?'

'No bloody way! I couldn't get rid of her quick enough. She is totally cuckoo. She just happened to be there at the museum.'

'She happens to be in an awful lot of places. Just look at the CCTV images. Right after the robbery she's got something big and multicoloured under her arm. It looks like a helmet.'

Blomberg pointed with a pen at the screen and laughed.

'That bulky thing, oh yes! You know what that is? That's her cloth bag. It's got a big floral pattern and it looks really weird. And guess what she has inside it? Fish food!'

'Fish food, are you sure?'

'Yes, I'm sure, and if you bring that old hag in one more time' – Blomberg searched for something he could threaten Carlsson with – 'then I'll move all your flower pots and change the furniture!'

45

The League of Pensioners could be exposed any day. The plants down in the garden were growing at great speed and the valuable gold was being covered by the longer and thicker roots. The group of friends waited patiently. The days passed and soon it was June, but neither the state, the city government nor anyone else had offered to pay any ransom money. What if a rabbit started to dig tunnels out in the garden and happened to kick up a gold necklace or a gold nugget? A new neighbour right at the bottom of the hill had acquired a horse. What if that got loose? No, it didn't feel at all safe having gold in the garden, and it hadn't given them any money either. In their big old house the pensioners were beginning to despair. They had written letters to venture capitalists and finance sharks but nobody, absolutely nobody, had shown the slightest interest in Sweden's cultural treasures.

'We should have written that we had a home-help service or a retirement home for sale, and then we might have got an answer,' Martha sighed.

'Or a school,' Brains added, and they all nodded in agreement and despaired a little longer.

The police, too, were remarkably silent. No new bulletins, not a word. The detectives had got nowhere, or perhaps they were sitting somewhere ready to pounce. The worry spread among them, and Martha had her hands full trying to keep up their spirits. She scheduled a few extra gym sessions to keep the gang in shape and tried to console each one of them with the claim that nobody would dig up a herb garden full of manure without reason. When the others didn't react, she raised her voice and said more forcefully:

'Especially not a herb garden that has an ants' nest in it too!'

At least Rake could agree that she might be right.

Nothing happened at the Stockholm docks either, and Martha and Brains began to wonder whether their plan had perhaps failed. Now and then they also discussed whether they should make a big announcement of their engagement just to break the stalemate. But then they wanted a party mood to surround their news, and that certainly wasn't present now. What was the point of proclaiming such good news if nobody felt like celebrating? No, first they must deal with the awkward situation they had put themselves in. Some of Sweden's finest ancient treasures were buried in their garden, and they couldn't remain there forever.

'There is something I didn't know about our new direction in life,' Martha said a little later in the evening when she and Brains sat talking in her room. Even though they hadn't told anybody about their engagement, they often snuck into each other's rooms. It was nice to have a visit, and a little more exciting like this when you didn't take each other for granted. Besides, Martha thought that it was a good thing Brains had his own room because he was extremely messy.

'New direction in life?' Brains said, kicking off his slippers. 'In what way?'

'Yes, we have changed from acting quickly to waiting. For that you need patience.' Martha put on her nightcap and reached out for her earplugs. Despite using a mouthguard, Brains snored something terrible.

'Perseverance and patience, that's what it's about. Patience, yes – such good training for you, my friend.'

'What did you say?'

'Hmm, well, that you look cute in your nightcap.'

'You are sweet, Brains,' said Martha, and she gave him a little hug.

At dawn, Brains was suddenly woken by mysterious sounds from down by the bay. Not motorcycles, no – it sounded like a large Evinrude outboard and a hot bulb engine. He shook Martha.

'Martha, I can hear boats coming into our bay.'

Martha and Brains hastily put on their bathrobes and looked out. From the balcony they could see a Pettersson boat and two luxury boats berthing at the jetty. Dark-clothed Bandangels members made fast and jumped ashore. The motorboats had only just arrived when new, unusual sounds could be heard.

'A Bentley,' Brains claimed confidently.

'What did you say, darling?'

'A Bentley, and oh my God – here comes a Jaguar too!'

'Goodness me,' said Martha.

Martha and Brains looked out towards the road. A parade of cars drove up the hill. Now everybody in the old house woke up and soon the rest of the gang joined them on the balcony while car after car and motorcycle after motorcycle drove past.

'Do you recognize those cars, Brains?' Martha asked as, despite being so tired, she wanted to know if their plan had worked. But her sweetheart was in a world of his own at the sight of all those fantastic vehicles, and she couldn't get a sensible word out of him.

'Here comes an old Model T Ford and here are some Harley-Davidsons,' Brains sighed, quite lyrical at the sight.

'Yes, what a fantastic convoy,' said Rake, and he rubbed his eyes. 'I've never seen so many luxury cars in one place all my life.'

Some of the luxury cars were parked on the Bandangels' land, but when the yard was full, the rest of the vehicles were directed across to their own land.

'They do just what they want – they are completely ruthless,' said Christina when she saw that car after car and trailer after trailer with boats of various sizes were being parked on their land.

'Shush, Christina. Let them be. This is what we've been waiting for,' said Martha.

Brains, who had been silent for a few moments, now started to pace nervously up and down the balcony.

'This is just crazy, Martha. I feel so terribly guilty. They seem to have emptied the whole warehouse at the docks. I wonder how they got hold of the keys, or have they hot-wired them all?'

Martha took his hand. 'Brains, dear. The shady deals that the Bandangels and Beylings are involved in are their own doing. You haven't done anything. You just spilled the beans.'

'Yes, I know, but I did it on purpose and I was the one who showed them where the goods were.'

'It will turn out well, just wait and see.'

'Hmm, if you say so,' said Brains, but he still looked rather unhappy. He had come to realize that this was more dangerous than he had anticipated. After all, he had seen all those cars and boats in the dock warehouse and now they were all on the way here. Tompa might figure out that he would recognize them and might even want to silence him. Brains pondered this, but didn't say anything to Martha. He didn't want to frighten her.

They watched for a long time as their land was covered with cars. In the end, it felt as if it was just noise and images. Exhausted, they went back in.

'I think we've had enough excitement now,' Martha announced, and she closed the balcony door. 'Let's go to bed again; we need all the sleep we can get.'

They all agreed this was a good idea, and retired to their rooms. It was quite a while before they could fall asleep again. It is hard to sleep when stolen goods worth millions of kronor have been put on your land.

46

They had a rather late breakfast the next day, and after drinking coffee and eating eggs, yoghurt and muesli, they were all back on form. Martha got up and took Brains upstairs with her. They had a look out of the window. The whole slope was a mess of tire tracks, and the most luxurious cars, trucks and boats were still outside.

'This is just crazy. A whole yard full of luxury goods,' said Brains.

'Yes, now is the time for you to act,' said Martha. 'You must make sure you get really angry now, Brains – make a hell of a fuss.'

'Angry? But that isn't so easy, Martha dear. I never lose my temper.'

'But can't you see! The whole yard is full of stuff that isn't ours. It would be strange if we didn't get furious!'

'But it's not that. How can I be really angry when I'm not? I'm just so happy and pleased that, well, you know, you and I . . .'

Martha heard what he said, felt a warm sensation deep inside and completely lost track of what she had been thinking. Suddenly the Great Plan didn't seem as important any longer. A hug from Brains and she would feel just as good as after a bank robbery. She was still for a moment.

'To think that I had to wait such a long time for someone like you,' Martha mumbled almost inaudibly. 'It really is so nice that we can do lots of fun things together. Cozy up and all that . . .'

'Yes, yes of course.' It's just that I find it hard to keep up with all your ideas, Brains thought, but he was diplomatic enough not to say it out loud. Instead, he smiled and pulled her towards him. Then suddenly they heard footsteps on the stairs, upon which they moved a few fumbling steps back, cleared their throats and mumbled something about a big and important task that waited. Then they went down into the kitchen.

'We must tie up the loose ends now,' said Martha, and she nodded to the others. 'It's high time we confronted the Bandangels, and we're going to manage it.'

'What are you talking about? I don't understand,' said Christina.

'We're going to try to give a nasty telling-off to a gang of bikers who have clubs and knuckledusters,' Brains explained, now looking decidedly pale in the face.

'Oh goodness me!' said Christina. 'You are brave.'

'Perhaps Gunnar can go along with you?' Anna-Greta suggested, and looked around her, but he had already disappeared.

'I'll sort this out. Sometimes you must make an extra effort,' said Brains, and he felt encouraged by their support, but, deep inside, he had never been so afraid in all his life. Martha saw the look in his eyes.

'I'll come with you,' Martha decided. 'It always feels better if there're two of you, don't you think?'

A little while later, Brains took Martha by the arm and together they walked up to the yellow house. Once there, they straightened their backs and hammered on the door with heavy, deliberate thumps. Tompa opened it and broke into a big grin when he saw his elderly neighbours. He didn't ask them to come in; he just stood there in the doorway.

'Well, it's about the vehicles on our land. That's our land,' said Martha.

'And?'

'Well, we need our land, quite simply,' said Brains, minding his words. 'We are somewhat angry over your having put a load of trash there.'

'Trash? What do you mean? Are you calling a Cruiser trash?'

'Not exactly, no, I didn't mean that, but the cars block the view and we can't grow our flowers and it's a bit hard to move around with all the vehicles you've parked there.'

'Listen! We're keeping our stuff there as long as we need to. Got it? You could have rented the land to us, but now it's too late. You've only yourselves to blame.'

'But it's our land,' Martha protested, in a firmer tone this time.

'Are you hard of hearing or what?'

'But how long are you going to leave your stuff there, then?'

'That's up to us.'

Jörgen appeared in the doorway too. His torso was bare and Martha saw that his entire chest was tattooed.

'Sorry, we haven't got time for you now. Get lost!' Jörgen said.

'Can you move it all by Monday?' Martha insisted.

'No way. We're going to Copenhagen. This'll take the time it takes.'

'But the lawn and the garden?'

'Listen, we're going to the AGM, do you get it? Just cool it; the grass will grow again, okay?' Jörgen started to close the door.

'But, please . . .' Martha attempted again.

'Get lost, I said.'

Martha and Brains withdrew, Brains took Martha by the arm again, and they walked slowly down the hill. When they got back inside their own house, they looked relieved.

'Just like we thought, and like it says on their website,' said Brains. 'They're going to the Mad Angels Annual General Meeting in Copenhagen. So we can get going straight away!'

'Should we really go ahead with this? What if somebody sees us?' Christina worried.

'Don't you worry. This is going to work, you wait and see,' Rake said to console her, and he put his arm around her shoulders. Then she looked at him in amazement, speechless. Rake was his old self again now, just like before that hocus-pocus woman turned everything upside down.

* * *

On Friday evening, the Bandangels left the yellow house, and motorcycle after motorcycle roared past Myrstigen in a cloud of exhaust fumes. The League of Pensioners stood on their balcony and watched the spectacle. When the last bike had left, Martha wiped her hands on her apron and looked very decisive.

'Now, my dear friends. I'm afraid there won't be any cloudberry liqueur this evening. We have too much to do.'

'Can we really be absolutely certain that they have all left the house? Can you guarantee that nobody will come back?' Christina was really worried.

'You can never guarantee anything in this life. But sometimes you have to take a risk. It's only then that things can change or develop into something better,' said Martha.

'Or worse,' Rake muttered.

'This time I reckon it's going to work fine,' Brains hurried to add. 'Don't forget that we have an awful lot to struggle for.'

'Health care, social services and retirement homes . . .' Anna-Greta started to say.

'Home-help visitors and culture,' said Rake.

'And schools,' Christina added, but at that point Martha cut her off.

'We can have a critical look at society later on. First things first, we've got to take the photos and get measuring,' she exclaimed. 'Brains and I will take pictures of everything, and you, Christina and Rake must make a list of all the details of makes and models, and measure everything in the garden and on the lawn. And don't forget the boats down by the jetty.' Martha handed over a tape measure stained with PVC plastic from Brains's image-stone castings.

'But what about Lillemor? She might start wondering,' Christina pointed out.

'There's no risk of that. She's at one of those Tarot séances all weekend,' said Rake.

'Ah, right, then she'll be in her own world. As usual, that is,' Christina snapped, still finding it hard to stomach the thought of the dark-haired gold-digger.

'Gunnar, perhaps you could help us transfer our photos to the computer as usual,' Martha continued without bothering about what her friend had said. Gunnar nodded in delight, pleased to be at the centre of things once again.

'We must make sure that all the details and product numbers et cetera match with the measurements and the right photographs. Well, you know what I mean.'

'Indeed,' he answered with a jocular salute.

'Righto, then, let's get going!' Martha commanded, but not before Brains had been up to the yellow house and made sure that nobody was home. Christina had informed Anders and Emma what was going on so that they would be available during the weekend should help be needed.

'Well, there's lots to do today, but at least we don't have a gym session,' remarked Rake.

They all set off and enjoyed the fact that it was June and light outside until very late in the evening. Making a note of all the names and details of everything, as well as measuring cars, motorcycles and motorboats worth alto-gether almost two hundred million, took time. The hours ticked by, and not until nine in the evening had they finished the practical work. Then it all had to be entered into the computer. Martha served coffee and tea with toasted sandwiches and after a little break they continued with their work. Close to midnight everything was finished, and by then they had put everything on the Internet sales website, including two paintings they had found inside the cabins of one of the yachts.

'Right, take the chance to get a bit of sleep now,' said Martha, 'because you never know. We might have an awful lot to do tomorrow.'

At that moment she didn't know just how true that would be.

47

Olle Marling was in a dreadful mood as he tramped around inside the Mad Angels' shabby old clubhouse in Orminge. He had touched a hot exhaust pipe with his foot and the burn had become infected – blood poisoning. The doctor had told him to rest and keep still, but of course he wasn't going to do that. Mad Angels clubs from all of Scandinavia would be meeting down in Copenhagen the next day and he had lots of things to organize for the AGM. He'd go down south on his bike with some colleagues later in the evening, as soon as he had finished. But he was so tired and his foot hurt like hell. He'd better fortify himself with a beer. He took a can out of the fridge and looked for the opener. Then he caught sight of the burned shop dummy.

'Oh!' he groaned to himself and held up the wretched mannequin. The leather clothes were hanging in tatters and one boot was missing. The dummy looked ridiculous. He slowly drank the beer and limped out of the clubhouse. Outside, the sun was shining and there wasn't a cloud in the sky. It smelled of grass and newly planted flowers, and the leaves fluttered lightly in the breeze.

Down in the garden a flock of birds was cackling. He limped across to the garden and waved his arms to frighten them off, but they just flew up a few metres, circulated several times and then landed again. They were eating the vegetable seeds. Olle Marling sighed. Angry, he went into the tool shed and fetched an old rake. From the toolbox he took out a knife and sharpened the end of the handle. Then he went into the clubhouse again and fetched the shop dummy. The head was loose, but he screwed it back on as best he could. Then he pushed the handle inside the dummy's half-burned leather gear. It wasn't easy and it took a while, but when he had finished he took a step back and looked at his creation with pride. A perfect scarecrow. Pleased with his work, he took the dummy under his arm and limped off back to the vegetable garden again. Once there, he stuck the rake handle into the ground and hammered it in place as firmly as he could. Then he stepped back and admired the result. A neat job, he just had time to think before the birds returned and started pecking at seeds the same as before.

He swore and decided to dump the wretched dummy in the garbage bin. He had had his fill of it. He remembered the party, when they'd made a fool of him in front of everybody: that embarrassing raffle prize, and how in his anger he had just grabbed the shop dummy when he left. Since then it had mainly just been in the way. It was high time to get rid of it. Or why not give the Bandangels something to think about? He found himself thinking about the mafia and how they left the chopped-off head of a horse as a sign. Yes, the Bandangels could get their dummy back, sure, and there was no doubt that the burned body would scare them. He couldn't imagine a better way to get his revenge. He laughed and went back into the clubhouse with the dummy.

Rake was busy out in the garden when he heard the noise from down the road. A motorcycle courier drove up the hill with a large packet. He got off his bike and rang the bell of the yellow house but nobody opened up. He tried once more but, as it seemed to be dead up there, he looked around and saw Rake lower down the hill. Then he got onto his bike again, drove down to the mailboxes and stopped at the gate. He waved to Rake to come to him.

'I've got a package for that lot up there. Do you know when they'll be coming home?' he asked.

'In two days,' said Rake, and he glanced suspiciously at the package. 'Actually, they asked me to take care of their mail and any deliveries while they're away. If you want, I can sign for it?'

The courier didn't seem to have any qualms about that; he pulled an electronic pad out from his leather vest and gave Rake a pen-like stick to sign with.

'Just a signature, that'll do.'

Rake nodded, scribbled something illegible, and handed the pad back. Then the courier untied the package from the carrier and leaned it against the fence.

'Well, then, have a nice weekend,' he said, and he kicked the motorcycle back into action. Rake raised his hand in farewell. Then he called to the others to come over.

'What was that?' Brains asked, as he looked at the man-size rectangular package.

'I think I know,' said Rake. 'Just look at that shape. What else could it be but our missing mannequin?'

'But how in the name of? Then we'll take that back right now!' Anna-Greta exclaimed.

Martha came forward and had a look. She carefully started to unwrap the package while the others stood around watching.

'Oh my God, it *is* our mannequin, but look, it's been burned!'

'What did you say?' Brains cut in, and then he, too, looked inside the wrapping paper.

'What if the banknotes have all burned up?' said Christina as she, too, approached cautiously.

'It must be a practical joke. Or some sort of revenge for what happened to Olle Marling at the party,' Rake said.

'Well, it doesn't matter anyway. The main thing is that the money has come back to us,' Anna-Greta added in a satisfied tone. 'All we have to do is empty the mannequin, right?'

'Do we dare do that?' Christina wondered.

'Oh yes. Then we can just put the mannequin back again so that nobody will know,' said Martha, and she started to unscrew the head. 'Oh, thank the powers above, this is our lucky day. Look, the banknotes are still there!'

'Right, then,' Anna-Greta announced, and she rolled up her sleeves and dug her hand down into the millions. A happy smile spread across her face while she felt the bundles of bills with her fingers. 'Oh, lovely banknotes. How wonderful. They feel as though they are real,' she sighed.

'No, stop, I know what. I've got a better idea,' Martha suddenly broke in.

'What now? There are several million kronor here!' Anna-Greta protested.

'The money from the Handelsbanken robbery is marked.'

'We can always launder it. Solvalla horse races!' said Anna-Greta nonchalantly, with both her hands now stuck deep into the mannequin.

'That's true, but sometimes it pays to think a step further,' said Martha, looking carefully around her. 'Now we'll take the mannequin up to our dear neighbours. It's what the Mad Angels wanted and I think it would be wisest for us to do that. I promise you, this is going to be the best thing for us too. Trust me.'

Anna-Greta opened her mouth to say something, but stopped herself at the last second when she saw Martha's determined expression. Reluctantly, she withdrew her hands from the bundles of banknotes and straightened her back. Then she looked on sadly as her friend screwed the head on again and put the mannequin back in the wrapping, after which Brains balanced the package on his walker and set off up towards the yellow house – with five million kronor.

Since the League of Pensioners had advertised on the Internet, people had been phoning like mad. Anna-Greta had written: 'Final sale from the estate of a collector', which was the sort of thing that attracted people's attention. Car or boat, motorcycle or tractor, it didn't seem to make any difference what she had advertised, every item that they had put on the website had attracted a swarm of eager buyers. To keep some sort of order during the day, they had taken turns manning the telephone and then planned the visits so that not all the speculators would turn up at the same time. It was a good strategy, but they doubted whether it would actually work.

'It's going to be a long day,' said Martha, and she put out four Thermoses of freshly brewed coffee in the lilac arbour. They had eaten a fortifying breakfast, and they would need the coffee and snacks to keep up their strength during the day. The cake tin was full of wafers, and on a bread board next to it there was some fresh bread. Besides that, they had stocked up with several kilos of apples, oranges and bananas, and for Rake – who preferred candy – there were several packets of his favourites. For Brains, she had put out some Fazer's lemon licorice and a strawberry cheesecake that she had made in the morning. Love evidently gave you oceans of energy. She had never before even dreamed of putting on an apron and baking. But since she had been engaged, she just loved it when Brains was happy.

It was lovely weather and there was no wind at all; the water was like a mirror and out beyond the bay you could see birds high in the sky. The first of the huge ferries from Finland was on its way into Stockholm and beside their own jetty there were three large luxury boats: the Pettersson boat, a yacht and a motor cruiser. Two luxury yachts that there hadn't been room for were moored out in the bay. Thankfully, Anders and Emma had promised to help with sales and that was a good thing, too, as it would make everything more credible when so many objects were to be sold. It was only Rake who thought their presence was unnecessary – as far as the boats were concerned, at any rate, because that was something he could best take care of himself. Being a former seaman was one thing, selling boats discreetly was quite another. Christina took a wafer and looked as if she was pondering something, then she said:

'You know what, I've been thinking about this. How can we explain that we own all of this?' She looked out across the garden and the field behind where the boats and cars had been parked so close to each other that you could hardly walk between them.

'Somebody has left it all to us in their will,' said Anna-Greta. 'After all, we wrote in the ads that they came from an estate. We could have inherited all this from a close relative who owned boats, car factories and the like,' Anna-Greta went on.

'That's smart,' Martha agreed.

'What about the art?' Christina wondered. 'One of the paintings is a Zorn.'

'We could have bought that when we were young. It's gone up in value over the years, you know,' said Anna-Greta.

'But then surely we should have sold it via an auction house?' Brains suggested.

The discussion went back and forth while the sun rose higher and the League of Pensioners waited for the first customers. They discussed the different lies they could trot out – but they didn't sound especially credible, so they decided to simply say as little as possible. Most of all, they were worried that one of the Bandangels might come home earlier than expected or that one of the customers would see through them and discover that it was all stolen property.

'In the criminal world things are always a bit uncertain.' Martha tried to smooth things over.

'It's best to just pile on the lies,' Rake added. 'If you tell enough lies, people will believe you.'

'I suppose we could pretend that we are politicians who've been to nightclubs and been caught?' Christina interjected.

'Yes, exactly, and we must improvise,' said Martha. She had hardly got the words out of her mouth when they heard sounds from down the hill. It was now eight o'clock in the morning and the first buyer of the day was on the way. Gunnar got up, ready with his computer printouts, and Anna-Greta had a firm grip on her notebook, where she was going to tick off all the items. Like Martha, she had a belt-bag around her waist where she could put the money when people paid in cash, as well as a shoulder bag with an iPad that she and Gunnar could use to provide the bank details for larger transactions.

The first customer was a man who wanted to buy a Bentley. Brains started up and talked so much about acceleration and horsepower that he completely forgot to sell the car, and if Martha hadn't come and helped at the last minute, they would have missed their first sale straight away. Two motorcycles, a Jaguar and one of the boats were, however, quite easy to flog, and Martha and Anna-Greta praised the Internet.

'It's really fantastic how easy it is to sell stuff!' Anna-Greta exclaimed, and she had to go inside and empty the overflowing belt-bag. Then she put the banknotes in envelopes marked 'Bentley', 'Jaguar', and so on, and hid the envelopes in an old linen trunk. If there were any crooks among the customers, then they wouldn't find the money among all the towels and sheets. The boats and the Bentley were, unfortunately, worth so much that they could only get a deposit and Anna-Greta had to use the iPad to give them a bank account number to pay into.

'I can see from your eyes that you are honest,' she concluded the deals, and then hoped that the buyers really would put the rest of the money into the account. When Rake was going to sell the Pettersson boat, there was some confusion, as nobody could find it. It wasn't there any longer.

'Perhaps it's already been sold?' Rake muttered. He hadn't made any notes as he thought he could remember everything anyway. They had to go down to the jetty while the prospective buyer paced impatiently.

'Well, you see, Pettersson boats are very much sought-after. Real vintage,' said Rake with the look of an expert. 'I think we had a customer here who wanted to take it for a test run.'

'So when will he be coming back?'

'Err, any minute now, I should think. It's a really beautiful boat, I can tell you that. Newly varnished, the mahogany interior has been completely renovated, the brass is polished bright. In fact, I'd really like to keep it myself.'

'A swindler must have gone off with it,' said Anna-

Greta fifteen minutes later when no boat had returned to the jetty. Then Martha remembered the discussion they had had about old decrepit wooden boats and she went right to the end of the jetty, put on her polarized sunglasses, and leaned over the edge. Yes, that was the explanation.

'We can give you a discount,' said Martha, pointing at the water where the Pettersson boat could be seen on the sea bed.

'I'm not here to buy a bloody submarine!' the customer hissed.

'But, my good man, it hasn't been there very long,' Anna-Greta attempted. 'It's just a little wet.'

It was not until they had radically lowered the price that a happy collector of vintage boats bought it anyway.

The telephones rang and one car after the other was sold from the hill. Business was brisk. Vintage cars, motorcycles and Jaguars sold just as well as the paintings that Martha had found in the cabin of one of the yachts. Besides the Zorn, there had been a Matisse, but that wasn't quite as easy to sell. However much Christina swore that it was genuine, people didn't believe her.

'Pull the other one; you've painted that yourself,' they said and shrugged their shoulders, and Christina did actually feel rather flattered. Later, a man who had been fired from his job as a curator at Moderna Museet came by, and he bought the painting at such a high price that Anna-Greta laughed and laughed. New customers were arriving all the time, and by the afternoon, Martha and her friends were completely exhausted. Now they started mixing up the ads and soon they had lost track of what they had sold and what was still for sale.

'What does it matter?' said Christina, exhilarated. 'This is really fun and the main thing is that we get some money in.'

'But selling a motorcycle from the thirties as a moped isn't very smart at all,' said Brains angrily.

'You have the nerve to say that after calling a genuine Zorn a watercolour by an unknown artist,' Christina was quick to counter. 'If I hadn't seen that, we'd have lost several million.'

'No bickering, we're doing our best. Soon we'll have some coffee and sandwiches, with cheesecake to follow,' Martha cut in, as she wanted to ensure that they all stayed on good terms and kept their spirits up. She tempted them with lemon wafers, too. Just that very moment, more people drove up to Myrstigen and the League of Pensioners had to take care of them. Since they'd had no time to have that fortifying afternoon coffee break, their sales got really confused. Anna-Greta didn't always have time to tick off the items on her list, and sometimes Brains sold the same item twice. In a moment of weakness he was about to sell Lillemor's car because he thought it was so ugly, but he restrained himself at the last minute when he realized it wasn't his. But it was Rake who made the worst blunder when he nearly sold the neighbour's horse by mistake. It was grazing in the ditch nice and peacefully and in the general rush he thought the horse was for sale too. Thankfully, Christina, who, after all, was the youngest and thus not quite so tired as the others, succeeded in preventing that sale at the last moment.

One way or another, one expensive car and boat after the other disappeared and, by the late afternoon, the land outside the yellow house, as well as their own land, had been emptied. They were all totally exhausted and Anna-Greta's horsey neighing laugh sounded much weaker than usual. But she was in top form, because she hadn't handled so much money in one day for years. With a smile she put yet another envelope of banknotes into the trunk, an eighteenth-century wooden chest, patted the lid, which said 'HOME SWEET HOME', and exclaimed: 'Now my trunk is full to the brim, and the money smells of lavender!'

'Yes, and it's such a delight to get back our Las Vegas money, albeit by a very roundabout route!' said Martha. 'Beylings have only themselves to blame for helping villains.'

'Not to mention Chief Inspector Blomberg,' Brains added.

'Yes, it's his own fault. Stealing our money like that!' said Christina.

'Can you imagine his face when he sees the empty warehouse?' Rake smiled.

'Let's drink to that,' Martha proposed, and the champagne came out. 'I'd like to see the Bandangels' faces when they come home. They can kick up as much fuss as they want, but they can't do anything about it. Everything has gone.'

Brains gave a slight shudder and Christina scratched with her index finger on the table top.

'I am a little scared, nevertheless,' she said in a feeble voice. 'They give me such a strict look sometimes. What if they think all that stuff is theirs?'

Then Rake suddenly stood up and looked quite horrified. 'Theirs! Yes, of course. Oh heavens above! We've made a terrible mistake!' he stuttered. 'They don't know that the goods in Beylings' warehouse were bought with our Las Vegas money. They're going to think we stole it all from them.'

'Oh, dear me, what a mess!' Anna-Greta exclaimed.

'Stolen from them? The thought never occurred to me. There is so much one needs to remember nowadays,' Christina moaned.

'Yes, I'm afraid that this must count as yet another of our crimes,' Brains said, with surprising calm.

'Now we're really in deep trouble,' Rake contributed.

'Perhaps it would be best if we give it all back?' said Christina, and she looked extremely worried. 'Or else we must think of something, and quickly too.'

'Think of something? Lord have mercy! This isn't going to be easy.' Anna-Greta sighed.

'It'll work out, don't worry. I've got everything under control,' said Martha, 'Or, at any rate, I ought to have,' she added in such a weak voice that nobody heard. 'We'll leave Värmdö for a while until things have calmed down.'

'Are we going to leave our house?' they cried out in unison. 'No, we've got everything so nice and cozy here.'

'Perhaps I ought to have said something earlier, but neither I nor Brains wanted to frighten you. We actually do have a plan.' Martha glanced at Brains and he gave her an encouraging nod. Martha took a deep breath, put the champagne glass aside and clasped her hands in front of her. 'Now listen to this. It doesn't sound good, but everything is perhaps not quite as dark as it looks.'

The five of them and Gunnar were so preoccupied that they didn't notice Lillemor. She had come home from her Tarot séance at a friend's and was walking up the hill looking really rather content. She was a bit unsteady on her feet and, if truth be told, she had enjoyed many glasses of wine, but it didn't look at all the same here as it did yesterday. The car that had been parked next to her fence had gone, as had Tompa's pride and joy, a Cruiser 16. It took a while before she realized what had changed. At first she stared once, then several more times, and she still couldn't believe her eyes. To make sure, she walked up to the Bandangels' yard to see if the goods were up there. But they weren't. With shaking hands she opened her handbag and pulled out her cellphone. It was hard to press the right buttons and her voice sounded decidedly slurred, but she did manage to say:

'Tompa, you know what? You're not going to believe this, but the yard and garden are empty. All your stuff has gone!'

Then she fell into bed, dizzy and drunk and quite lost to the world.

48

It is decidedly unwise to steal from a notorious motorcycle gang. Anna-Greta, Gunnar, Christina and Rake had gathered around the kitchen table, horrified at the realization of what they had just done. They tried to calm themselves with a cup of hot chocolate, and Martha and Brains tried to console and encourage them as best they could, but they, too, understood that the situation was serious. The most likely outcome was that the Bandangels would think that their nearest neighbours had stolen the bikers' property. So now all the members of the League of Pensioners must be prepared to flee, perhaps even to pack all their stuff and leave the old house for good.

'I'm sorry, but it looks as if we must get out of here, whether we want to or not,' Martha summarized, and she gave the others a serious look. 'And what's more, I don't think we've got much time to do it in. But you don't have to worry. Brains and I have arranged a place where we can hide for the time being, and Anders and Emma will certainly give us some help.'

'Where will we move to? You must tell us,' Rake grumbled.

Martha lifted up her floral-patterned cloth bag and searched for the folder. Although it was plastic, the papers inside had got all wrinkled. She had sniffled and cried a little because she, too, liked living in the old house, and now she had a bad conscience for forcing her friends to move on once again. In the future, she must plan things better. If they were going to commit more crimes, then she must make sure it didn't lead to such turmoil in their lives.

'It *is* a pity that we must leave Värmdö, but we can come back again later. Anyhow, just have a look at this place; it isn't bad at all, don't you think?' Martha said, opening the folder and pulling out some papers. 'Brains and I looked on the Internet and we found this. I think the prospects are good that we can stay hidden yet still be quite comfortable.' She unfolded a map on the table and laid out some photos that showed both the house and the area surrounding it.

The others were a bit grumpy because they hadn't been involved in planning this from the beginning, but then they realized that they had had more than their hands full as it was, and that perhaps it was, after all, for the best that Martha and Brains had planned for them. Towards midnight, the friends agreed on what course of action they should take, and could allow themselves a few hours of sleep. Now it was a question of sink or swim.

'We must pack all our stuff secretly so that the Bandangels don't realize that we are leaving. And not only that, we should have everything ready before they come back,' said Christina, a tremble in her voice.

'Yes, indeed, but we'll manage that,' said Rake, and he patted her on the cheek. His little 'affair' with Lillemor, and Christina's strong reaction, had made him want to look after her better. He had been egotistical and stupid, and even though it had been exciting to be with Lillemor, he didn't want to risk losing Christina for good. Of course he liked his Christina best! He always had. Strange that she couldn't grasp that!

Early next morning, they started to pack. A red-eyed Anna-Greta had been forced to abandon her vinyl record collection and even though they had promised that she could take one box of her favourites, that didn't really help much. After all, she had twenty large boxes full of LPs that she would now have to leave behind in the old house.

'When everything's calmed down we can come back and fetch the boxes,' Martha said to console her. 'Besides, we're moving far from Stockholm, so you'll be able to devote lots of time to Gunnar. That will be nice, won't it?'

Reluctantly, Anna-Greta agreed to pack all her records away in the cellar, and then muttered something about how criminal activities had started to destroy her private life. She and Gunnar got on so nicely in the old house and they had looked forward to many evenings together where they could have eaten well, surfed the Internet and listened to their records together. He had introduced her to Jussi Björling and Harry Brandelius, as well as to Telemann's and Verdi's fantastic compositions. Now she would have to put it all in the cellar and she could not even take her old treasury of horn music with her. At the next meeting she would raise the question of their private lives and insist on lowering the level of their criminal ambitions. They couldn't just keep going on with robberies and ransom demands. Of course they ought to do everything they could for those who found themselves in difficult circumstances, but surely they didn't have to be in such a hurry, like stressed-out teenagers.

There was a lot of stuff that had to be moved. Anders and Emma came to help. They arrived in a Volvo station wagon and had even attached quite a large trailer. The personal belongings of the League of Pensioners were loaded into the back of the Volvo, but there wasn't room for it all. Anders would look after the rest and drive it out to them later. They needed the trailer for another purpose. Together with Rake, Anders attached the trailer to the minibus and then they filled it with all the whisky they had left in the earth cellar, and topped that with some bottles of liqueur and champagne.

'Pity about all the booze,' said Rake, and he patted one of the boxes sadly.

'Okay, ready? I'm starting up now,' said Anders, and he rolled down the hill until he got as far as the corner at the road. They had gathered there earlier in the morning and discovered that that was the only place where you couldn't see either their own big old house or the yellow house. That way, nobody would be able to see that the cars and boats were gone. Anders pulled up the parking brake, got out of the minibus and looked about him.

'Yes, this should do nicely – just a little bit farther,' he noted, before getting back into the bus again. Then he reversed a bit closer to the ditch so that the trailer was leaning over at an ominous angle and now blocked the road.

'Right, that's perfect,' he said, pleased, and got out again. Then he went round to the back of the bus and opened the doors. Together with Brains and Rake, he pushed out some cartons of whisky, which fell onto the road. Then he opened the hood, took out the spark plugs and gave them to Brains.

'Now the most depressing part.' Rake sighed and pushed out some more boxes of champagne and liqueur, which fell onto the whisky so that many of the bottles got smashed. Slowly the precious drink dripped onto the gravel and seeped down into the ditch.

'This is just too sad,' muttered Rake, who always found it hard to see precious drops going to waste. He purposefully went up to the trailer and dipped his hand in one of the aromatic puddles. Then he licked his fingers and thumb for a long time, savouring the taste.

The Copenhagen meeting had gone on a bit longer than expected, but in the end the committee made the decision that the Bandangels had waited for, for such a long time. Their club had been admitted into the Mad Angels as full members. The Bandangels' success in emptying the warehouse at the Stockholm docks had tilted the decision in their favour. Beylings had lost everything when they hadn't paid out those ten million, and now the motorcycle gang had acquired lots of goods worth so much more. Tompa and Jörgen cheered when they heard the decision and then knocked back so many beers that they had to sing and roar out all the time. On the Saturday evening, the celebrations knew no bounds. The bikers ran riot along the Ströget, and in the early hours of the following morning, Tompa, now drunk and crazy, had put a bathing suit on a statue of the Little Mermaid, making her look quite ridiculous. She didn't look any better when he added a hat and sunglasses, and painted her lips with motor oil. In the end, Jörgen had been forced to stop him, when Tompa carved the Bandangels logo on her tail fin and added an 'I love you'. Luckily, Tompa was always in a happy mood when he was drunk, so he had nothing against Jörgen removing the logo, and, singing joyfully, they wandered along the shore until they finally collapsed on a park bench. When they woke up at dawn, they hobbled back to the hotel during a lovely sunrise, fell asleep and didn't wake up until lunchtime, when they had more or less recovered. Tompa was lying half awake, looking rather the worse for wear, when his cellphone rang.

'Who's ringing now?' he complained, picking up the phone.

'Lillemor,' he said, and he pointed at the phone when Jörgen gave him a questioning look.

'Oh yeah, the hocus-pocus woman,' mumbled Jörgen, and he watched as Tompa listened with half-closed eyes and hummed and hawed now and then without saying much.

'Sure, we'll come right away, old girl!' Tompa said finally, and he smiled and put the phone on the bedside table. He turned towards Jörgen. 'She's quite a laugh, that Lillemor. She sounded totally pissed and said that all our stuff had gone.'

'What if she's right? What if Beylings have been there and taken all their stuff back?'

'She was pissed out of her mind. Nope, cool it.'

'But to be on the safe side, I think we'd best leave now,' said Jörgen. And that's what they did.

It was early evening when Tompa, Jörgen and four other Bandangels members came roaring into Myrstigen. On their way up the hill they could see that something was wrong and they screeched to a halt. The oldies' minibus was stuck there with one wheel in the ditch while the big trailer blocked the road. Here and there boxes and broken bottles lay in the road, and some whisky bottles of the very finest sort had rolled into the ditch.

Tompa exclaimed, 'Those old people shouldn't be allowed to drive!'

The bikers got off their bikes and looked at the mess.

'Well, perhaps it's not such a bad thing? Just look at what they've left: whisky and champagne. Let them keep on driving! Let's just take a few bottles!' Jörgen suggested.

'Yeah, we'll just help ourselves!' said Tompa, grabbing a bottle. The boys started to walk round the trailer to see how they could lift it off the road. Then there was a sudden rustling in the bushes and Martha came out from down by the beach.

'Oh dearie me, sorry about this, it all went wrong! I tried to drive and I shouldn't have done,' she started to explain, throwing up her hands. 'But we've phoned for a tow truck so it'll all be sorted soon. Why not have a drink

389

with us down in the sauna in the meanwhile? We've got some pickled herring and vodka too.'

Tompa and Jörgen looked at the trailer, thought it over and glanced down towards the bay.

'You can just leave your motorcycles here. That's all right. They're not in the way. Take a bottle, we can't drink it all by ourselves,' Martha went on, and she pointed at the damaged cartons of whisky.

'Herring and vodka. Yeah, why not? What do you say, boys?' Tompa turned to the others.

The bikers who had driven all the way from Copenhagen and only had two breaks were hot and tired and had absolutely nothing against going straight to a table with food waiting. Herring, and vodka to wash it down – that was never wrong. The old girl was right. They could leave their bikes at the bottom of the hill and perhaps go for a swim afterwards, too. Several hours in that black leather gear had left its mark. They all stank of sweat.

'Okay, then,' Tompa and Jörgen mumbled, and the others nodded in agreement. They took off their helmets and followed Martha down to the beach. There on the terrace outside the sauna stood a long table with various sorts of herring and several bottles of vodka. Koskenkorva from Finland, some flavoured Swedish varieties and a Smirnoff glistened in the sun, and from the sauna you could smell the burning birch logs. It all smelled very inviting.

'Well, now, boys, just help yourselves. There's nothing as delightful as an early summer evening. One should enjoy it!' said Christina briskly, and she tried to hide the fact that her legs were trembling and her kneecaps were shaking out of step. The boys combed their sweaty hair, mumbled a thank-you and looked on with amusement as the old ladies filled their schnapps glasses. Brains and Rake, for their part, served fancy buns and freshly baked bread while Martha put out serving dishes filled with herring, sliced eggs and beets.

'Did you know, boys, that we oldies used to sing in the same choir? Now, let's all join in and sing a traditional drinking song together!'

'*Helan går, sjung hopp fallerallan lej,*' Martha started in a jolly tone and then the rest of the League of Pensioners, including Gunnar, sang in parts and the Bandangels joined them as best they could and with general amusement. '*Skååål!*' they all shouted out across the water as they raised their glasses and then downed their drinks in one gulp. The herring, bread and appetizers made the rounds, and they had hardly started eating before it was time for a new toast.

'Now we shall sing the bumble-bee song,' said Anna-Greta with her thunderous voice, and she held up her schnapps glass. 'Are you ready, boys?'

And whether they were ready or not, Anna-Greta soon smothered any objections when she started singing.

'*We are little bumble-bees, that's what we are, bzzzz, bzzzz. We are little bumble-bees, that's what we are, bzzzz, bzzzz.*' At this point she started giggling. '*We are little bumble-bees and here's a toast for you, we are little bumble-bees . . .*' Then she burst out laughing and lost the thread.

Now Christina took over: '*We are little angels, that's what we are, swoosh, swoosh. We are little angels, that's what we are, swoosh, swoosh. We are little angels and here's a toast for you . . .'*

Then Martha, who realized that these giants would need more than a few glasses of schnapps to get drunk, took over and in quick succession proposed toasts to the sauna, the coming summer, the birch trees, the cowslips and all the whisky that had spilled on the road, while Rake went round after round and made sure that the schnapps glasses were never empty. After a while, when the Bandangels had toasted more times than they could remember, the leather gear started to feel sticky and the smell of sweat spread.

'What about it, boys? We were going to go for a swim before dinner, right? Come and join us!' Brains exclaimed, and he started to take off his shirt.

'Yes, you go for a swim, and I'll start making dinner,' Martha added. 'What about something on the grill? I've got some lovely lamb steaks . . .'

'No,' said Jörgen.

'Now listen, boys. We're still waiting for the tow truck and you have had such a long journey. What do you say? This evening we neighbours can provide dinner. So you can have a sauna and go for a swim. That would be nice, wouldn't it?'

'Well, I'm not sure that . . .' said Tompa, hesitating. He thought about the telephone call from Lillemor and that perhaps he ought to go and check that everything was as it should be. Oh, but if he went to see her now, she would surely insist on telling his fortune and he wouldn't be able to get away. She'd been drunk and would probably still be sleeping off her hangover. Anyway, if anything serious had happened, then the oldies would have said something, wouldn't they? A bit of grub first would do no harm. Lillemor could sometimes be a real fusspot. They were better off with these old folks, and that Martha, she wasn't nearly as weird as Lillemor.

'A bit of grub and a sauna would just fit the bill,' Tompa decided, and Jörgen and the others soon expressed agreement. Relieved, they started to take off their sweaty leather waistcoats and dirty boots.

'Right then, we girls will go and prepare the food,' said Martha, and she started to walk up towards the road. 'Rake, you can help us to get the grill going.'

Rake nodded and followed after the ladies while Brains and the bikers got undressed. They threw off their clothes in the room outside the sauna just like Brains, and then went in and sat on the benches. Brains poured some water onto the hot stones and put all his concentration into not spilling it. Even so, he did spill most of the water because, to tell the truth, he had never been so nervous in all his life. Here he was, sitting naked with six drunk Bandangels bikers, as Martha had instructed. What idiotic idea had she thought up now? Did she care so little about him that she could put him at such risk? Brains tried to keep his spirits up by talking about motorcycles and trips he had made when he was young. Besides, he and Rake had put a whole crate of beer in the sauna outhouse earlier that day, and now and then he nipped out to fetch a few bottles, which he handed round. The atmosphere became all the jollier and everybody was having a good time, although it gradually got far too hot.

Brains ladled some more water onto the stones and loudly announced: 'Time for a swim, boys, right?'

'It's hot in here,' Tompa agreed and the Bandangels members made their way, on somewhat unsteady legs and with merry shouts, down towards the bay. At that moment, Brains suddenly remembered that the luxury boats were no longer there and started to panic. Now Tompa and the others would see what had happened.

'Listen, guys, it's much better to swim from the shore over there,' he said and pointed in the other direction. 'Just run across and throw yourselves in!'

'That's it. I'll race you!' Tompa roared out.

'You go and enjoy yourselves, you youngsters. I must take it a bit easy and have a shower instead,' said Brains, and he stayed behind.

'We're grilling a large joint of lamb. Do you want fries to go with it?' Martha called out from higher up the slope.

'Oh yeah, that'd be great,' Tompa yelled merrily and took the lead down to the beach. 'Last one in is a sissy!' he shouted out, and then dived in head first. Brains watched, and when they were all out of sight, he put on his clothes and hurried up to the road.

'Roast lamb!' he shouted, and that was the signal to the others. Straight away, Rake, Christina and Anna-Greta came out from behind the bushes and hurried to the sauna. They grabbed the bikers' clothes and boots as quickly as they could and stuffed them into large plastic bags from the supermarket. Then they ran as fast as they could up to the minibus, where Anders and Emma were just unhooking the trailer.

'Have you got the old clothes trunk?' Anna-Greta asked when she climbed into the bus.

'Yes, we've put that inside,' Emma answered, a little out of breath.

'The luggage too?'

'Yes, we've packed everything,' said Anders.

'We're ready, then. Time for action!' said Brains, and he opened the hood and put back the spark plugs while Martha climbed in and took up position behind the steering wheel. Many a year had passed since she first got her driver's licence, but she knew how to steer. As soon as Rake and the girls were installed on the back seats, she started the engine and grabbed the steering wheel. The minibus roared into action, and turned so quickly that they almost ended up in the ditch and jerked to a halt again.

'Goodness, it is fast!' said Martha, and she opened the door so that Brains, too, could jump in. 'Hang on, everybody!'

'Yes, what do you think we're doing?' Rake muttered, taking a firm grip with both hands on the door handle. 'Why didn't you let Anders drive?'

'He's got the Volvo. He and Emma have just driven off with the last of our stuff and they're waiting for us farther on.'

The previous evening, Martha and her friends had realized that they must leave the old house and had decided to hide at a place where nobody would look for them, let alone find them. Rake was in charge when they dug up the gold in the garden, but as they were in such a hurry, they were rather careless. The plants had grown so many roots that soil and worms as well as manure and seeds followed along in the rush, and even half an ants' nest full of pismires. But, finally, Rake and Christina could level out the ground again and put all the gold in new black garbage bags which they – with considerable effort – managed to pack in the car.

It had not been easy to make the decision to leave their house, and Martha mourned the fact that she couldn't take her gym equipment with her. Rake had smiled and looked unusually happy. Clothes, toiletry articles, kitchen equipment and everything else they needed, it was all squeezed into the car, which, in the end, was so full that Anders and Emma hardly fit in themselves. But now the brother and sister would, at any rate, be waiting for them at the parking lot just after the Skuru Bridge, so that they could travel together. If everything went according to plan, that was.

Martha drove out towards Värmdövägen at a crazy speed and, already on the first straight bit of the road, she pulled out her cellphone and handed it to Christina.

'Please phone the police!'

Christina keyed in 112.

'Is that the police? Well, it's about the money from the Handelsbanken robbery. You can fetch the money and the villains at Myrstigen 3, Norra Lagnö,' Christina said, disguising her voice. 'The boys are in the sauna at the moment and, if you're quick, you'll be able to nab them straight away. The money? That is hidden inside a shop dummy. It is slightly burned, but don't let that fool you. That's where the thieves have hidden their loot. Hurry now, before those villains have time to escape!'

Christina ended the call and pulled out the pay-as-you-go SIM card.

Lillemor gave a start when she heard the police sirens. Her head ached and she regretted that she had yet again drunk too much cheap wine. She never learned. Nowadays she didn't have a good head for alcohol. Anyhow, it was too late now and she had already slept away the whole day. Clumsily, she rinsed her face in cold water and went into the living room to see what had happened. She opened the door to the porch. Oh, there were the boys' motorcycles, how nice – they had followed her advice and returned from Copenhagen. How strange that they had parked their bikes by the ditch down the hill. And the police sirens, what a dreadful noise! It sounded almost as if the pigs were on their way to her house! A moment later, the sirens were silenced, and two police vans screeched to a halt and deliberately blocked the road. What was going on? Admittedly, the Tarot cards had said that she would experience some exciting events this week, but this was really a bit much! Lillemor went to the edge of the porch to get a better view.

The police officers jumped out of the vans with guns in their hands and ran down towards the sauna by the bay. It took a while before she took in what was happening, but then she immediately went out onto the road. She looked down towards the beach just in time to see Tompa, Jörgen and the others running up the hill with the police after them. They were all sweaty and red and ran as fast as their legs would carry them, with the towels around their waists fluttering like laundry on a clothesline in a storm. One after the other, the wet towels fell to the ground but the boys kept on running. In the end the police caught up with them and managed to handcuff each and every one. Lillemor had never seen so many half-naked, sweaty guys at one time, let alone all being chased by the police. She stared at Tompa and felt sorry for him when two burly officers pushed him into the van together with the other boys from the Bandangels. Then the police checked that nobody was hiding up in the yellow house.

Up there, they didn't find any more bikers, but they did find a shop dummy with burned leather clothes. It looked really hilarious when a policeman came down the hill pulling the shop dummy behind him. And then, just as he was approaching one of the police vans, something weird happened. The head fell off and a bundle of banknotes fell to the ground. Banknote after banknote was caught by the wind and it was quite a while before the policeman realized it.

The driver wound down his side window and shouted: 'Blomberg, damn it, be careful with the dummy. Can't you see the banknotes? The money from the robbery, that's what she said, the woman who phoned. And just look at that! I think she was right!'

'Yes, yes, okay!' Blomberg muttered.

'But run after those banknotes, then, and pick them up!' Carlsson gesticulated wildly.

'And you can shut up!' Blomberg retorted. Nevertheless, he ran after the money, put it back in the dummy and obediently screwed the head back on. Then, still swearing, he carried the dummy the last few paces to the van and asked Carlsson to unlock the back doors.

Lillemor stared. Perhaps not so much at the police as at the half-naked Tompa in one of the vans. While she studied his flabby body, she consoled herself. She hadn't succeeded in seducing him, but perhaps she hadn't missed so very much after all.

The Volvo with its trailer roared along at a decent speed on Värmdövägen and it was not long before the Skuru Bridge appeared before them.

'You must turn off after the bridge,' said Emma, and Anders nodded. Below them the water glistened and the fancy old country houses – reminiscent of the one they had just abandoned – climbed up the steep banks. On the horizon they could see the first yachts of the season and the shores were rich in greenery. Soon nature would be at its most beautiful, but just now they didn't have time to enjoy it. They were on the run, and the oldies would arrive any minute. As soon as they had passed Skuru Bridge, Anders turned off to the right, then took another right turn and finally came to a halt beside the ditch. He kept the engine running.

'Righto, now all we have to do is wait,' he said.

'I'm getting out for a smoke,' Emma answered, and she lit a cigarette, opened the door and stepped out. She put the lighter back in her pocket, inhaled the smoke and started to cough. They could have been out sailing now, but instead Martha had instructed them to 'prepare the next phase'. They were accomplices in a crime, and now she was reminded of that fact. Thank God there wasn't so much more to do. Soon the League of Pensioners would leave the big city and be able to lead a peaceful existence. And Emma did have little Malin to look after, didn't she? There was really a bit too much criminal activity, and five or six oldies to look after, too. On the other hand, Martha had actually given her a million, so later in the summer that sailing holiday would indeed happen. Anders got out too, begged a cigarette and lit it. They stood there smoking quite a long time while they waited.

'Do you think we'll have a calmer life when they leave town?' he asked.

'Well, to be honest, with that bunch you never know what can happen.'

'No, you're right about that. Never!'

When Martha skidded to a halt in the parking lot she saw, to her relief, that Anders and Emma were ready and waiting. They had fastened a sticker to the Volvo with the name SENIOR CLEANERS on it, and everything seemed calm. She drove up beside them and wound down her side window. The two stubbed out their cigarettes.

'Everything's ready, but it was a tight fit getting the cleaners' cart in,' said Anders, pointing at the Volvo.

'And what about the plastic bags?'

'Oh yes, everything's under control – we put them in the trailer.'

'Fine, then we'll change places,' said Martha, and she got out of the minibus. Christina got out too.

'Goodbye, everybody, and keep your fingers crossed that it'll all work out. See you!' she said and she waved to the others in the back seats.

'Yes, we wish you good luck,' said Brains and Anna-Greta in unison, and Rake leaned forward and urged Martha to take good care of Christina.

'But of course, you can rest assured,' she answered. 'We have actually practised this, Christina and I. Practised in secret.'

So when Anders and Emma left the station wagon and got into the front of the minibus, Martha got in the driver's seat of the Volvo. She started the car and was just about to drive off when Christina grabbed the door handle.

'Don't forget me,' she said, and she squeezed herself in with her mop and brush and pan.

'No, no, no way, and that's excellent that you've got all your cleaning equipment,' Martha mumbled, ashamed because, being in such a hurry, she had almost set off without her friend. 'You do have your pills to keep your blood pressure up?' she asked to be on the safe side, because you never knew with Christina, who had a tendency to faint as soon as things started to get complicated. 'Of course,' said her friend, looking in her pockets. But the pills weren't there; she had indeed forgotten them. But then, thankfully, she became so irritated that her blood pressure went up anyway.

Martha took the lead into Stockholm with the mini-bus discreetly keeping its distance two or three cars behind her. When they got close to the Historical Museum, Anders steered in towards the parking lot on Narvavägen to wait while Martha turned into the museum and parked in the drive. There she opened the car door and she and Christina got out of the car as best they could. They went round to the back doors, opened them and pulled out the cleaners' cart with the garbage bags, dusters, cleaning fluids and two red buckets. Martha looked around her and noticed some children on their way in through the entrance, but otherwise it was all quiet. Christina put the cleaning materials on top of the garbage bags and then the two elderly cleaning ladies walked towards the entrance. When they were about to go inside, Martha noticed something strange about Anders' car. She stared at it a long time before she saw what it was. On one side it said SENIOR CLEANERS but, on the other, they had put the sign saying CONTROL UNIT FOR STANDARDS IN RETIREMENT HOMES. Oh dear, oh dear, they'd got it wrong in the rush, but Martha consoled herself with the fact that Control Unit for Stan-dards in Retirement Homes and Senior Cleaners did at least sound as if they might be part of the same organization. With renewed courage, she and Christina went in through the door and made their way to the Gold Room.

'Now we just walk nice and calmly and try to avoid attracting attention,' Martha whispered on their way in, but she had hardly said that before she heard a strange noise behind her. She turned round but, despite looking in every direction, she couldn't see anything close to her. It was not until she rolled the cleaners' cart towards the Wishing Well that she noticed she was trailing a cord. By mistake, they had taken the mop with Brains's built-in compass saw and now the cord snaked along on the floor behind them. If only it had been the battery-driven mop, but this was the first prototype, the one with a cord. Thankfully, the museum had so few staff that nobody noticed anything. There wasn't a guard in sight.

'Don't say we've got that robot vacuum cleaner with us too,' Martha mumbled, but then she remembered that Emma had taken care of that. For a short while she felt relieved, until she noticed that there was something about the long brush. It felt unusually heavy. But perhaps she was just imagining things because she was so nervous, and, besides, there was nothing she could do about it now anyway.

'Right, I think we'll start by cleaning around the Wishing Well,' she said and she tried to sound calm and controlled.

Christina nodded, and the two ladies made their way as discreetly and nonchalantly as possible towards the Wishing Well with their cleaners' cart. The water glittered magically and in the low light you could see the shining coins that museum visitors had thrown in. It was here and now that they should start their much-practised cleaning session and make use of the well. First sweep and wipe the floor, and then in with the gold! Everything ought to work nicely. It was just that when Martha put down the brush, she realized that things were not right. The floor brush was not an ordinary floor brush, but a battery-driven lawnmower. Brains had long since decided that lawnmowers were too large and unwieldy for ladies and had thought up a new variety. To make it especially attractive for women, he had designed it to look like cleaning equipment, and this was evidently just such an apparatus. As everyone knows, you should never be in a hurry when you pack things, and now Martha – unaware of the error – put down the heavy but elegantly designed floor brush and the apparatus started up with a hop, followed by a deep roar, which would have frightened a horse to death. With a noisy clinking and clonking sound, the apparatus set off across the stone floor at a wild speed with Martha hanging on for all she was worth, like a tail. She tried to make it stop, but the floor brush was not even an ordinary lawn-mower; it was evidently a souped-up version.

'What's going on?' Christina shouted in a shrill voice.

'I'm chasing a floor brush,' Martha hissed in reply.

At that moment, in the middle of the thunderous racket, a school class stormed into the room. The noise from the school children drowned the sound of the lawn-mower just as effectively as an underground explosion. The entire room vibrated.

'Oh look, wow that's great!' a girl shouted out the very same moment that the floor brush rammed the railings around the Wishing Well and got stuck. The engine was racing but finally Martha, with shaking hands, managed to find the on/off switch. Still somewhat shocked, she leaned against the railings to get her strength back, only to be resuscitated quickly by Christina.

'Martha, I think there's one thing we've forgotten,' her friend said.

'Just one thing?' Martha answered.

'Just feel this, and then you'll see. The garbage bags are too heavy. We're not going to manage to lift them over the railings and throw them into the Wishing Well.'

'Oh God, not that too!'

Martha fumbled in her pockets for find her phone so that she could call for help but then she realized she had forgotten her iPhone in the car. She and Christina had, of course, only intended to walk past the Wishing Well with their cleaners' cart and discreetly slip the garbage bags of gold into the water when nobody was watching, and then get out of there. Now they were standing, dressed in their white cleaners' overalls, with the cart full of stolen gold while the room was filling up with raucous schoolchildren. Christina started to fumble for her blood pressure pills and Martha searched in her pockets for her Jungle Roar lozenges. Then a gang of shouting boys rushed up to them making enough noise to wake the dead.

'A lady as old as you can't work as a cleaner, can she?' said the oldest with a cap and braces, pointing at Martha. His friend, who was chewing gum, grinned widely.

'No, when you are as old as me, then you're dead,' Martha answered and gave him a piercing look. 'Listen to me, son, I am at least working, but you and your friends are just shouting and making a disturbance. I bet you can't even lift up a garbage bag!'

'Oh yes, I sure can!' The youngster laughed out loud and his friend smirked.

'That's just empty boasting. You couldn't even lift this up out of the cart.'

'What? You think that's heavy?' His friend came to life.

'We can lift up those garbage bags and throw them into the well, but you can't! I bet you don't dare throw them into the Wishing Well!' Martha said scornfully.

She affected a superior laugh, and more than that was not needed. The boy waved to his friends and the next moment they had rudely pushed her aside.

'I'll show you!' said the boy with the braces, and he gave her a challenging look. Then he grabbed hold of one of the bags, lifted it up and threw it down into the well. That was the signal for the others, and now they, too, threw in the rest of the bags to the accompaniment of gorilla-like roars.

'What about that, then, Granny?' The boy with the braces grinned.

'Oh goodness me! Gosh, you are strong, you boys, aren't you!' said Martha, and clapped her hands in pretend admiration.

Then she walked off with Christina, with the mop cord trailing behind them. The two ladies discreetly withdrew towards the entrance and this time when Martha went out to the street, there were, thankfully, no policemen waiting for her. She and Christina could calmly walk back to the car. They put the cleaners' cart in the back, made sure the brush-cum-lawnmower and the mop-cum-saw were pushed in too, and closed the door. Then they drove off and honked when they passed Anders and the others on Narvavägen. Admittedly, nobody had started to chase them yet, but both Martha and Anders drove out of town as fast as they possibly could. Because, even though they had actually given back Sweden's ancient gold treasures, the League of Pensioners was still guilty of many spectacular robberies. It would probably be best to lie low for a while until everything had blown over.

Epilogue

The depressing November darkness rolled across the district early in the afternoon and the rain was cold and heavy. In the dusk among the fir trees, the landscape was deserted except for a tiny flickering light far away. Deep in the forest, if you got close enough, you could see a building with some weak light visible from the windows, as if somebody actually lived there in the middle of this rocky terrain, which was almost entirely covered with forest. If you dared to go closer, you could indeed see an old dry-stone wall around a little smallholding. Behind it was a well-maintained cottage and, behind that, a little yard with a minibus and a Volvo station wagon. Candles were burning on the windowsills. Outside the little town of Vetlanda in southern Sweden, there had been yet another power cut.

'It is rather cozy with candles, don't you think?' said Martha. 'But, Brains dear, perhaps you can start up the generator? We want to get onto the Internet.' She patted the lifeless computer, where they had now run out of battery power. Since Anna-Greta had taught her a bit about computers, she was always wanting to surf the web, and that wasn't so easy here in deepest Småland.

'Yes, Brains, darling, we must get online. It's important that we make our payments in time,' Anna-Greta added.

Their plans for Project All Inclusive were fully underway and it was important to keep the payments up to date. They used gift vouchers and bank cards, which were handed out every week via a flower delivery service to the country's retirement homes and other needy parties. The Las Vegas money – or rather the profit from the sales of the Beylings warehouse goods (depending on how you looked at it) – had meant that they could buy three apartment buildings in good locations in the posh district of Östermalm in Stockholm, and the money they got from rent was used for charity purposes. Gunnar and Anna-Greta saw to it that the money went directly to retirement homes, nursing homes, schools, theatres, museums and other institutions they wished to support, and the recipients received the money together with a bunch of flowers. The flower delivery was not really necessary, but Martha thought it was so much nicer to hand out money that way, even though the League of Pensioners sometimes varied the routine, and sent the money together with a basket of fruit. The Las Vegas income had also been sufficient to pay for a little old forest farm in Småland for themselves, and they had a delightful old building with outbuildings, including a stable, a woodshed and a large workshop where Brains could experiment. They intended to lie low here until the hunt for the gold robbers was over, because even though they had taken the loot back, you never knew what the police might do.

They all missed their big old house on Värmdö, and

the excitement of their life there, but they also knew that the Småland farm was only a temporary solution. Brains hadn't seen a real Harley-Davidson for several months and he consoled himself by going online and looking at pictures of them. Rake, for his part, said nothing about Lillemor, but you could see that he sometimes brought out his Tarot cards. Christina sighed to herself but let him be. Then she realized that she could teach him to pick wild mushrooms, and, after patiently going over all the different varieties in the forest around them, they had gone on long walks together. He became something of an expert and it wasn't long before he was almost keener than she was. Anna-Greta and Gunnar spent most of their time sitting in front of the computer. It was mainly their responsibility to make sure that all the money transfers worked properly, and they liked giving away so much money. They often played their new vinyl records very loudly so that you could hear the music in all the upstairs rooms, but as they had tired of Jokkmokks-Jokke's 'Gulligullan' and horn music, it didn't matter so much. Now they often listened to gospel and Verdi, and the others liked that too.

Martha herself had calmed down a little. Since she didn't have access to all the gym equipment, she settled for a thirty-minute daily session. To keep the others in good shape, she urged the gang to go for a one-hour walk every day, and since Rake hoped to find some mushrooms on the way, he didn't protest like he certainly would have done otherwise.

Indeed, a great deal had happened since those dramatic last days out on Värmdö almost six months ago. In her repentant moments Martha might feel a bit sorry for the Bandangels who had been framed with the Handelsbanken robbery, but people who made threats and engaged in extortion really deserved all they got. It would be decidedly good for them to spend a few years in prison, and to get some nourishing food and be able to get fit. For beefy types like Tompa and Jörgen, a bit of exercise would do a world of good. She had even heard that a stint in prison only served to improve the status of bikers in such gangs, so perhaps the boys weren't so angry after all.

However, Anders and Emma were not exactly in the best of moods after having been tasked with selling the big old house and storing the household effects that had been left behind in the rush. And they were worried about Christina and her friends, who were now stuck deep in the forests of Småland, so they had to visit them now and then to keep an eye on things. Martha had reassured them that this was just a temporary solution and had given them a few hundred thousand kronor each. Then she had added that as soon as everything had quieted down, they would buy a new house and engage in more projects to improve society. But exactly what they would be, and how they would go about it, she kept secret. One thing at a time, that was her rule.

Then there was the engagement. In some way that had come to fill a larger and larger portion of her thoughts, and one day, after she and Brains had had a really good time, she had even forgotten the obligatory daily gym session! It was surely high time to tell the others, she thought, but then she remembered that Brains didn't think they should do that until they were back living in normal circumstances, and not obliged to be hiding out in the forest. Yes, there were a lot of consequences that followed a crime – life became much more complicated than she had expected. If truth be told, there were lots of things to keep track of.

Martha sighed and went to make some coffee. For a change, she was going to serve coffee with egg liqueur. So much of the cloudberry liqueur had ended up in the ditch on Myrstigen that day they left Värmdö, and she hadn't been able to find anything similar in the nearest liquor shop down here. They had even discussed starting to distill their own, but Anna-Greta had said that home distilleries smelled awful and that it would be better to buy liqueur on the Internet since the liquor monopoly would actually deliver to your door. But, as it was probably wise to lie low a bit longer, they voted against that and instead made do with Bols Advocaat Original and egg-liqueur ice cream. And that wasn't bad at all. A bit of a change was always stimulating.

Martha yawned and happened to catch sight of the local newspaper, *Vetlanda-Posten*, which lay on the table. It had been there since yesterday, but nobody had got round to reading it yet. She started to look through the pages and was just about to put it aside when she noticed a little item. It was about the Historical Museum.

The museum staff had made a strange discovery inside the Gold Room. Shortly after the happy day when a guard had found all the missing gold treasure in the Wishing Well, ants had started crawling around inside the room and the maintenance man had to call in Anticimex. And down in the Wishing Well itself, the water had turned murky. An unusual variety of the Rose of Jericho had grown up among the coins and there were even rumours that a museum visitor had seen water lilies and a cannabis plant down in the well – although this was said to be a tall tale. Nobody could explain how those plants came to be there, although the police had vague suspicions that it was in some way connected with the return of the gold by the robbers. Martha read this little news item quickly, but gasped when she came to the final lines:

With the help of samples of soil taken from the well, the police hope to be able to trace the robbers and link them to the crime.

'Oops,' said Martha, and she dropped the newspaper on the floor. Had they succeeded with everything else only to be caught by such a tiny detail? But then she decided not to worry. Nobody would find them here deep in the forest. They could certainly lie low a bit longer. Emma and Anders could drive the minibus and the Volvo to Denmark and put new registration plates on them there. Anyway, the police would certainly think that the gold robbers had fled the country long ago. Martha picked up the newspaper and put it back on the table. Then she went up to the new espresso machine and put in a chocolate-flavoured coffee capsule. After that she fetched the egg liqueur and put out cups and plates. New habits and new tastes. It was a matter of not stagnating, but keeping moving on, she thought. They had a new way of making coffee, and they had given up cloudberry liqueur – now espresso, egg liqueur and new crimes were the order of the day.

When they had all eaten breakfast and were in a good mood, she would summon them to a meeting. She had a plan. The League of Pensioners would renew itself and in the future be able to donate more money than ever. And then, perhaps, she and Brains could tell the others about their engagement . . .

It was late in the autumn, but Customs Officer Carlsson had never given up the hunt for the robbers. In the garishly designed room in the police headquarters at Kronoberg, the grey steel spotlights constantly shone over his busy head. The dove grey tone went nicely with the new red curtains and the colour of the walls. This time he had asked the caretaker to paint everything bright red because that was such a good contrast to black. The chairs were black, as were the desks, while the cushions were in different shades of grey, blue and purple, so the room looked really chic.

He had also brought in two new fish tanks – although neither of them was as fancy as the old one. For some strange reason they lacked the same glittering lustre. Perhaps it was to do with the gravel? He must be sure to get hold of some more of those nice shiny small stones again.

He thumbed absentmindedly through the printouts of the results from the lab. He was forever trying to get the lab people to hurry along with their analyses of the samples from the scene of the crime, but they were always so slow. But perhaps there was something in this batch of reports? He browsed through all the reports and suddenly gave a whoop.

'Yippee, now we've nailed them! Caught them at last!' Carlsson shouted in a falsetto when he saw the report on the soil sample. 'Blomberg, here's the proof!'

'What? What did you say?' Blomberg said in a tired voice, looking up from his computer.

'I said that we've caught them at last, we can arrest those oldies. I think the crime has been solved.'

'Has it?'

'Yes, aren't you pleased? You don't seem to be really with us, Blomberg. What's the matter? Can I do anything for you? You've been looking decidedly down in the mouth the last few months.'

'Have I? I don't know about that,' said Blomberg and he blushed. 'Well, some business deals, that's all. I lost a bit of money, you know how it is. That can always make you a bit depressed.'

'Yes, of course,' said Carlsson. 'In fact, I asked them to re-paint the room in brighter colours to cheer you up. We must have pleasant surroundings where we feel cozy. You only live once.'

Blomberg looked utterly miserable.

'But at least, Blomberg, you can stop worrying about money. When they raised my salary, I asked them to raise yours too.'

Blomberg gave a start and swallowed several times but managed to restrain himself.

'That was most kind of you,' he said, and he felt as if he might explode at any moment. The irritation was building up inside him to danger level. But at the same time, really, he ought to be grateful. Beylings had not had time to insure all the goods in the dock warehouse and he had thus lost everything. At least that's what Birgerson had told him, but that bastard of a lawyer had just bought himself a new car. A Bentley, no less. Carlsson saw Blomberg's grim expression.

'But you know what? I've got something else that might cheer you up.' The former customs officer got up, went into the corridor and returned with his face all lit up.

'Nice, isn't it?' He patted the black leather clothes. 'It was down in the cellar and nobody knew what to do with it, so I thought I could try to do something.' He held the burned shop dummy, which had been stuck onto a Christmas-tree stand. 'Whatever the room you are designing, it can be simply super to have a special feature; it gives that final touch.'

'Oh heavens above, not that mannequin too!' Blomberg sighed.

'What? Don't you like it? But, Blomberg, life is about giving and taking. I have had to put up with your pussy cat.'

'Oh, yes, Einstein.' Blomberg became quiet and immediately felt guilty. Since that day when Carlsson had installed two fish tanks in their office, he had got his own back by starting to take Einstein with him to the police headquarters. But Carlsson hadn't got the message; he had simply continued with his fish and just made sure that he kept a cat-proof lid on the fish tanks.

'What about if we started doing a little work, instead of talking nonsense. What did you just say, something about us finally being able to nail them? Something about the pensioners?'

'Yes, the gold robbers, of course. You know what? The soil samples from the Wishing Well in the Gold Room have the same components as the soil from the garden of that big old house out on Värmdö. The Bandangels said they had taken the shop dummy from the oldies' earth cellar, so we had to investigate that. We couldn't find any traces of it in the earth cellar itself, but the sample of soil from the garden was interesting. The level of phosphate in the garden soil and in the soil found in the Wishing Well was exactly the same. What makes this especially interesting is that one of the oldies who lived there is that old lady whom we saw on the CCTV images.'

'Oh no, not her again!'

'Oh yes, Blomberg, now it's serious. I've looked through all the CCTV images in great detail. She was there at the Handelsbanken robbery, when the gold was stolen from the museum, and even when the gold was taken back again. And that shop dummy has been in the earth cellar next to the house where she lived.'

'But we've already solved the Handelsbanken robbery.'

'Err, I'm not so sure about that. The Bandangels categorically deny all involvement, even though they were convicted for that crime. And there is a problem. Half of the ten million that was stolen is still missing.'

'Yes, of course, you do have a point there,' said Blomberg, and he picked up Einstein. Having the cat on his lap helped to keep him calm and prevented him from having a nervous breakdown.

'Just come and have a look at this. I've got all the CCTV images here. That old lady turns up everywhere. It's not been possible so far to prove that she was involved in the crimes, but now with the soil samples we've finally got the evidence we need.'

Carlsson put the soil sample on the table and leaned closer to the computer. Reluctantly, Blomberg put Einstein down in the cat basket and went across to his colleague. The customs officer had taken over the work on the big robberies, while Blomberg himself had been asked to deal with some small break-ins and purse-snatchers. Their boss, Strömqvist, had been of the opinion that Blomberg was no longer the most suitable detective for the task, and had quite simply handed the investigation over to Carlsson. If it hadn't been for the fact that Blomberg only had two months before retiring, he would have blown his top – but now, he managed to behave stoically. He would soon be out of this wretched police station for good, and he was more or less fully occupied transferring valuable information to his USB drives. He was collecting material for lots of future crime thrillers. He must earn money from something now that he had lost everything at the docks.

'All right, then, what have you got to show me?' he said, and he scratched the back of his neck.

'Just look at this!' Carlsson clicked on a folder icon with 'The Gold Room' next to it.

The pictures that came up showed the old lady called Martha walking round and round the Wishing Well.

'And what is so remarkable about that, pray tell?' Blomberg yawned.

'Can't you see that she's looking suspiciously often at the display cases? As if she was examining them.'

'No, she's looking for her husband,' Blomberg muttered.

'Well, what about this, then?' said Carlsson eagerly and he clicked on another icon labelled 'Handelsbanken'. 'And isn't it rather weird, too, that some of my folders about Handelsbanken have acquired new icons that I don't recognize?'

'That happens. The benefactors must have something to occupy themselves with after three in the afternoon,' said Blomberg.

'But look at these icons here, for example,' said Carlsson, and he moved his pointer to 'Handelsbanken AB Gibralter' and 'Handelsbanken AB Småland'.

'Careful, don't click those.' Blomberg was quick to react. 'You never can tell.'

'Okay, I'll delete those, but look at this. The old lady . . .'

'She's called Andersson,' Blomberg pointed out.

'Yes, look how she's standing outside the Handelsbanken branch on Karlavägen the very same day the robbery took place, and she's talking on her phone, several times. I've checked those calls and they were made to the police. And look at this, here it looks as if she is going into the bank herself.'

'What? She's actually going in herself?' said Blomberg, now suddenly interested, leaning forward. 'Yes, well, well, that's one for the books! You might have found something there. You know what, I want us to go through all those CCTV images together.'

Carlsson beamed with joy. 'Lovely, that'll be great. But there are quite a lot. What about a cup of coffee first?'

'Yes, that's a hell of a good idea, in November one needs plenty of coffee to be in peak form.' Blomberg went off in the direction of the kitchen, now feeling rather pleased with himself. Perhaps he would retire with quite a good reputation after all, because it looked as if they had now finally nailed those villains. He smiled to himself, fetched a filter for the coffee, put some ground coffee in, and then turned the coffee machine on. Carlsson did his bit by fishing out some pastries from his briefcase and hurrying after Blomberg, but in his haste he bumped into the cat basket, rudely waking Einstein. The horrible cat hissed at him and he glared back at it. Oh how he hated that cat! It really was time he had a serious talk with Blomberg. That overfed monster had sharpened its claws on the fancy designer sofa and had shed all over his purple armchair and that was not at all nice. Muttering to himself, he went off to the kitchen and got the cups out.

Back in their room, Einstein climbed out of his cat basket and started to slowly and methodically lick his paws. Then he stretched himself out at full length and looked expectantly at the delightfully warm keyboard that had just become available. With an elegant leap he was up on the desk; the sample of soil fell to the floor, and the cat was now next to the computer. Then he lay down over the keys, his tail hovered over Enter, and his right paw above some function keys. Purring loudly, Einstein now started to stretch his paws and extend his claws, as cats tend to do. The Handelsbanken AB Småland icon was firmly clicked and this was followed by a paw on another key so that the Handelsbanken AB Gibralter icon also opened a folder.

Shortly afterwards, the computer started to work away all on its own and this destruction of the arduously gathered information would go down in police history. One after the other the files disappeared from the screen, the CCTV images and all, and the virus that was later traced to deepest Småland was totally unknown to the IT experts. Which meant that they couldn't block it either. And the strange thing was that it didn't wipe out everything, only the folders and files about robberies and coups that had taken place over the last two years. But, weirdest of all, and what really confounded the police IT department, was that even their recipe for tasty coffee wafers disappeared.

Acknowledgements

I have been writing *The Little Old Lady Strikes Again* for more than a year – a task that was endlessly more fun with the help of all those who have supported me en route. First and foremost I am really grateful for all the valuable help I have received from my Swedish publishers, Bokförlaget Forum. Thank you, Teresa Knochenhauer, my publisher, who has gone through my manuscript with a fine toothcomb. Thank you, Adam Dahlin, head of the fiction department, for your encouraging words. Thank you, too, Liselott Wennborg Ramberg, Åsa Ernflo and Anna Cerps for all the time you have spent working on my text and the improvements you have suggested. And thanks, too, to Anna Käll and Nils Olsson for yet another great cover to the Swedish edition.

I would also like to thank Göran Wiberg, Bernt Meissner and Bo Bergman of Bonnier's sales department for all the work you did with this and my earlier books, and I would similarly like to extend my warm thanks to Sara Lindegren, Annelie Eldh, Barbro Almgren and Karin Eklund from the marketing department for help over many years with my books. Apart from the publishing house, I have had my own private test panel of readers who have given their views while I was working on the book. They include Inger Sjöholm-Larsson, whose encouragement and joyful laughter have been a delightful source of inspiration, and Lena Sanfridsson, who quite simply has been wonderful to try out ideas on AND A GREAT SUPPORT. My warm thanks, too, to Barbro von Schönberg, whose support and encouragement have contributed to the joy of writing this book, and to Ingrid Lindgren, who was always just as quick and ready in every situation to share her opinion on what I had written.

My thanks go also to Mika Larsson for all your wise, professional views and for when you have openly criticized and praised with the same joyful verve; Isabella Ingelman-Sundberg for your NICE AND FRIENDLY support and all the times you have read the manuscript and given me your quick and insightful comments; Gunnar Ingelman, who has been there and supported me while I've been writing this book; and Henrik Ingelman-Sundberg for your always unsentimental, critical and direct comments, which have been worth their weight in gold.

Thanks also to Magnus Nyberg for reading, reflecting and commenting. Your laughter and views often influenced how I then worked on the manuscript! And my thanks to Kerstin Fägerblad for yet again reading from the very first version to the final book, and, together with Marike Ollner, for helping with research out at Solvalla racecourse. I would also like to thank Solbritt Benneth, Bengt Björkstén and Karin Sparring Björkstén for your invaluable help. I have also benefited from quick and inspiring opinions from Ingegerd Jons, Anna Rask and Agneta Lundström, comments that I greatly value. Thanks also to Peter Östman and Malin Elgborn, who have given me valuable feedback.

Last but not least I would like to thank Maria Enberg, Lena Stjernström, Peter Stjernström, Lotta Jämtsved Millsberg and Umberto Ghidoni at Grand Agency. Thanks for all your help with selling *The Little Old Lady Who Broke All the Rules* to more than twenty countries.

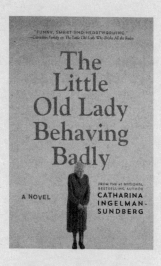

Don't miss the League of Paensioners' next hilarious adventure in Saint-Tropez, where they cheat billionaires out of luxury yachts.

#1 bestselling author Catharina Ingelman-Sundberg

'Ingelman-Sundberg deftly orchestrates the foibles of real life . . . and captures the rebelliousness percolating just under the surface of ignored, shuffled away elderly folks.'
—*Kirkus Reviews*

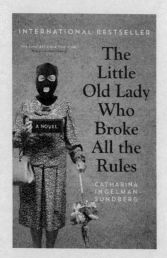

Find out how Martha and her friends escaped their dull, drab life in a retirement home and got their start robbing banks.

Over 2 million copies sold!

'A good-natured, humorous crime caper.'
—*The Independent*